Praise for *The Adept* Novels
by Bestselling Authors
KATHERINE KURTZ
and
DEBORAH TURNER HARRIS

"Admirable, elegant . . . A constantly absorbing story that features excellent pacing, a frequently compelling sense of place, and an equally compelling emotional impact."
—**Booklist**

"This series is the finest use of the 'occult detective' theme since Manly Wade Wellman."
—**Chicago Sun-Times**

"A fast-moving and suspenseful tale by an unusually adroit duo."
—**Publishers Weekly**

"One of those rare books that, once you start reading, you can't stop."
—**SFRA Newsletter**

"Fast-paced . . . fun . . . devoted Anglophiles will delight in the details of the life and times of Sir Adam Sinclair."
—**School Library Journal**

"Starts at a high pace and never lets up . . . The characters, unusual as they are, are carefully crafted and thus quite believable."
—**Australian SF News**

W9-BRE-053

THE ADEPT SERIES
by Katherine Kurtz and Deborah Turner Harris

*Also available from Ace Books by
Deborah Turner Harris*

DAGGER MAGIC

A Novel of *The Adept*

KATHERINE KURTZ
DEBORAH TURNER HARRIS

To Duncan —
Best wishes
Katherine Kurtz

▲

ACE BOOKS, NEW YORK

This Ace Book contains the complete text of the original hardcover edition.

DAGGER MAGIC

An Ace Book / published by arrangement with the author

PRINTING HISTORY
Ace hardcover edition / May 1995
Ace mass-market edition / February 1996

All rights reserved.
Copyright © 1995 by Katherine Kurtz and Deborah Turner Harris.
Cover art by Joe Burleson.
This book may not be reproduced in whole or in part,
by mimeograph or any other means, without permission.
For information address: The Berkley Publishing Group,
a member of Penguin Putnam Inc.,
200 Madison Avenue, New York, New York 10016.

The Penguin Putnam Inc. World Wide Web site address is
http://www.penguinputnam.com

Check out the Ace Science Fiction/Fantasy newsletter,
and much more, at Club PPI!

ISBN: 0-441-00304-4

ACE®
Ace Books are published by The Berkley Publishing Group,
a member of Penguin Putnam Inc.,
200 Madison Avenue, New York, New York 10016.
ACE and the "A" design are trademarks
belonging to Charter Communications, Inc.

PRINTED IN THE UNITED STATES OF AMERICA

10 9 8 7 6 5 4

For Christopher Seal,
without whom we might never have known . . .

ACKNOWLEDGMENTS

The authors offer grateful acknowledgment to the following people, who have greatly enriched the background authenticity of this novel by their generous contributions of time and information:

The Reverend W.C.H. Seal, for background on *Phurbas* and Tibetan black magic, as well as orthodox Tibetan Buddhism, and for checking the final manuscript for accuracy; any errors that have crept in are ours, not his;

Mr. Thom McCarthy, administrator for the Holy Island Project, Samye Ling Tibetan Centre in Scotland, for his warm welcome and reams of information at Samye Ling, and for helping arrange our visit to Holy Island;

Mr. Harry Lloyd, Northern Fisheries Board, Ballyshannon, who allowed us to inspect and photograph inflatable patrol craft and survival gear used by Fisheries officers; also, Mr. Ronan Flynn, Central Fisheries Board, and Mr. Bryan Murphy, of OceanTech, Dun Laoghaire, for more specific information on the Avon inflatable boats used by the Irish Department of the Marine;

P.C. Stephen Stewart (Alexandria), Detective Sergeant Alasdair Barnett (Campbeltown), and P.C. David White, Strathclyde Police, for guidance on police procedure;

Mrs. Elaine Ennis, Scottish Department of Social Work, for insights on rehabilitation procedures for spinal injury patients;

Chief Engineer Gordon W. Whitehead, for invaluable technical expertise regarding submarine operation;

Mr. Simon Martin, for sharing his practical knowledge of marine salvage work;

Dr. Richard Oram, our resident authority on Scottish history, who was able to paint us a graphic picture of seventeenth-century Hawick;

Mr. Ken Fraser of the St. Andrews University Library, for being ever ready to find all manner of obscure books on demand.

PROLOGUE

"THE weather in the far north of Ireland will continue unsettled for at least the next twenty-four hours," came the crackly voice of the radio weatherman. "... occasional outbreaks of rain and northeasterly winds gusting up to forty knots ..."

The rest of the marine forecast dissolved in a hiss of static that was lost in the roar of twin Yamaha outboards and the slap of water against black and orange sponsons as the big inflatable boat punched through the waves off the north coast of Donegal. Irish Fisheries Officer Mick Scanlan grimaced as he scanned ahead with a pair of powerful marine binoculars, one arm looped through the boat's A-frame to brace himself. Amidships, sitting astride the pillion seat behind the control console, his partner, Lorcan O'Haverty, throttled back slightly to compensate for the wave chop.

The sky overhead was a dirty shade of grey, looking more like February than early May, and the two officers were dressed for weather. With their bright orange crash helmets and regulation life-vests, both men wore the distinctive orange-and-black survival suits called Polar Bears that could keep a man alive for several days in these waters, whose winter temperature often dipped to near-Arctic levels. Even in May, though the water had begun to warm, hail and sleet might accompany the squalls and storms so prevalent in this area. To be caught out unprepared could be fatal.

Not that today was too bad, as days went in early May. The wind was brisk, but the sun looked poised to break through the cloud cover for at least a little while. A hundred yards off to port, the outbound tide was peeling back on itself lethargically from the sheer base of a long line of sea-cliffs, leaving the exposed rock-faces festooned with streamers of stranded kelp.

Scanlan shifted his weight and continued to scan. Off to the seaward side, shadowed and uncertain under the receding tidewash, the dark lurk of submarine rocks posed a threat to conventional craft venturing in this close, but the rigid inflatable boats used by the Irish Department of the Marine drew only inches of water, and had proven highly effective for this kind of patrol. Weighing hardly more than a ton, a six-meter boat like this one could be trailered where needed and launched within minutes—a godsend for men like Scanlan and O'Haverty, charged with protecting the coastal fishing rights of a country heavily dependent upon its maritime industries. While much of their routine work was done ashore—either shuffling reports in the local fisheries office or else conducting routine inspections on the docksides of fishing ports from Inishfree to Malin Head—field investigations were not at all uncommon.

This morning they had launched from Downies to check a report of illegal fixed nets in the area. Their backup boat had developed engine trouble and would try to catch up later, but their land-based backup would be shadowing them from the shore in a Land Rover, also linked by radio. Scanlan had spotted him as they passed Dunfanaghy, and expected to pick him up again after they rounded Horn Head.

The radio chatter ebbed and flowed against the background bluster of wind and waves, and Scanlan automatically scanned the shoreline as O'Haverty skipped their nimble craft past a succession of small inlets gouged out of the coastline by the action of the North Atlantic tides. But as O'Haverty brought the boat around the point of the headland, a sudden and unexpected stretch of calm water stretched before them along a narrow crescent of sandy beach adjacent to the rock cliffs. Taking closer notice now, Scanlan saw that the outbound swells were coated with the greasy rainbow film of spilled oil.

"Uh-oh," O'Haverty said, glancing back at him.

"Yeah, I see it." Scanlan swung his binoculars along the

sweep of shoreline and adjusted the focus. "We'd better have a closer look."

As O'Haverty nosed the boat toward the beach, the slick became visible as a V-shaped stain fanning out across the flattened waves, apparently coming from a waterline cleft in the base of the cliffs that marked the western end of the beach.

"Looks like it's coming from those rocks up ahead," O'Haverty said.

"Yeah." Scanlan lowered his binoculars for a few seconds to peer with unassisted sight, then resumed his study. "I don't see any signs of a wreck, though. Maybe an oil barrel's gotten washed against the rocks and broke open. Let's go in, and I'll check it out."

Without comment, O'Haverty brought the boat around with a spin of the wheel and gave a brief rev to the engines to propel them in toward the shore while Scanlan shed his binoculars and helmet and moved into the bow, ruffling a hand through sandy hair. As soon as the boat's snub nose nudged sandy bottom, Scanlan threw a leg over the side and stepped onto the sand and shingle, grabbing an anchor and coil of line. Sea water washed and tugged at the legs of his survival suit until he won free of the retreating surf and bent to set the anchor behind a cluster of rocks a few yards higher on the beach. Behind him, O'Haverty pulled up the slack and snubbed it off.

"We'd better make this quick," O'Haverty called, shouting to make himself heard above the boom of the surf. "Tide'll be turning soon."

Grinning, Scanlan gave his partner a thumbs-up sign and turned to begin trudging toward the promontory. The tide-lines to his left suggested that the strip of beach was only exposed to view at low tide—which explained why he did not remember having seen it before, even though he and O'Haverty had passed this headland many times on routine patrol. He was halfway to the base of the cliffs, heading for the area from which the oil seemed to have come, when a flicker of color and movement drew his gaze upward.

About halfway up the cliff-face, a small flurry of sea gulls exploded into flight from the mouth of a jagged fissure in the rocks. That alone was hardly surprising, but as the birds wheeled away screeching, a slight, shaven-headed figure in flowing orange robes suddenly appeared from behind them.

The sight was startling enough to bring Scanlan up short, to send him scuttling into the shadow of the cliff-face to his left—though if the man looked down, he was sure to notice the bright orange upper half of Scanlan's survival suit. Scanlan could not have said why it seemed important that the man not see him. Even as he craned to get a cautious better look, hardly able to believe his eyes, a second man emerged from the fissure's mouth, a slightly more wizened version of the first. Both were well past middle age, and obviously of Oriental extraction.

What the hell? Scanlan thought.

Their attire reminded him of the Hare Krishna votaries he had seen now and again in Dublin and London, handing out flowers and pamphlets on street corners or dancing and singing in the streets—except that these two were much older than the usual Hare Krishna, and far less scruffy-looking. Part of the difference lay in the high-collared black tunics they wore beneath the saffron-orange outer robes, almost like a priest's cassock—a feature that Scanlan couldn't recall ever seeing before. But that sartorial difference paled to insignificance before the incongruity of *anyone* so garbed being present on this bleak, windswept stretch of Donegal coast.

The two glanced back into the darkness of the cave and conferred briefly, whatever words they spoke whisked away in the wind and the boom of the surf, then moved off along a ledge that slanted away toward the landward summit of the cliff. As they disappeared behind a screen of boulders, they seemed not to have noticed that they were being observed from shore and boat.

Scanlan backed away toward the water's edge, trying to discover where the pair might have gone, but he could see no trace of them. More mystified than ever, he shifted his puzzled gaze back to the mouth of the cave. What could they have been doing in there?

Glancing back at O'Haverty, who lifted both arms in an exaggerated shrugging motion, Scanlan waved a hand at his partner in a gesture to stand by, and started up the rocks. He unzipped the neck of his survival suit as he climbed, reaching inside for the small but powerful emergency torch he always carried. The cave warranted a quick look.

He gained the ledge without mishap, sidling carefully along it till he reached the narrow cave mouth. After a last glance over his shoulder to assure himself that O'Haverty was still watching from the boat—and scanning the cliffs beyond with the binoculars—Scanlan ducked into the opening and switched on his torch, poking the powerful beam back into the darkness.

The cave appeared to extend some distance into the cliff-face. The dank iodine-tang of the seashore prickled at his nostrils as he started edging forward, scything the beam of the torch before him as his eyes began to adjust to the darkness. A dozen cautious steps took him to the brink of deeper darkness, where his torch probed out across the echoing vault of a much larger cavern.

The vaulted expanse was not wholly dark. Here and there pale lances of daylight pierced the shadows, filtering down through scattered chinks in the roof and the seaward wall. The cave alone was unusual enough, but not far below, the sweep of his torch and the fugitive glimmers of daylight picked out the dark, deadly outline of a great torpedo shape slumbering in the gloom, with a more angular shape thrusting upward from the center. It almost looked like—good Lord, could it be?—a beached submarine!

"Jayzus, Mary, and Joseph!" Scanlan muttered under his breath.

His words echoed in the confines of the sea cave like an untimely intrusion in the hush of some vast cathedral. He fell silent as he played his torch along the length of the thing, noting the faint gurgle of water stirring sluggishly about its armor-plated flanks. The sound suggested that the cave itself was accessible to the tides from outside, but he could see no other openings above ground save the one through which he himself had just come. Nor could he make out any underwater glow that might indicate a passage below the waterline to the sea beyond.

"Jayzus," he breathed, more softly this time. It was difficult to make any very accurate estimate of the sub's size, but he guessed she must be close to two hundred feet long, maybe more. She looked like all the photos his father had shown him of German U-boats he had helped to sink during the Second World War, when he served on a British frigate. The lines of her were right, from the graceful, deadly bow, with its jag-toothed net-cutter and lethal torpedo tubes, to the stubby conning tower and snorkel, to the deck guns mounted fore and aft. And just readable, as he played his torch across the slight curve of the conning tower, was the white-painted designation *636*.

U-636. He wondered how she had come to rest here. What little he could see of her did not appear to be damaged. And she must have been lying here in secret for nearly half a century.

Suddenly avid to have a closer look, Scanlan hunkered down and flicked his torch over the rocks below, seeking a way down. A narrow ridge meandered gently along the side, slick with sea wrack but perhaps rendered less treacherous by a profusion of barnacles. A series of outcroppings presented him with a ready-made set of stepping places and handholds, and should bring him within a few feet of the foredeck.

Exhilarated at the prospect of exploring the vessel, he hooked his torch to a clip on his life-vest and began his descent toward the cavern's watery floor. The air in the cavern was moist and heavy, the tang of brine laced with a musky hint of something else that reminded Scanlan curiously of church incense. The water lapping along the hull looked to be perhaps waist-deep. He was not quite sure whether the tide had turned yet, but he should have a few minutes in reasonable safety.

He reached the bottom of the cavern without mishap and sprang lightly to the sub's foredeck, unclipping his torch to play it before him as he started aft. He brushed one hand along the rusted length of the sub's big 3.5-inch deck gun just before he skirted the conning tower, again shining the torch on the painted numbers, *636*. The ladder going up into the back of the conning tower was heavily rusted, but it looked sound enough—and was.

He climbed carefully, lest he cut his hands or damage his suit, and emerged on the command bridge. Forward, the wheel that dogged down the hatch drew him almost irresistibly, but when he tried to shift it, it stubbornly resisted his efforts.

"Shit," Scanlan muttered. Though he had not really expected it to open, he still was disappointed. Panting a little from the exertion, he shone his torch around the inside of the conning tower again and noticed something he had missed in his first inspection: an irregular grey packet about the size of his two hands, lashed to the inside of the nearest bulkhead by grey webbing straps.

The straps fell to bits as he tried to loose the buckles. The packet itself was sheathed in a double layer of oilskin, mildewed and brittle with age, that cracked and all but disintegrated as he peeled it back to expose a folded bundle of scarlet material. It was musty and damp, but when Scanlan gingerly shook it out, the mass of red became a German *Kriegsmarine* flag—red and black and white.

He caught his breath at the sight of it—once-fine scarlet wool boldly ensigned with the distinctive black cross of old Germany behind the newer white roundel and black swastika of the Third Reich. He almost dropped it in sheer reflex, for the associations of evil that it held.

Again he found himself wondering what might have brought *U-636* to her present resting place. His first thought had been that her captain must have been using this cave as a base from which to sally forth and harry Allied shipping. That seemed unlikely, though, for he could not imagine that the cave had ever offered safe access to and from the outside.

Had she fled here for sanctuary, then, pursued by her enemies? Again, how? He recalled hearing how stragglers from North Atlantic wolf packs sometimes had taken refuge in the depths of Tory Sound, not far away, though far more subs had ended up on the bottom than had escaped. He had even heard tell of a German sub from the First World War, said to lie on the floor of Donegal Bay, farther south. In those days, German submarines had used mercury for ballast—lots of it. There was talk of trying to salvage that ballast, for mercury in such quantities was extremely valuable; and such a salvage might also avert a later rupture, with its accompanying ecological implications.

Belatedly, he remembered the oil slick he had seen from outside. Surely this was its source. Had the sub limped here damaged, then? Shining his torch along her off side, he could see nothing overt, but who knew what lay below the water-line? More probably, however, the slick he had seen could be attributed to a leak in one or more of the fuel tanks, their fabric failing at last after five decades of progressive deterioration.

But why had she been beached here in the first place, and how? More mysterious still, now that Scanlan stopped to think about it, was the matter of the two Hare Krishna types he had seen emerging from the cave. Recalling them now, he wondered what possible connection such individuals could have with a German submarine. What were they even doing in this part of the world?—in Ireland, of all places. Had they stumbled across the cavern purely by chance? Somehow Scanlan doubted it.

A gurgling sound like the lapping of waves recalled Scanlan from his speculation, and he flashed his torch over the side again. The tide had turned. The water level in the cavern was rising—further confirmation that there must be an underwater channel leading to the outside. He had better get out of here, if he didn't want to get trapped or maybe even drowned.

Clipping the torch to his vest again, Scanlan set about refolding the flag. He was well aware that the sub's presence would have to be reported to the proper authorities. After this long, her salvage value was probably nil, but if she still held torpedoes, there was no telling how unstable they might have become in half a century. And there was the oil-spill question; who knew how much fuel might still reside in her tanks, set to trigger yet another ecological disaster?

In the meantime, however, there was no reason why Scanlan should not take the flag for himself as a souvenir. Stuffing it into the front of his survival suit, up under his life-vest, he zipped up again, then swung himself down out of the conning tower and set about retracing his route to the exit.

The grey light of the overcast day seemed glaringly bright after the dimness of the cavern's interior, even though a heavy fog bank had begun to roll in with the incoming tide.

Scanlan emerged squinting from the cave and fetched up short as his half-dazzled gaze picked up a blur of bright orange out on the ledge a dozen yards to the landward side of the cave entrance.

Even as Scanlan gasped, the blur resolved itself into one of the Hare Krishnas—or maybe he was some sort of Oriental monk, come to think of it—gazing expectantly in his direction. Startled, Scanlan looked around for the second one and spotted him down on the beach below, standing ankle-deep in the water right next to the boat, a brighter orange against the deeper shade of the inflatable craft. He could not see O'Haverty.

"Hey, what are you doing?" he shouted, gesturing with his torch toward the man in the water. "Lorcan, where are you?"

O'Haverty did not answer, but the second monk glanced up at him with placid indifference. Only then did Scanlan realize that both men were holding odd-looking daggers with heavy, triple-edged blades, perhaps a foot long overall. The weapons looked dull and clumsy, hardly capable of inflicting much damage unless one were hit over the head with the pommel, but Scanlan found himself gripping his torch more tightly, wishing it were bigger, heavier. He had never heard of Hare Krishnas being other than peaceable and nonviolent, but there was something not right about these two. And where was O'Haverty?

Almost without realizing what he was doing, Scanlan began to back away from the nearer monk. As he did so, the one down on the beach thrust his dagger into his belt and jerked loose the anchor that was holding the boat in place, beginning to gather in the mooring line. His movement gave Scanlan a clearer look at the interior of the boat—and the crumpled splash of black and brighter orange lying in the stern, awash in a sea of crimson.

"Lorcan?" Scanlan whispered, the color draining from his face.

The monk in the water paid him no heed, merely continuing to coil the mooring line. The fog bank swallowed up the sun in that instant, and the temperature seemed to drop by at least twenty degrees.

Before Scanlan could summon the will to move, to do *something*, the monk on the ledge turned his impassive gaze back to the cave from which Scanlan had just emerged and clasped the hilt of his dagger between his palms, point downward. Then, as the thin lips began to move silently, the agile hands began rolling the hilt of the dagger between the palms, the black eyes quickly losing focus and rolling back in the hairless head. As Scanlan edged away from the man, trying to decide which one was the greater threat, the monk on the beach tossed the anchor into the bow of the boat and moved back amidships. His expression, as he turned his face toward Scanlan, was one of mild reproof.

"Curiosity can be very costly," he announced, in heavily accented English.

He must have done something to the boat's controls then, for the engines suddenly roared to life, the bow swung around, and the boat began heading away from the shore.

"Hey!" Scanlan shouted, starting to skitter down the ledge in pursuit.

Even as he said it, already aware that he had no chance of catching the retreating boat, the monk up on the ledge raised the point of his dagger toward the entrance to the cave, continuing to roll the hilt between his palms—and suddenly released the weapon.

It sprang from between his hands, launching itself through the air like a tiny guided missile to strike the top of the cave opening with explosive force. With a crack like a thunderclap, the rock above the opening gave way, raining down rubble to bury the passageway under a descending weight of earth. Within a matter of seconds, the cave mouth had vanished, erased under tons of broken stone.

The concussion staggered Scanlan to his knees. Now nearly to the beach, he scrambled up and wheeled around in time to see the strange dagger come flashing back to its owner's hand like a boomerang.

Scanlan's eyes flew wide in blank incredulity. Even as his mind groped in vain for a logical explanation for what he had just witnessed, he realized that the second monk now was rolling his dagger the same way the first had done—except that its point was directed right at Scanlan!

The sight made Scanlan's blood run cold. Backing off a few steps in horror, he turned to bolt for the imagined safety of a tumbled ridge of boulders, skirting close to the edge of the cliff-face. A lightning scramble up over the rocks took him some distance above the level of the beach. But before he could take shelter behind any of the outcroppings, the monk on the beach released his dagger.

Running for his life, Scanlan had no further warning before the blade thudded home between his shoulder blades, piercing to the hilt. The pain transfixed him as he screamed and staggered, his torch flying from his hand as he toppled forward into the sea. His head cracked against a rock enroute and he knew no more. Where he landed, the water for an instant was dyed crimson, but then the surf took command, dispelling the red as it rolled his body to and fro.

For a moment the monk on the beach gazed impassively at the tumbled form, at the occasional glimpse of the dagger's hilt protruding from the bright orange of his victim's survival suit—which would not permit its wearer to survive this assault, no matter its sophistication. When the monk raised his hand in a gesture of summons, the dagger pulled itself free with a slight shudder and snapped back to the summoner's hand like the flick of an adder's tongue. Briefly the dagger pointed again at Scanlan, and his body caught an eddy of current and began to drift eastward, against the direction of the incoming tide.

The monk nodded and turned his back on his work, scanning for his companion. Up on the cliff-face, the other monk was picking his way back down to the beach, having finished inspecting his handiwork. Of the former cave opening, only a tumble of rubble now remained, indistinguishable from all the other tangle of rockfall on this face of the promontory. Offshore, the blank wall of incoming fog had already swallowed up the sight and almost the sound of the retreating boat, and the smaller speck of the floating body's life-vest and survival suit had very nearly disappeared.

The monk from the cliff rejoined the one on the beach. Facing eastward, the two stood shoulder to shoulder and prepared themselves, daggers grasped in their right hands with the blades pointed downward toward the sand at their feet.

Together they began to mouth the words of a whispered chant, faster and faster, until abruptly the eyes of first one and then the other rolled upward in trance. Faces rapt, lips still moving, they then set out along the shrinking beach in a series of lengthening bounds.

They gathered speed as they went, their pace accelerating to carry them forward in smooth, fluid leaps, each one longer than the one before. As they travelled, the two made rhythmic, forward-reaching motions with their right hands, driving their dagger-points toward the ground as if propelling themselves off the surface with the aid of unseen walking sticks. They struck out across the water when they came to the end of the sand, just skimming the flat surface for half a dozen strides, their movements blurring into invisibility just when they would have disappeared into the fog beyond.

CHAPTER ONE

"OH, why do photographers have to take so long?" said
Lady Janet Fraser, as she peered up the avenue leading toward Sir Adam Sinclair's gracious country house.
"Adam, I'm dying to see the look on Julia's face when she
sees the painting."

Behind them, ranged on the front steps and broad front
lawn of Strathmourne Manor, nearly a hundred well-dressed
wedding guests were chatting amiably and sipping champagne from crystal flutes on this sunny Saturday in May.
Many of the men wore kilts and day-wear jackets; the ladies
were resplendent in spring frocks and fanciful hats.

Earlier, they had gathered at St. Margaret's Episcopal
Church in Dunfermline to witness the marriage of Peregrine
Lovat, one of Scotland's most talented young portrait paint-
ers, to the lovely Miss Julia Barrett; now they prepared to
celebrate those nuptials with a formal reception and luncheon, here in the gardens of Strathmourne, Scottish seat of
one of Peregrine's more prominent patrons. Over on the
south lawn, a vast yellow- and white-striped marquee had
been erected to accommodate the guests. Half a dozen wait-
ers in Stewart tartan trews and white mess jackets circulated
among them with silver drinks trays, offering liquid refreshment before the bridal party arrived from the church.

Even as Janet spoke, there was a sudden flash of reflected
sunlight among the tall beech trees that lined the avenue
leading to the house. More flashes followed in quick succession, winking in and out among the beech leaves on the long
approach.

"They're coming!" Janet declared, as her surgeon-husband, Sir Matthew Fraser, brought her a glass of champagne.

Adam smiled and glanced in signal at his stableman, John Anderson, kilted and filling in as domestic staff for the day. Anderson, in turn, beckoned to another kilted man, the teen-aged son of one of Adam's tenant farmers, who nervously brought out a pair of ancient-looking broadswords. The two took up posts to either side of the entryway, swords at rest before them, as the first of three sleek Daimler limousines came into view, deep claret coachwork gleaming in the mid-day sun.

At a pace both stately and efficient, the first car eased to a stop at the foot of the steps and disgorged the bride's aunt and uncle and both mothers. Adam welcomed them gra-ciously, deftly directing them to one side as the first car was replaced by the second, which carried the best man, Julia's matron of honor, and the two little flower girls. Other family members followed in the third car, and the tardy photogra-pher bailed out of a hastily parked Volkswagen van and be-gan setting up. As the newcomers availed themselves of champagne and joined the rest of the wedding guests begin-ning to congregate closer to the entrance to the house, the bridal car appeared at the far end of the drive and made its slow approach.

Rather than another hired Daimler, it was Adam's own classic Mark VI Bentley that carried the newlyweds, lent for the occasion along with Adam's valet-butler, Humphrey, in his well-accustomed alternate role as chauffeur. Though Humphrey rarely displayed much emotion, as befitted his sta-tion as manservant in a distinguished household, Adam thought he detected more than a hint of a smile on Hum-phrey's normally impassive face as he brought the big blue car to a smooth halt in front of the steps and came around to open the door.

"Oh, don't they make a handsome couple?" Janet mur-mured as the kilted Peregrine handed his bride out of the car, to a smattering of applause from the assembled guests. "And Julia's gown is absolutely stunning!"

The gown in question was an Edwardian confection of

creamy silk taffeta, with wide skirts billowing from around Julia's tiny waist. Antique lace framed the wide neckline and frilled the puffed sleeves at the elbow, and dozens of tiny buttons marched down the back of the close-fitting bodice to a bustle-effect above a modest train. In keeping with the romantic mood set by the gown, Julia had pulled back her red-gold curls in a cascade caught at the crown, with a wreath of creamy-yellow silk roses securing her veil. Peregrine's cobalt-blue velvet doublet was frothed at the throat with an heirloom lace jabot, above a kilt of brown and blue and green—the hunting sett of his customary Fraser of Lovat tartan.

"Oh, I do love weddings!" Janet declared as the pair kissed for the photographer's benefit. "One of these days, Adam, I hope to see *you* getting out of that car with a lovely bride on your arm."

Adam shot her a forbearing smile and returned his gaze to the bridal couple, now posing for a more conventional photograph with Humphrey, beside the car. He hoped Janet was not going to bring up the subject of Ximena. On this day, of all days, he did not need reminding of his own domestic frustrations. A physician himself, he had met Dr. Ximena Lockhart in a hospital emergency room, after sustaining minor injuries in a car crash some eighteen months ago. Despite this inauspicious beginning, which had proven to connect with one of the highly unofficial investigations he pursued from time to time with the local police—and which had even brought Ximena herself into danger—his relationship with the lissom, dark-haired American had flourished in the next six months, leading both of them to begin entertaining serious thoughts of marriage.

But news of her father's terminal illness had summoned Ximena back to California the previous summer to nurse him in his final months—which now had stretched on to nearly a year. Adam could not begrudge them the time together, but he still cherished hopes that, when all was resolved, she might be moved to return to Scotland. Meanwhile, he must not let his own nostalgia for her company darken his enjoyment of Peregrine Lovat's wedding day.

The said Peregrine was looking very pleased with himself

as he led his bride up the steps of Strathmourne, hazel eyes shining behind his gold-rimmed spectacles, the fair hair slightly breeze-ruffled. Behind them, Humphrey took the Bentley silently off to its garage in the stableyard, and ahead of them, beyond Adam, Anderson and his young partner came to attention and brought their swords smartly to salute.

"Welcome to Strathmourne, Mrs. Lovat," Adam said, gallant words to match his dark good looks and courtly manners as he bent smiling over her hand in a graceful swirl of red Sinclair tartan.

After clasping Peregrine's hand in more hearty congratulation, he invited the pair of them to follow him into the house. The swordsmen remained at salute until he had passed through the arched doorway, then smartly extended the blades in a sword arch for the happy couple, to the obvious approval of the wedding guests.

"Well done," came a murmured commendation from a distinguished-looking older man with a military moustache.

Anderson knew the speaker well; and when he and his partner had closed the arch behind the couple and returned to "shoulder arms" and "dismiss," he came back to attention and gave him a precise military salute. It was General Sir Gordon Scott-Brown who had given Anderson the recommendation that led to employment with Adam for the past ten years. Until invalided out from injuries sustained in a terrorist bombing, John Anderson had been a trooper in the Household Cavalry.

"Good to see you again, Mr. Anderson," the general said, coming to shake the man's hand. "I'm glad to see you haven't forgotten everything they taught you."

"No, sir," Anderson said with a smile. "And young Andrews has proven as a good a student as I ever had. May I present him to you? I've been trying to talk him into a career in the military."

Inside, Peregrine was drawn aside to answer a question from the caterer, and Julia glanced back over her shoulder appreciatively as Adam led her farther into the flower-banked vestibule.

"Oh, Adam, the swords were a wonderful touch," she said. "Peregrine told me you'd arranged a sword arch, but I expected the usual Scottish basket-hilts. Those look very old. Are they ancestral Sinclair treasures?''

''After a fashion,'' Adam conceded, smiling. ''The blades were once used in the service of the Knights Templar—and as you know, both Strathmourne and Templemor were once Templar holdings.''

He left unsaid that her new husband had been among those who helped acquire the swords, whilst in pursuit of thieves attempting to locate and plunder a secret Templar strong-room. It was but one of the instances in which Peregrine had aided Adam in his work, on many levels. The public and social face presented by Sir Adam Sinclair, Baronet, declared him a patron of the arts, an antiquarian of some repute, and an aficionado of classic motor cars. Professionally, Dr. Adam Sinclair was well regarded as a psychiatrist and sometime consultant to the Lothian and Borders Police. Only a handful of people, many of them present today, knew anything of his dedication to more arcane pursuits, as white-occultist, Adept, and Master of an esoteric fraternity known as the Hunting Lodge, charged with enforcing the higher laws of the Inner Planes.

''Well, then,'' said Julia, who was *not* aware of these other facets of her husband's patron and mentor, ''we have the Templars to thank for the swords, I suppose. And thank *you*, Adam, for making all this possible. Peregrine says you always think of everything, and I'm beginning to see what he means. This whole day . . .'' She gestured around the flower-banked vestibule with a happy sigh. ''I still can hardly believe we're having our wedding reception here. You've made it especially magical for us.''

''It's my pleasure,'' Adam assured her. ''Consider it part of my wedding present to the pair of you. I only wish the restoration up at Templemor could have been farther along. It would have been a marvellous tribute to your new husband's artistic talents, to have held the reception in the great hall. I very much doubt we'd be even as far along as we are, if it weren't for his artistic vision.''

''But Templemor wouldn't have been nearly large enough,'' Janet Fraser said, come to whisk Julia away to freshen up before joining the receiving line. ''The great hall *here* isn't even big enough. Julia, this is an absolute fairy tale. Just wait until you see the marquee! Come upstairs, and you can look down on the lawn from one of the south bedrooms.''

As the two women disappeared up the stair, chattering animatedly, Adam reflected that it was probably as well neither had any idea just how far Peregrine Lovat's range of artistic talents exceeded the norm. It was those particular talents that had commended him to Adam's attention in the first place—and soon had earned him a place as one of Adam's most versatile and useful Huntsmen, a preferred teammate on many an unusual investigation. Adam's Second, Detective Chief Inspector Noel McLeod, had come to value Peregrine's unique talents in a forensic capacity as well, so that on occasion, Peregrine, too, served as a consultant in police investigations that ranged beyond the conventional.

Adam spotted the grey-haired inspector and his wife just outside the door, McLeod uncharacteristically kilted and looking none too happy about it. As he lifted a hand in greeting, Jane McLeod saw him and also raised a hand to wave.

Jane was a rare gem. Adam hoped that Peregrine would be as fortunate in his choice of a mate as McLeod had been—and that *he* would be as fortunate. Though Peregrine would have been as forthright with Julia as he could be, about the demands sometimes placed upon him—and much could be explained away by the need for confidentiality, when off about police business—the more specific work of the Hunting Lodge was not something that could be readily accepted and understood by those who were not themselves initiates. Nor was it fair to expect active participation from those who had no calling in what, essentially, was a vocation. Given a spouse not so called, mere loving support and unquestioning acceptance were great blessings; and even those were not always granted to those who served the Light. It took a special kind of spouse to accept such an arrangement on trust.

McLeod's Jane was one such spouse—supportive but not herself directly involved—and Adam guessed that Julia would also rise to the challenge. He hardly dared to hope that perhaps, in time, Ximena might be able to do so as well—if the two of them ever got together again for more than a forty-eight-hour flying visit. As for an equal partnership in the Work, like that shared by Christopher and Victoria Houston—he dared not even dream that he might be that fortunate.

A sudden outburst of squeals and childish laughter broke in on his reverie. Glancing back, he saw that Peregrine was playing at being a snapping crocodile for the delighted benefit of Ashley and Alexandra Houston, aged seven and four, Julia's two little flower girls.

"Just offhand," said a crisp contralto voice at Adam's shoulder, "I'd say that Peregrine possesses all the right qualifications for future parenthood, wouldn't you?"

"I would, indeed," Adam agreed, smiling. The speaker was the children's mother, Victoria Houston, whose clergyman-husband had officiated at the wedding in conjunction with the elderly parish priest resident at St. Margaret's. Only their fellow Huntsmen would have been aware that Father Christopher had added one or two special touches of his own to ensure that Peregrine and Julia's marriage received not only the blessings of the Church, but also the benisons of the Inner Planes.

"I would also say that the girls have earned their sport with Uncle Peregrine," Adam added. "They were perfect little ladies for the ceremony, utter models of decorum."

"Goodness, don't say that!" Victoria said in mock alarm. "The next thing you know, they'll be trying to climb the wedding cake!"

"Those little cherubs?" Adam said with a droll grin.

"Well, the early indoctrination *might* hold," Victoria allowed. "Years of sitting still in church and watching Daddy parade around in fancy dress helps. Actually, they can't wait until they're old enough to be in the choir, so they can wear those flashy red cassocks and little white ruffs!"

Adam laughed aloud at that. Hearing him, Christopher excused himself from a conversation with Julia's mother and uncle and came over to join them, snagging a fresh glass of champagne on the way, dapper and elegant in his clerical suit and collar. He spared an amused look for his daughters, then asked in a conspiratorial undertone, "Has Julia seen the painting yet?"

Adam shook his head. "Not yet. I've had Humphrey put it on an easel right beside the head table. She'll get her first glimpse of it when Peregrine leads her to her place."

"So it's still a surprise. Good." Christopher grinned like a schoolboy. "I hope that photographer will be around to catch the expression on her face!"

As soon as Julia rejoined them, the members of the wedding party reconvened in the vestibule and entry hall to receive their guests before retiring to the marquee for lunch. Following several of Julia's school chums, one of the first to come through the line was a fragile, elderly woman in a wheelchair, lifted up the steps, chair and all, by Anderson and Andrews. She was swathed in a graceful sari of sapphire silk shot with silver, with a paisley shawl draped over her lap. A handsome sapphire set in a golden scarab graced her right hand, and Indian bangles circled both wrists. A somewhat younger companion accompanied her, guiding the chair. Peregrine's face lit up at the sight of the pair.

"Lady Julian!" he exclaimed, going to her. "And Mrs. Fyvie! I'm so glad you could come!"

"You know I wouldn't have missed this day for the world," Lady Julian said, smiling as she gave Peregrine both her hands and accepted the salute of his kiss on her cheek. "Julia, my dear, you look positively radiant, as all brides should. Are you pleased with the rings?"

Slipping one arm through Peregrine's, Julia leaned down to display her left hand, for Lady Julian, an accomplished jeweller, had made both their rings. Peregrine had opted for a plain gold band lightly etched with a Celtic interlace design; Julia's narrower band nestled close to the heart-shaped ruby she wore as an engagement ring. The latter had belonged to Peregrine's grandmother.

"They're absolutely wonderful," Julia said, eyes shining, "and all the more special for having been made by you. I look forward to wearing mine for a lifetime."

"You have my prayers that that lifetime may be a long and happy one, my dear," Lady Julian said.

"I promise you, I shall do everything in my power to make it so," Peregrine replied, with an adoring glance at his bride.

The cheerful buzz of conversation swelled as guests continued to present themselves, passing through the drawing room then and onto the terrace, with the marquee beyond. Some of Peregrine's guests were former schoolmates, but many were his former clients and patrons.

Perhaps most prominent among the latter were the Earl and Countess of Kintoul. The earl was closer to Adam's age than to Peregrine's, but Peregrine had been close friends with the earl's younger brother, the Honourable Alasdair, tragically killed in a motoring accident shortly after both young men left university. After Alasdair's death, his mother had adopted Peregrine as a surrogate son, and had become his first really important client and patron as his career began to take off. She sadly had not lived to see the flowering of his friendship with Adam, following her introduction, but she had remembered him in her will with a modest bursary and the bequest of a beloved and valuable vintage motorcar. The dark green Alvis drop-head coupe parked near the marquee, poised for the honeymoon getaway, had been known affectionately as "Algy" by the Kintoul family.

"The best of all good wishes to you and your enchanting bride," the earl said to Peregrine, shaking his hand as Lady Kintoul gave Julia a fond hug. "Julia, has he let you drive Algy yet?"

Julia rolled celestial blue eyes and pulled a mock pout. "Not so far, I'm afraid—though, in fairness, I must admit that my esteemed husband has been having the engine gone over so that Algy will be ready for our wedding trip. I shan't tell you where we're going, but he *has* promised me a turn at the wheel once we get away in the countryside—and I intend to see that promise gets kept!"

"I shall look forward to your assessment of the old bus," the earl replied, laughing as his wife poked him in the ribs and said, "Shame on you, David Kintoul! Algy is not an 'old bus'! Julia, you're going to love it. Just don't let Peregrine bully you into thinking that driving vintage cars is an esoteric sport, reserved only for men!"

Of a slightly different tenor was the brief exchange with General Sir Gordon Scott-Brown, John Anderson's benefactor, soon to retire as Governor of Edinburgh Castle. He was escorting his wife and younger daughter, both of whom had sat for Peregrine to paint their portraits in the past year. A prominent Freemason, the general had been of material assistance to Adam and his associates some months past, when a lodge of black magicians had set about killing off Freemasons. Since then, Peregrine had received several important commissions on the strength of the general's recommendation. Now Sir Gordon shook Peregrine's hand vigorously and tipped him a jaunty wink.

"Come and see me when you get back from your honeymoon, Mr. Lovat," he told the young artist. "My Lodge is celebrating its centenary this year, and we're hoping to have a group portrait painted for the occasion. I've let it be known that you're the man for the job."

When it was time for the wedding luncheon to commence, the Earl of Kintoul's personal piper struck up "Mairi's Wedding" and led the newlyweds out to the marquee. The photographer had been alerted, and was standing near a large gilt-framed oil painting set on an easel near the head table. Peregrine said nothing as he led his bride across the parquet floor, but Julia noticed the painting almost immediately. She caught her breath as they came abreast of it, half in delight and half in awe.

"Peregrine, did you do this?" she exclaimed, as the piper finished his tune.

Peregrine acknowledged responsibility with a sheepish grin. "Let it never be said that romance is dead," he told his bride. "I hope you like it."

"Like it? I *adore* it!" Julia exclaimed—and threw both her arms impulsively around his neck, to the delight of the watching guests and a smattering of applause.

It was a unique wedding gift, that only Peregrine himself could have created for his bride. In composition and technique, the painting was a faithful reflection of a nineteenth-century work by the Scottish artist Alexander Johnstone. The original portrayed a romanticized Bonnie Prince Charlie meeting Flora MacDonald for the first time, with the kilted

Prince seated beside a rustic table in a rough stone cottage. Before him, outlined against the light from an open doorway, stood the legendary heroine who had helped him elude his English pursuers "over the sea to Skye."

Peregrine had re-created every detail of the original with consummate skill and deliberation. In his version, however, the features of the principals had been altered to mirror a cast of familiar faces. The Flora MacDonald of Johnstone's original painting now wore Julia's fair visage and a fanciful conjecture of her wedding gown, which Peregrine had never seen before today. The latter was a close likeness, suggesting that Peregrine might have had a conference with his bride's dressmaker.

Peregrine himself had assumed the identity of the Bonnie Prince, kilted in his customary Fraser of Lovat tartan, hazel eyes brimful of adoration as he gazed up at his fair rescuer. In a puckish display of humor, the glint of his wire-rimmed spectacles was clearly visible. The handsome laird who was presenting Flora by the hand displayed the darkly handsome features of Adam and wore his Sinclair tartan. Other figures in the painting were clearly recognizable as Matthew and Janet Fraser and Julia's Uncle Alfred, all of whom had been present when the newlyweds first met. Casting her gaze over the detailing, Julia gave a little crow of laughter and clapped her hands in delight.

"Oh, Peregrine, it's wonderful. I hate to think how much time you must have spent toiling over this when you might have been doing other things. Whatever gave you the idea?"

Smiling, Peregrine captured one of his wife's hands and raised it to his lips with a smile.

"I thought the spirit of our first meeting should be preserved, and the Johnstone painting seemed somehow an appropriate model," he declared. "You have made me a prince among men, dearest Julia, and just as Bonnie Prince Charlie placed his life in Flora's hands, so do I place my happiness in yours."

"Hear, hear!" someone shouted approvingly as applause broke out again; and Janet Fraser murmured, "Who said that chivalry was dead?"

The luncheon menu began with a salmon mousse in shells

of fresh melon and worked through a tomato bisque, breast of duck in a marinade of orange and ginger, and an accompaniment of new potatoes and garden vegetables, along with appropriate wines. Once the remnants of the main course had been cleared away, Humphrey wheeled in the wedding cake on a silver serving trolley: a glistening triple-tiered confection in white sugar icing. Decorating the top tier, in place of the traditional figures of a bride and groom, was a miniature scene from a fairy tale: a knight on a white horse doing battle with a dragon while his lady looked on from the turreted window of her castle.

"How lovely!" whispered Janet Fraser to her husband. "To be married in the spirit of chivalry . . ."

Once the cake had been cut, using a Victorian cavalry sword carried by the groom's great-grandfather in the Zulu Wars, there followed the traditional round of speeches while the cake was distributed and coffee was served. After the addresses had been concluded, Adam rose from his seat at the top table and gave his crystal champagne flute a chiming tap with a silver coffee spoon. As the buzz of conversation settled, he lifted his glass.

"My lords and ladies, honored guests, friends and family of the happy couple," he proclaimed. "Before we adjourn to the garden, please join with me in pledging Julia and Peregrine our best wishes for a happy, healthy, and prosperous future."

The toast signalled the formal end to the meal. Thereafter, the guests filtered out to the gardens while Lord Kintoul's piper played again and the marquee was cleared for the dancing that would follow. Adam, his formal hosting duties now done, circulated freely among the guests, enjoying the sunshine of the terrace and the chance to chat with friends.

Eventually his perambulations brought him round to the rose arbor, where he found Noel McLeod sitting alone on a stone bench in the shade, polishing his gold-rimmed aviator spectacles on a handkerchief. Something in the inspector's manner suggested that he might have been waiting for Adam.

"Hello, Noel," Adam said, wondering what the reason might be. "Don't tell me you've tired of the festivities already, when there's still some country dancing to be done."

Scowling beneath a wiry grey moustache, McLeod settled his spectacles back on his face and ran a hand through thick grey hair.

"Not tired, just hot," he said with a grimace. "I had to wear my winter-weight kilt." He picked up a pleat in distaste. "Jane discovered only yesterday that the moths had been at my summer one, and you know how women are, when they get something in their heads: She wouldn't even entertain the thought of me wearing a suit."

Adam smiled. "If you wore your kilts more often, the moths wouldn't have as much chance to get at them."

"Och, I know that." McLeod raised a hand in dismissal. "I could have hired one, I suppose, but things have been so hectic at the office lately that I haven't had much time to spare for anything apart from police business. As a matter of fact, the next time you've got a free moment, there's something I'd like to talk over with you—just to see what you think."

McLeod's tone was casual, but the very fact that he had broached the subject of business at a purely social gathering made it clear that the matter to which he was referring had been weighing on his mind.

"I suppose I could make a bit of time just now," Adam said, "so long as it isn't anything *too* complicated."

"Well, the *telling* isn't complicated," McLeod said as Adam sat beside him. "You remember Donald Cochrane?"

"Of course." Cochrane was McLeod's chief assistant.

"Well, about a week ago, Donald handed me the file on a case that had come over from Traffic Division. It seems that in the course of the past four months, for some unknown reason, a particular stretch of the Lanark Road west of Currie has suddenly become the scene of a whole string of serious traffic accidents, with several fatalities.

"I say 'for some unknown reason,' " he went on, "because that bit of road has never been a problem before. I've driven it many times myself, and I can tell you that it's just a straight stretch of plain tarmac—no curves, no roundabouts, not many access roads—no potential hazards of any kind. As far as these recent accidents are concerned, there are no reports of any particularly adverse weather conditions on the days in question, likewise no unusual traffic congestion.

"Nor have we been able to make any human correlations. Investigators from Traffic Division checked over the medical records of the various victims and couldn't find any medical anomalies affecting any of the drivers. And yet, for all these *noes*, there have been no fewer than nine people killed or injured along this roadway since the beginning of the year. It's getting so bad that the media have begun referring to this bit of road as Carnage Corridor."

During McLeod's recital, Adam had become aware of something stirring at the back of his mind. It was a sensation he had experienced many times before, and invariably signalled that there was more to a given situation than might meet the eye. Without having any special idea what he might be plumbing for, he asked, "What can you tell me about the accidents themselves?"

McLeod pulled a scowl, setting both hands on the stone bench to either side of him and studying his black brogues and kilt hose.

"The first crash occurred on New Year's Day," he said. "Three local lads were on their way home after an all-night Hogmanay party when the driver ran his car off the road. The vehicle overturned into a ditch, killing the driver outright. One of the passengers died a few days later; the other survived, but is still in a coma. They haven't much hope that he'll ever wake up. Everyone involved in the investigation assumed that it would turn out to be a clear-cut case of drunk driving, but the post-mortem showed that the man at the wheel had a blood alcohol level well below the legal limit."

"Asleep at the wheel, then?" Adam ventured.

"Maybe. But the hostess of the party says that all three lads had caught a few hours of sleep in the wee small hours, and they'd had a solid breakfast before setting out for home, with lots of strong coffee."

"Go on."

"Since then, there have been four more accidents, occurring roughly at three- to four-week intervals," McLeod continued, "each of them attended by at least one fatality. They form enough of a pattern to suggest that there must be *some* common factor—but so far, nobody's been able to figure out what it could be. Given the fact that all logical avenues of investigation have failed to turn up an answer, I've begun to wonder if maybe the explanation we're after is one that defies conventional logic.''

"The situation certainly would seem to border on the uncanny," Adam agreed. "Have you any theories?"

McLeod pulled a wry face. "Nary a one. That's why I thought it might be worthwhile to let you have a go at it. If you've any chinks in your schedule this coming week, I'd appreciate it if you could come down to the station and look over the reports for yourself, just to see if you get any feel for what might be at the bottom of it all.''

Adam nodded, considering. "Monday's actually not too bad," he told McLeod. "I've got my usual rounds at the hospital, together with some late-morning appointments, but I should be free by noon. Why don't I meet you at your office after lunch?"

"That would do nicely," McLeod said. "Maybe you'll be able to spot something I've missed. It's just too uncanny to be mere chance.''

"What's uncanny?" said an interested voice from behind Adam's back.

Both Adam and McLeod looked around to find Peregrine Lovat standing on the path.

"Nothing that need concern anyone who's about to take off on his honeymoon," McLeod said sharply. "Believe me, you've got far better things to do than meddle in the affairs of Traffic Division.''

"*Traffic* Division?" Peregrine looked briefly nonplussed at the possibility of anything unusual occurring under the jurisdiction of that generally humdrum aspect of law enforcement. "But if you've really got a case you think we should look at—"

"We don't know yet," Adam said firmly. "We won't know until I've had a chance to look over the paperwork, if then. And even if something does turn up that might prove worth our investigating," he continued, raising an eyebrow, "don't you think you might trust Noel and me to handle it in your absence?"

Peregrine had the grace to look sheepish. "All right, I can

take the hint," he told his mentors. "But if anything interesting happens here while Julia and I are off in the Western Isles, I'll want to hear the whole story when I get back."

"Don't worry, you will," McLeod promised. "Now, away you go and dance with that pretty wife of yours. I hear the Ceili band tuning up. A man's wedding day doesn't last forever, so don't waste another minute of it standing around talking to us."

CHAPTER TWO

"Salutations to the Buddha!
  In the language of gods and in that of the demigods,
  In the language of the demons and in that of men,
  In all the languages which exist,
  I proclaim the Doctrine!"

THE words of the ancient Buddhist invocation resonated across the courtyard of the monastery like a flourish of temple bells. As the echoes died away, there arose a sonorous, long-drawn exchange of horn-calls signalling the commencement of evening devotions. In the windows belonging to the apartments of the monastery's abbot, a string of moving lights appeared as the abbot himself, together with his attendants, processed toward the *tsokhang*, the community's vaulted meditation hall. Elsewhere throughout the monastery, a subdued patter of sandalled feet likewise converged on the hall, arrested outside the door as the ordinary monks paused to shed their footwear before padding inside to take their places for prayers and meditation.

The traditions governing these observances dated back to ancient Tibet. This monastic community, however, was located not amid the towering crags of the Himalayas, but deep in the heart of the Swiss Alps. Most inhabitants of the neighboring villages assumed that this settlement was merely an extension of the respected and much better-known Buddhist colony located at Rikon, near Zurich.

In fact, nothing could have been further from the truth. Though many honest seekers from both East and West daily found their way here, none of these ever suspected that this innocent-seeming retreat from the world was home to a select group of individuals who, for nearly half a century, had concealed the shadowy nature of their true powers and ambitions behind carefully maintained masks of sanctity.

Nowhere was the illusion more complete than in the meditation hall of the temple. Lofty as a cathedral vault, the interior was illuminated mostly by an array of elaborately jewelled and enamelled butter lamps. On every side, the walls and pillars were decorated with frescoes and scrolls of painting, some of them showing the manifold images of various Buddhas, others devoted to the depiction of a wide range of saints, demigods, and demons. At one end of the hall, enshrined behind another row of butter lamps, glittered the gilded images of lamas and former abbots. Beneath these statues reposed a collection of gold and silver stupas, reliquaries containing their mummified remains.

A stir at one end of the hall, together with a sudden brightening of the lights, heralded the arrival of the abbot's procession. Those monks who were still standing hurriedly fled to their stations and settled themselves cross-legged on the floor. A moment later, the abbot himself appeared, flanked by two of his senior attendants. Four lesser acolytes hovered behind them with thuribles of incense, ready to perfume the hall with the fragrances of balsam and musk.

The abbot and his aides were arrayed in caftan-like *chubas* of black brocade, the loose folds belted and bloused, with shoulder fastenings of gold. Over this, each member of the trio wore a short coat of heavy orange silk, surmounted by a toga-like mantle of the same material. The features of the two attendants were unmistakably Oriental, but the abbot himself was a Westerner. His ice-blue eyes and pale, regular features proclaimed Nordic blood, though his head was shaven clean, like those of his companions.

As the congregation of his humbler followers respectfully abased themselves before him, he led the way across the floor to a raised dais on the east side of the room. An expectant silence fell as he folded himself cross-legged onto the low, gilded throne which awaited him there. Before his two senior attendants took their places to either side of him, they paused at the edge of the dais to kindle two more lamps. As the twin lights flared, a deep-toned chant broke out from all sides.

The liturgy was conducted in the language of Tibet. The abbot himself led the chanting in a voice devoid of any trace of a Western accent. To the chorus of voices was added the occasional music of a small consort of Tibetan instruments—reed-like *gyalings* and trumpet-like *ragdongs*, played to the rhythm of a pair of kettledrums. Over all wafted the fragrance of incense mingled with the fumes from the lamps.

At the conclusion of the service, the abbot paused briefly to salute the statues of his predecessors before departing from the hall. A serving brother was waiting just outside the door and bowed low, joined hands pressed to his forehead.

"Pardon if I intrude, *Rinpoche*, but Kurkar-la and Nagpo-la have returned. I am instructed to ask if you will speak with them now or at some later time."

"I will see them now," the abbot said coolly. "Bring them to me here."

With another bow, the serving brother departed. When he returned a moment later, he was followed by two very senior-ranking monks, one of exceedingly venerable years. The abbot's blue eyes narrowed slightly as he searched their faces, but after a moment, his chiselled features eased.

"Come," he said, also instructing the serving brother to bring refreshment to his chambers.

The apartment to which he led them was opulently appointed. Butter lamps of gold and silver filigree flooded the room with wan, flickering light. The febrile glow of the flames picked out the jewel-like weave of a number of Oriental carpets warming the polished wooden floor on which they lay. Incense smoke from several gem-studded braziers filled the air with a heavy perfume redolent of opium and sandalwood.

Each of the four corners of the room was dominated by the presence of a heavy, triple-edged dagger standing as tall and bulky as a man, set upright by its point in a stand fashioned in the shape of an equilateral triangle. Thus positioned, the daggers had the look almost of sentries on guard. The pommel ends of the wooden daggers bore intricate traceries of carving, in patterns reminiscent of grinning masks. The wavering light of the butter lamps lent the carvings a disquieting illusion of movement, as if the weapons themselves harbored some malevolent life of their own. Though clearly made of wood, not metal, in all other respects they bore a kindred resemblance to the smaller metal daggers the two newly arrived monks were carrying thrust through the backs of their belts.

Entering the room behind the abbot, the two monks paused to offer each of the standing daggers a formal salute. Hands pressed flat together, they bowed low from the waist, lightly touching the tips of their fingers to forehead, throat, and heart in a gesture of reverence.

On the side of the room opposite the door stood a low dais, luxuriously carpeted and strewn with flat cushions of rich brocade. To this the abbot mounted, seating himself cross-legged on one of the pillows and beckoning his two subordinates to places before him. As they settled, a servant dispensed Tibetan tea laced with butter and salt into bowls of fine porcelain ornamented with gold leaf. Only after he had withdrawn did the abbot speak, lifting his bowl in salute.

"You have returned in good time," he said, in his fluent, unaccented Tibetan. "Tell me how you fared in your mission."

"The news we bring is mixed, *Rinpoche*," said the younger monk. "Finding the cave presented no difficulty. The signs were all there to be read with the eyes of knowledge. We entered and found the submarine resting where the records said she would be. Regrettably, however, our visit did not go unnoticed."

The abbot's brow furrowed. "Explain."

The elder monk inclined his head. "A man came ashore from a boat. A second remained with the craft. They must have glimpsed us from the water and become curious enough to investigate. An unfortunate trait. Both have been eliminated, and will cause no further interference."

"And what of the submarine itself?" the abbot asked.

"The vessel appears to be intact," the first monk allowed, "but we were unable to gain entry."

"The hatches are rusted fast," the second monk explained.

"We were reluctant to apply such force as was available to us, lest we risk damage to what lies within."

The abbot paused to consider this piece of reasoning, then nodded his agreement.

"Your decision was wisely made. This is a task requiring ordinary tools, and men who know how to use them properly. Furthermore, they must be Westerners who will not arouse suspicion by their presence in the area where the submarine is hidden. I want no further instances of local people getting curious."

The two monks traded glances. The younger one pulled a slight frown, the first trace of emotion he had shown since his arrival.

"Where are we to find such men, *Rinpoche*? If we hire such from the immediate vicinity, there is no way to ensure their silence."

"There are other difficulties, as well," put in his counterpart. "Now that we have seen where the submarine is hidden, it is clear there will be problems with transport. There are no roads readily accessible from the area in question. Moreover, we are given to understand that the political situation in this area is one that will demand careful handling."

He directed an inquiring look toward his superior. The abbot did not immediately respond, but after a moment's thought, he squared his broad shoulders.

"At dawn, I will instruct Lutzen to consult the oracle," he declared. "In the meantime, you have done well, and have earned your rest. You may retire until morning, when I trust I shall have further instructions for you."

CHAPTER THREE

ON the Monday following Peregrine's wedding, Adam breakfasted early before driving off to the Royal Edinburgh Hospital, where he ranked as a senior psychiatric consultant. Checking at his office before his first appointment of the day, he found a message on his desk from one of the secretaries, informing him of a telephone call from Noel McLeod half an hour before.

The inspector says not an emergency, the secretary had written, *but would be grateful if you could ring him back at your earliest convenience.*

Adam frowned slightly, wondering what was afoot, but a glance at his pocket watch confirmed that he had only a few minutes before he was due to see his first patient. The relevant case file was lying on his desktop. Since he wanted to review his notes from the last session, he decided to take McLeod at his word and leave off returning the call until after this morning's session.

He skimmed the top few pages from the file, then headed for the treatment room, while memory supplied the background details of the case. The patient, a young man named Colin Balfour, was suffering from an acute form of obsessive behavior. Morbidly repelled by dirt, he would spend hours washing his hands, sometimes scrubbing until his skin was rubbed raw. In the crisis that had led to his hospitalization, he had taken lye to his hands; fortunately, a neighbor had heard his screams and gotten help. The hands would heal with little scarring, but the psychic scarring that had prompted the attempted mutilation would require more delicate treatment.

It was not a question of finding the underlying cause. That had become clear very early on in their work together. As a child of about seven or eight, Balfour had been sexually abused by an older cousin, who had terrorized him into keeping silent with threats of reprisals. Now, some fifteen years later, Balfour was desperately trying to wash away the psychic residue of shame, confusion, and misplaced guilt.

"Just thinking about it makes me feel unclean," he had told Adam, the day he finally had opened up about this shadow from his past. "I feel grimy right down to the marrow of my bones. I keep asking myself how I could ever have let myself be used that way, if some part of me didn't want it to happen. I mean, I let it go on and never told anyone. So I was as guilty as my cousin, wasn't I?"

The questions Balfour had posed for himself were ones Adam had encountered elsewhere in similar cases. For this young man, as for many other victims of abuse, the traumatizing effects of the experience itself had been exacerbated by anger and a soul-sickening conviction that somehow he must have been at least partly to blame for what had happened to him. Adam had helped him work through much of the rage in their earlier sessions; today, he hoped to begin working on the misplaced guilt.

That entailed getting at Balfour's memory of the traumatic episodes, which would have been distorted by time and his growing obsession. Fortunately, hypnosis offered one effective means by which the patient himself could bring the important details of the past into focus, whilst deriving needful comfort and support from the companion-presence of his therapist. Adam had explored the possibility of hypnotic regression at their last therapy session, and Balfour had agreed, though without much enthusiasm.

As soon as Adam entered the therapy room, however, he could see that his patient would be needing some renewed encouragement. Balfour was slumped despondently in his chair, bandaged hands resting listlessly in the lap of his tan hospital-issue dressing gown. Adam greeted him cordially, without alluding to the other man's moody behavior. Moving round to the chair on the opposite side of the desk, he made a relaxed show of sitting down and consulting his notes.

"Well, it seems we've got plenty of work to do today," he observed genially. "Are you still willing to try that experiment we spoke of last time?"

Balfour seemed to hunch down even further between his shoulder blades, like a turtle retreating into its shell.

"I suppose so," he mumbled. "I guess it couldn't hurt." His expression was morose, his manner withdrawn.

"Oh, it certainly won't *hurt*," Adam said with a fleeting smile. "On the contrary, I have high hopes that it might very well be of some help. Have you any questions you want to ask me before we begin?"

Balfour gave a shrug, not meeting Adam's eyes. "I guess not," he said in a flat voice. "If you want to play Svengali, it's up to you."

"We'll proceed as planned, then," Adam said calmly, coming around to sit on the front edge of his desk. "Why don't you put your feet up and make yourself comfortable? But if you're expecting me to don a long black cloak and make mystic passes in the air before your eyes, I'm afraid you're going to be in for a disappointment. Clinical hypnotherapists are a notoriously unimaginative bunch when it comes to stage properties."

Balfour gave him an odd, faintly skittish look, but did as he was told.

"Just don't touch me; I don't like to be touched," he murmured.

"I know that, and I know why," Adam said. "So I'll just ask you to lay your head back and have a look at that spot on the ceiling, just above your head. Do you see it?"

"Yes."

"Good. I'd like you to fix your gaze on that spot and just let yourself listen to the sound of my voice. The first part of this exercise has to do with distracting your conscious mind, so that your unconscious can come to the fore—because your unconscious is very clever and very observant, and if we can establish communication with your unconscious, it can give us valuable information that will help your understanding of what's been bothering you."

Balfour's gaze had flicked only reluctantly to the spot, but as the low voice droned on, he began visibly to relax.

"That's right," Adam murmured. "Let your conscious attention stay focused on that spot, while your body relaxes and another part of your mind just begins drifting with the sound of my voice. If your eyes get tired after a while, you can close them. There's really nothing to see with your eyes anyway, because we're far more interested in seeing what your unconscious memory might show you, as you relax more and more, drifting, floating . . . very comfortable and relaxed. . . . "

Speaking softly and calmly as a father to a frightened child, Adam soon was able to lull the younger man into a state of relaxation bordering on sleep, and from there to guide him toward those deeper levels of awareness which could open up the long-locked doors to the past.

Balfour proved a ready subject, and the next half hour yielded far more fruitful results than Adam had dared to hope. When he brought his patient back to full consciousness, it was immediately apparent that Balfour had achieved some fresh insights into his situation, both past and present. After brief discussion, Adam left him with instructions to reflect on what he had learned until their next session, later in the week. But when he went back to his office to telephone McLeod, it was not McLeod who answered, but his assistant, Sergeant Donald Cochrane.

"Sorry, Sir Adam, but the inspector's gone off to the Royal Infirmary," Cochrane said. "I was to tell you that he'd appreciate it very much if you could arrange to meet him there, the sooner the better. Are you ringing from home?"

"No, from Jordanburn," Adam said, giving the psychiatric facility the name by which it was known locally. "Did the inspector happen to mention what this is all about?"

"Aye." Cochrane's voice sounded a little pinched. "He did tell you, didn't he, about that stretch of road they're starting to call Carnage Corridor?"

"Yes."

"Well, it's claimed another victim, maybe two. A man was killed there earlier this morning, and another's undergoing emergency surgery. The inspector's standing by, in case he regains consciousness, but it doesn't look good.''

''I see.''

''Here's the part you're going to love,'' Cochrane went on. ''The man who's in surgery was still conscious when the police arrived. He claimed he'd veered off the road to avoid hitting a man and a pregnant woman—kept asking, 'Did I hit them? Did I hit them?'

''The problem is, none of the witnesses the police interviewed can recall seeing any pedestrians on the scene. Given the fact that the crash occurred in broad daylight, you'd've thought *somebody* would have seen the couple in question, but so far nobody's come forward with any descriptions. If I were a superstitious man, I'd be starting to wonder if maybe the driver of the crashed car might have seen a ghost.''

As Master of the Hunting Lodge, Adam had known far stranger things to happen, but he forebore from saying so aloud. Though Donald Cochrane had received some peripheral esoteric instruction through his training as a Freemason, and McLeod had pegged him as a potential future recruit for the Hunting Lodge, his direct experience with the supernatural thus far had been solely in a support capacity. Adam himself was rapidly becoming convinced that there was more involved in the present case than malignant coincidence, but if things were about to shift into a more overt brush with the unknown, best to keep Cochrane at arm's length until they knew more.

''Well, it's reassuring to know that you aren't a superstitious man, Donald,'' he allowed. ''I shouldn't think we'll find a ghost involved, but the situation does seem to go beyond mere coincidence. Do you happen to know the name of the surviving victim?''

''Aye, the inspector left it right here on his desk pad,'' Cochrane said. ''The name's Malcolm Stuart Grant, with an address in Lanark. That's all I've got, though.''

''That's enough for now,'' Adam replied, jotting the name on a notepad. ''I just need to know who to ask for when I get to the Royal Infirmary.''

''You'll go, then.''

''Aye. Whatever the cause of these accidents, the effects would seem to be getting out of hand. I'll see what I can do to reshuffle my appointments for the rest of the morning. In the meantime, if Inspector McLeod should happen to check in, tell him I've received his message and will rendezvous with him at the hospital as soon as possible.''

Uncertain how long he might find himself detained once he and McLeod met up, Adam rescheduled his two remaining patients for appointments the next day and postponed his usual morning rounds for later on in the afternoon, after which he signed out and headed for the car park.

He decided to risk the traffic on Morningside Road, and was relieved to find the route relatively uncluttered. Carrying on north and east along Bruntsfield Place, he bore right at the Toll Crossing onto Lauriston Place, whence a string of signs pointed the way toward the casualty department of Edinburgh's Royal Infirmary. He parked the Range Rover in a physicians' car park and headed toward the entrance.

It was not a hospital he normally frequented in his psychiatric practice, but its casualty department was reputed to be one of the two best in Scotland; Glasgow had the other. It was here that injured police officers and firefighters were most apt to be brought; he had watched with McLeod through several lonely nights when men's lives hung in the balance. He had been here once as a casualty himself—and Dr. Ximena Lockhart had been the on-call surgeon who had patched him up.

Shaking off the memory, he eased aside to let an ambulance crew wheel an empty gurney out of the building, then slipped inside and headed for the registrar's desk. He was reaching for his credentials when a breezy voice hailed him from farther along the corridor.

''Dr. Sinclair?''

Turning, he saw the familiar white-uniformed figure of Reggie Sykes, the orderly Ximena had been training in emergency-room procedures. Sykes's coffee-colored face split in a broad grin as he approached.

''I thought that was you, sir!'' he exclaimed, the musical lilt in his voice proclaiming his Jamaican origins. ''It's been a long time. Say, what you hear from that pretty lady of yours? How's her daddy gettin' on?''

The subject was one Adam would have preferred to avoid,

but he knew Sykes had doted on the attractive American "Dr. X."

"I gather he's holding his own," he replied, not without some private reservations. "The last time we spoke on the phone, she described his condition as 'stable.'"

He hoped that Sykes would interpret the term optimistically, but the orderly pulled a grimace.

"Only stable, huh? With what he's got, that's not so good."

Adam shrugged. Ximena had told him that her father was comfortable enough, if rarely lucid, because of the painkillers they gave him, but it was only a matter of time. In fact, Ximena and her father between them had already accepted that his chances for recovery were virtually nonexistent. Her mother and brothers, however, were still determined to cling to hope, however faint and misplaced. It was as much for their sake as for anyone else's that Ximena was committed to remaining at her father's bedside.

"I could certainly wish the prognosis were better," Adam agreed. "Unfortunately, the situation is out of both our hands."

Sykes gave a sympathetic shake of his head. "Well, the next time you talk to her, you tell her from me that she ought to come back here soon, okay? Things haven't been the same since she left."

"I can attest to that," Adam said with a faint smile. "And I'll certainly pass the word along."

"Thank you, Doc," Sykes said, with another of his fleeting grins. "There aren't many like Dr. X. around. Come to think of it," he added, cocking an eye at Adam, "you haven't said what brings you here this morning. You sure didn't come all the way cross town just to see if we've had the walls repainted since your last visit."

"True enough. Actually, I'm looking for a patient by the name of Malcolm Grant. He would have been brought in several hours ago—car crash."

"Another statistic for Carnage Corridor," Skyes said with a grimace. "We get most of 'em. He's up in surgery. Don't know if it's going to help him much, though—not the state he was in when he arrived. I helped get him over to X-ray, and I don't know when I last saw anybody that bad who could still breathe at all. They brought his buddy in dead.''

"Yes, I'd heard there was at least one fatality.''

Sykes gave a darkling shake of his head. "I tell you, Dr. Sinclair, it's spooky business. You may not believe it, but this must be the fifth or sixth big crash we've had along that stretch of road since New Year's, all with fatalities. If I had any reason to drive to Lanark just now, man, I'd damn sure go round about by way of Livingston, just to be on the safe side.''

He paused for an exaggerated shiver, then directed a curious look in Adam's direction. "But, what's your interest in this case, sir, if you don't mind my asking? Last I heard, psychiatrists don't normally do casualty work.''

"You just said it yourself,'' Adam replied. "That bit of road has claimed far more than its share of casualties, and all in a very short time. The police are doing their best to see if they can come up with a pattern, even to the extent of calling in a psychiatrist—me—to see if anything in the victims' psychiatric profiles might point to an underlying cause. To that end, I'm supposed to be meeting one of their special investigators, a Detective Chief Inspector McLeod. Do you know him?''

Sykes pursed his lips. "Is this Inspector McLeod a big fellow with grizzled hair and glasses and a military-looking moustache?''

"That sounds like him.''

"Then you'll probably find him up in the lounge next to the operating theatres. If he isn't there, I don't expect he's gone far.''

"If he has, I can always have him paged,'' Adam said. "Thank you, Mr. Sykes, you've been a great help. The next time I talk to Dr. Lockhart, I'll be sure to let her know you were asking about her.''

He lost no time getting up to the surgical wing. Here he learned that Malcolm Grant was out of surgery and had been transferred to Recovery, just down the hall. He found McLeod propping up the wall to the left of the nurses' station, moodily sipping tea from a hospital-issue mug. Through the round porthole windows in the double doors opposite,

Adam could catch just a glimpse of bustling medical activity as he approached.

"Is he still with us?" Adam asked, as the inspector pulled himself erect and shelved the mug on the desk with an air of mingled relief and misgivings.

"Aye, but I don't know how long that will continue to be the case. Thanks for coming. Sorry about dragging you out earlier than we'd planned, but I hadn't reckoned on this. And it may be wasted effort. But if he does regain consciousness, I didn't want to miss it—and you might pick up something I'd overlook."

"You don't sound optimistic."

"I don't think there's much cause to be optimistic. Have a look. He's pretty smashed up."

As he spoke, McLeod moved to one of the portholes, and Adam joined him at the other. Four of the six bays in Recovery were occupied, the respective patients linked up to an assortment of monitors and life support units. A man and a woman togged out in green surgical scrubs were standing at the foot of the bed nearest the door, where lay a supine figure cocooned in bandages and surrounded by the metal frames of traction apparatus. The woman was scribbling orders on the patient's chart as the man looked on.

"That's our man," McLeod murmured, pointing the way with a jerk of his chin. "He's only just come out of surgery. I was waiting until they'd finished getting him settled before pressing for a prognosis, but any questions on that account are probably better coming from you, anyway."

As two uniformed nurses busied themselves around the patient, the female surgeon concluded her notes with a brisk flourish and presented them to her male colleague, pausing long enough to answer a brief inquiry from one of the nurses before making for the exit. Adam and McLeod stepped back from the doors as she came through, and she nodded to McLeod and pulled off her surgical cap to ruffle a hand through short, curly dark hair.

"Will I get to talk to him?" McLeod asked.

She glanced back at the doors swinging closed behind her and shrugged. "I wouldn't say the chances are very good—certainly not right away. We're waiting to see what will result from his head injury; we may have to go in again. Meanwhile, he's got a definite concussion, some cracked ribs, two broken legs, he's probably lost the sight in one eye, and he was bleeding internally. We had to remove his spleen—''

"Tell Dr. Sinclair, if you please," McLeod interrupted. "He's a special police consultant."

"Dr. Stirling," a voice called from the recovery room, as a nurse poked her head through the door. "Could you take a look at Mrs. Bell? She's looking a little shocky; she might be hemorrhaging."

"On my way," the surgeon said, giving Adam an apologetic shrug. "Sorry, Doctor. If you want, you can go ahead and have a look at Mr. Grant's chart, but I don't expect it will make much difference, one way or the other."

Murmuring his thanks, Adam snagged a spare hospital gown, plus one for McLeod, and pulled it on over his suit before following the surgeon into Recovery. The other surgeon and one of the nurses had already gone to tend the ailing Mrs. Bell, and the remaining nurse continued to adjust an IV drip as Adam picked up Grant's chart. He now could see that Grant was also on a respirator, not just oxygen; and the vital signs being monitored on the bank of machines to one side described a patient very ill, indeed.

"Bad, huh?" McLeod murmured, close by Adam's elbow.

Gravely Adam nodded, eyes scanning the chart. "I can only say that he must have a tremendous will to live. He might make it, though."

Behind them, Dr. Stirling and her colleague were preparing to wheel Mrs. Bell back into surgery, and most of the medical staff were congregated at that end of Recovery, including the nurse who had been monitoring Grant.

"Well, I very much doubt he's going to be able to talk to us, so maybe I'd better see if I can go to him," Adam said softly, replacing the chart at the foot of the bed. "This will be quick and dirty, if it works at all, but we'll see what we can pick up."

Moving closer to the head of the bed, Adam prepared himself with a single deep breath to ground and center himself, at the same time framing a silent prayer of petition to the spiritual guardians who ruled the Inner Planes. He must be very careful, for one of the nurses had just come back. Despite that distraction, however, he could feel the first faint glimmerings of rapport with the soul resident in the shattered body before him—and knew that the link of soul to body was tenuous, else he would not have been able to perceive it so clearly.

But before he could stabilize the forming bridge between them, the beep of the pulse-rate monitor increased in tempo and Malcolm Grant shuddered and roused, his one unbandaged eye snapping wide in a sudden, agitated return to consciousness. Simultaneously, he started gasping, fighting the ventilator that had been helping him breathe. Alarms began going off on all his monitors as his heartbeat faltered.

"Code Blue!" the nurse shouted. "I need a crash cart!"

Even as she moved in to begin administering CPR, and other medical personnel began converging on the patient, including Dr. Stirling, Adam bent to the stricken man's ear, both hands gently steadying the thrashing head.

"You aren't choking, Mr. Grant," he murmured. "There's a machine helping you breathe. Let it do the work. Just try to relax."

But Grant deteriorated quickly, despite the efforts of the crash team, and slipped back into unconsciousness even as a nurse wheeled a defibrillator into place and Dr. Stirling positioned the paddles on his chest.

"Clear, everyone!" she ordered, and everyone else fell back.

But though she shocked the patient several times, the monitors one by one went flat. Watching helpless and silent from behind the circle of technicians fighting to save Grant's life, Adam sensed the fraying of the silver cord that was Grant's spiritual lifeline. Powerless to knit it back together, he felt a kindred psychic wrench at the moment when the cord parted. In that same instant, the fleeting image came to him of two stricken faces, a man and a woman, staring back at him in frozen horror through the windscreen of an onrushing car.

The image exploded on impact, even as an invisible breath of psychic breeze wafted past Adam—Malcolm Grant's immortal soul winging free of his broken body. The release was untimely, leaving behind tasks undone and promises unfulfilled. All Adam could do was wish the retiring spirit Godspeed in his own heart of hearts, trusting to the wisdom of the Light to redress the balance in the fullness of time.

Lost momentarily in these reflections, he only belatedly became aware that the nursing staff had abandoned their efforts to resuscitate their patient. Even as he lifted his bowed head, one of the nurses leaned in and gently drew the sheet over the face of the deceased.

"Dr. Sinclair, was it?" said a woman's voice behind him.

As he turned, Dr. Stirling offered him Grant's chart and a pen.

"Could we have your particulars, in case there's an inquiry?" she said. "I actually expected to lose him on the table, but the hospital needs to have all the details, just in case any question comes up later."

He would have preferred to retreat at once to some quiet place where he could consider what he had experienced and bounce his impressions off McLeod. Even more, he wished that Peregrine had been here to sketch the faces, either direct or from Adam's description. Holding onto the images as best he could, he jotted down his sparse observations, commending the crash team for their efforts, then signed with his particulars of consultancy and licensing and handed the chart back to a nurse. He was shaking his head as he headed out of the recovery room, where McLeod had withdrawn at the first sign of medical crisis.

"Well?" McLeod said. "Were you able to pick up anything at all?"

"Something, but I'm not sure what it means," Adam said, stripping off his gown. "Here's not the best place to discuss it, though. Why don't we head on down to the hospital chapel? That's as private a place as we're likely to find on the premises."

They found the chapel empty, and settled into a pew in the rear. Closing his eyes, Adam conjured the mysterious faces and described for McLeod's benefit what he himself had shared of Malcolm Grant's experience.

"I believe Grant was telling the absolute truth when he told the officers at the scene that he'd seen two pedestrians step out in front of his car," he told his Second. "Whether or not there was anything actually there, however, is another story entirely."

"A ghost story, maybe?" McLeod said.

What his Second meant was not lost on Adam. It was a fact, affirmed by their experience as Huntsmen, that people and incidents, especially violent ones, could generate emotional and imagistic resonances that could be inadvertently apprehended by anyone sensitive enough to pick them up.

"I wonder if, perhaps, it is," Adam said thoughtfully, glancing back at McLeod. "Tell me: Were there pedestrians involved in any of the other accidents covered by this investigation?"

McLeod shook his head. "No, they were all car crashes."

"Hmmm." Adam gave the patrician bridge of his nose a thoughtful rub. "I wonder, then, if Malcolm Grant saw a ghostly manifestation of something that predates the onset of these accidents."

McLeod turned to look at him more directly. "What are you saying? That we're not casting our nets widely enough?"

"Something like that," Adam said, with a thin flicker of a smile. "From what you've been telling me, I gather that Donald and his Traffic colleagues have been spending long hours sifting through the accident reports themselves in search of a common denominator. If they haven't found one, that could be because it isn't there. I wonder what they might turn up if they were to work backwards from the first of the year, looking for any other unusual occurrences along that stretch of road—perhaps something involving pedestrians."

"That's a very interesting notion," McLeod said. "I'll pass it on to Donald, and authorize the archival work. You really think you're onto something?"

"I don't know," Adam said. "But if Donald turns up anything promising, be sure to let me know."

"Aye, so I will," McLeod said. "I'd like to see us crack this case before Carnage Corridor claims another set of victims."

CHAPTER FOUR

"SAINT Columba's footsteps," Julia Lovat murmured, looking up from the pages of her much-thumbed guidebook. "Do you suppose those marks we saw on the top of that rock by Kilcolmkill Church really are the imprints of his feet?"

Peregrine had his portable campstool firmly planted in the sand a short distance away, his travelling easel propped up on its tripod in front of him. He was overlaying thin washes of watercolor to a developing study of his wife where she sat perched above him on a large flat-topped boulder, with the intense blue-green waters of the North Channel for a background. Julia's question came just as he was trading the fine sable brush in his hand for one finer still. Lifting his hazel gaze from the paintbox, he gave her a grin.

"Given the way the currents run in these waters, I suppose this stretch of shoreline is as likely a place as any for an Irish-born saint to have made his landfall. As for the footprints themselves—I don't know about you, but I am a firm believer in miracles."

The fond look that accompanied this declaration left Julia in no doubt as to the romantic nature of his meaning. She accepted the tribute with a chuckle and said wryly, "I hope that's not meant to be an assessment of my driving ability."

"Not in the least!" her new husband averred. "You and Algy are getting along famously."

The dark-green Alvis so named was parked at the side of the narrow road overlooking the beach where the couple had just finished picnicking on oatcakes, smoked salmon, and "truckles," a creamy variety of local cheese. It was the third day of their honeymoon, the second since their arrival in Kintyre, a wild and scenic peninsula on Scotland's west coast. Among the places they had explored since leaving their guesthouse in Campbeltown earlier that morning was the spot where the seventh-century Irish missionary, St. Columba, was purported to have preached his first sermon on Scottish soil. A set of footprints visible on the flattened summit of a rock near the local village of Southend was said to be a permanent memento of that historic visit.

From Southend the pair had driven west along a road that was little more than a paved one-lane farm track, making for the point at the southwestern tip of the peninsula known as the Mull of Kintyre. From where they were sitting now, they had a view of the Kintyre lighthouse, built in 1788 and one of the first of its kind to be erected by the Trustees for Northern Lighthouses. Julia's expression turned meditative as she surveyed the lighthouse's turret-like outline, rising off its rocky base like some seagirt tower out of a Scottish folk tale.

"I always thought I'd like to live in a lighthouse," she observed dreamily. "To live balanced between the land and the sea and the sky, and to listen by night to the songs the silkies sing . . . "

Silkies were the mer-people of Scottish legend, gifted with the ability to shed their seagoing skins of seal-fur in order to go about ashore in the likeness of men. Softly Julia began to sing the ballad of the Great Silkie, which told how this lord of the sea had fathered a child on a woman of the land, returning from the waves thereafter to claim his son. Clear as a crystalline bell, her soprano voice floated up over the surrounding rocks, carrying with it the words of the Silkie himself:

> "I am a man, upon the land,
>   An I am a silkie in the sea;
> And when I'm far and far frae land,
>   My dwelling is in Sule Skerry. . . . "

Had they been at home, Julia would have accompanied herself on the harp, but even without the delicate counterpoint of harp strings, her rendition of the melody had the power to arrest Peregrine in the midst of his work. As he listened, he was reminded how it had been her singing which first had captivated him, even before he ever set eyes on her.

The occasion had been a sad one: the funeral service for Julia's godmother, the same Lady Laura Kintoul who had made Peregrine a present of the Alvis in her will. A mere apprentice then in the use of the Deep Sight which was now second nature to him, Peregrine had come to the church with Adam, half-dreading to find himself confronted by spectres of the dead. Instead, he had found not only peace but a new direction, for which Adam had been the catalyst and of which Julia was the living embodiment.

The silvery lilt of her voice lingered in his ears even after she had finished her song. He roused himself from contemplating a host of pleasant memories to discover that she had gone back to her guidebook. Bestirring himself to return to his work, he asked, "Where are you proposing that we should go tomorrow?"

"If it's all the same to you," she said, " I rather fancy taking the ferry across to Arran to see Lochranza Castle and King's Cave. That's where Robert the Bruce reputedly met the famous spider."

Peregrine smiled. Every schoolchild in Scotland was familiar with the legend of how Bruce, discouraged and demoralized after a string of military reversals, had drawn fresh resolve from the sight of a small grey spider painstakingly rebuilding a shattered web.

"That sounds fine to me," he said. "Brodick Castle might be well worth a visit as well. After that, weather permitting, we might even try to hire a boat and have a look at Holy Island."

Julia's sea-blue eyes turned quizzical as she lowered her guidebook. "Didn't I read somewhere that Tibetan Buddhists recently bought that island? It strikes me as odd, you know, that Buddhists would want to buy a Christian holy site."

Peregrine shrugged, not looking up from his work. "I understand the local folk felt that way, too, at first. But from what I hear, the order that bought it have been well-established and respected in the Borders for nigh on twenty years now, and they made it clear from the start that their purpose was to preserve the historic spiritual character of the island, to make it a place that would welcome seekers of all faiths.''

''Well, that's refreshing, in these days when people are killing one another over religion.''

''Aye, but the Buddhists have always been known for their tolerance. As you might expect, they're also very focused on the ecological aspects of the place. I understand that most of the island will be maintained as a nature preserve for the protection of the island's wildlife. I thought I might do some sketching. They've got all kinds of rare birds, about a dozen Ersikay ponies—which are the original Celtic horse—and even a small flock of Soay sheep.''

''Soay sheep?'' Julia looked at him in some disbelief. ''Do they really?''

''That's what I hear. They're a very ancient breed, aren't they?''

''Aye, Bronze Age. They look rather like small goats, and you don't shear them—you pluck them. I don't know what kind of yarn the wool makes—though you can spin almost anything. I've got a cousin who's very keen on spinning and weaving.''

''Well, maybe we can bring back some wool for her,'' Peregrine said. ''See what the guidebook says about the island.''

As she consulted the book, Peregrine carried on with his painting, considering Julia's comment about Buddhist interest in a Christian holy site. Though a formerly lukewarm childhood faith had been kindled to a sustaining flame through his association with Adam and the Hunting Lodge, and he was content for it to be so, Peregrine felt drawn to the island with a keenness that he was somewhat at a loss to explain.

Wondering what the lure might be, he allowed his gaze to wander out to sea. A gauzy haze was forming on the western horizon, blurring the distinction between sea and sky. Even as it occurred to him that he had better finish his painting before the light changed, his eye was drawn to a curious patch of shadow bobbing up and down among the swells of the incoming tide.

Peregrine's first thought was that it was probably just a large patch of kelp. Unlike kelp, however, this object seemed to keep to a solid shape, and was showing disconcertingly unnatural flashes of bright orange as it rolled closer in the surf. Whatever it was, it was attracting the attention of the gulls and other birds feeding along the shoreline.

With a pang of sudden foreboding, the young artist laid aside his brush and got to his feet to go take a closer look. His movement was abrupt enough to divert Julia's attention from her book.

"What's the matter?" she asked. Her expression was more curious than alarmed.

"Probably nothing," Peregrine said, with what he hoped was a reassuring smile. "Just stay where you are. I'll be right back."

He made his way down toward the water's edge just as an incoming swell swept the object into the shallows, tumbling black and bright orange amid the expected sea-wrack. One reluctant glance was enough to confirm Peregrine's worst misgivings. The object was the body of a man, encased in the black-and-orange neoprene of what looked like a wet suit.

Reluctantly he bent closer. The corpse was more than a little battered from its passage through the rocks. It half-floated face-down in the surf with arms and legs loosely out-sprawled like the limbs of a sodden rag doll. The bloated hands were starting to show evidence of decomposition. Peregrine decided it was probably just as well that he couldn't see the face.

Calling on his forensic training with McLeod, he made himself draw breath and distance himself a little as he continued to note first impressions. Alive, the man probably had been fit and sturdy. The short hair that capped his skull was a uniform shade of sandy-red, and thick, indicating that he had been relatively young. A serious laceration laid open the back of his skull, but the sea had washed away any blood. From the wet suit, Peregrine wondered if he might have been a diver, or possibly a wind-surfer met with mishap.

Even as the possibilities crossed his mind, a muffled exclamation from behind him made him start around. Julia had come down off her perch to join him, and was staring at the corpse with an expression of mingled pity and horror. His own squeamishness momentarily forgotten, Peregrine went to take her in his arms, at the same time trying to block her view with his own body.

"Julia, I'm sorry," he said lamely. "I didn't mean for you to see this. Let me take you back to the car."

He made a gentle attempt to steer her away, but somewhat to his surprise, she resisted his efforts. Her gaze partly averted, she murmured, "Poor soul! I wonder if he's the man who went missing off the Irish coast at the weekend."

Her observation put Peregrine in mind of a news bulletin he had picked up in the car on his way to the church on their wedding day. Dimly he recalled something having been said about a vessel from the Irish Department of the Marine being found adrift off Malin Head, with a dead man aboard.

He glanced uneasily down at Julia. She was looking rather white about the lips, but he saw with some relief that her face was otherwise composed. After a moment's pause, she drew herself up and asked, "Shouldn't we be thinking about telephoning an ambulance or something?"

"Not an ambulance," Peregrine said with a shake of his head. "We'll want the police back in Campbeltown. They should have the facilities to deal with this. How would you feel about driving Algy all on your own?"

Julia registered a blink. "More confident than I would have felt a week ago. Why?"

"I want you to go find a phone box and report what we've found," Peregrine said. "Southend is the nearest place where you'd be likely to locate one. Failing that, however, you may find yourself obliged to drive back to Campbeltown. I realize the road's none too good. Do you think you're up to it?"

"I suppose I'd better be, hadn't I?" Julia said with a small grimace. "What will you be doing in the meantime?"

"Keeping an eye on the body," Peregrine said. "I don't want to handle it, if I can help it, because if this turns out to be more than a simple case of death by misadventure, the procurator fiscal won't thank me for doing anything that might compromise the evidence. At the same time, the tide is going to be turning soon, and we don't want our unfortunate friend to be carried back out to sea again before the police can retrieve him.''

"Certainly not if we're going to call them out on a round trip drive of thirty miles,'' Julia agreed with feeling. She glanced over at the body on the shore and hurriedly looked away again with a shiver. "Thanks for giving me the easy job.''

"Don't mention it,'' Peregrine said wryly. Gathering his bride into his arms, he added, "I really am sorry about this. I hope it hasn't ruined your honeymoon.''

Julia nestled into his embrace and smiled. "Darling, it's *our* honeymoon—and do you really think anything could do that?''

This declaration earned her a lingering kiss. Resisting an impulse to repeat it, Peregrine fished in his trouser pocket for the car keys.

"Here you are,'' he told her as he handed them over. "Take as much time as you have to, for your own safety. I'm certainly not planning to go anywhere else between now and when you get back—and neither is he.''

He followed her with his eyes as she made her way up through the rocks toward the road, where the Alvis stood waiting. Before climbing into the driver's seat, she vouchsafed him a wave and a kiss blown from her hand. He heard the smooth growl of a well-tuned engine as she turned the key in the ignition. A moment later, the Alvis swung around in a compact U-turn and headed back up the road in the direction of Campbeltown.

Left alone, Peregrine spent the next few minutes pacing uneasily up and down at the water's edge. He found himself wondering if he would ever achieve the degree of fortitude he had seen Adam and McLeod display when confronted with a corpse. As he reflected back over the experience he had gained in their company as a forensic artist, it occurred to him that it might not be a bad idea on this occasion to take some photographs for the record. Satisfied that the body on the shore was in no immediate danger of floating away, he went to retrieve his camera from amongst the rest of his artist's paraphernalia.

He removed the lens cap from his Pentax as he returned to the water's edge, casually framing up a cover-shot as he walked. But when he paused to take it, adjusting the zoom lens, he had trouble getting it to focus.

"That's odd."

He shook his head, blinked, and tried again. His efforts brought no improvement to the imaging. A quick inspection of his glasses showed nothing to account for the fuzziness. Clucking his tongue impatiently, he unscrewed the lens and held it to the light from both directions—perfectly clean— then replaced it and looked again. The results were still no better. Though his vision by itself seemed clear enough, the picture seen through the lens remained curiously blurred.

Perplexed, Peregrine went ahead and shot several different angles of the body, focused as best he could, then sat back on his heels and scowled as he contemplated this peculiar development. The absence of anything like a logical explanation aroused hitherto dormant suspicions, and made him begin to wonder what would happen if he were to try his luck with a sketch.

He decided to test his perceptions before going to the bother of fetching his sketchbook. For Peregrine, the act of drawing was the means by which he could both activate and direct his own distinctive powers of psychic perception. Laying the camera on a nest of sea grass behind him, he settled gingerly on a rock beside the body and composed himself, momentarily closing his eyes. Calling now upon the training given him by Adam, he drew several deep, measured breaths. The centrifugal whirl of his thoughts and emotions fell away, leaving him centered in an island of calm. Grounded in that calm, he opened his eyes again, simultaneously willing himself to See.

For a moment, he could envision nothing but the piebald shape of the corpse itself. As he continued to watch, however, another, hazier image began to form, hovering over the body like a ghost. Insubstantial as mist, it assumed a vaguely human shape. But as soon as Peregrine attempted to bring that shape into sharper focus, it abruptly dissolved.

With a hard-won patience born of self-discipline, he set himself to try again. Before he could re-establish any degree of perception, however, a sudden surge in the tide lifted the dead man's body from its grounding on the beach. The wave's backwash started to pull the corpse with it, tumbling it back in the direction of the open sea.

Peregrine roused himself with a jerk and made a hasty lunge to recapture it. A splash of cold brine left him wet to the knees, but he managed to get a hand around one orange-clad wrist. While he was struggling to maintain his grip, his eyes lighted for the first time on an irregular three-cornered tear in the back of the man's wet suit.

A wound?

His curiosity piqued, Peregrine towed the body back to its resting place at the waterline, then bent down for a closer look. He could see no immediate evidence of any wound beneath the tear, but he refrained from poking and prodding. Even if his work with McLeod had not taught him a healthy respect for proper forensic procedure, he was strongly disinclined to have anything more to do with the dead man's remains than he absolutely had to. He took the minimal measures necessary to get the body beached, retrieved the camera and put it away, then sat back on a nearby rock to guard the body and await reinforcements.

A full hour passed before the distinctive purr of a familiar engine brought him to his feet. When the Alvis swung into view, Peregrine was relieved to see that it was accompanied by a white Range Rover bearing the fluorescent yellow side stripe and door insignia of the Strathclyde Police.

Julia stopped the Alvis where she had parked before and sprang out as the police car slowed to a halt a yard or two behind the Alvis' rear bumper. Two uniformed policemen alighted and came to join her on the shoulder, falling in behind her as she led the way down to the beach. As soon as she reached the sand, Julia broke away from her escort and ran forward to greet her husband.

"Sorry it took me so long," she said. "I couldn't find a public telephone anywhere between here and Campbeltown, and once I got there I had a bit of trouble finding the police station. This is Sergeant MacDonald, and that's P.C. Williamson." Turning back to the two police officers, she added, "This is my husband."

"Gentlemen." Peregrine acknowledged the introduction with a nod. "Thank you for coming out."

"Not at all, Mr. Lovat," the sergeant replied, directing his subordinate toward the castaway corpse. "Sorry you and Mrs. Lovat have had your stay here in Kintyre so rudely interrupted. I'm thankful to say we don't get many calls like this. We'll try to run through the formalities as quickly as possible, so that you and your wife can get back to your holiday."

Delving into the breast pocket of his police tunic, he took out a notebook and pen.

"Mrs. Lovat has already given us a statement," he told Peregrine. "While we're waiting for the ambulance to arrive, I'd appreciate it if you'd give me your version."

Peregrine was familiar with the procedure, having witnessed McLeod in action on the scene of more than one investigation. Knowing full well what to expect, he responded to the ensuing series of questions with a conciseness consistent with police methods. At the end of their dialogue, the sergeant gave him a quizzical look over the top of his notebook.

"Have you given evidence before in a police inquiry, Mr. Lovat?"

"Yes, I have," Peregrine admitted. "I occasionally do freelance work as a forensic artist for Detective Chief Inspector Noel McLeod of the Lothian and Borders Police."

Sergeant MacDonald's blue eyes registered a spark of lively interest. "That wouldn't be the same DCI McLeod who headed up the investigation into those so-called jack-o'-lantern killings last October?"

"The very same, I'm afraid."

MacDonald pulled a wry grin. "Gets all the strange ones, does your Inspector McLeod. Well, I guess somebody has to tackle them. Were you involved with the case?"

"Only in a very minor way," Peregrine said evasively. He did not add that, in seeking to apprehend the killer,

McLeod had drawn—unofficially—on the collective resources of the Hunting Lodge.

MacDonald favored Peregrine with a speculative look, but any further comment on McLeod's apparent notoriety in police circles was forestalled by the return of P.C. Williamson.

"Sergeant, I think this might be that Irish Fisheries officer who went missing over the weekend," he said. "Scanlan, I think the name was. They use this kind of survival gear. He's got a wound in the back to match his partner's."

MacDonald pursed his lips in a brief, soundless whistle, then gave a deprecatory shake of his head. "Well, that rules out a fight between the two of them," he said. "They can't both have stabbed one another in the back. And he had to wash up on our beat."

The subdued rumble of another vehicle approaching heralded the arrival of the ambulance. Conscious of a growing sea chill in the air, Peregrine wrapped an arm around Julia's shoulders and gathered her close to him as two ambulance attendants made their way down from the road to meet them. Under the supervision of the two police officers, they zipped the remains into a black body bag and shifted the bag onto a portable stretcher for conveyance up to their car, Sergeant MacDonald lingered long enough to exchange parting words with the Lovats.

"Once again, let me express my regrets that you should have had your visit interrupted by a thing like this," he told them. "I hope the rest of your trip goes smoothly."

"So do I," Julia said solemnly. "This certainly wasn't on our agenda!"

"We were planning to leave Kintyre in the morning," Peregrine said, with a glance down at his wife's upturned face, "but I suppose we could stay on for another day or two, if you think you might need us as witnesses."

"I don't think that will be at all necessary," MacDonald assured them. "You've done your bit, and admirably. I don't anticipate our having to trouble you again. Best wishes to you both. Enjoy the rest of your holiday."

"We fully intend to," Peregrine said, giving Julia a hug. The two men traded handshakes before MacDonald took his leave. Once the police and the ambulance men had departed, the Lovats began gathering up their things. It was only when Peregrine had to shift his camera bag that he remembered the photos he had taken of the dead man.

He said nothing to Julia, but he made a mental note to see about having the film processed as soon as possible, and also have the camera checked out. With the camera misbehaving, he doubted the photos would be of much help to the police, but at least he wanted to be sure that further photos of the wedding trip were not ruined—and it would be fun to see the photos they had taken thus far.

Putting the camera out of mind, he packed up his paintbox, then paused to contemplate the unfinished painting still mounted on his easel. He was debating whether or not to crumple it up and consign it to the nearest rubbish bin when he felt Julia's arms encircle his waist from behind.

"I hope you're not thinking of getting rid of that," she said.

Peregrine turned to her in some surprise, circling her shoulders with his arms. "Are you saying you'd like me to *keep* it?"

"More than that, I'd like you to *finish* it, if you can," Julia said. Seeing that her husband was still looking dubious, she went on. "It's true I had a bit of a shock today, darling, but the experience was also something of a revelation. I got to see a side of you that I'd hitherto only heard about secondhand—the side of you that only comes out when you're working on a case with Adam and Noel McLeod. Since you're obviously going to continue in that association, it's important to both of us that I should come to understand that aspect of your life. This was the first step toward my achieving that understanding, and I want to remember it."

Peregrine gazed down at his wife's earnest face with something approaching wonder. "Julia, are you sure? The kind of enforcement work I get involved in from time to time can often get pretty harrowing."

Even as he spoke, it cost him a pang to think of some of the uglier sights he had seen. But Julia's blue eyes never wavered from his.

"You don't have to tell me all the gory details," she conceded. "But you don't have to shield me completely, either. Our lives are now inextricably intertwined. If each of us doesn't grow with the other, both of us will wind up stunted. Trust me to know my own mind in this, darling, and promise me you'll keep that painting."

Peregrine had never heard Julia speak so seriously before. "I promise," he told her. And sealed it with a fervent kiss.

CHAPTER FIVE

FOLLOWING their conversation in the hospital chapel, Adam and McLeod went their separate ways. Although both men were now committed to solving the riddle of Carnage Corridor, McLeod had other cases awaiting his attention back at police headquarters, and Adam still had a belated series of rounds to perform at Jordanburn.

Back at the hospital, however, he found it more difficult than usual to concentrate on the reports being rendered him by the nursing staff. Though one half of his mind remained dutifully attuned to the welfare of his patients and concerns of staff, the other half kept wandering back to the unanswered questions concerning how Malcolm Grant, and all those before him, had met their deaths.

He finally finished his rounds just after four o'clock. Faced with the better part of another hour to update his case notes, he resigned himself to the prospect of having to start home during the Edinburgh rush hour and wrote out a set of fresh orders for the nursing staff before starting back toward his office to finish up. Passing through the hospital foyer, a headline caught his eye at the small news kiosk adjoining the reception area:

CARNAGE CORRIDOR CLAIMS TWO MORE VICTIMS

Catching up short, Adam stepped over to the kiosk and picked up the top copy of the *Edinburgh Evening News*, skimming over the lead story. A cursory reading revealed nothing of substance that he did not already know from his briefing with McLeod and his stint at the Royal Infirmary. There was, however, a black-and-white photograph taken at the scene of the accident. Without knowing quite what he was looking for, Adam bent to examine it more closely.

Prominent in the foreground was the twisted wreckage of the late model Austin Rover that Grant had been driving at the time of the accident. The attendant caption labelled the car a "commuter's deathtrap." Several spectators hovered slightly out of focus in the background, but as Adam continued to study the photo, his attention kept returning to one of them: a woman's pale figure in the upper left corner of the frame.

He stifled an exclamation, already fishing out pocket change to pay for the paper, for the face, though blurred, was one Adam was not likely to forget in a hurry. He had seen it at the moment of Malcolm Grant's death—the last thing Grant himself had seen before the car crash that eventually cost him his life. He could feel his pulse quicken in dawning excitement as he took his trophy back to his office.

Once seated behind his desk, he spread the newspaper on the desktop in front of him, switched on the desk lamp, and delved into the upper right-hand drawer for a small magnifying glass. Leaning forward slightly, he brought the lens to bear on the suspect corner of the photograph, focusing his attention on the pale-faced figure. The resolution was coarse and grainy, but left him with little doubt that it was, indeed, the same woman. Under magnification, her image seemed slightly detached from the rest of the background, almost as if someone had superimposed a solo photo on top of the crash scene.

Whoever she was, she appeared to be in her mid- to late-twenties. The eyes that stared out of the picture were hollow and piercing, their expression disturbingly intense, as if their owner were searching for someone or something. What, Adam wondered, had impelled her to step out in front of Grant's car? And where had she disappeared to afterwards?

Laying aside his magnifying glass, he reached for the telephone and punched in the number of McLeod's direct line at police headquarters. The inspector's voice answered after three rings.

"No, I've not seen the *Evening News*," he replied, in response to Adam's initial inquiry. "Why? What's afoot?"

"Well you may ask," Adam said. "If you could manage to lay hands on a copy, there's a photo on the front page that I think you ought to see."

Swiftly he gave McLeod the gist of his discovery. "I'd be willing to wager a small fortune that this woman in the picture is the same one Malcolm Grant went out of his way to avoid," he informed his Second. "Do you think you might pull the accident report and check to see if anybody fitting the description I've just given you is mentioned among the witnesses?"

"Can't do that right now," McLeod said. "It won't be in the system yet. I'll put Donald on it first thing in the morning, though. Of course, this mysterious lady of yours won't be in our records at all, unless she came forward to offer testimony. And she might well have avoided doing that, if she had reason to believe she was to blame for the accident."

"Perhaps. But I have a feeling the situation is far more complicated than that," Adam said. "I wonder if the photographer might remember seeing her. We need to know who she is, Noel."

"I won't argue that," McLeod agreed. "Shall I see if I can track down the photographer? They'll know how to reach him over at the *Evening News*."

"By all means," Adam said. "I'll be here in the office for at least another hour. Let me know what you find out."

He cradled the receiver and sat silently for a moment, hand still on the receiver, then set himself to finishing his case notes while he waited for McLeod's call-back. Only ten minutes went by before the phone rang again.

"Our photographer's name is Tom Lennox," McLeod announced without preamble. "He's got a flat in Langton Road. That's not a mile from where you are now, on the other side of Blackford Hill. I'd have gotten back to you even sooner, but while I was on the line, it occurred to me that our man might still be in the building, so I asked the receptionist to have him paged. There was a bit of a delay, but eventually he checked in. The long and the short of our conversation is that he's quite prepared to cooperate with us so far as he's able."

"What have you told him?"

"The truth, if not all of it," McLeod said. "That there are one or two people in the background of his photo that the police have reason to believe may be potential witnesses, but haven't yet been able to identify. I told him we'd like to stop by later this evening to discuss the matter in person, and he suggested round about seven o'clock."

"That would suit me," Adam said. "You want to meet me here at about six forty-five?"

"Sounds fine to me. I'll go grab a bite to eat and see you then."

Once the inspector had rung off, Adam rang Strathmourne to inform Humphrey that he would not be dining at home, then made a brief pilgrimage out to the hospital cafe for a sandwich and some coffee, which he consumed while he returned to his case notes. He had just finished up when McLeod arrived to keep their appointed rendezvous.

Langton Road lay on the western perimeter of a housing estate made up of blocks of flats. Lennox's address was midway along the street in a three-story walk-up virtually indistinguishable from all the others in its row. Adam and McLeod left the latter's black BMW parked at the curb outside and let themselves into the building through a ground-floor foyer that smelled of disinfectant. From there, two flights of concrete steps took them up to the topmost floor, where they found themselves in an enclosed landing between two doors.

Lennox's flat was the one on the left. McLeod led the way to the door and knocked smartly. Somewhere else in the building a small dog began to yap belligerently. Trading wry glances with Adam, McLeod knocked again.

After an extended pause, a couple of thumps resounded from inside, followed by the hurried tattoo of approaching feet. They heard the click of a lock being unsnibbed, and the door opened to reveal a lanky, sandy-haired young man in jeans and a T-shirt with "Dundee College of Art" scrolled in black letters across the chest. At the sight of the two men on his doorstep, his goodnatured face split in a grin.

"Sorry if there was a bit of a delay. I was up in the loft, where my darkroom is, developing some prints. You're Inspector McLeod?"

"That's right." McLeod presented his warrant card for the other man's inspection. "My associate is Dr. Sinclair, a special police consultant." At Lennox's wave, McLeod tucked the ID back into the breast pocket of his coat.

"Well, you're both very welcome," Lennox said, with a cordial inclination of his sandy head. Backing away from the threshold, he beckoned the way into an untidy hallway lined on one side with a crowded array of bookcases. "Please come in. The sitting room's the second door on your left."

Together they made their way along the passageway into a large, square room, comfortably if somewhat haphazardly furnished. Waving his visitors toward two mismatched overstuffed chairs by the fireplace, Lennox flopped down on the davenport by the window and propped his elbows on his knees. Lacing his fingers together under his chin, he favored his two visitors with a look of inquiry.

"Now, then," he said briskly, "tell me which of the faces in that photo of mine are the ones you're interested in."

Taking his cue from McLeod, Adam produced the photo he had torn from his copy of the *Edinburgh Evening News* and laid it on the coffee table in their midst.

"Actually, there's only one," he told Lennox. "It's this woman here."

Turning the photo around so that Lennox could see it, he pointed out the figure that had claimed his attention earlier in the afternoon.

"As you're probably well aware," Adam continued, "today's accident out on the Lanark Road was the sixth incident of its kind since the beginning of this year. Given the circumstances, the police are interested in interviewing anyone who was present at the time the crash occurred. So far, this woman remains unaccounted for. Since you managed to catch her on camera, we were wondering if perhaps you might have some idea who she is."

Lennox was staring at the photo. When he looked up a moment later, he had an odd expression on his face.

"It's funny you should ask about her," he told his visitors. "She's the one I call my *phantom lady*."

McLeod remained carefully noncommittal. Without taking his eyes from Lennox's face, Adam asked, "Why is that?"

Lennox pulled a grimace. "Are you sure you really want to know? As stories go, it's pretty weird."

"You'd be surprised how often a so-called weird story can provide just the clue the police have been looking for," McLeod said. "Tell us what you know, and we'll make the best we can of it."

Lennox looked slightly dubious. "All right. But don't say I didn't warn you."

He rocked back in his seat, his face screwed up in a reminiscent scowl. "Beginning last December, I drew duty as part of a two-man team assigned to carry out a weekly survey of local traffic incidents. The survey was intended to supplement an editorial feature on defensive driving over the holidays, but it didn't stop there. When the first of these Lanark Road fatalities occurred, on New Year's Day, my mate Bill and I got sent out to cover the story. When we got back to the photo lab with my film, this woman you're interested in turned up amongst the spectators.

"At the time I didn't think anything of it," he went on. "She was just another face in the crowd. But then, about a month later, the second accident occurred. That same afternoon I'd been out with a couple of pals to see a football match over in East Kilbride. We were heading home along the Lanark Road when we saw the emergency vehicles converging on the scene. Since news is news, we stopped to investigate, and I took the usual battery of photos. You can probably imagine how surprised I was when I got this second lot of photos developed and spotted the same woman hovering in the background of nearly every shot."

He paused and bit his lip. "Maybe you're going to think I'm crazy, but ever since then, each time Carnage Corridor claims another victim, I've made a point of getting out there to take photos for the record. I always keep my eye out for the phantom lady, but I've never yet glimpsed her in the flesh. I don't know her name, still less what she could possibly be doing there. All I know is that when I get back home and develop the film, she's always present somewhere in the pictures."

He broke off with a hollow laugh. McLeod was quick to catch Adam's eye.

McLeod said, "Could we maybe see these photos of yours, Mr. Lennox?"

The photographer eyed him askance, then relaxed when he saw that neither of his visitors looked the least bit dubious or amused. Shrugging, he said, "Sure, why not? This thing's been eating at me for months. Maybe you people will be able to come up with a rational explanation."

He got to his feet and left the room. When he returned a few moments later, he had with him an accordion folder bulging with prints and notes.

"Here you are," he said, presenting the folder to McLeod. "If you have a look, you'll see for yourself I'm not making any of this up. I'll go make us some coffee."

He left them alone to go over the contents of the folder while he went through to the kitchen. The photos were clumped into chronological groupings, each grouping labelled and dated. Adam and McLeod shared the groupings out between them. Lennox's phantom lady was a ubiquitous presence throughout, a pale figure haunting the borders of nearly every scene.

In addition to the expansive collection of standard-sized prints, there were also a number of enlargements. The quality of the imaging was much sharper in Lennox's own prints that it had been in the newspaper version, affording Adam with a more detailed impression of a high-browed oval face framed in a shoulder-length mop of thick, dark curls. It was a face that would have been pretty, had it not been white and drawn with some inner tension, even pain. But Adam was quick to discern something else more worthy of comment than that.

"Noel," he murmured, "have you noticed that in all of these pictures, this woman appears to be wearing the same sweater?"

The sweater in question was a light-colored cardigan, open down the front.

"Aye," McLeod muttered back. "It's pretty much what you might expect, this time of year."

"Yet she never seems to change it, regardless of either the season or the weather," Adam observed. "Take this photo from the batch labelled February fifth. Everyone else in the picture is heavily bundled up against the cold. But here's our phantom standing in the midst of them in only a sweater. No hat, no scarf, no gloves . . .''

He broke off as Lennox returned from the kitchen with a trio of mugs balanced on a tray. Overstepping one or two photos that had escaped onto the floor, the lanky photographer plumped his tray down on the coffee table before quirking an eyebrow at his visitors in mute inquiry.

"I can well understand why this case has fascinated you so," Adam said. "Your phantom lady constitutes almost as big a mystery as these recurrent accidents."

"In other words," said Lennox, with a rueful twist of his lips, "you don't have any answers about her either."

"Not yet," Adam admitted. "However," he added with complete candor, "you've furnished us with something new to think about. Perhaps, if we're lucky, this angle on the case may lead us to the solution we've been looking for."

"An obvious next step," said McLeod, "is for us to try and put a name to this phantom lady of yours. Do you think we might borrow some of these prints?"

"Take any ones you want," Lennox said. "I've got all the negatives." He added with a grimace, "You know, if either of you had asked me six months ago if I believed in ghosts, I'd've told you no. Lately, though, I'm not so sure."

Adam and McLeod stayed long enough to drink a cup of coffee. Shortly thereafter, they took their leave, armed with a collection of prints culled at random from Lennox's personal archives.

"Curiouser and curiouser," Adam remarked, as he and McLeod made their way out to the car. "Two hours ago I was prepared to shelve the notion that we might be dealing with some kind of apparition. Now I'm not so sure."

McLeod clucked his tongue in mild frustration. "Ghost or no ghost, this woman has to have a history," he said. "Somewhere, there's got to be a record of her existence. All we have to do is look in the right place."

CHAPTER SIX

ADAM pondered the problem all the way home. Back at Strathmourne, he took time out for a shower and a change of clothes before retiring to the privacy of his library to scribble down some of his ideas. He had been at his desk for scarcely a quarter hour, however, when the in-house telephone emitted a buzz.

Adam lifted the receiver. "Yes, Humphrey, what is it?"

"Pardon the disturbance, sir, but you've a call from Mr. Lovat. Shall I put him through?"

"By all means."

He had a brief instant in which to wonder why Peregrine should be phoning, before the young artist's voice came on the line.

"Hullo, Adam. Hope I'm not interrupting anything."

"Not at all," Adam assured his young protégé, "though I fancy *you* must be interrupting something. I seem to recall that you acquired a new bride only a few days ago. Is everything all right?"

"Oh, it's swell, where that's concerned," Peregrine said, though there was an edge of strain to his voice. "I'd have called earlier, but I wanted to wait until Julia was out of earshot. She's off having a bath just now, so I thought this would be as good a time as any to have a word with you."

"A word about what?"

"Well, we ran into a spot of unpleasantness earlier this afternoon," came the reluctant response. "We were having a picnic down on the beach at Mull of Kintyre, when a dead body washed ashore."

"A body?"

Briefly, Peregrine went on to relate the events as they had occurred earlier that afternoon. After completing his narrative, he came back to the subject of the ghostly image he had seen hovering over the body.

"It was only there for an instant—too short a time for me to catch more than a fleeting impression. But the fact that it was there at all made me curious at the time. When Julia and I got back to the guesthouse, I decided to try a sketch or two, to see if I could recapture the image and bring it into focus. I couldn't—but I can't seem to shake the conviction that the image I'm missing is not only real, but important."

"What do you think it means?" Adam asked.

"I don't know. I can't explain it logically, but I have this gut feeling that there's much more to this man's death than meets the eye. If I'm right about that, perhaps I ought to offer my services, such as they are, to the local police. On the other hand, all of this could just be my imagination working overtime. I didn't want to discuss it with Julia—it's been beastly enough for her as it is, to find a dead body on our honeymoon—but I thought it was probably worth phoning you up to ask for your advice."

Adam considered the situation before speaking.

"Your impressions notwithstanding," he said, "there doesn't appear to be anything about this case that an ordinary police investigation wouldn't be able to handle—not on the surface, at least. If you're concerned, though, I can have Noel check into it further. Kintyre is outside his official jurisdiction, of course, as you've noted, but his reputation is such that I doubt your local police there will object to sharing information with him. You've already said that invoking his name elicited recognition. If the victim's death does turn out to have esoteric implications, Noel will be in a position to evaluate the police findings and decide whether or not we ought to consider getting involved."

"That sounds fair enough to me," Peregrine said. "I'm not really *eager* to interrupt my honeymoon, but if I'm needed—"

"I understand," Adam said, smiling to himself. "I certainly can't fault you on your sense of duty. Where are you staying, on the off chance I should need to get back to you this evening?''

"Right. It's called Glenbarr Abbey—a sort of castle, actually, but they take paying guests. Let me give you the telephone number."

He reeled off a set of digits.

"I've got it, thanks," said Adam. "In the meantime, why don't you see if you can arrange to take Julia a bottle of champagne in her bath? From what you've told me, she's richly earned it."

"I couldn't agree with you more," Peregrine said fervently. "Good night, Adam. And thank you."

In the ensuing quiet after Peregrine rang off, Adam weighed up the possible import of everything the young artist had said. Despite his own professed reassurances over the telephone, he had an uncomfortable feeling that neither he nor Peregrine had heard the last of this case. He toyed briefly with the idea of telephoning McLeod to discuss the matter then and there, but a glance at the clock on the mantel made him think better of it; the matter would keep safely until morning.

Thus satisfied, he returned his attention to the enigma of Lennox's phantom lady. Setting his notes aside, he opened his briefcase and took out the sheaf of photos he had borrowed from the photographer's personal files, setting one of the clearest enlargements on the desktop before him.

"Who are you?" he murmured aloud, as he contemplated the pale face. "What is it that draws you back time and time again to these scenes of destruction?"

After a moment, he found himself recalling Donald Cochrane's comment of earlier in the day, and wondered whether perhaps the young detective had hit closer to home than he realized.

If I were a superstitious man, Donald had said, *I'd be starting to wonder if maybe the driver of the crashed car might have seen a ghost. . . .*

It was possible, of course—and if they *were* dealing with an emanation of some spent life, the reason was likely to prove elusive, at least so far as conventional methods of investigation were concerned. Fortunately, however, Adam and his colleagues had access to unconventional sources of information, not normally available to more orthodox investigators.

Gazing at the haggard face of the woman in the photograph, he decided that it would be worth an excursion onto the astral to try to discover the underlying cause of her suffering. Such profound tension should not and could not be allowed to continue, if a means could be found to alleviate it.

This conviction crystallized rapidly into a resolve. Contacting Humphrey on the house telephone, he issued instructions that he was not to be disturbed for any reason until otherwise notified. Then he cleared the top of his desk of everything but the photograph of his nameless subject, which he propped up on a carved wooden bookrest directly in front of him. Having done as much, he fetched a candlestick from the mantelpiece and positioned it carefully to the right of the picture, lighting the candle from a book of matches resident in the center desk drawer. Dimming the room lights then, and before he sat back down in his chair, he reached into his trouser pocket and drew out a handsome gold ring set with a large oval sapphire.

Considered purely as an example of masculine jewelry, it was as fine a piece of work as could be found in any craftsman's studio. As far as Adam was concerned, however, the ring was beyond price—not only a symbol of his authority as a member of the Hunting Lodge but also one of the most important working tools of his vocation as Master of the Hunt. Slipping the ring onto the third finger of his right hand, he folded his hands on the desktop before him, the ring-hand uppermost. Then, following the dictates of a discipline he had practiced since his youth, he took a measured succession of slow, deep breaths to compose and center himself for the work he had set himself to do.

Poised on the threshold of an interior calm, he tilted his hand so that the ring caught the flickering light of the candle. Bending his gaze on the pure, cerulean depths of the stone, he closed his mind to the distractions of the waking world and turned inward in trance to confront the subtler realities of the Inner Planes.

At the heart of the Inner Planes lay the Akashic Records, the imperishable chronicle of all lives for all times. Like the mystical rose of Dante's *Paradiso*, the Records were eternal and ever-unfolding, the living mirror of all creation. Somewhere among that infinite array of archive chambers would be preserved the records belonging to the woman in the photograph. Using her physical likeness as a focus, Adam hoped to gain access to the psychic identity that went with it.

His body shed its weight. No longer fettered to his chair, he allowed himself to float free. An opalescent shimmer filled his mind's eye. Into the midst of that luminous field of inner vision he projected the mental image of the woman he was seeking, simultaneously uttering the Word of power that would enable him to pass through the portals to the Akashic vaults.

There was a sudden blinding flash, as of an actinic flare. The image before him was abruptly polarized, reverting in the wink of an eye to its photographic negative. Fluid tinctures of light washed over it like ripples of water in a pail. Bathed in that light, the woman's image began to re-emerge with the progressive clarity of a developing photographic print.

The scene that took shape around her was no longer that of a still photo. Invested now with life and movement, she was strolling along a grassy embankment at the side of an open stretch of road. Beside her, holding her hand tucked fondly through the crook of his arm, was a pleasant-faced young man. The sky overhead was dark, but the three-quarter moon hovering above their heads shed sufficient light for Adam to make out that the couple were laughing and talking as they walked along. Though he could not hear what they were saying, it was plain from the looks exchanged between them that they were very much in love.

A flaring set of headlamps appeared in the distance. The dual points of light converged along the road with a swiftness that proclaimed a dangerous turn of speed. The young couple checked in their tracks as the onrushing glare erupted into sudden blinding radiance. The man made a desperate, valiant attempt to shove the woman out of the way as the speeding car rocketed off the tarmac and hurtled straight for them.

The scene exploded, reverberating with her scream. Caught by the backlash, Adam instinctively flung up a hand to shield his eyes from a blustering whirlwind of flying shards. The ensuing darkness seethed with colored splinters. Even as Adam struggled to regain his bearings, the darkness collapsed upon itself and burst into flames.

Fierce as burning phosphorus, the fire roared up like a curtain. The ensuing wave of heat bore Adam backwards. An archway loomed above him, half-wreathed in curling smoke. Breathless and half-blinded, he tumbled through the gap and fetched up short against a stone wall.

The wall was cool and smooth beneath his outflung hands. More than a little shaken, he drew himself up and looked around. The marble corridor in which he found himself stretched away from him in both directions until it lost itself in a maze of turnings and distances. Those selfsame intimations of infinity told him he was now inside the halls of the Akashic Records.

The air near at hand was full of hissing and crackling, like the venomous mouthings of a giant salamander. Pivoting toward the sound, Adam found himself confronting an open doorway on the opposite side of the corridor. Tongues of fire were lashing furiously about the inner edges of the door frame. Looking beyond the archway, he saw that the whole of the chamber beyond was in flames.

A melodious voice spoke to Adam's back.

What signs of the chase do you follow, Master of the Hunt? it asked.

Hearing that voice, Adam experienced a thrill of recognition. Turning, he was not surprised to see a prismatic column of dancing light materialize out of thin air before him. The presence embodied in that light belonged to one Adam knew as the Master, an entity sufficiently evolved and perfected so as to no longer need the physical vehicle of human incarnation. Adam bowed low in respect and reverence before venturing to speak.

I am following the trail of a troubled spirit, in the hope that if I find it, I may give it peace.

Peace for such a one is never given; it is only found, the Master said. *The soul you are seeking still has far to go to find that peace.*

Adam acknowledged this declaration with an inclination of his head.

I had no way of knowing before now whether or not the soul I am seeking was presently incarnate. Since you give me to understand that she is still in the flesh, is it permitted to ask her name?

The glow of the Master's presence grew sharper. *The question is permitted. But the answer must not be sought with me.*

Where, then, must I seek it?

In both worlds. The Master's voice was calm. *If the knowledge you require has thus far eluded you on the earthly plane, that does not mean it cannot be found there. Here among the Inner Planes, it resides there—in the chamber of fire.*

Adam redirected his gaze toward the burning room. Peering through the furnace reek, he could dimly make out the shape of a raised lectern at the center of the room. Mounted on the lectern was an open book. Flames billowed round it in a rising hurricane, yet the book itself was unconsumed.

Will you choose to dare the fire, Master of the Hunt? the Master asked.

Heat from the open doorway beat harshly at Adam's face. The blistering touch of it stirred up a host of fearful memories from his own past lifetimes. Repressing an inward shudder, he asked, *What makes it burn like that?*

Anger, came the Master's response. *Anger and bitterness. Together they have been allowed to become an all-consuming passion. If this passion remains unslaked, ultimately the soul will devour itself in its anguish. Nor will it be the only sufferer. Already, this fire reaches out and has destroyed other lives.*

Can it be quenched?

Only if the soul itself can be persuaded to will it so, said the Master. *Have you the strength, Master of the Hunt, to endure the peril of such an encounter?*

It would not be the first time that I have tasted fire, Adam said grimly. That much was true: Once incarnated in the guise of a Knight Templar, he had suffered burning martyrdom during the attempted dissolution of his Order.

If there is no other way to resolve this matter, he continued steadfastly, *I will do whatever must be done. But knowledge must come first.*

Then seek it elsewhere, before you seek it here, the Master advised, *for the time is coming when you will have need of all your strength.*

This announcement was as ominous as it was unexpected.

The Patrons of Shadow begin to move anew, the Master continued, the melody in his voice roughened now by a note of grim misgiving. *An old evil rises once more, an evil that threatens to encroach upon the balance of the powers of Light at work in the mortal world. The adherents of this evil have made their first foray into those created lands that lie under your protection. If they should succeed in establishing a firm foothold, then the Huntsmen and their charges will rapidly become the hunted.*

This was disturbing news indeed.

What signs must I look for? Adam asked.

A Teacher will come when you have need of one, said the Master. *There is that which sleeps in you which, if it can be awakened, will know how to read the Teaching offered.*

The light that betokened the Master's presence was fading. Sensing his superior's imminent withdrawal, Adam asked urgently, *How can what sleeps be awakened?*

The answer came faint and faraway, like an echo out of receding distances.

It must be called forth by one skilled in the reading of souls. The die is already cast. . . .

The words faded away as did the Master's presence, amid a dissipating shimmer like the last gleam of a vanishing rainbow. Simultaneously, the corridor in which Adam was standing began to dissolve around him. Pinpoints of light shone through the thinning fabric of the walls, like jewels seen through a veil of fine gauze. Brighter they shone, and brighter still, until the walls disappeared altogether, leaving Adam suspended in space amid a firmament of stars.

The starry firmament turned on its axis. The sudden shift

in the stellar configurations took Adam's breath away. For a dizzy moment he hung in limbo, surrounded by comet-blurs of wheeling lights. Then all at once he plummeted.

A supple skein of silver materialized in front of him, coiling round him as he fell. Recognizing the line of his own lifetime, Adam reached out and seized it with both hands.

His headlong plunge slowed to a floating descent. Below him now he could see the foreshortened outline of his physical body, sitting relaxed in its chair. He followed the cord down in an ever-tightening spiral until, with a slight, disorienting jolt, his travelling soul was once again reunited with its corporeal complement.

He took another moment to settle back into his body before opening his eyes. The candle beside the photograph had burned down almost to the sconce, indicative that nearly two hours had passed since he first entered into trance. Now that he was back to full awareness, he became sensible of a chill in his bones and a hollow feeling in his midsection. It was further proof, if he needed it, of how far afield he had ventured on the astral this night.

Drawing a steadying breath, Adam reached for the house phone and buzzed for Humphrey. The promptness of the latter's response suggested that his faithful valet had been anticipating his summons. After requesting his usual fortifying snack of hot ham sandwiches and cocoa, Adam rang off with a heartfelt word of thanks, indulged in a languorous stretch, and sat back in his chair to contemplate the import of his exchange with the Master.

He centered his thoughts first on the matter of Tom Lennox's phantom lady. Since the Master had strongly intimated that the key to this woman's identity was to be found on this side of the astral, Adam resolved to redouble his efforts to learn who she might be. He was prepared to take seriously the Master's pronouncement that this woman was presently posing a danger not only to herself but also to others who might come into contact with her. Certainly those who had died in Carnage Corridor could attest to that danger. His resolution was unshaken by the prospect of having to share in her suffering, though the nature of that particular ordeal had been made only too plain to him during his astral journey to her place in the Akashic Records.

Of more disquieting concern was the Master's cryptic warning that the equilibrium of the Light was once again in danger of being destabilized by forces of darkness. Lacking any clues to work from, he could do nothing for the moment but watch and wait.

A knock at the library door roused him from his reverie, heralding Humphrey's arrival with a laden tray.

"Here you are, sir," the butler said. "Will you take your refreshments at the desk, or by the fireside?"

"By the fireside, thank you," Adam said. "And then I hope you'll take yourself off to your bed."

"Very good, sir." Humphrey raised a dubious eyebrow. "Are you sure you won't be needing me any further?"

"Quite sure," Adam said firmly. "I would, however, be grateful if you could have breakfast ready for six o'clock. Tomorrow promises to be a very busy day."

CHAPTER SEVEN

DAWN broke pale over the Swiss Alps. Initially the light touched only the outer walls of the remote Buddhist monastery perched on the heights. Inside the compound, the early morning quiet was broken intermittently by the subdued clatter from the kitchen wing. The still air carried the mealy fragrance of cooked *tsampa* porridge mingled with the scent of wild thyme.

A diaphanous mist filled the gaps between the buildings, leaving a fine glaze of moisture on everything it touched. Deep in the heart of the compound, in the sheltered formal garden adjoining the abbot's private apartments, the mist had limned each individual leaf and twig with silver. Soft on the foggy air came the muted sound of a door opening and then closing as the man known to his flock as Dorje *Rinpoche* turned his back on his quarters and moved silently along the pebbled pathway, approaching a small domed structure at the center of the garden.

The edifice was a temple in miniature, its exterior densely ornamented with grotesque carvings of demons, demigods, and other denizens of the spirit world. As Dorje drew near, a small, stooped figure in orange robes detached itself from the shadows and hobbled forward to meet him, bowing over a box of black lacquerwork cradled to its chest. No word was spoken, but the abbot returned the old monk's bow and beckoned him forward, leading the way up into the shallow porch that fronted the entrance to the shrine, where both men shed their sandals.

A groined doorway admitted the pair to a square meditation chamber. The flickering yellow glare of four butter lamps quartered the room, picking out the tarnished sheen of metallic embroidery amongst the ancient-looking tapestries that overhung the walls. The floor was of black marble, its center covered by a darkly patterned carpet of silk brocade. A number of flat brocaded cushions had been scattered around the carpet to provide seating.

More glints of silver and gold showed up from the chamber's vaulted ceiling. Here, a mosaic had been executed in tiny, many-colored tiles, depicting a wrathful, multilimbed deity wreathed in sulphurous clouds of fire and smoke. Two crimson eyes like molten rubies glared down into the room out of a skull-like face. Any initiate of Tibetan mysticism would have recognized the figure as that of Shinjed, the dread Lord of Death.

In the northwest corner of the chamber stood a small dais covered with a pall of crimson brocade. Centered on the dais, its point supported in a triangular stand, stood a large triple-edged dagger as tall as a man, with a hilt made of carved faces. The dagger was flanked by a pair of bronze incense burners in the shape of two coiled serpents, whose smoke left the air inside the chamber heavy with the musky, aromatic tang of burnt spices.

Approaching the dais, Dorje and his companion abased themselves before the dagger, then withdrew to the center of the room. As they drew up cushions and sat down opposite one another, leaving an open space on the carpet between them, Dorje fixed his chilly, china-blue eyes on the age-withered face of his companion.

"I am troubled, Lutzen," he said, addressing the other man in fluent Tibetan. "Almost fifty years have passed since you and your brother brought me here from Germany. Tell me, how much do you recall of the days leading up to our flight?"

The old monk's expression showed faint surprise. "How should I not remember, *Rinpoche*? It was a time of great uncertainty. The war was going badly for our patron. Daily the talk grew of impending defeat. Eventually it was decided that you should be brought away to safety. And so it was done."

"Indeed." Dorje's tone conveyed no warmth. "How would you evaluate that decision by your predecessor?"

"He did as his wisdom dictated," Lutzen said. "Thanks to his foresight, you were safely out of Berlin when it was taken by the Allies."

"Do you think this was well done?"

The old monk shrugged. "You are here, *Rinpoche*. And now that the Treasure Texts have at last been located, there will be no further impediment to your fulfilling your destiny as Keeper of the Keys to Agarthi."

"That destiny might well have been fulfilled half a century sooner," Dorje said coldly. "As you rightly observe, I am the Keeper of the Keys. Had I been allowed to remain in Germany, I might have unlocked Agarthi's gates and summoned the hosts of chaos to defend the Fatherland. As it was, I was absent at the very time when I was most needed."

"You were only a child," Lutzen reminded him. "The signs of your true identity were undeniable, but you had not yet regained your full stature as the Man with Green Gloves."

Dorje gestured impatiently for silence.

"Bermiag *Rinpoche* should not have been so quick to underestimate me. Had he allowed the Treasure Texts to go with me, it is conceivable that I might have been able to do something, even from exile, to salvage the fortunes of the Reich."

"Bermiag *Rinpoche* did not agree." Lutzen's tone was without any audible shift in emotion. "When you were sent to safety, all of us believed the war could still be won—that though our beloved Green Gloves was not yet fully restored to us in function, some other worthy might be found to unlock at least a part of the Treasure Texts' secrets.

"Sadly, that did not prove to be the case. When it became clear that nothing could save our German patron, Bermiag did his best to place the Texts beyond the reach of our enemies by sending them out of Germany by submarine."

"And in so doing, he placed them beyond my reach as well!" Dorje retorted. "The messenger who brought the news of the sub's launch should likewise have been entrusted with the vessel's intended destination."

The old monk shrugged again. "There was always a danger that the messenger might have been captured. Bermiag *Rinpoche* had more than once encountered interference from Adepts at work in the Allied camp. Those most senior amongst them would have had sufficient power to force a full accounting of the facts from almost any prisoner under interrogation."

"Perhaps that is true," the abbot conceded. "As it stands, Bermiag's caution has cost us valuable time. The search might have gone on indefinitely if Sidkeong had not undertaken to locate the submarine by dowsing. And the effort cost him his life."

"I have not forgotten, *Rinpoche*," Lutzen said. "The lives of the Irishmen were justly forfeit by way of recompense."

"Recompense is not yet complete, and finding the submarine only continues the quest," Dorje stated, his lean features like a carving in marble. "The cargo still must be retrieved—and for that, we shall need outside assistance. You know what is required, Lutzen. Have you made adequate preparation to perform the necessary exercise with the *kyilkhor*?"

The elderly monk gave an inclination of his hairless head. "I am quite prepared, *Rinpoche*. I am confident that the oracle will yield us the guidance we are seeking."

"Excellent." Dorje's tone was one of dispassionate approval. "In that case, let us proceed."

"As you command, *Rinpoche*."

So saying, the aged monk turned his attention to the lacquerwork box in his lap, swiftly shifting a succession of trick panels embedded in the box's lid and sides. The box opened to reveal two compartments within, the first containing a sheaf of rice papers, a bamboo brush pen, a small ink flask of pale green jade, and a piece of rock crystal in the shape of a pyramid. The second, larger compartment held several closely packed stacks of square lacquered tiles.

Taking out the brush and the ink flask, the monk proffered them to his superior, along with a square piece of rice paper the size of his palm. Accepting these three articles, the abbot lapsed briefly into silence, his expression intense and abstracted, as if he were attempting to identify some curious object glimpsed at a distance. After a long moment, he roused himself to unstopper the ink bottle and dip the pen, after which he swiftly wrote out an inscription in Tibetan. Seen by the amber light of the butter lamps, the writing fluid showed up not black but a dull shade of dark red. The abbot paused briefly to contemplate his work before handing it over to his subordinate.

"As the diviner, it is for you to read what has been written," he told the old monk.

Lutzen took the page and held it up to the light. Signalling his comprehension with a curt nod, he carefully placed the paper on the carpet in front of him, then removed the crystal pyramid from the lacquerwork box and set it on top of the paper with a finely judged precision that indicated the importance of its placement. This done, he returned to the box and began lifting out the layers of lacquerwork tiles.

There were sixty-four in all, each tile having one side blank and the other inscribed with a symbolic pictograph. Lutzen turned all the tiles blank side up on the carpet before giving them a randomizing shuffle. Satisfied with his preparations, he folded his palms together and touched his joined fingertips to his forehead, throat, and breast. Then, raising his eyes to the vault above his head, he spoke.

"Hail, Shinjed, Lord of the Dead and Devourer of the Living. We who are initiates sworn to your service do pray that you will look with favor on our present enterprise. We ask that, being secured of your guidance, we may recover the treasures our forebears hid, receiving like them earthly power in exchange for feasts of slaughter."

Lowering his gaze, he turned to Dorje. "The pattern lies within your grasp, *Rinpoche*," he said, indicating the strewn array of tiles. "May Shinjed guide your hand."

Dorje reached out and plucked a tile from the midst of the pile. Turning it face-up, he placed it on the floor next to the crystal pyramid. While the old monk looked on, he chose a second tile, overturning it with a flick of his wrist and setting it directly opposite the first, on the other side of the crystal.

A further six tiles were added in turn, arranged in opposing pairs so as to leave an octagonal space at the center of the configuration—the pattern known to practitioners of this form of divination as *The Lotus Wheel*. When all eight tiles were in place, Lutzen leaned in to scan the array of symbols displayed there. After prolonged consideration, he drew a deep breath and began to expound, tracing lines of association as he did so.

"The Stranger and the Fortress," he intoned. "Taken together, they point to a man outside our immediate fellowship, yet sometimes under our protection. The Gambler—here—indicates one who is both ambitious and desirous of material wealth. The companion symbol, however, is the Broken Ox Cart, signifying a recent reversal in fortunes."

Dorje's blue eyes narrowed thoughtfully. "An interesting combination. The man we require evidently has prior associations with this order. It would appear that he is someone who has tasted disappointment in the not-so-distant past. So much the better if his fortunes need mending. If he is hungry, he will rise the more readily to any bait we offer him. Continue."

Lutzen bent his gaze on the pattern again. "As for the formative elements of the future, we have first the Serpent and then the Hunter. These symbols denote agencies in opposition. The Serpent is guileful and defends itself with venom. The Hunter, for his part, is a reader of signs and a tireless pursuer. These two elements can never be reconciled. I read the interference of a long-time adversary who must be killed if he cannot be eluded."

This revelation drew a frown from Dorje. "An inauspicious complication. What of the remaining signs?"

Lutzen returned his attention to the Lotus Wheel. "Success is denoted by the Fruitful Vine. But it is paired with the sign of the Fool, indicating random influences at work. Whether those influences will manifest themselves as a person, an object, or an event is beyond my ability to determine. All that can be said at this time is that a successful outcome to this venture is probable, but not certain."

"Then we must proceed with great caution," Dorje said. "Until this enterprise is safely concluded, nothing must be left to chance. In the meantime," he continued, "there is still this morning's work to be completed. Let us see what final sign the oracle will show us."

Dorje bowed his head over the pattern of tiles on the floor and focused his eyes on the crystal pyramid at its center. His breathing slowed, and with it his heart rate, as he lapsed into trance with the ease of long practice. The meditation room, with its gilded hangings and jewelled mosaic ceiling, faded into obscurity. The pyramid correspondingly seemed to expand to fill his vision, blotting out everything else until he could see nothing but the cone-shaped crystal.

As he continued to gaze fixedly at the pyramid, a point of light appeared at its apex. Dorje narrowed his concentration so that it centered on that light. As he did so, he was drawn out of himself toward the point of illumination. At the instant of contact, the light blossomed round him, leaving him floating in the midst of what seemed to be a large, well-appointed library.

Sunlight was flooding into the room through a lofty set of windows, their roundel arches set with Moorish tiles. The light pooled brightly around a large, ornately finished desk in the center of the floor. Seated at the desk was a tall, slender man in a dark suit of impeccable cut. His interest quickening, Dorje moved closer in spirit to take note of the face.

The man at the desk looked to be slightly younger than Dorje himself, with silky fair hair going thin at the top and brushed back at the sides. The pale features were almost ruthlessly refined, the light grey eyes fixed in utter absorption on an age-worn manuscript written in Arabic. One well-manicured finger traced the lines of writing with possessive care.

Another time, Dorje might have taken an interest in the manuscript. At this moment, however, he was far more concerned with the identity of the reader—for the face was one Dorje knew well.

Grimly satisfied, he relaxed his grip on the image before him and allowed himself to be drawn back to his corporeal body. After a blurring of his inner senses came a slight, dizzying jolt. Dorje allowed the momentary sensation of vertigo to subside before opening his eyes. Lutzen was watching him closely.

"I have been shown the face of the man who is to carry out our mission," Dorje informed the elderly monk, allowing himself a thin smile. "It is none other than our own Gyatso, who calls himself Francis Raeburn."

Lutzen's seamed face registered bemusement and some doubt. "Raeburn?"

"More properly, Francis Tudor-Jones," Dorje said in some irritation. "Surely you remember him."

"Tudor-Jones . . ." Lutzen gave the name a curious twist in pronunciation as he nodded. "Ah, yes, I remember both the father and the son, *Rinpoche*. The father was instrumental in keeping a valuable book of spells from falling into the hands of our British enemies—though his motives for doing so remain open to question. You forbade the son to continue his studies with us."

"He was altogether too ambitious," Dorje murmured, "though a worthy successor to his father. As Lynx-Master, he was making serious inroads in Scotland. Unfortunately, he ran afoul of a White Lodge there."

"At some cost to us," the old man agreed.

"Then you will agree that he owes us this service," Dorje replied. "He resides now in Spain. I shall send Kurkar and Nagpo to bring him here without delay."

"He will not welcome this charge."

"Of course he will not," Dorje replied. "But I trust he will not be so foolish as to resist the edicts of Shinjed. Nor can he deny that a debt is owed us in recompense for past benefits—and past failures. He will do as we require of him, or suffer the consequences."

Chapter Eight

ADAM'S Tuesday began early, as planned. By ten o'clock, he had made his rounds and seen his first patient, rescheduled from the previous day. He was ensconced in his office, reviewing his notes for a noon lecture, when the phone rang.

"I've got some news for you," McLeod said, an edge of satisfaction to his voice. "We've got a make on Lennox's phantom lady. Your suggestion that we start working backwards paid off. It turns out that the accident back in January wasn't the first Carnage Corridor fatality. There was a pedestrian incident about this time last year—man killed, woman critically injured. Donald pulled file photos, and the woman appears to match up with the phantom lady in Lennox's pictures."

"Indeed?" Adam sat forward, reaching for a pen and scratch pad. "Please go on."

"Our files give the woman's name as Claire Alison Crawford, aged twenty-seven," McLeod said. "On the night of May sixteenth of last year, she and her husband John were walking home from a *ceilidh* when a drunk driver ran them down. John Crawford was killed instantly, but Mrs. Crawford survived. Their address will interest you. It's about three blocks away from the stretch of road now known as Carnage Corridor." He paused to let this piece of information sink in.

"I see," Adam said as McLeod's pause lengthened. "I gather there's more to come. What happened to the driver?"

"They never caught him," McLeod replied. "The car

turned out to have been stolen; it was found abandoned in a ditch about five miles north of Carnwath. The joy rider himself must have been on a right bender. The floor of the passenger side was littered with empty cider bottles.''

''But there was nothing to identify the driver,'' Adam said.

''Nope. There were plenty of fingerprints left all over the car, but none of them checked out against criminal records. If the bastard ever commits another offense, we'll have him nailed for hit-and-run manslaughter, but unless and until that happens, he's off the hook.''

''All right, back to Mrs. Crawford,'' Adam said, jotting down notes. ''You say this incident took place about a year ago?''

''Aye.''

''Where's Mrs. Crawford been since?''

''After she left hospital,'' McLeod said grimly, ''she spent the better part of six months down at Stoke-Mandville.''

The significance of the name was not lost on Adam. The Stoke-Mandville Centre had been established expressly for the treatment and rehabilitation of patients suffering from varying degrees of paralysis.

''I see. How badly affected was she left by the accident?''

''She still has the use of her arms and upper body,'' McLeod said, ''but she'll be confined to a wheelchair for the rest of her life.''

Adam allowed himself a heavy sigh as he contemplated the havoc that could be wrought on innocent lives as a result of one man's criminal self-indulgence.

''You say Mrs. Crawford spent six months in rehab. Do you know where she went after she got out?''

''Aye, we do. She went home,'' McLeod said. ''She moved back into her house a few days after Christmas—not a week before the first of our current series of Carnage Corridor accidents.''

After a moment's pause, McLeod asked heavily, ''What are you suggesting? Could this woman somehow be responsible for causing these people to run off the road?''

Adam nodded slowly, even though he knew McLeod could not see it.

''I think it's possible,'' he said carefully, ''though if she is, I very much doubt that she's consciously aware of what she's doing. At the same time, however, it's quite possible for unconscious rage to break loose as psychic phenomena, when the potential is there and it's fuelled by a conscious sense of grief and injustice. I can't say for certain that this is what's at work here, but it certainly warrants further investigation. How would you feel about our paying a house call on Mrs. Crawford?''

''I'd consider it a very worthwhile expenditure of the taxpayers' money,'' McLeod said. ''When were you thinking of going?''

''The sooner, the better,'' Adam replied. ''After lunch, perhaps? I've got a lecture just before.''

''I don't foresee any difficulty there,'' McLeod replied. ''Do we make this an official police visit?''

''Not in the sense that you should phone ahead,'' Adam said. ''In this instance, I think it would be better if we were to take the casual approach and simply drop in. First impressions are likely to be important in a case like this. If Mrs. Crawford does have latent psychic ability, I don't want to give her time to mask her feelings.''

''Good point,'' McLeod muttered. ''All right, why don't I meet you there at the hospital around two?''

''That ought to do nicely,'' Adam said.

He was about to ring off when abruptly he remembered his telephone conversation with Peregrine the night before.

''By the way,'' he continued, ''while I've got you on the line, I probably ought to mention that I had a call last night from Peregrine. Yesterday he and Julia found a dead body washed up on the beach at Mull of Kintyre.''

''You don't say! What a wretched wedding present.''

''I agree. Julia seems to have taken it in stride, though.''

Adam went on to relate, in as few words as possible, what the young artist had told him concerning the corpse itself and his misgivings that there might be more to the incident than mere misadventure.

''He thinks he might have Seen something, without being able to make out clearly what it was,'' Adam concluded. ''I told him I'd ask you to follow up on the case.''

''I'll be glad to,'' McLeod agreed. ''Mull of Kintyre, you

say? That means the body will probably go to Dumbarton. I'll ring my friend Jack Somerville and see what he can find out. Jack and I go way back. If I tell him I'm interested in this case, he knows me well enough to not mind sharing information.''

''Nobody could ask more than that,'' Adam said. ''I'll leave the matter in your capable hands, then. See you at two.''

With these words he rang off. A glance at his watch told him he still had twenty minutes before his lecture—time enough, hopefully, for what he had in mind to do. After checking his desktop directory, he punched in the number for the Stoke-Mandville Rehabilitation Centre.

''Good morning,'' he said to the cheery receptionist who answered. ''I'd like to speak with Dr. Miles Heatherton, extension 593.''

''Thank you. One moment, please,'' she responded.

There was a brief pause while the call was transferred. After two buzzes came the click of someone lifting a receiver.

''This is Dr. Heatherton,'' said a brisk baritone voice. ''What can I do for you?''

Passing over the question for the moment, Adam said, ''Hello, Miles. This is Adam Sinclair.''

''Adam? Good Lord, this is a pleasant surprise! It seems like donkey's years since we last spoke. How have you been?''

''Very well, thanks,'' Adam responded cordially. ''What about you and your expanding clan? Last I heard, you and Lorraine were well on your way to parenting your very own rugby team.''

''Only half a rugby team!'' Heatherton protested with a rueful chuckle. ''I'm beginning to think the only way we're ever going to get ourselves a daughter is to adopt one. But what about you? Are you still keeping company with that exceedingly fetching American lady you introduced me to at the Birmingham conference?''

''I'm afraid she's back in the States at the moment,'' Adam said, ''but I'm hoping to lure her back here, once her commitments there are at an end. Look, Miles,'' he continued before Heatherton could question him further, "I've got a lecture in a few minutes, but I need some information. I wonder if you can tell me anything about a woman who was admitted to the institute about a year ago—a Mrs. Claire Crawford. She was—"

"Claire Crawford?" Heatherton interrupted. "I know exactly who you mean. She was one of my patients. If you don't mind my asking, what's your interest in her case?"

Adam had anticipated the question, and said easily, "Oh, just academic curiosity. I'm hoping to put together an article on the long-term emotional consequences of disability. I heard about Mrs. Crawford through a police contact of mine, and thought she might be a good subject for research."

"Well, there's no doubt about that," Heatherton said, in a tone that conveyed more than a hint of reservation. "How much do you know already?"

"Only the barest essentials," Adam replied. "That she was admitted to the institute on a referral from Edinburgh Royal Infirmary. That she stayed six months before being released. What I need to hear from you is an account of her progress, together with your evaluation of her psychiatric state when she left."

Heatherton's immediate response was a dissatisfied grunt.

"I wish I could say she was one of my success stories, but that would be telling a lie. I don't know whether the problem was me, or whether the complications of the case were simply too severe. All I know is that successful psychiatric counselling is a matter of give and take. If your patient doesn't choose to cooperate with you, for whatever reason, there's not a whole lot more you can do."

Adam pricked up his ears. "We've all encountered patients like that at some time or other. I'd still be very much obliged if you could give me chapter and verse where Mrs. Crawford is concerned."

"Chapter and verse? All right." Heatherton paused for breath before launching into his narrative. "If ever I saw an individual in need of professional counselling, this woman was the one. For her, the problem of learning how to deal with being paraplegic was severely compounded by bereavement. If you've read the police reports, you'll have a fair idea of the kind of emotional trauma we're dealing with here. There is something ultimately unjust about having your husband wiped out of existence by some drunken lout you didn't even know.''

''Indeed,'' Adam concurred soberly. ''Murder with a motive might almost have made more sense. Even a bad reason for something happening is better than no discernible reason at all.''

''True enough,'' Heatherton agreed. ''Anyway, all these people we deal with here at the institute are challenging cases. Most of them are angry; some are suicidal. It isn't enough to teach somebody how to cope with a crippling disability; in some cases you've got to convince the individual that it's worth trying to find a reason to keep on living. Some people find it; some don't. I can't honestly say I'm surprised that Mrs. Crawford turned out to be one of the latter. She didn't even have the consolation of seeing her baby survive.''

''She lost a baby?'' Adam was genuinely shocked at this revelation.

''Didn't the police reports mention that? Claire Crawford was seven months pregnant at the time of the accident. The trauma sent her into premature labor. The baby was born alive, but died a couple of days later of respiratory complications. As far as she was concerned, that was the ultimate cheat of her entire existence.''

Adam found himself recalling his vision of the previous night with fresh and discerning clarity. The flames he had seen raging within the Akashic chamber of record constituted, he saw now, a far-reaching destructive force. How he was going to deal with it was going to depend on what further information he could glean from his colleague.

''What was Mrs. Crawford's state of mind when you first met her, Miles?''

Heatherton's own unhappiness over his patient's welfare was plainly audible in his voice.

''She was completely withdrawn when she arrived. It was a month before anyone could get her to speak. And when at last she did break silence, it was like a volcano erupting. It wasn't anything in the words she said, but being in the same room with her was like being out in a hurricane. You felt as if you were being psychically battered about from all sides.

"Eventually the storm seemed to blow itself out of its own accord," he continued, "but I'm not sure whether it actually subsided or simply changed form and went underground. Either way, Mrs. Crawford eventually checked herself out of the centre. At last report, she'd gone back to her home in Scotland."

"Then you didn't actually discharge her?"

"By no means." Heatherton was vehement. "If I could have found a way to keep her here, I would have done so. Not that I could boast that we were doing her any good," he added gloomily, "but at least here, she was assured of a stable environment with somebody keeping an eye on her to make sure she didn't try to take her own life."

"Do you think that a likely possibility?" Adam asked.

Heatherton sighed gustily. "I only wish I knew. Most of the resentment and hostility she displayed here was outwardly directed, but now and then, during our sessions, she would let fall a remark that gave me cause to suspect she was angry with herself as well. There's no doubt in my mind that she has enough poison in her soul to kill twenty people. If that poison ever boils over, what outlet it will find is anybody's guess."

The other's statement only served to reinforce Adam's worst misgivings. Carefully masking his own feelings, he said, "I gather you haven't heard anything further about her progress since she left?"

"Not much, I'm afraid," Heatherton said. "About three months ago, I had a routine report kicked back to me by the Social Works Department, but I can't say I found it terribly illuminating. Let's face it, very few district nurses are qualified to deal with psychiatric disorders of the kind we're talking about here."

"No, that's quite true."

Heatherton coughed a little nervously, then said, "Adam, I realize that your interest in this case is purely academic. I will, of course, be quite happy to furnish you with transcripts of my case notes, subject to all the usual restrictions regarding confidentiality. At the same time, it would ease my mind considerably if I could persuade you to go and talk to this poor woman—maybe see if you could breach the wall of anger she's built around herself since the accident. Who knows, you may be able to succeed where I failed.''

CHAPTER NINE

AFTER his lecture, Adam caught a sandwich in the hospital cafe with several of his students, then returned to his office to find McLeod there before him. The inspector closed a manila folder and presented it to Adam as he rose.

"No luck reaching Somerville yet, about Peregrine's dead body, but here's the full file on Claire Crawford," he told Adam. "You already know the basic facts, of course, but I thought you might want to look over the details on the way out to her house—just to see what, if anything, your intuitions have to say."

"I'll do that," Adam said, slipping off his starched white lab coat and exchanging it for his suit coat. "I've also spoken with her therapist at Stoke-Mandville. I find it interesting that he was my *only* contact at Stoke, and she'd been his patient. The connection tends to reinforce what I learned last night, on a little astral foray."

He told McLeod about it on the way down to the car, keeping his terminology carefully neutral whenever someone was in earshot.

"If the opportunity presents itself, I want to try regressing her to the night of the accident. Every instinct tells me increasingly that we're dealing with a psychic talent gone wild."

Cochrane was waiting for them outside, at the wheel of an unmarked police car. Leaving McLeod to take the passenger seat up front, Adam slipped into the back with his briefcase and took out the manila folder. He had the Lennox photos as well. By the time they pulled out of the car park, heading west toward the Lanark Road, he was already absorbed in skimming over the additional background.

Prior to the accident, Claire Crawford had been a junior teacher at a local nursery. John Crawford had taught mathematics at Merchiston Castle School, a much-respected institute of secondary education in central Edinburgh. Their shared hobbies had included canoeing, hill-walking, and a variety of other outdoor activities. Realizing just how much Claire Crawford had lost in the space of so short a time, Adam found it all too easy to understand how she could have plunged to such depths of grief and rage.

But however justified such emotions might be, nothing good could be gained from letting them rule the remainder of her life. On the contrary, there was every reason to believe that such passions had already done considerable harm. If so, Adam's very first priority must be to ensure that no more innocent people died.

"The house number we're looking for is thirty-five," McLeod said, jarring Adam from his troubled contemplation as they turned off the Lanark Road. "Pull over right there, Donald. That's got to be the place."

Cochrane complied without comment, setting the brake and switching off the ignition.

"You want me to keep trying Somerville's number, Inspector?" he asked as McLeod and Adam got out of the car.

"Aye, give him another half hour, if we aren't back by then. His sergeant said he'd be back between three and four."

Claire Crawford's house was a detached modern bungalow fronted by a small terraced garden. From the street it looked spruce and trim, the white harling of its outer walls neatly contrasting with the slate-blue paint of the woodwork.

Upon closer inspection, however, it seemed almost too well kept. All the bedding plants were rigorously confined to their borders, and the miniature boxwood hedge had been ruthlessly squared off. The spaces between the plants had been filled in with small colored stones for easy keeping. The effect was well-groomed to the point of severity.

Considering the pattern he was starting to detect, Adam followed McLeod up the garden steps, briefcase in hand, skirting a concrete ramp to the right that gave wheelchair access to the front door. The small brass plaque above the letterbox was inscribed with a single name: C. A. CRAWFORD. Trading glances with Adam, McLeod reached out and thumbed the doorbell.

A distant buzz elicited a light scuffle of movement from inside, followed by the rattle of a lock being unsnibbed. The young woman who opened the door, however, was demonstrably not Claire. Standing no more than middling tall, this woman was stockily built, with shoulder-length light-brown hair, dark eyes, and a pale, clear complexion.

"Oh," she said, faint disappointment in her tone. "I was hoping you were the plumber."

McLeod already had his warrant card out, and presented it with an apologetic shrug.

"Afraid not," he said. "I'm Detective Chief Inspector Noel McLeod, Lothian and Borders Police, and this is my associate, Dr. Sinclair. We'd like a word with Mrs. Crawford, if it's not too inconvenient. Is she at home just now?"

The woman gave an affirmative jerk of her head. "Yes, she is. She's out in the back garden. Was she expecting you?"

"No," Adam said, summoning a reassuring smile. "I'm afraid this is a somewhat impromptu visit. The only excuse I can offer you is that the inspector and I sometimes have difficulty coordinating our respective work schedules, and decided we'd better seize the present opportunity, even if it meant stopping by unannounced. Are you a relative of Mrs. Crawford's?"

Disarmed by the gentleness of his manner, the young woman returned his smile. "I'm her sister-in-law. My name's Ishbel—Ishbel Reid. Claire's late husband was my brother. My own husband is away a lot—he works on the oil rigs—so I'm staying with Claire just now, to help out while she finishes up a secretarial course."

She looked as if she might have added something more, but then seemed to think better of it. After a glance over her shoulder, she stood aside and said, "Won't you come in?"

"Thank you," Adam said. As he and McLeod entered, Ishbel closed the door behind them.

''Can you tell me what this is all about?'' she asked, turning to conduct them through the house. ''I thought the police closed the books on Claire's accident a while back, when it proved impossible to track down the person responsible.''

''The books are far from closed,'' McLeod replied. ''In fact, that's the main reason Dr. Sinclair and I are here—to got back over anything and everything your sister-in-law can remember from the night of her accident. It's possible we may be able to turn up a clue the previous investigators have overlooked.''

Ishbel looked dubious. ''I wish you every success, of course, but I probably ought to warn you that you may not find Claire very receptive. I'm afraid she's developed a rather hostile attitude toward the police—and who can blame her? It's been almost a year, Inspector, and so far as I know, you're no closer to catching the man who ran down Claire and my brother.''

''I certainly understand your frustration, Mrs. Reid,'' Adam said. ''And hers. Once we've spoken to her, perhaps we'll be able to persuade her that she has nothing to lose and everything to gain by helping us prove her wrong.''

''Well, you're certainly welcome to try, so far as *I'm* concerned,'' Ishbel said. ''Come this way, and I'll take you to her.''

With Ishbel leading the way, they moved off down the hall. A door at the opposite end of the passage let them through into a sunny, open-plan sitting and dining room. At first glance, the place seemed a model of good housekeeping, fitted out with a tasteful array of new drapes, furnishings, and wall-coverings. At the same time, Adam was left with the distinct impression that there was something missing.

He took a second look around the room, then realized that the missing ingredient was what Peregrine might have termed the human element. There were no keepsakes or decorative objects left casually around on the tables. Though there were several prints hanging on the walls, these were all geometric abstracts without any reference to human form. Most significant of all, to Adam's way of thinking, there were no family photographs.

''I see your sister-in-law has recently had this room redecorated,'' he observed out loud.

"Yes.'' Ishbel's acknowledgement had a note of constraint in it. "It was done in conjunction with having alterations made so that someone in a wheelchair could live here. I still haven't quite got used to the new decor. If you'd seen this room a year ago, you'd hardly believe, to see it now, that it could be the same place.''

"In what way?'' Adam asked.

Ishbel pulled a slight grimace as she turned back to face them.

"In almost every way you could think of, actually. You know, of course, that Claire used to be a nursery teacher? Well, what your records and reports probably didn't tell you is how much she loved her job. She was wonderfully dedicated, and so clever with her hands. She used to spend all her free time making things to use in her lessons—hand puppets, models, mobiles, posters—just about anything you could think of that children would enjoy. And this room is where most of the work got done.''

She sighed wistfully. "What with all the clutter of paints and glue pots and half-finished projects lying about, the place usually looked as if it had been hit by a cyclone. On top of that, Claire kept a virtual menagerie of small pets for the children—cats, budgies, guinea pigs, gerbils, goldfish—you name it. Back then, the house was always messy. But it was a lively, happy mess, and I rather liked it.''

"What did she do with all the animals?'' McLeod asked.

Ishbel turned her gaze his way. "She gave them away to various play groups and schools round about. All except the cats. Funny, they're the only things she's kept, when nothing else about the house has been allowed to remain the same. The way this room looks now is very neat and pretty, I suppose, but I can't say I feel at home in it.''

"Sometimes it takes a while for a newly furnished room to look lived in,'' Adam remarked, the casual lightness of his tone masking the intensity of his interest in Ishbel's revelations. "I have no doubt that once your sister-in-law has had time to get a few more of her own things out of storage, the place will start to seem more familiar. It's been my experience that even so small an addition as a photo or two can sometimes make all the difference.''

Ishbel's soft lips tightened. ''I wouldn't even dare to suggest such a thing to Claire. After the accident, she asked me to gather up all the photographs in the house and put them in a suitcase. I thought she wanted to take them away with her to Stoke-Mandville, but it turned out that wasn't it at all. When I presented her with the case, she just stared at it for a long moment. Then she ordered me to take it out and have it burnt.''

''Indeed?'' Only Adam's rigorously acquired self-discipline prevented him from reacting outwardly. Keeping his voice studiously devoid of expression, he asked, ''And did you?''

Ishbel gave him a swift, searching look. Apparently satisfied by what she saw, she allowed herself a small, strained smile and shook her head.

''No, I didn't. But please don't let Claire know. When I asked why she wanted me to do that, she claimed it was because she wanted to put the past completely behind her, but it seemed to me that it was a decision she might later regret. So instead of packing the suitcase off to the incinerator, I stowed it away in the loft at my house. I hope the time will come someday when she can deal with the memories of her life before the accident. And if that time comes, some part of her previous life will still be waiting for her to reclaim it.''

''I share your hopes,'' Adam said gently. ''And your secret is safe with us, I promise. When that time comes, I'm sure your sister-in-law will thank you for not acting in accordance with her wishes.''

''I hope you're right,'' Ishbel said. ''It's been almost a year now, and so far she's shown no sign of changing her mind. But maybe if the police could catch the man who did this to her, and she could feel that justice had been done . . .''

''Believe me, Mrs. Reid,'' McLeod, ''we're as eager as you are to see justice done. May we see her now?''

''Of course.''

So saying, she led them on through the dining area into the kitchen, from which a small glass-walled conservatory gave access to an outdoor patio set with paving slabs. The garden beyond was large, fenced in on either side, with a high hedge at the back. The view beyond the hedge was partly screened by the spreading branches of two sturdy-looking apple trees that had been planted in opposite corners of the yard.

A paved path, wide enough for a wheelchair, extended out from the patio to a small arbor laced over with close-clipped tendrils of honeysuckle. At the end of the path, parked in the sun beside an ornamental fishpool, a figure in a wheelchair sat with head slightly bowed. The face in profile was that of Tom Lennox's phantom lady. Her nearer hand was moving slightly, scratching the ears of a large grey and white cat draped across her rug-covered lap. Her wide-open gaze appeared to be fixed on nothing in particular.

At the sound of footsteps on the path, the cat started up and made a bound for the nearest patch of shrubbery. Roused from her private reverie, Claire turned her head. A stony expression descended over her features as she caught sight of her sister-in-law and the two visitors, warning Adam that he and McLeod were likely to have their afternoon's work cut out for them.

"You weren't asleep, were you, Claire?" Ishbel asked, summoning a determined smile. "These gentlemen are from the police. This is Detective Chief Inspector McLeod, and this is Dr. Sinclair, his associate. They want to talk with you about the accident."

McLeod displayed his warrant card again and murmured a vague apology for dropping in unannounced, and Adam took a moment to study their subject. On her feet, Claire would have been tall. She gave the impression of having been strongly built, but her frame was now more bones than flesh. Her hair was as luxuriant and dark as it had appeared in Lennox's photos, but it had been cropped brutally short in this present time. The bright blue eyes were deeply hollowed, their expression restlessly introspective.

"You won't be needing me, will you, Claire?" Ishbel asked, breaking into Adam's preoccupation. "I'm still waiting for that pesky plumber, and I don't want to miss him, in case he comes or calls."

She turned around and retreated toward the house without giving Claire a chance to object. Claire Crawford spared her sister-in-law a single, unfathomable glance, then shifted her attention back to Adam and McLeod.

"It's been months since the police last demonstrated any interest in my case," she said, speaking for the first time. "May I ask what lies behind this sudden renewed curiosity?"

"You certainly may," McLeod replied. "We're attempting to tighten up our procedures for dealing with drunk drivers. To that end, you can probably appreciate the value of our reviewing and reappraising any and all unsolved drunk-driving incidents still on the books. Since the accident involving you and your late husband constitutes one of the most glaring offenses on recent record, it seemed worthwhile for us to sit down with you yet again to review everything you can remember from the night in question."

Claire heard him out in a tight-lipped silence, her measured stare never deviating from his face.

"I don't mean to be rude, Inspector, but I've already said all I have to say on that subject. Since offering up my testimony almost a year ago now, I've been working very hard trying to put the whole affair out of my mind and start my life over again. I can't even get it out of my dreams! I hope you'll understand me when I say I see nothing to be gained from raking over old ground."

"Normally, I would be inclined to agree with you," McLeod said with gruff frankness, exchanging a glance with Adam. "That's why, in this particular instance, I've enlisted the assistance of Dr. Sinclair. Besides being a highly qualified psychiatric physician, Dr. Sinclair has had considerable training and experience as a hypnotherapist. He's helped us out in numerous cases. We were hoping you might agree to let him use hypnosis to help you remember more about the accident."

"Hypnosis?" She repeated the word in a tone of incredulity.

"You needn't feel threatened, Mrs. Crawford," Adam said. "If you know anything at all about it, you'll know that it can be an effective tool for assisting the subject to remember things he or she may have otherwise forgotten or overlooked.''

Even as he spoke, he could sense Claire's growing resistance and see fire beginning to smolder behind her eyes. Gripping the arms of her wheelchair with taut fingers, she countered his gaze with a withering look before turning the full force of her anger on McLeod.

''Is *this* what passes for police work these days?'' she demanded harshly. ''No wonder you people haven't caught the man who murdered my husband and child! Haven't I had to put up with enough official incompetence already, without being asked to submit to this charade? If you want to play cheap stage tricks, go and do it somewhere other than here!''

The suppressed violence in her tone was nothing compared to the accompanying blast of psychic reverberations as she spun her chair away from them. Moved to wonder at the raw force of Claire Crawford's emotions, Adam mentally braced himself to withstand the rising storm, exchanging another glance with McLeod.

''I can't blame you for being skeptical, Mrs. Crawford,'' he said quietly. ''No doubt you know your own mind. If you're so opposed to the idea, it's doubtful we would have much success anyway. Before we take our leave, however, I wonder if I might ask you to at least take a look at a few photographs—so our trip won't have been a complete waste of time.''

Claire turned her head to eye him with suspicion. When he did not flinch from her gaze, she said grudgingly, ''All right. Provided that afterwards you'll agree to go away and leave me in peace.''

Breathing a tiny mental sigh of relief—for the concession was a foot in the door—Adam said, ''Thank you. The photos are in my briefcase. Inspector, if you'd be so good as to give me a hand?''

As McLeod wordlessly complied, supporting the case from beneath, Adam tripped the catches and retrieved Lennox's brown envelope. Abstracting three of the most recent photographs, he passed them over to Claire.

''Here you are,'' he said casually. ''I'd be obliged if you'd tell me what you think. These were taken at the scene of yesterday's accident. I'm sure you must have heard about it.''

Two of the photos were overall shots of the smashed Austin Rover, the third a detailed enlargement. Claire gave the pictures an initial cursory glance, then stiffened in her chair and subjected them to a closer look. The color drained from her face.

''What kind of stupid hoax is this?'' she whispered.

Adam had been watching her intently. Warning McLeod to silence with a quick glance, he said to Claire, ''It's no hoax, I assure you. Does the name Tom Lennox mean anything to you?''

''No.'' Claire gave her head an emphatic shake. ''I've never heard of him before. Who is he?''

''A professional photojournalist who works for the *Edinburgh Evening News*,'' Adam said. ''He doesn't know you either. But for the past six months, he's been doing the photo coverage for all the accidents along Carnage Corridor. And ever since the beginning, your image has been turning up in his photographs.''

So saying, he handed over the rest of Lennox's pictures. Claire leafed through them, her fingers none too steady, only staring at the last photo for a long moment before absently squaring up the stack.

''I don't understand,'' she murmured, not looking at him. ''I was nowhere near the scene of any of these accidents. This can't possibly be me. How could it be?''

She was visibly shaken. Adam decided to take the plunge. ''I have a theory about that,'' he told her. ''But I'll warn you right now it's going to sound a bit unorthodox.''

''Tell me anyway.''

''All right. First answer me this, though: Would you consider yourself a religious person?''

Claire's jaw tightened. ''There was a time when I would have said I was. Now . . .'' She broke off with an embittered shrug.

''Let me rephrase the question, then. Do you believe that you possess an immortal soul?''

Swallowing audibly, Claire bowed her head and looked away. ''I don't dare believe otherwise,'' she said with bleak candor. "If I thought this were all the life I was ever going to have—" She shook her head bitterly. "What has any of this to do with your theory?"

"Perhaps everything," Adam replied, dropping to a crouch to put himself more on her level, aware that he was embarking on precarious ground. "Allow me to lapse into my lecturer's mode for a moment. If we grant that a soul exists at all, then it is not stretching credulity too far to suggest that it exists as a subtle emanation of energy. Researchers into the paranormal have demonstrated time and again that photo and X-ray films both are sensitive to such emanations. Given the present circumstances, I'm tempted to suggest that what Mr. Lennox has inadvertently captured on film are images of what students of modern occultism would call projections of your astral self. Or, if you prefer, your wandering soul."

When Claire offered no comment, only looking off into the fishpond, he forged ahead.

"It's a documented fact that many people have experienced the sensation of their souls parting company temporarily with their bodies. By virtue of special training, the ascetics and holy men of the Far East profess themselves able to control the comings and goings of this spiritual aspect of themselves.

"Here in the West, where such experiences are not governed by any formalized religious tradition, such periods of astral separation tend to occur spontaneously and unconsciously, usually in response to acute physical pain or intense emotional stress. I expect you may have heard of out-of-body experiences in connection with near-death episodes. The individual doesn't necessarily have to believe in the possibility of astral travel in order to experience it, if the triggering circumstances are sufficiently extreme."

Claire's gaze hardened incredulously. "Is that what you think I'm doing? Astral travelling?"

Adam raised an elegant eyebrow. "I'm suggesting that it *could* account for your likeness in these photographs."

"But—this is crazy!" Claire protested. "Even if you were right—which I don't believe for a minute!—what possible reason could I have for wanting to visit the scenes of these accidents? Believe me, that's the last place I want to be!''

''That's precisely what I've been wondering myself,'' Adam said. ''It may be worth noting that all of these accidents have occurred in almost the exact same place as your own. Perhaps your astral self is being drawn to the scene of these later accidents because you need to search out and retrieve some forgotten piece of evidence that would help the police track down the driver of the car that hit you.''

Claire was shaking her head, as if in blank denial. The look in her eyes, however, told Adam that she was almost convinced.

''This whole thing is insane,'' she muttered. ''Even if I *were* astral travelling, wouldn't I have some memory of having done it?''

''No conscious memory, perhaps,'' Adam said. ''What the unconscious mind records may be another matter. Hypnosis might allow me to test the theory. If you could bring yourself to reconsider it.''

Claire was silent for a long moment, nervous fingers plucking at the rug over her lap. The silence drew itself out until every small sound from the surrounding garden seemed strangely amplified.

''All right,'' she finally whispered, her voice almost inaudible. ''I don't know what's going on, but I want to find out.''

CHAPTER TEN

"I was hoping you'd see it that way," Adam said gravely. "Shall I take those photographs back now?"

Wordlessly Claire handed the prints back to Adam, who rose and returned them to their envelope, stowing it away again in his briefcase. McLeod, meanwhile, fetched two white plastic lawn chairs from the patio and brought them into the shade of the arbor. Claire watched these preparations without comment, but made no move to join them.

"Would you prefer to stay in the sun?" Adam asked, handing his briefcase to McLeod.

She shrugged and glanced at the fishpond, where a dragonfly was humming just above the surface, its wings barely stirring that water.

"Does it matter?" she said.

Retrieving one of the chairs, Adam brought it over beside her, angling it slightly toward her before sitting. She was not making this any easier.

"Not really," he replied. "Wherever you're most comfortable. I can certainly understand your apprehension, but please allow me to reassure you that nothing is going to happen without your consent. Despite what the makers of a B-grade horror movies would like you to believe, hypnosis has nothing to do with brainwashing or mind control. Only your cooperation will make any kind of success possible. My role, as physician and therapist, is simply to be your guide and companion." He smiled slightly. "Shall we begin?"

She shrugged, feigning indifference, but her hands were clasped tightly in her lap.

"Very well," he said easily, aware of McLeod settling a few feet behind them, still in the shade of the arbor. "The most important initial rule is always to relax. So before we do anything else, I'd like to make sure you're quite comfortable. Take a deep breath and let it all the way out, as far as you can. Close your eyes and feel the warmth of the sunlight on your face and hands. Unclasp your hands and let them just lie there in your lap . . . that's right.

"Next, I'd like to run through a simple breathing exercise with you," he went on. "The pattern is this: Take a deep breath in for a count of five, hold it for a count of five—and then exhale as fully as you can, also for a count of five, and feel the tension draining out of your body each time you repeat the sequence. Let's do it together a few times. In for five—hold for five—out for five . . ."

He made a soothing litany of the instructions. Under the calming influence of his voice, Claire showed signs of beginning to unbend, but her eyes kept flickering open to see what he was doing. Noting her distraction, Adam casually slipped the pocket watch from his waistcoat pocket and unfastened the fob and chain from the buttonhole.

"That's fine," he murmured. "Feel yourself becoming more and more relaxed as you sit here soaking in the sunshine. And now I'd like you to fix your gaze on this pocket watch, if you would." He dangled it at the end of its chain and set it gently turning. "As you can see for yourself, there's nothing particularly unusual about it—just an ordinary gold pocket watch, if a bit old-fashioned. I'd like you simply to use it as a focal point. Watch it spin; see how it catches the sunlight. We're going to use it to distract your conscious mind—the mellow flicker of sunlight on the gold. It's very pleasant sitting here in the sunshine. . . .

"And as you find yourself more and more comfortable, more and more relaxed, you can feel yourself growing drowsy, your eyelids growing heavier and heavier as the sunlight dazzles your eyes. You can even feel the warmth of the reflected light. It's so much more peaceful just to let your eyelids close, and float on this calm, tranquil tide of well-being. You're safe and warm and secure and very relaxed and comfortable . . . so relaxed, your thoughts subsiding, floating, drifting . . . too much effort to think very much. You just drift and float, like a leaf on the surface of the pool. No strife, no danger, just peaceful silence all around you . . . Let your eyes close if you want. You can feel yourself becoming more and more relaxed, more and more at ease. . . . ''

His voice continued to soothe and reassure. She was more resistant than most, and for a while Adam was not certain she would let go enough for any useful work; but gradually her eyes closed and her breathing steadied, some of the lines of tension easing from face and shoulders. When she seemed to have settled, he pocketed his watch and shifted his approach slightly, easing into a standard induction for deepening trance.

''I want you to imagine now that I'm holding the string of a helium balloon, just between us. The balloon is about twice the size of my head, and it's made of shiny silver mylar that flashes in the sun. Can you see it in your mind's eye, floating just above our heads?''

''Yes,'' she replied, after a slight hesitation.

''Very good. Now I want you to imagine that I'm pulling the balloon over closer to you, and I'm going to tie the string around your left wrist. You'll feel just a light touch as I attach it.'' He lightly stroked across the back of her wrist with a fingertip.

''And now you can feel the tug of the balloon against your wrist, pulling at it, making it lighter and lighter, so that any second now, your hand will begin to float free of your lap. You can feel the tug of the balloon, and your hand is becoming lighter and lighter. . . . ''

Under such guidance, her left hand soon began to float free of her lap, slowly rising toward her face. As it touched, at his suggestion, she seemed to relax even more deeply into her chair, indicative that she finally had slipped into trance. Satisfied that the depth probably was sufficient to be of use, Adam gently clasped her wrist and eased her hand back to her lap.

''That's fine,'' he said softly. ''I've removed the balloon now, and your hand can lie easy in your lap again. Can you hear me clearly?''

''Yes.'' Her voice was scarcely louder than a whisper.

"Excellent," Adam murmured. "Now, you're very deeply relaxed, but you're also perfectly well aware of who and where you are, sure of yourself and your surroundings. Even with your eyes closed, you will always retain some sense of being solidly anchored to your familiar environment, relaxed and safe and secure. That underlying security will abide with you, whatever else may happen here today, and wherever our inquiries may take us.

"Now, we've agreed that we'll try to discover what reason you might have for wanting to revisit the scene of your accident. To explore this question, I should like to take you back to the accident itself. Will you allow me to do this?"

A flicker of uncertainty passed over Claire's hitherto quiet face, suggestive of conflicting impulses at work. Adam half held his breath and waited. After a moment, however, she gave a dreamy nod of acquiescence.

Adam allowed himself to breathe again, though something in her manner made him wonder whether the simple regression he had in mind would be sufficient. Even relaxed in trance, the strength of Claire's anger and fear remained as an almost palpable tension. As much to safeguard himself as to focus his own powers, he dipped into his trouser pocket to slip his sapphire ring onto his finger, mentally pausing to pay homage to the Light as he touched the stone to his lips.

"Thank you, Claire. Now, I'd like you to picture yourself poised at the threshold of a doorway," he said, himself building a mental image of what he described. "This doorway represents a portal to the past, and in a moment I'm going to ask you to open the door and step inside. The place and time we're about to revisit is the occasion of your accident. The difference in this instance, however, is that I will be present as well, ready to lend you all the support I can. And you will have the authority to alter the scene at any point you desire. I'm going to take hold of your wrist now, so that you'll know I am truly with you."

When Claire made no demur, he reached out with his left hand and gently encircled her near wrist, setting his fingertips on the pulse-point. Claire trembled slightly at his touch, but made no attempt to pull away. His own breath coming calm and slow, Adam let himself sink into trance as well, waiting until his pulse synchronized with hers. Then he closed his eyes and let himself enter the scene he had built in his mind's eye, hopefully well-matched with Claire's.

Sensory impressions from his own body receded into hazy obscurity. The transition was like overstepping a stream. A momentary sensation of imbalance gave way to a sense of firm footing as he settled into the scene, standing before a tall portal half-shrouded in shimmering silver fog.

And standing beside him, her spirit-form unconfined to any wheelchair, Claire was gazing up at the door, head flung back.

"Tell me what you see, Claire," he murmured aloud.

Ignoring his request, Claire put her hand to the door and lifted the latch, which yielded without a sound. The door opened when she gave it a push, and to his surprise, she stepped boldly across the threshold.

Adam darted after her, preparing to intervene, but he found himself out-of-doors, beneath the dim sweep of a nighttime sky. The grass beneath his feet was flecked here and there with cast-off bits of litter, and gave way to a ribbon of tarmac an arm-span to his left. Houses were visible on the opposite side of the road a quarter of a mile away, their rooftops dimly silhouetted against the amber glow of a distant row of street lamps. Though Adam had not yet been to the scene of Claire's accident in the flesh, somehow he knew it would be exactly as he saw it.

"Now, don't tell me you didn't enjoy yourself tonight!" a woman's voice said in the darkness. "Once the baby arrives, you'll be glad we made the most of these last few opportunities to slip out for the evening."

It was Claire Crawford's voice, both in reality and in his visualization—and he saw that the Claire standing beside him in vision was the same who had appeared in Tom Lennox's photographs, her shorn locks restored, wearing a light-colored cardigan over a denim smock, her body gently rounded by advancing pregnancy. She was smiling, her dark curls bobbing in the breeze, and Adam realized that she was speaking to him in place of her dead husband.

Even as the setting registered, a set of headlamps appeared in the distance and began to converge with frightening speed, flaring like strobe lights. As the glare expanded to encompass them, Adam saw the woman at his side make a sudden lunge, calculated not to carry her out of danger, but to place herself squarely in the path of the onrushing car.

In that same instant Adam was gripped by a sense of genuine peril. Without time to analyze the situation, he yielded to instinct and tried to wrench her back.

"No!" she gasped, head wildly shaking in denial as she fought him. "Let me go! I must see the driver! *I must!*"

The car was almost upon them. Brakes squealing, it made as if to veer aside. Exerting all his strength, Adam forced her back onto the grassy verge just as the car flashed on by. Its passage raised a gale of wind and grit, and left him with racing pulse and pounding heart.

"Why did you stop me?" Claire demanded hoarsely, aloud as well as in their shared vision. Vision-fists pounded impotently against his shoulders as she rounded on him with blazing eyes and angry tears. "You should have let me *see!* What happens to me doesn't matter. All I'm trying to do is get close enough *to see his face!*"

The truth dawned on Adam like a thunderclap. In that instant of revelation, he realized that the scenario into which he had just been pulled had been drawn not from Claire's memory of her original accident, but rather from a follow-up dream born of unfulfilled compulsion—the desperate yearning to identify her husband's killer.

The situation at Carnage Corridor suddenly became crystal clear. Given focus by the longing embodied in her dreams, Claire Crawford was returning on the astral to the scene of the accident, unaware that the cars she was now confronting were real. So convincing was her astral presence, powered as it was by her own emotional turmoil, that the drivers involved were being wholly taken in by the illusion. To avoid hitting her, they were swerving off the road to their deaths.

And had Adam's own intervention a moment earlier perhaps narrowly averted yet another tragedy? Even as he considered that possibility, Claire's voice broke in sharply, high and strained.

"Why did you stop me?" she demanded again. "Don't

you understand? Until the driver of that car is caught and punished, my husband and my baby won't be able to rest easy!''

Her fierce accusation conjured a brief but poignant vision of John Crawford laid out in his coffin, the tiny form of his infant daughter cradled in one arm.

''Damn you!'' Claire cried, her fingers digging into his arm. ''*You should have let me see*!''

Her sudden fury was like a blast of burning wind. The sheer, undisciplined force of it staggered Adam, and the surrounding dream-landscape shrivelled away like so much burning celluloid, plunging him into sudden darkness.

As good as blind, he raised the focus of his right hand and the ring it wore and cried out the Word of power that was his to command on the astral. His utterance called forth a spark of blue flame from the ring's stone, which expanded and fragmented, sending javelins of sapphire cleaving outward in all directions. Before that light, the darkness fell back, showing him a vaulted tunnel stretching off into murky distances.

Stalactites and stalagmites lined the passageway like ranks of dragon's teeth. The floor was pooled with black wherever their shadows overlapped. Straining his eyes to penetrate the gloom, Adam caught sight of Claire Crawford's fleeing form. Determined to stay with her, he held his ring-hand before him to light the way, and set out after her.

A red glow materialized ahead, growing brighter as he approached. Claire's racing figure showed up as a black silhouette against the glare. The light intensified, volcanic in its jewelled radiance. Like a meteor drawn toward the sun, Claire abruptly vanished into the midst of it.

Fearing he might lose her in this labyrinth of dreams, Adam plunged on after her. A rift opened up before him, a scarlet slash in the surrounding rock. Waves of hot air hissed and roared through the rift like the sulphurous fumes from a lava pit. Shielding his face with his right arm, Adam pressed forward as far as the opening, then stopped short at the sight that met his eyes.

He was standing at the cavernous edge of a lake of fire. Out on the lake, wild torrents of flame leapt and seethed like magma in a cauldron, around an island ringed with blazing whirlpools. Standing alone on the island was Claire Crawford.

Fire roared around her like a cyclone. On a lectern before her lay an open book, its pages alight with tongues of dancing flame. The sight of it told Adam where he was—back in the hall of Akashic Records, catapulted thither by the spontaneous rapport he had formed with Claire Crawford, translated past her mind's inner defenses into the raging core of her heart-of-hearts.

That psychic link was represented here as a slender bridge of stone overarching the fiery lake. Clinging fast to the lectern, Claire gave a wild, despairing cry—the cry of a soul in torment. Hearing it, Adam reached out to her—and began gingerly moving out onto the bridge.

Fire rose to meet him, raging round him with hurricane force. The blistering furnace of the flames erased all distinctions between body, mind, and spirit, leaving only pure agony, but he clung to his purpose and struggled on. Halfway across the bridge, he felt its fabric shudder under him. He tried to quicken his pace, flinching at each fresh explosion, but he was forced to a standstill only a few paces from the shore, choking on fire.

His whole being felt blasted and flayed. Beaten to his knees, for a moment he could go no further. The excoriating heat conjured up a tortured memory out of his own past. In as agonizing wrench of perspective, he was suddenly a fourteenth-century Templar knight, reliving fiery martyrdom at the instigation of the French king, Philip le Bel. . . .

His chains held him fast to the stake as the flames licked hungrily up his legs, surrounding him with pain. Assailed by the stench of his own burning flesh, he flung himself against his bonds, hearing his own voice moaning in mortal—

"NO!"

With a supreme effort of will, Adam wrenched himself back to his present purpose, pressing his ring to his lips as he forced himself to remember who he was and what he was doing here. With a puissant lunge, he broke free of the chains and burst from the flames, at last gaining the refuge of the shore.

Claire was slumped over the lectern. Once more in command, Adam made his way to her side. No time now to wonder how he had been drawn so completely into her visualization—though a part of him knew it betokened contact with a far older soul than he first had thought. Could it be that Claire Crawford, like Peregrine when Adam first had met him, was a damaged fledgling?

He caught hold of her arm, intending to lift her clear and bring her back to her senses. But before he could invoke the necessary controls, his senses wrenched again and the scene around them blurred and vanished in an accompanying pang of dizziness. When Adam's vision cleared, he discovered that he had been cast into yet another scene conjured up from the well of Claire's personal unconscious.

CHAPTER ELEVEN

THIS one, at least, was more tranquil. Adam was standing alone on a gravelled path in the midst of a broad churchyard. On either side of him, the lush grass of early summer was broken up by grave slabs, with here and there a raised table-tomb to indicate the resting place of someone of more substantial means. In front of him the ground sloped away downhill toward the junction of two rivers, one broad and smooth, the other narrow and swift-running. At the lower end of the burial green, within the shelter of the yard's freestone wall, half a dozen ewes were placidly grazing while their lambs frolicked about in the sun.

The attendant church was large, stone-built in the cruciform plan of the late medieval period, with a high tower at its western end. The columns and friezes flanking the west door showed a gothic wealth of carving. Beyond the church, past the meeting of the waters, the noonday sun glanced off the crowstepped gables and grey slates of a modest-sized town. Between church and town, an L-plan tower-house jutted against the sky, encircled by a bawn wall of moldering stones.

The carts and wagons going into the town gave Adam his first clear indication that he was no longer operating within the confines of present time, and the wealth of detail suggested that this was more than a mere stage set devised by Claire's imagination to serve as backdrop for some romantic daydream. On the contrary, Adam realized with a rising wave of excitement that he was almost certainly dealing with a vision drawn not from fantasy, but from the memory of a historic personality—Claire Crawford's.

That Claire should possess a historic past was a discovery of no mean significance. Genuine experience of past lives was one of the hallmarks of individuals with Adept potential. That Claire herself seemed unaware of her historic past reinforced his earlier speculation that Claire might be a wounded fledgling—which made it all the more imperative that she should be healed and brought back into harmony with the Light.

Spurred on by this possibility, Adam surveyed his surroundings, trying to deduce where he might be, and when. Scotland, certainly; the crowstepped gables of the town roofs were a distinctive feature of Scottish architecture. And in a town of some consequence, given the presence of the tower house and the size of the parish church. Probably no later than the mid-seventeenth century, judging by the fact that the burial ground contained only grave slabs and table-tombs. Standing monuments, he recalled, had not become a feature of Scottish burials until shortly before the turn of the eighteenth century.

His interest deepening, Adam left the path in order to examine the inscriptions on some of the newer tomb-slabs. A preponderance of Scotts and Douglasses amongst the names suggested a location in the central Borders area. The most recent date he could find was 1640. Before he could begin to speculate further, the sound of a door opening behind him made him turn his head in time to see a tall, dark-haired woman emerge from the church porch with a flat basket of flowers looped over one arm.

She was dressed in a style that reminded Adam at once of portraits executed by the seventeenth-century Scottish painter George Jamesone. Her full-skirted gown was a blued-grey shade of plain, dark wool, but the quality of the cloth itself proclaimed her a member of the gentry. About her shoulders she wore a shawl of fine Flemish lace, with more lace frilling the cuffs of her full, elbow-length sleeves. The face beneath the sweep of a broad-brimmed chapeau was striking rather than pretty, and unfamiliar, but the eyes gazing out across the churchyard belonged to Claire Crawford.

She had three children with her, two small boys of perhaps

five or six, and a girl who looked to be several years older. Shooing them off with a smile to go play with the lambs at the far end of the churchyard, this Claire-who-had-been left the path and picked her way decorously across the grass toward a handsome granite table-tomb on the south side of the church door. When she reached it, she paused a moment with her head bowed as if in prayer, then knelt and began arranging flowers in a stone sconce at the foot of the tomb.

Adam drifted over to join her. Halting a discreet distance behind her, he took a moment to glance over the Latin carved on the face of the tomb. Thomas Maxwell of Hawick, aged thirty-one, had been buried here with his three children: James, Margaret, and Eilidh, the last a mere infant. The year was the same for all four: 1636.

He needed nothing further to tell him how the four had died. Like the rest of Europe, Scotland had been visited by periodic outbreaks of plague from the fourteenth century onward. Prior to the turn of the seventeenth century, those outbreaks had been confined largely to the coastal ports, but with the stabilization of the English border in 1603, the increase of overland trade had brought the plague inland. One such outbreak had ravaged Hawick in 1636.

At that moment, the woman kneeling at the tomb glanced around and gave him an inquiring look from under the brim of her hat.

"Good day to ye, sir," she observed pleasantly, the lilt of the Borders in her accent. "I dinnae think I know ye. Are ye a stranger here?"

In his vision, Adam shook himself out of his reverie, amazed that she could see him.

"In a manner of speaking," he said. "My name is Adam Sinclair."

"And mine is Annet," she returned with a smile. "Annet Maxwell."

There was nothing in her manner to suggest she found anything at odds with his appearance. Adam could only infer that just as Claire's imagination had lent shape to her earlier visions, so her submerged memories must be coloring her present perceptions. And the fact that he had been drawn into her vision at all suggested that Annet Maxwell had something to convey to him, having recognized another soul with a historical past.

"If your name is Maxwell, then these people buried here must have been your family," he said, directing his gaze toward the tomb. "I'm sorry. Was it the plague that took them from you?"

Annet Maxwell nodded wistfully. "My Thomas was an attorney-at-law. He had dealings with many folk from outside our borough. When the plague came, he was one o' the first to take sick, and our bairns with him. Why I wasnae ta'en too, I dinnae know. But I count myself fortunate that my daurlins found room here in the churchyard, with Our Lady herself to watch o'er their rest."

Her gaze flicked toward the frieze above the church door. Looking more closely, Adam saw that the scenes carved there depicted episodes from the life of the Virgin. But he glanced back at Annet as she stood up and shook her skirts back into place.

"Were ye looking for anyone in particular?" she asked. "If none o' the names here belong to ye, ye might try the burial ground across the river, on the north side o' the common. Many o' the later plague victims found rest there, when there was nae more ground left here to take them. It was a grim, bare place at the time, but the grass has since grown o'er the mounds, and the dead sleep there at peace."

"I thank you for that suggestion," Adam said, adding, "You sound as if you have come to terms with your loss."

Annet shrugged. "What would ye, sir? I couldnae bring the dead back to life again by any excess o' grieving. Besides, the kirk teaches that we shall all be reunited at the Resurrection on the Last Day. An' in the meantime, there are others who need me."

It was a more vigorous response than Adam had dared to hope for. If Annet Maxwell's words were any true indication of acquired inner strength, the potential resources available for Claire Crawford might well be considerable. Curious to see how far that strength might be tested, he asked, "Did you never wonder who might have been responsible for bringing the plague to town in the first place?"

"Ye mean, did I look for someone tae blame?" Annet

smiled and shook her head. "Looking for some scapegoat wouldhae been so much wasted effort, when sae many people were dying. An' e'en if the spread o' the disease could hae been traced back to one man," she continued reflectively, "what good would that hae done? That one man would ne'er hae willed this disaster upon us knowingly, e'en had it been within his power to do so. And where there is nae premeditated will, e'en if the grief that follows is great, surely we were better advised, for the good of our own souls, tae forgive rather than tae demand retribution."

So saying, she turned away and waved a hand to attract the attention of the children playing down at the far end of the green. The girl was first to notice, and called the two boys to order. Watching as the three began picking their way up the hill through the grass, Adam was moved to ask, "Whose children are those?"

Annet answered him over her shoulder. "Mine, now. The same plague that left me childless left them without parents. Between us, we manage to make up our losses. But then I've heard it said that a will to love will always find a worthy object."

As she spoke, Adam noticed a telltale blurring in the air along the peripheries of his sight. When he looked out beyond the river's embankment, there was no longer anything of the town to be seen. With a smiling nod of farewell, Annet Maxwell turned away and went to rejoin her adopted sons and daughter. A moment later, their forms disappeared from view in a wave of silvery mist.

Adam's return to his senses was gentle. When he opened his eyes, his left hand still lightly clasping Claire Crawford's wrist, Noel McLeod was standing over him, looking more than a little concerned. As soon as he saw that Adam's eyes were open, an expression of relief crossed his craggy features as he mouthed silently to Adam, Are you all right?

Adam blinked and nodded. Though the sunlight was still warm, he felt chilled all over. It was one of the common aftereffects he had come to associate with astral travel; nevertheless, he could not repress a slight shiver. He glanced over at Claire Crawford, but she was still sitting quietly, her face becalmed in deep trance.

"Claire, I want you to rest for a few minutes now," he murmured, holding a finger to his lips to caution McLeod. "Take a very deep breath and go deep asleep as you let it out. Hear nothing until I take your hand again and call you by name."

As she complied, her head nodding onto her chest, he released her wrist and got shakily to his feet, momentarily leaning on McLeod's shoulder as they withdrew into the shade of the arbor.

"I'm fine," he assured his Second. "Just give me a few seconds to settle. Did I give you a turn, there?"

"Not exactly," McLeod said. "But there at first, I wasn't sure you were totally in control. This last bit was a fairly straightforward conversation with someone called Annet Maxwell, who I can only assume was a past-life persona, but before that, you suddenly cried out, "No!""

Adam nodded. Remembering the flashback to fiery martyrdom as a Templar Knight, he could well believe that the pain's reliving had found expression in his voice.

"I hope I didn't make myself heard as far as the house," he remarked with a grimace.

"No, no, it wasn't all that loud—and you calmed immediately. But you did give me a start. I even considered trying to bring you out." He cocked his head at Adam. "What did you find out?"

"Well," Adam said, "I'm certainly satisfied that this unhappy lady is, indeed, the cause behind what's been happening at Carnage Corridor. She's been trying to see the face of the driver who hit her and her husband. But instead of going back in memory to the accident itself, she's been looking into real cars in contemporary time—and the drivers swerve and crash, trying to avoid hitting her."

Pursing his lips in a silent whistle, McLeod shook his head.

"That's only the beginning," Adam went on. "She has a historic past that could have a significant bearing on this present crisis. But to use it, we'll have to find a way to break down the barriers that Claire Crawford has since erected in her own mind, between the past and the present."

In as few words as possible, he related his experiences on

the astral, including visual details of his churchyard encounter with Annet Maxwell. By the time he had finished, McLeod was looking both extremely interested and extremely concerned.

"So this is not the first time she's had to cope with multiple bereavement," he said thoughtfully. "I can certainly see how Annet Maxwell's experience might throw some beneficial light on this present situation—both for what she's lost and for what she's done inadvertently—but bringing together those two aspects of herself could take a while. And in the meantime, what's to stop her from causing further accidents?"

"*We'll* have to stop her," Adam said with bleak candor, "and there are no easy answers. In the short term, I could probably leave her with a posthypnotic suggestion to forbid dreaming about the accident, waking or sleeping—but that's a stopgap measure, at best. In the long term, that kind of repression would only lead to more trouble—maybe even plunge her into psychosis—which would only make her that much harder to reach.

"No," he continued, "the impetus to stop these astral forays has got to come from Claire herself, by breaking this compulsion of hers that she *must* find that driver. We all hope he'll be found, of course, but not at the expense of more innocent lives."

"So, what do we do?"

"Well, just now, she's under the illusion that she's doing nothing more than reliving her own accident. So what I must do is to strip away that illusion, to lay bare the underlying truth."

"Do you think she can handle that truth?" McLeod asked dubiously. "How is she likely to feel when she finds out she's inadvertently killed nine people?"

"We'll deal with that issue when we come to it," Adam said. "Right now, our main priority is to ensure that no more innocent people get hurt or killed through no fault of their own. Let's see what we can do."

Returning to Claire, Adam eased himself back down into the chair beside her and gently touched her wrist.

"Claire, listen to me," he said softly. "You've done very

well so far—so well that I'd like to venture a bit further. You understand that you've been reliving your accident in your dreams. Could I clarify a few points? May I ask you a few more questions?''

Claire's cropped head made a slight movement up and down.

''Thank you,'' Adam said approvingly. ''Now, the police reports say that your accident took place shortly before midnight. Is that correct?''

''Yes.''

''And the car that struck you and your husband was red— a red Mercedes, wasn't it?''

''Yes.''

''Was there anyone else in the car besides the driver?''

''No.''

''Good. That all tallies so far. Now, leaving aside the recall work we did earlier, I'd like you to tell me, please, when you last had the dream.''

A small furrow appeared in Claire's smooth forehead. ''It was yesterday morning,'' she murmured. ''It woke me up.''

''About what time was that?''

''It was seven minutes past eight,'' she replied. ''I looked at the clock.''

Adam exchanged a glance with McLeod, for the time coincided almost perfectly with the reported time of Malcolm Grant's accident.

''Claire, I'm going to count backwards from three,'' he told her. ''On *one*, I'll touch you lightly on the forehead. That will be your signal to begin reliving that dream again— the same dream you had yesterday morning, as if it were a film being projected against the insides of your eyelids. When I touch you a second time, those dream images will become translucent, like stained glass windows. At that moment, you will see through the dream itself to glimpse the reality that lies beyond it. The dream will begin as I count three . . . two . . . *one*.''

As he spoke the final word, he tapped her lightly between the eyebrows. Claire's eyelids trembled as a sigh escaped her lips, and her shoulders stiffened.

''Tell me where you are,'' Adam instructed.

"On the south side of the Lanark Road." Claire's voice was soft, intense. "It's getting late. John and I are walking home. We're talking about the music."

"And then what?"

"Several cars pass us by. It's very dark for a bit. Then we see headlamps in the distance."

She caught her breath. "High beams, coming fast. Engine roaring . . . speeding . . . coming on like an express train. Jump for the bank—no, too late! The car's almost on top of—"

"Stop!" Adam ordered, touching her forehead again. "Freeze the action!"

Claire paused in mid-sentence. Her hands were white at the knuckles where they gripped the arms of her chair.

"Listen to me, Claire," Adam said urgently. "A year has passed since the accident you're envisioning. Look beyond the dream and tell me what you saw yesterday."

As he spoke, he laid his right hand briefly across her forehead again. Claire's lips parted with a slight gasp, and her blue eyes snapped wide-open, but she stared past Adam with an expression of bewilderment on her face.

"What is it?" Adam demanded. "Tell me what you see."

Claire seemed more than a little confused.

"Same stretch of road, but not dark," she muttered dazedly. "Not night—broad daylight."

"Do you see a car?"

She nodded, looking even more perplexed. "Not a red Mercedes. Yellow. A yellow sedan, with two men in it—"

She raised a distracted hand to her brow. Adam reached out and clasped her other hand gently. She recoiled with a gasp, then all at once seemed to become aware of his presence.

"What's going on?" she murmured disjointedly. "Where am I?"

"Safe at home," Adam assured her. "Take a deep breath to ground, and come fully back to normal waking consciousness. You were dreaming, remember?"

"About the accident, yes." Claire still seemed bemused. "I've dreamt about it before. Only this time—where did that yellow car come from?" She scanned Adam's face as if seeking enlightenment.

"It belonged to a man named Malcolm Grant," Adam said, as gently as he could. "Yesterday morning, just after eight o'clock, he and a friend were driving in to work along the Lanark Road. Just where your accident occurred, they went off the road and crashed. When the ambulance first arrived at the scene, Grant told the attendants that he'd veered off the road to avoid hitting a pregnant woman. Nobody else could remember seeing such a person on the scene—but she turned up later in the news photographs taken by Mr. Tom Lennox."

Claire gave a small choked cry, her eyes darting to Adam's briefcase, then lapsed abruptly into white-lipped silence. Adam let the silence stand. After a moment, she roused herself to look at him fearfully.

"Did they die?" she asked.

Adam nodded. "I'm afraid so."

"It was me that man saw, wasn't it?" she said.

Her face was white as chalk. Without waiting for Adam to offer either confirmation or denial, she added in a hollow voice, "That's not the first time I've had that dream. Do you suppose—does this mean that—I'm somehow responsible for all those accidents? All those deaths?"

Adam's response was measured. "As to that, it's too soon to tell. We may yet discover an element of coincidence—"

"No." Claire cut him off. "Coincidence wouldn't account for that many accidents taking place in exactly the same place—"

She broke off short, unable to complete the sentence. Then she said, "I don't understand. Why should I want to kill people I didn't even know?"

"The obvious answer to that question is that you didn't," Adam said. "When I first took you back in trance to your dream about the accident, you spoke of wanting *to see the face of the man who ran you down*. I can only guess that your repeated excursions on the astral are the result of that burning desire. Unfortunately, that desire is so intense that every now and then it escapes the confines of conventional dreaming, allowing your astral image to manifest itself at the actual physical location where the accident took place."

"And innocent motorists think there really is someone

there," she whispered. "And they—"

She drew a deep breath and passed a hand across her eyes, as if to shut out the image conjured up by her own thoughts.

"There is more power in the human spirit than is ever likely to be fathomed by science," Adam told her quietly. "Emotion without an outlet is like water building up behind a dam. If that accumulating energy can't be channelled off to some constructive purpose, it becomes potentially destructive. Sooner or later, either the reservoir will overflow or the dam will burst.

"In your case," he went on, "you've built your bulwarks too strongly, and the dam itself has refused to break. But there is a limit to what it can contain, and the excess, ungoverned, has found its own release, creating in the process an illusion powerful enough to deceive the unwary observer. There's no denying that you're probably indirectly responsible for a number of unfortunate accidents. On the other hand, it certainly wasn't intentional. And now that you know, you can stop it."

"But you just said yourself that I didn't realize what I was doing," Claire protested. "If that's true, how can I stop it, when I don't seem to have any conscious control over the situation? It's worse than possession! How can I even go to sleep, knowing that I might kill some one else?"

Adam had already been giving some thought to precisely this problem. "To begin with," he said, "I should like to admit you to hospital."

"I spent six months at Stoke-Mandville," she retorted, turning her face away slightly. "It didn't help those people who died."

"Perhaps not—but these auxiliary tragedies didn't start occurring until after you came back from Stoke-Mandville. This would seem to suggest that the dreams have more potency—or you yourself are more susceptible to them—the closer you are to the site of the original trauma.

"So I'd advise putting some physical distance between you and this stretch of the Lanark Road—which may enable you to gain some psychological distance as well. And I'd also like to prescribe some appropriate medication at night, to take you quickly past the normal transition between wakefulness and sleep, in which you're most apt to dream. If there *is* some strange connection between your dreams and the accidents, this should stop it.''

Though he did not say so aloud, it also was in the back of his mind that he and McLeod could probably arrange to ward Claire's hospital room in order to prevent her spirit-self from venturing too far afield.

''Beyond that,'' he continued, ''I should very much like to continue working with you, using hypnosis. One of the functions of hypnotherapy is to assist a subject to retrieve detailed information from memory. This being the case, it offers an effective means of redirecting your desire to 'see' what there is to remember from your accident. There's no guarantee that you will be able to 'see' the driver of the car that ran you down,'' he allowed. ''However, I would be prepared to conduct a session with a forensic artist present. From your description, it's possible he might be able to produce a recognizable drawing of the perpetrator. This could even aid the police in locating him.''

At his glance, McLeod said on cue, ''I'll be glad to arrange it. Just tell me where and when.''

''You want to hospitalize me, then,'' Claire murmured, wringing her hands. Then, after a long pause, she added abruptly, ''What about my cats?''

Adam breathed a mental sigh of relief. ''I expect your sister-in-law would be willing to look after them and your house. She seems to be quite devoted to you.''

She looked away, tight-lipped, then returned her glance to Adam.

''How long would I have to stay?''

''I can't begin to predict that yet,'' Adam said honestly. ''The sooner we begin, however, the sooner we'll find out just how much work we have to do. Are you willing to make the effort?''

Claire drew herself up, once more taut and angry.

''I don't have much choice, do I?'' she said with brutal bluntness. ''I don't want to be a murderer.''

Adam let this piece of self-condemnation pass without comment.

''My medical practice is out of Jordanburn,'' he said quietly. ''That's part of the Royal Edinburgh Hospital. If you'll allow me to use your telephone, I'll make the necessary arrangements to have you transported cross-town. Assuming that you have no objections, I would advise that we start work first thing tomorrow morning.''

Claire gave a perfunctory nod. She was staring off into space, her gaze fixed upon some distant point.

''That bastard has a lot to answer for,'' she muttered. ''Because of him, it seems I'm not only a widow, but also guilty of manslaughter. I find myself asking, Is forgiveness possible?''

The tone of her question, however, left Adam wondering if she was thinking of herself or of the unknown driver of a red Mercedes.

CHAPTER TWELVE

McLEOD met the ambulance at the curb when it arrived half an hour later. Ishbel Reid accompanied Claire and Adam to the door, carrying Claire's overnight bag.

"Here you are," she said, looping its strap over the back of the wheelchair. "I'll be along to visit you tomorrow, once you've had time to get settled in. If you think of anything else you need or want in the meantime, just ring me and I'll bring it with me when I come."

"Thank you," Claire murmured. Her tone was very subdued. "Please be sure to phone the polytechnic and let my instructors know I've been recalled to hospital."

"I will," Ishbel promised. "And don't worry about Bogart and Bacall. I'll do whatever it takes to get them in at night, even if it means bribing them with salmon. Maybe I'll even smuggle them in for a visit, if Dr. Sinclair will turn a blind eye."

As Ishbel glanced sidelong at Adam, only half-serious, a crooked smile touched Claire's pale lips.

"I don't know what I'd do without you, Ishbel," she said—and held out her arms.

Ishbel's gaze widened. Stepping forward, she bent down to exchange a heartfelt hug with her sister-in-law, who then turned her chair about without saying anything more and wheeled herself down the garden ramp to the curbside, where the ambulance attendants were opening the rear doors. Left alone on the doorstep with Adam, Ishbel gave him a strange, rather awed look.

"You must be some kind of magician," she murmured.

"That's the first time since the accident that she's shown affection to anyone but the cats. What on earth did you say to her out there in the garden?"

"Sometimes it isn't a matter of words, but of timing," Adam said evasively, biting back a smile. "Let's hope that this means your sister-in-law is beginning to wake up to her true self."

"You think she'll be all right, then?"

"I think the chances are excellent," Adam replied.

With these words, he bade her goodbye and went to join Claire in the ambulance for the cross-town ride back to Jordanburn. McLeod likewise offered her his courteous best wishes before closing the rear doors and making his way back to his waiting police car.

Donald Cochrane was slouched behind the wheel reading over a copy of *Motorsport*. At the sound of McLeod's approaching footbeats, he tossed the car magazine into the back and straightened up. The cellular phone was resting in the passenger seat beside him, together with McLeod's scribbled note of his colleague's office phone number in Dumbarton.

"Any luck getting through to Somerville?" McLeod asked, opening the door.

Shaking his sandy head, Cochrane scooped up the phone and note so McLeod could get in. "No, sir. He's still in a meeting that was supposed to have ended twenty minutes ago. I tried again, just before the ambulance arrived. Shall I give it another go?"

"Thanks, I'll do it." McLeod took the phone. "Why don't you head us back to the office?"

As Cochrane started the engine and pulled into traffic, McLeod belted up, consulted his note, then punched in the Dumbarton number, which answered on the first ring.

"Inspector Somerville here," said a gruff Glaswegian voice.

McLeod's brow cleared, and he gave Cochrane a thumbs-up. "Hello, Jack. This is Noel McLeod."

"Oh, aye? My sergeant told me you've been trying to get in touch with me. What can I do for you?"

"I'm hoping you can give me some information," McLeod said. "What, if anything, do you know about a dead man who was washed up yesterday on Mull of Kintyre?''

"You seem pretty well-informed already," Somerville said. "*I* only got the case this morning."

"The young couple who found the body are friends of mine," McLeod said. "They asked me to find out if the police have been able to identify the man."

"I suppose you told them that that's classified information, for as long as the police choose to withhold it?"

"No need for that. Young Lovat's no stranger to police work. He's a professional artist—a damned good one—and he does forensic work for me now and again. You can take it from me that he knows how to keep his mouth shut."

"I'm damned glad to hear that," Somerville said frankly. "I was dreading the thought of having this whole thing leak to the media before we'd got a chance to piece some answers together."

"That sounds ominous," McLeod said. "What have you got?"

"A damned nuisance!" Somerville replied. "This is strictly off the record, but we're all but certain the dead man is an Irish Fisheries officer, name of Michael Scanlan, who went missing several days ago off the coast of Donegal. His brother's flying in tonight from Belfast in order to make a positive ID, but no one's in any serious doubt about it, including the Irish government. They're sending along a representative from the Garda Siochana, who will liaise between us and our opposite numbers in Dublin."

"It's turning into an international incident, then, if you've got the Irish police involved," McLeod said. "I take it that we're not talking about a simple drowning."

There was a pause.

"We'll just have to wait and see," Somerville said. "Listen, sorry to cut you off short like this, but my watch is telling me I'm three minutes short of being late for an appointment. Where are you just now? Out in the car?"

"Aye."

"In that case, why don't you find a public phone box and call me back in half an hour? By that time, I'll be at the number two phone box I usually use when I'm out of the office. You know, the one *on the square*."

The phrase carried significance amongst members of the Order of Freemasonry to which both McLeod and Somerville belonged. To any uninitiated listener, the words would have conveyed nothing more than a set of directions. To McLeod, it was an indication that something more was afoot than Somerville was prepared to discuss over an open line.

"I know exactly the phone box you mean," he told his colleague. "I'll talk to you again in half an hour."

Slowing for a traffic signal, Cochrane watched his superior return the portable phone to its place in the glove box.

"Where to now, Inspector?" he asked. "You still want to go back to headquarters?"

McLeod's shrewd blue eyes were half-lidded in thought behind his gold-rimmed aviator spectacles.

"Not just yet," he told his young assistant. "Let's make a detour to Jordanburn. I have a feeling that Dr. Sinclair and I may have some further business to discuss."

On their way back across town, McLeod kept an eye out for a public telephone and finally spotted one outside a neighborhood grocery shop. Directing Cochrane to pull over, he got out of the car and went over to the call-box, fishing coins from his pocket. After consulting his pocket directory, he lifted the receiver and dialled.

Somerville's voice answered promptly. "That you, McLeod?"

McLeod fed a selection of coins into the slot. "Aye, it's me. Now, suppose you tell me what this is all about."

From the other end of the line came a deep intake of breath, like a weightlifter getting ready to heft a heavy set of barbells.

"Sorry about the cloak-and-dagger tactics, but I don't suppose I have to tell you how easy it is to scan a cellular phone. I meant what I said earlier about your friend Lovat. It's damned lucky for us that he was the one who found the body, not some other hapless member of the public. The last thing anybody needs is for the press to get wind of what I'm about to tell you."

McLeod was fully on the alert now. "I'm listening."

"Well, for starters, this Scanlan fellow didn't just fall overboard and drown. He was helped along by a knife in the back and a clip on the head."

"Some brush with illegal fishermen, perhaps?" McLeod asked, for incursions of foreign fishing boats into British and Irish waters had led to more than one violent clash in recent months.

"That's what we thought at first," Somerville replied. "Their control said that Scanlan and his partner were going out to check reports of illegal fixed nets, but he lost them when a fog came rolling in. The next anyone heard from them was the next day, when Scanlan's partner was found adrift in their boat."

"And what does the partner have to say?" McLeod asked.

"Nothing," Somerville said bluntly. "He had a matching knife wound."

"Ouch. Could he and Scanlan have gotten into a fight?"

"With each other? Not impossible, but bloody unlikely," Somerville said. "The word from the Northern Fisheries Board is that the two men had been working together for the better part of four years. Nothing to indicate that there was ever any friction between them."

"Which brings us back to square one."

"That's right. And it gets worse. The weapon that inflicted the wound in Scanlan's back wasn't your usual switchblade or hunting knife. This was something out of the ordinary: heavy, with a triangular blade, probably a good eight to ten inches long. Preliminary examination indicates that it pierced the lung. Even if Scanlan hadn't landed in the sea, he probably would have died of internal hemorrhaging within a matter of minutes."

"I see," McLeod said. "What about the partner's wound?"

"Pretty much the same, so far as we know."

"And the blow to Scanlan's head?"

"Probably not sufficient by itself to be fatal," Somerville said. "It's possible he got it falling out of the boat—hit his head on a rock or something. Actual cause of death may turn out to be drowning—not that it much matters to Scanlan. We'll know more after the post-mortem."

"When's that?"

"As soon as possible, if I have anything to say about it," Somerville growled. "I'll let you know exactly when and where, as soon as the arrangements have been made. You and that psychiatrist friend of yours—what's his name, Sinclair?—might well want to be present."

"Oh?"

Adam Sinclair's role as a police consultant was well documented, especially with respect to some of the stranger cases that came the way of the Lothian and Borders Police. Somerville's suggestion was enough to kick McLeod's internal warning system into full operation.

"What makes you think Adam Sinclair might have anything to contribute to this case?" he wondered out loud. "For that matter, is there any particular reason why we shouldn't just wait to read the medical examiner's report when it comes out?"

"I've saved the best for last," Somerville said. "What do you suppose they found on Scanlan, when they were looking him over for identification?"

"From the sound of your voice," said McLeod, "I shouldn't be able to guess if I lived to be a hundred. A winning ticket for the Irish Lottery?"

Somerville gave a gallows chuckle. "Not even close, Brother McLeod. It was a flag—and not just any flag. This was a World War Two *Kriegsmarine* flag, apparently off a German U-boat. It has *U-636* stencilled along the canvas of the hoist."

"He had a Nazi flag on him?" McLeod asked, astonished.

"Yep. The thing was wadded up inside the breast of his survival suit—waterlogged, as you might well expect, since the suit had been breached, but otherwise intact. The experts haven't had a chance to examine it yet, but it looks damned authentic to me. And if it *is* authentic," he finished, with dour relish, "this Scanlan bloke was messing about with a ghost ship."

"How's that?"

"Official naval records list *U-636* as having been depth-charged by Royal Navy frigates in April of 1945, some ninety miles northeast of Donegal."

"Are you sure about that?"

"Sure am. I checked the stats myself."

McLeod was prepared to take Somerville at his word. A war games enthusiast, the Strathclyde inspector had made a special study of Nazi regalia.

"I'll grant you, this is an odd one," he replied. "But ghost ship or not, no ghost stabbed Scanlan in the back. Have you considered the possibility of a tie-in with the IRA or some other terrorist group?"

"Aye, we have—and from a purely pragmatic point of view, I'd go so far as to say that may be our best line of further inquiry. Depending upon the state of preservation, a German U-boat could be a source of weaponry for terrorist activities. If Scanlan and his partner did inadvertently stumble across something like that, the organization involved would certainly have taken steps to make sure they didn't live to tell about it. . . . "

As he paused, McLeod said, "You don't sound entirely convinced."

"I'm not," Somerville admitted. "I'd be more sure of myself if Scanlan had been shot. Knives aren't the IRA's favorite toys; they like to play with guns and explosives. And even as knife-killings go, this one is queerly atypical. I'll be interested to hear what the pathologists have to say."

"Me, too," McLeod said. "And you're quite right that Adam Sinclair may very well be the man to help us out on this one. I'll have a word with him and let him know what's in the wind—"

He was interrupted by a beep on the telephone line, warning him that his time was up.

"Don't bother putting any more coins in the box," Somerville said. "That's all I've got for now. I'll get back to you as soon as the post-mortem is scheduled. It'll probably be tomorrow or the next day."

"Right you are," McLeod said. "Thanks, Jack."

The connection was broken on his last words. McLeod's expression was thoughtful as he returned the receiver to its cradle. Somerville's latest investigative headache promised to become contagious—and something about the possible Nazi connection sent cold shivers up McLeod's spine. Ruefully aware that he himself was already partially committed, the inspector stumped back to the car and directed Cochrane to proceed on to Jordanburn.

✦ ✦ ✦

Adam had arranged for Claire Crawford to be installed in a private room. Leaving the nursing staff to make their new patient comfortable in her hospital surroundings, he withdrew to the nurses' station and settled down to write up his orders for the night, including appropriate sedation for Claire. Under cover of this commonplace activity, he also set about the more subtle task of erecting a psychic barrier around the room, to prevent her errant spirit-self from straying abroad. When he was finished, he bade Claire good night and retired to his office. He had been at his desk for barely ten minutes when a knock at the door announced the arrival of McLeod.

"I got through to Somerville just after you went away in the ambulance," he announced, coming in to flop into the chair opposite Adam. "From the sound of things, Peregrine and Julia may have uncovered a hornets' nest."

In as few words as possible, he related all that Somerville had told him regarding the case that was building up around the dead man the Lovats had found on the beach. Adam refrained from comment until McLeod had wound down.

"That's a very interesting wrinkle," he said thoughtfully. "No wonder Peregrine was picking up odd twinges. We must next ask ourselves how and where Scanlan came into possession of a Nazi flag. Since this isn't an object most people normally carry about their persons, we have to assume that he found it while he was out on patrol. Is it possible he could have stumbled onto the actual wreckage of a U-boat? Could it just have broken loose from wherever it sank, and washed ashore?"

"It's possible, I suppose," McLeod said, "but according to Somerville, the flag is minty. I can't see how something as perishable as a piece of cloth could survive fifty-odd years of weathering and immersion in salt water."

"Neither can I," Adam admitted. Leaning back in his chair, he made a steeple of his forefingers and tapped them thoughtfully against his lower lip. "All right, then, suppose the wreck was somehow sheltered."

"Lying on the rocks somewhere for fifty years?" McLeod said. "I doubt that. I'm sure every inch of the Irish coast has been combed more than once in half a century. I do remember an uncle of mine saying that during the war, Nazi sympathizers tried to claim that the Germans had built secret submarine pens along the Irish coast. Do you suppose it might have been true?"

Adam shook his head. "I don't see how. I've certainly never heard of any such installation being found. Besides, it simply isn't credible that construction on that scale could have gone unnoticed—not to mention the equally conspicuous problem of fuelling and provisioning such bases, once they were built. Nor can I imagine that the Irish would have violated their official neutrality to sanction such an operation by Germany."

"Yes, but Irish independence was hardly a generation old, when the war broke out," McLeod said. "Adam, they're *still* killing one another over that legacy of bitterness."

"True enough," Adam agreed. "But while it's all very well to quote that old adage about 'My enemy's enemy is my friend,' I don't think even the most rabid Irish Nationalist could have had any illusions about what would have happened to 'neutral' Ireland, if England had fallen to Germany. I think we can discount the notion that there were actual submarine pens."

"All right," McLeod conceded. "What are our other options, then?"

Adam thought a moment. "Well, that part of the Irish coast is quite rugged. It's not inconceivable that the occasional lone U-boat might have sought—and found—shelter there amongst the coves and sea caves."

"Aye." McLeod fingered his grizzled moustache. "There are certainly caves along the Scottish coast that might be big enough to hide a submarine, so who's to say there couldn't be equivalent formations to be found up in Donegal?"

Adam nodded, his mind leaping ahead to explore further possibilities. "Assume that Scanlan *did* find the sheltered wreck of a German U-boat," he said. "Assume that he took the flag as a souvenir of his find. The next question is, Who could possibly be sufficiently interested in such a vessel to kill a man in order to prevent the secret from leaking out?''

''I suppose that would depend on what they wanted it for,'' McLeod mused. ''Somerville suggested that the IRA might be interested in salvaging the weaponry on board, or possibly even the sub itself, to be used in terrorist activities.''

''I certainly wouldn't dismiss that notion,'' Adam said. ''But the IRA isn't the only terrorist organization in the world. There are others I can think of who might consider themselves entitled to a prior claim on a German submarine and its contents.''

McLeod stiffened slightly. ''A neo-Nazi group of some kind?''

Adam cocked an eyebrow. ''That would certainly explain how they knew where the sub was likely to be found in the first place.''

As he spoke, he was thinking back to his recent astral encounter with the Master, and the cryptic warning he had been issued concerning an old evil once more on the rise. *The adherents of this evil*, the Master had said, *have made their first foray into those created lands that lie under your protection.* Was the mysterious death of Michael Scanlan merely a passing move in some much bigger game, one in which the opposition had already stolen the first march?

It would not be the first time that Adam and his fellow Huntsmen had encountered the resurgent spectre of Nazi evil. It was an evil that seemed capable of renewing itself time and time again, changing its form but not its substance.

On the other hand, neo-Nazis were not the only exponents of darkness at work in the world, and a dead man with a Nazi flag did not necessarily presage a neo-Nazi plot. Without more concrete information to go on, he and the other members of the Hunting Lodge might as well be shooting arrows in the dark. He could only hope that the investigation into Scanlan's death might yield up a telltale clue to what was really going on.

''All right,'' Adam said, thinking out loud. ''If this *is* some neo-Nazi operation that Scanlan interrupted, I'd be willing to bet that they don't know he took the flag—which means they won't be expecting anyone to make a connection to them. I can't make that connection yet, but the flag could be the means. There's also the matter of that odd stab wound. I think we ought to attend that post-mortem—and have a look at the flag.''

McLeod nodded. ''Can do. When Scanlan rings back, I'll set it up. It probably won't be before tomorrow afternoon—maybe even Thursday.''

''That's fine,'' Adam agreed. ''In the meantime, we have responsibilities closer to home. I want to follow through as quickly as I can with Claire Crawford. Right now, she's eager to cooperate; but I don't want her getting frightened and checking herself out of the hospital before we break that dream cycle for good. How soon can you make good on your offer to provide a forensic artist?''

''How about first thing in the morning?'' McLeod replied. ''We've always got someone on call. If I've got the duty rota right in my head, it should be Peterson tomorrow. He's just a straight forensic artist—not up to Peregrine's standards—but I've watched him work. He's a little eccentric, but he's pretty good.''

'' 'Pretty good' ought to be sufficient, if Claire does manage to come up with a physical description,'' Adam said. ''I wouldn't mind having you there as well, if you can force a gap in your morning agenda.''

''I'll be there, with Peterson in tow,'' McLeod promised. ''When do you want us?''

''Would half past nine be too early?''

''Not for me,'' McLeod said sturdily. ''As for Peterson, it won't do him any harm to conform to the schedule.''

''You're a hard man, Noel.'' Adam chuckled. He glanced at his pocket watch. ''If we're going to be meeting up again first thing tomorrow, it's probably time we both called it a day. Just let me file these papers away and then I'll walk you out to the car park.''

CHAPTER THIRTEEN

T HE dagger brooding in the Spanish sun was palpably ancient—a dark, heavy implement of meteoric iron, so blackened with age that the runic markings inscribed on its leaf-shaped blade were scarcely discernible without the aid of a strong light and a magnifying glass. Set near the edge of a large mahogany desk, it rested sullenly on its pillow of white silk like a toad squatting on a white marble grave slab, its sleeping presence suggestive of old bloodshed and primitive violence.

Overlooking the desk from the creamy stuccoed wall behind it was a black-and-white drawing of a similar artifact, a torc of the same dark metal, its iron density highlighted in silver by strange zoomorphic designs that troubled the eye with their interweaving lines. An accompanying set of runic inscriptions reinforced the probable close kinship of torc and dagger, not only as to their origin but likewise their purpose.

The arcane nature of that common purpose was no secret to the dagger's present keeper. The torc was now lost, but Francis Raeburn had witnessed firsthand the elemental powers it had been fashioned to focus through its wearer. Both terrible and exquisite, the allure of such power was seductive, addictive, despite the cost. Since acquiring the dagger, Raeburn had spared no effort in attempting to decipher the kindred mysteries bound up in the sorcerous patterns of its runes. With one or two significant breakthroughs now behind him, he was confident that it was only a matter of time before those mysteries would be his to command.

His study of the dagger, however, did not prevent him

from taking an interest in any other intriguing artifacts that might happen to come his way. Just now, sitting in the book-lined solitude of what might have been a library of the late Renaissance, he was carrying out the daily ritual of sifting through the morning's mail. Off to his right, a recessed pair of doors stood open to the tiled courtyard beyond, where a small fountain played softly amidst an array of potted ferns and ornamental orange trees.

Deaf to the subdued music of the water, Raeburn abstracted a large envelope bearing an assortment of German stamps and set the rest aside. As he reached for the ivory-handled Moorish dagger that served as his letter opener, a fugitive gleam of sunlight from one of the east windows glanced off the signet ring he wore on the third finger of his right hand. The stone was a bloodred carnelian, cut square in the form of a cartouche, bearing the device of a snarling lynx head.

Carefully he slit open the German envelope and extracted its contents: a cover letter and half a dozen photographs. A cursory glance at the photos produced a thin smile as he sat back in his leather chair to read the letter.

It had been over eighteen months since he had traded the Victorian refinements of his Scottish country house for the equal opulence and greater security of his present residence, a walled villa on the south coast of Spain. Outside, beyond the terraced terracotta rooftops of the town, the Mediterranean sun was laying down a pattern of dazzle across a blue bay the color of a Madonna's robe. Inside, a shadowy cool prevailed, redolent of Moroccan leather, Spanish cedarwood, and the pungent fragrance of lemons wafted in on the breeze from a neighboring citrus grove. Oblivious to the scents and sounds of his Andalusian retreat, Raeburn cast his avid gaze over the correspondence at hand.

The letter was from an associate in Berlin, acting as his agent. The attendant photographs were studies of a grail-like golden cup, taken from various angles. The sides of the cup were embellished with swastikas and other runic symbols. The provenance—or so the present owner claimed—was directly traceable to one of the black lodges known to have been working actively on Hitler's behalf in the late 1930s.

The item, as might be expected, was not readily available. Indeed, it was not for sale at any price. Klaus Richter's contact, a man named Hans Grausmann, professed to have reliable knowledge of its present location, but a third man held actual possession. In light of the cup's potential worth, the price Grausmann was asking for sharing that knowledge was high, but not excessive, in Richter's opinion. More than a little tempted by the proposition, Raeburn was just weighing up the financial considerations of the enterprise when his contemplation was jarred by a sharp, peremptory knock at the door.

The summons was sudden enough to bring Raeburn upright in his chair, annoyance furrowing his fair brow.

"Yes, what is it?" he snapped.

A rangy, dark-haired man in khakis poked his head into the room apologetically and then entered—Barclay, Raeburn's pilot, driver, and general factotum. Like Raeburn, he wore a carnelian lynx ring—and also a .45 automatic stuck into his waistband.

"Sorry to disturb you, Mr. Raeburn, but I thought you ought to know you've got a couple of visitors."

"Visitors?" A scowl pulled at the corners of Raeburn's mouth. "You know full well I don't have any appointments scheduled for this morning. Tell them to go away."

"They're—ah—already in the entrance lobby, sir. I saw 'em on the security monitor. I can't explain how they got past the gate. And Rosita and Jorge are in another part of the house; they didn't let 'em in."

"You mean they just—appeared?"

"Yessir."

Raeburn's pale gaze flicked to the pistol in Barclay's waistband, suddenly aware of the pilot's uncharacteristic uneasiness.

"Who the devil are these people?" he asked softly.

"They look like Oriental monks, sir," Barclay said. "Not exactly Buddhist, but something like it. I remember seeing robes like that when I was out East in Nepal. Something to do with shamanistic rituals—"

"Tibetan black *ngagspas*." Raeburn used the native term for "sorcerers" with biting certainty. Fully alert now, he slipped Richter's letter and photographs into the top drawer of his desk, partially masking the presence of the .32 caliber Biretta lurking amongst the secretarial clutter of pens, envelopes, and stationery. Leaving the drawer discreetly ajar, he was just drawing breath to give Barclay instructions when two exotic figures clad in orange and black stepped into the doorway.

They were small and wiry by Western standards, and definitely Tibetan. The older one had a face seamed and chiselled like a carving in old ivory; the younger looked to be about of an age with Raeburn. As Barclay turned in challenge, reaching for his pistol, the younger monk raised his right hand and touched the pilot lightly behind his right ear with the tip of a triple-edged dagger.

Barclay's eyes went blank, all resistance fading away. Mouth slightly agape, he lapsed into passive immobility, his hands sinking slack to his sides, face wiped clean of all expression, swaying slightly on his feet. Raeburn had half come to his feet in alarm, but made himself sit again as he glared at the two intruders and considered the desk drawer.

"What is the meaning of this?" he demanded coldly. "What have you done to my associate?"

From far too close, the monks regarded him with a mixture of indulgence and faint disdain.

"Your servant has not been harmed," said the elder of the pair. "He has merely been rendered inactive."

"As for you, Francis Raeburn," the other instructed with bland authority, "you will please to keep your hands in plain sight."

Both monks spoke English with a strongly inflected accent. Looking from one to the other of the pair, Raeburn saw that both possessed the heavy daggers with triple-edged blades. The nature and purpose of such daggers was not unknown to him, nor was he ignorant of the kind of damage they could do in hands trained to manipulate such mysteries. Cautiously he eased himself back in his chair, ostentatiously displaying his empty hands.

"Who sent you?" he demanded. Then supplied the answer himself. "Siegfried—or perhaps I ought to have said Dorje," he amended, when neither of the monks appeared to recognize the German name.

"Dorje *Rinpoche*," the elder of the monks corrected gently. "He wishes to speak with you."

"Does he?" Raeburn's thin smile just missed a sneer.

"Your presence is required at Tolung Tserphug," the younger monk stated. "You will prepare to leave for Switzerland at once."

Despite his outward show of bravado, Raeburn felt his pulse surge in sudden apprehension. It had been thirty years and more since he last had visited the remote Alpine monastery where, as a boy, he had acquired most, if not all, of his working knowledge of Eastern ritual magic. In those days, his nearest contemporary had been a tall German youth, slightly older than himself, whose undeniable affinity for power had been matched only by his towering arrogance.

That arrogance had been fuelled by his having been acknowledged within the monastery as the most recent reincarnation of a supreme Tibetan sorcerer known throughout the ages as "Green Gloves"—a claim which had yet to be proven to Raeburn's satisfaction. Because of that claim and that title, however, Siegfried—or Dorje *Rinpoche*—had been accorded a degree of instruction denied the monastery's less exalted initiates. And it was this, more than anything else, that Raeburn had resented.

Nonetheless, though he had not seen Siegfried/Dorje since leaving Tolung Tserphug, he had followed some of his activities, and had cause to be wary concerning some of his own activities in recent years, where they touched on Dorje's concerns. While he did not accept Dorje's authority over him, the rumors of his power could not be denied. Nor could this cavalier summons—which gave every indication of being a command, not a request.

"This invitation comes at a rather awkward time," he ventured cautiously, eyeing the two monks. "I'm involved in several important projects. What if it doesn't suit me to accept?"

The elder of the two monks elevated a disinterested eyebrow. "The question is without substance. If any resistance is offered, we are empowered to do whatever is required to ensure that the wishes of Dorje *Rinpoche* are carried out.''

The answer was not so much a threat as a statement of intent. Raeburn had no doubt that the monks could carry out their master's wishes. However much it galled him to admit it, he appeared to have no choice but to go along, at least in the short term. Otherwise, he was apt to wind up like Barclay. He was just promising himself the satisfaction of staging a rebellion at the first viable opportunity, when the younger monk spoke again.

"Time grows short. *Rinpoche* is aware that you have not the mastery of *lung-gom*—you would call it speedwalking. Therefore, it will be necessary that you travel to him by more conventional means. You have access here to air transport.'' It was not a question but a statement.

"I have a helicopter at my disposal,'' Raeburn admitted. "As to whether it is capable of flying to Switzerland on such short notice, we shall have to ask my pilot—assuming, of course, that your interference has left his faculties intact,'' he added with a touch of sarcasm.

The younger monk countered this veiled accusation with a faintly superior smile and a touch of the point of his dagger to Barclay's temple. The pilot sucked in a gulp of air and gave his head a bemused shake.

"Are you all right?'' Raeburn demanded.

Barclay was blinking rapidly, as if to clear his vision. In response to his employer's question, he gave a mute nod.

"I hope you're quite sure you've got all your wits about you,'' Raeburn said, "because I need a few quick answers. Has the chopper got the range to make it to Switzerland?''

Barclay drew a steadying breath as he gave another nod. "No problem, sir,'' he muttered huskily. "We'd have to do it by stages, of course, but she'll make the trip easily.''

"And what about *you*?'' Raeburn asked. "Are you sure you're fit to fly?''

"I—think so, sir,'' the pilot replied, apparently steadying by the second. "Yeah, I'm fine. Just a little lightheaded for a few seconds there.''

Raeburn would have preferred to stall for time, if only on principle, but Barclay's answer deprived him of any effective excuse for delay. Resigning himself to accept the inevitable, at least for now, he asked, "How long will it take you to get her ready to fly?"

Barclay considered, eyeing the monks sidelong. "That depends on how many passengers, sir, and precisely where you intend to go in Switzerland."

Raeburn glanced at the monks.

"We shall accompany you," the elder monk said. "And your course should be plotted to Bern, though we shall not go that far. We shall direct you from the Swiss border."

"You heard the man," Raeburn said to Barclay. "Four it is, going toward Bern."

The pilot dipped his head in agreement. "Right, sir. I'll need to do some book work first, to figure out the stages. The first part's easy enough, but fuel efficiency drops dramatically once we have to start climbing over mountains."

"How long before we can leave?" Raeburn interjected. "I trust you to deal with the logistic arrangements."

Barclay swallowed visibly, darting a glance at their orange-robed "visitors."

"With standard preflight, fuelling—say, maybe an hour or two."

"Then I suggest you get started right now," Raeburn said. "And have Pilar pack us each a bag. It appears that you and I have some unscheduled business waiting for us in Switzerland."

CHAPTER FOURTEEN

T HAT same morning, unaware that an old adversary was being drawn back into combat by a new one not yet met, Adam Sinclair braved the early rush-hour traffic into Edinburgh to keep his appointment with McLeod. A tail-back on the Forth Road Bridge delayed him, so that when he pulled the big blue Range Rover into the hospital car park, a few minutes later than he had planned, the inspector's familiar black BMW was already angled into a visitor's space.

He found McLeod waiting on one of the couches near the news kiosk in the lobby, looking over the latest edition of *The Scotsman*. As soon as he caught sight of Adam, the inspector flicked the paper shut and laid it aside on the nearest coffee table, murmuring something to a denim-clad individual with a wiry red ponytail—a hatchet-nosed, thirtyish-looking man with piercing blue eyes and a prodigious crop of freckles, who towered over McLeod by nearly a head as both men got to their feet. The stranger stubbed out a cigarette and eased the strap of a battered art satchel over one shoulder as Adam came over to join them.

"'Morning, Adam," McLeod said. "This is Alec Peterson, the police artist I mentioned last night. Alec, this is Dr. Adam Sinclair, one of our psychiatric consultants."

Proffering a smile and a handshake, Adam said, "Hello, Mr. Peterson. Sorry I'm a few minutes late. Has Inspector McLeod explained to you what it is we're hoping to accomplish today?"

"Aye, sir." The artist's voice was softer-spoken and far deeper than Adam had expected. "He tells me you're going to interview a hit-and-run victim under hypnosis, to see if she can remember enough to give us a description of the driver. With luck, I may be able to reconstruct a recognizable likeness.''

He sounded more than a little intrigued at the prospect, and McLeod gave him a darkling glance.

"I'll warn you again, laddie: Don't let your imagination run away with you. This is a clinical procedure we're talking about, not a stage-magic act.''

"No, sir. I mean, yes, sir, Inspector.''

Adam bit back a smile, prepared, for his part, to make allowances for the uninitiated Peterson.

"Relax, Mr. Peterson—or may I call you Alec? The outward form of what you're going to see may seem a trifle unorthodox, but I assure you its object is quite consistent with normal investigative procedures. The only restriction I'll impose on you is to ask that once the session is in progress, you must make no attempt to address Mrs. Crawford directly, unless I give you permission. She shouldn't be able to hear you, but it could be distracting. I realize that there'll be a need for interaction, once you've established your preliminary sketch. All I ask is that you let me facilitate the dialogue.''

"I understand, sir,'' Alec said meekly. "I'll be ever so quiet.''

The party repaired first to Adam's office, where he stopped long enough to slip on a lab coat and check his desk for messages. Having taken note of a staff meeting scheduled for the following week, he led his companions along to the low-security wing, where Claire's room was situated. The charge nurse was seated at the desk, making out a list of medication orders from a stack of charts at her elbow, but she looked up with a smile as Adam approached.

"Good morning, Dr. Sinclair. Here to see your new patient?''

"I am, indeed. Thank you,'' Adam said as she handed him Claire Crawford's chart. "Did she have a quiet night?''

"I believe she did, Doctor. It was a quiet night for the entire floor. Oh, and young Mr. Balfour asked if he might have a word with you. He's looking very cheerful, these last few days.''

Adam paused in his perusal of Claire's chart and looked up. ''Colin Balfour is looking cheerful? We *are* making progress. I'll have a quick look-in after I've seen Mrs. Crawford, probably just before lunch. Will you tell him that for me?''

''Of course, Doctor.''

''Thank you. In the meantime, I'll be working with Mrs. Crawford this morning, in her room.'' He handed back the chart. ''These gentlemen are from the police. Mrs. Crawford has agreed to let them sit in on this session, which essentially is a victim interview. I'd appreciate it very much if you could ensure that we're not interrupted for any reason other than a genuine emergency.''

''Certainly, Doctor.''

Having thus disposed of any staff curiosity about police interest in Claire Crawford's case, Adam led the way toward her room, which was located at the far end of the adjoining corridor. As they went, he unobtrusively moved his sapphire ring from his trouser pocket to the more accessible pocket of his lab coat. Claire's door was ajar, but the vital, invisible tingle in the air about the doorway confirmed that the wards he had set the night before were still in place and still intact. He rapped lightly on the door frame before stepping across the threshold.

''Come in.''

Claire was sitting by the window in her wheelchair, awake and fully dressed, and swung herself around as her visitors filed in. During the ensuing exchange of greetings and introductions, Adam made note of her appearance. She seemed sternly in command of herself, but he was uncertain whether to regard this as a good sign or a bad one.

''Well, you're looking rested and alert this morning,'' he said easily. ''How did you sleep?''

Claire shrugged. ''Not too badly, thank you. I took the sedative you prescribed. It seemed to help.''

''Good. That's why I ordered it. Let's take a quick moment to look you over, and then we'll go work.''

He began by taking Claire's wrist and timing her pulse-beat with his pocket watch. While he performed the reassuring ritual, designed to begin setting the stage for what he planned to do, McLeod surveyed the room in preparation for the next phase. The furnishings were limited to the bed itself, a movable writing table, a cabinet on wheels for holding personal effects, and two starkly functional chairs upholstered in orange vinyl.

"Obviously in keeping with the rule, 'only two visitors at a time,' " he observed drily, starting to move one of the chairs closer to Claire. "Alec, why don't you see what you can do to scrounge us up an extra chair?"

The police artist set aside his satchel and disappeared outside, returning a few minutes later with a folding chair. Leaving McLeod and his subordinate to arrange the seating, Adam went to shut the door and set a DO NOT DISTURB sign in place, unobtrusively dismantling the wards as he did so.

"I think we're about ready to begin," he remarked, coming back into the room. "Noel, if you and Mr. Peterson would care to get yourselves situated, I'll see to the lighting."

He made a show of adjusting the venetian blinds while he also dismantled the wards about the windows, tilting the louvers upward to diffuse the morning sun. Returning to join the others, he saw that McLeod had positioned himself and Peterson slightly behind and to Claire's right, where their presence would be least likely to distract. Nodding his approval, Adam moved the remaining chair directly in front of Claire and sat down, almost knee to knee with her.

"I think we can begin now. Are you comfortable?" he asked.

She shrugged, obviously apprehensive, but far less tense than she had been the day before.

"I suppose."

"Good. Now, we touched yesterday on your recurrent dreams about your accident. Today, however, we'll try to bypass those dreams and have a look at the accident itself. The specific purpose of this exercise is to sharp-focus your memory of the accident and see if it's possible for you to give us a physical description of the driver. From that description, Mr. Peterson hopes to produce a sketch that will help us find the man who's to blame. And once *that* happens, there's a strong likelihood that the associated dreams will spontaneously come to an end.''

Because of Peterson's presence, Adam left unsaid that once the dreams stopped, so would the accidents along Carnage Corridor. Certainly, that was their highest priority in the short term—to ensure that no more innocent lives were lost.

But a longer-term priority had to do with Claire herself. While, at a very basic level, Adam's duty as a physician was to help Claire achieve what peace of mind she could, with regard to her losses—at least to make her functional— Claire's case went beyond the usual mandate of psychiatric medicine, because of the psychic aspects. And even though, in his role as a sometime enforcer of cosmic justice, he could hardly object to justice being exercised, where Claire's drunken driver was concerned, he found it profoundly unsettling at a deeper level, as a physician of souls, that Claire should feel so compelled to catch and punish the person responsible for her situation. Such compulsions were not the hallmark of a maturing soul.

Yet the very existence of Claire's unformed psychic talent, coupled with Adam's brush with the persona of Annet Maxwell—probable evidence of at least one previous incarnation—suggested that Claire possessed greater potentials. But Annet Maxwell had achieved a serenity not yet granted Claire Crawford, also bereft by the loss of husband and children. If Claire was to progress as a soul and achieve the potentials being presented in this life, eventually she, too, must find a healthier way to come to terms with her losses.

Meanwhile, finding John Crawford's killer was, indeed, one of their priorities—if only to remove the impetus that kept triggering Claire's unschooled psychic powers. And to do that, an artist's sketch might well provide conventional law enforcement authorities with just the tool they needed to succeed. Alec Peterson was waiting with pencil and sketch pad poised—and for this, at least, the procedure was fairly straightforward, even if the more complex resolution of Claire's anger might have to wait.

"Having established the ground rules, then," Adam went

on, "let's begin with a variation on the same procedure we used yesterday. Claire, you remember what it felt like yesterday, relaxing and settling into trance. You'll find it much easier this time. I'd like you to close your eyes, if you would, and let yourself begin returning to that comfortable, relaxed state of mind. You'll recall that we did some breathing exercises to begin, so I'd like to take you through them again, as you breathe in for a count of five . . . hold for a count of five . . . and exhale for five. . . . In for five . . ."

A hush settled in the room as he soothed his patient into a state of receptive calm. Though aware that he must exercise some caution in what he said, because of Peterson's presence, he felt confident that the younger man probably would overlook any but the most blatant deviation from "normal" procedure, through not knowing what "normal" was. It was also quite possible that Peterson himself might slip into trance—which would only make matters easier when they finished and it was time to tidy up all the loose ends.

The artist became an anonymous blur as Adam, too, settled into a light trance, as was his usual wont when working with a patient in this manner. He was peripherally aware of McLeod's supportive presence next to Peterson, towering and strong, but everything besides Claire was fast receding into temporary obscurity. At first, Claire's eyes showed an occasional, fugitive glint of blue through her lowered lashes, but gradually the lines of tension ironed out of her face and she relaxed. Her breathing slowed to a whisper, her hands motionless in her lap.

After taking her through several short exercises to deepen her trance, Adam decided it was time to progress to the next stage. A glance at Peterson suggested that the artist was, indeed, coming along inadvertently for the ride—eyes slightly unfocused, pencil poised only loosely over the sketch pad on his knees.

"You're doing very well, Claire," Adam murmured, returning his attention to his patient. "In a moment now, I'm going to ask you to return to the night of your accident. Before that, if you will, I'd like you to imagine that you have before you a very special video machine, with the control beneath your hand. This video machine makes a perfect, three-dimensional recording of everything that happens to you—and it recorded what happened that night of your accident.

"Now, you said that you and your husband had been to a pub earlier in the evening, so in a moment I'm going to ask you to press the Rewind button, to go back to that time, as you're leaving the pub. The very special thing about this video machine is that once you return to that scene and then press the Play button, you will actually be *in* the recording, reliving that experience. In all respects, you will be back walking along that stretch of road with John, reliving all the sights and sounds and smells—every detail of that night, just as it was when you actually experienced it. It will be *exactly* the same, in every detail but one. Shall I tell you what that difference is?"

She nodded slowly, passion stirring behind the closed eyelids.

"The difference is that a small part of you is going to remain aloof, as if it's sitting back and watching the tape," Adam went on. "This detached part of you has its finger on the Pause button—which means that as you relive that night, and this detached part of you watches the tape, you have the ability to stop the action, to freeze-frame, just before the moment of impact, and take a good, long look at the man behind the wheel of the car that struck you. And from that look, you'll be able to describe him to me. If you're willing to do this, please nod your head."

Slowly her head nodded, her right hand shifting position in her lap, as if poised over unseen control buttons.

"Very good," Adam whispered, sitting forward in his chair. "I'm clasping your left wrist now, as I did yesterday, so you'll know that I'm with you, that you've no reason to be afraid. However frightening it may seem, to relive what happened that night, you're perfectly safe—and remember, you're going to stop the tape just before you can be hit; you don't have to relive the actual accident. Are you ready to give it a try?"

Again she nodded.

"Good. Now, on my signal, I want you to push the Reverse button, so that the tape begins rewinding, going back to that night of the accident, starting—*now*. Watch the screen flicker, too quickly for you to see anything, but you'll know when you've reached that point, right after you and John left the pub. Let the flicker of the screen take you more and more deeply focused, so that you'll know exactly when to push the button. . . . And when you've gone back far enough, push the Freeze-frame button. . . . ''

He watched for nearly a minute as her eyelids flickered, watching the screen he had constructed in her mind. Then, all at once, lips pressed firmly together in concentration, she stabbed at an imaginary button with her right forefinger.

''Good,'' Adam whispered, giving her other wrist a reassuring squeeze. ''Now tell me what you see, frozen there. Describe the scene in as much detail as you can.''

Her lips parted, her eyes moving behind her closed eyelids as if surveying what she saw.

''It's the Lanark Road, not far from our house,'' she murmured. ''It's the way we always come back from the pub on Wednesday nights. It's a mild night for May; it isn't even raining. There's a three-quarter moon, so we can see the road quite clearly. It's two lanes here, with a gravel footpath on the side where we're walking—the north side—and a gorse hedge grown up along a barbwire fence that marks the edge of an open meadow. There's a little burn running just the other side of the hedge. I can hear it chuckling over the stones, it's so quiet this time of night. No traffic; just the gurgle of the burn and our footsteps crunching on the gravel . . .''

''Go on,'' Adam said quietly, when she did not speak for several seconds. ''Tell me about yourself, and John.''

''We're walking with our arms around one another's waists. We're very happy; it's been a good evening. I can smell his aftershave, and the smoke from the pub clinging to our clothes, and just a hint of beer on his breath . . . and the scent of gorse mixed with petrol fumes. . . .''

She smiled faintly. ''He's just teased me that soon I won't be able to see my feet anymore. We're so excited about the baby. The doctor told us just last week that it's a girl; we wanted to know. John is secretly pleased, even though everyone says that men are supposed to want sons first. He told me before we were even married that he always wanted a little daughter. We think we might call her Heather, or maybe Alison. We've got plenty of time to decide, though. She won't arrive for a couple more months. . . . ''

"It's time to go *into* that Claire now," Adam prompted softly, when she wound down again. "A part of you remains aloof, fingers poised on the Slow-motion and Pause buttons, but you're walking along that road now, and headlights are approaching. Tell me what you see."

As he spoke, he commended his soul to the protection of the Light and let himself reach out to perceive what he could of what she was experiencing, once again lowering the psychic barriers between them. Though he did not close his eyes, all his own bodily sensations faded, save for the point of contact where his hand still clasped Claire's passive wrist. For an instant he floated dizzily outside himself, momentarily blind and disoriented. Then suddenly he was in the scene Claire had been describing.

A host of new sensations burst in on him from all sides— the gurgle of the waters in the burn, the cool touch of the night breeze, the scent of gorse mixed with a hint of petrol. Even as these sensations registered, a set of headlamps appeared ahead in the distance.

"There're headlights coming," Claire murmured. "They converge like a set of flares. We can hear the roar of the engine, and John grabs me by the sleeve and starts to push me out of the way."

" 'That bloke's going too bloody fast!' " she said urgently, mimicking her husband's words. " 'We'd better move back.'

"He pulls me away from the verge, but we can't go far because of the gorse hedge. We can hear the engine noise redoubled as the car bears down on us—it's weaving back and forth across the center line—the guy must be drunk! Squealing brakes—it swerves and ploughs right into the verge!

" 'Jesus, he's heading right for us!' " The tone made it clear that again, these were John Crawford's words.

"He pushes me behind him, trying to shield me," she went on, breathing hard, "but there's no place to go! I can feel the gorse tearing at my legs, and the fence behind it hard against my waist, but we're pinned like moths against a windowpane, caught in his headlights—''

"Go to Slow-motion!" Adam ordered, right beside her in the vision and fighting his own instinct to recoil. "Slow it all you want," he went on, as one of her fingers jerked spasmodically. "You've got time to watch now. You know you can stop the action, just before it happens, but let the car get as close as you possibly can. You want the best possible look at the driver. It's ten yards away—nine, eight, seven, six, five, four, three, two—*Freeze-frame!*" he ordered sharply.

CHAPTER FIFTEEN

ON the knife edge of a scream, the world shuddered to a halt. Claire's eyes were open now, wide and glazed like those of a hare mesmerized by fright, staring straight into the glare of the remembered headlamps. Her pupils were even contracted, her lips parted for the scream Adam had interrupted. Seizing upon that moment of paralysis, he moved in with surgical delicacy to direct her perceptions.

"Can you see him?" he asked softly. "I know there's a glare from the headlights, but can you see his face behind the windscreen?"

"Too bright," she murmured. "And still too far away . . ."

"Adjust your video machine," Adam urged. "It can do all kinds of things that an ordinary machine can't do. You can step down the light level, filter it, zoom in on his image. . . . Make the necessary adjustments, Claire. You *can* see him. . . . "

Adam could not see the face, try as he might. For Claire, however, her adjustment of perception seemed to achieve the desired effect.

"It's *him*!" she murmured breathlessly. "I can see him now—see him clearly!"

"Describe him to me, then," Adam ordered. "Tell me what he looks like, in as much detail as you can manage."

He could not spare a glance for anyone but Claire—indeed, had almost forgotten the presence of McLeod and the enrapt Peterson—but McLeod was already glancing back at the artist—who was leaning forward avidly, his eyes slightly glazed, pencil poised above his sketch pad. A shiver passed through Claire's seated body before she began haltingly to speak.

"He's young—early twenties, maybe . . . clean-shaven . . . hair straight and dark, cut longish . . . good-looking, actually. The face is square, with hollow cheeks and high cheekbones. . . ."

"Alec, are you getting all this?" McLeod whispered to Peterson, whose response was a distracted nod. The artist's pencil flew, executing swift strokes across the page as he strove to capture what Claire was describing.

"Full lips . . . longish nose, narrow at the bridge, with nostrils a bit flared . . . There's a—a sort of a bump, like he might have broken it once. . . ."

Peterson kept drawing for several minutes after she had wound to a halt, at length passing the sketch pad over to McLeod.

"Is it possible for her to look this over, see if I'm getting it right?" he asked in a shaky undertone.

McLeod glanced at the drawing in his hands, then passed it to Adam. The face that looked back at them from the paper was that of a spoilt, impetuous youth.

"Claire, I'd like you to take a look at Mr. Peterson's sketch and tell me what you think," Adam said quietly. "Keep the actual image on your video screen strongly before you, then compare it with the sketch."

He put the sketch pad into her hands. Dispassionately the blue eyes tracked down to the drawing, flicking across it without reaction as she slowly nodded.

"It's very close," she said. "The chin needs to be sharper and the ears neater. And the hair's a little too clean-cut. It should be a bit longer on top, like a pop star's. It's quite dark, by the way—maybe black. And the eyes are light; I couldn't see the color."

When she made no further comment, Adam reclaimed the sketch and returned it to Peterson. Tongue between his teeth, the police artist went back to work. After a short interval, he returned the amended sketch for Claire's inspection. Again she pointed out necessary refinements, which Peterson dutifully made. It took four tries before she pronounced herself satisfied.

"That's the man," she said, holding it at arm's length before her. "That's him exactly."

"Excellent," Adam said. "Close your eyes now, and relax for a few minutes. Go deep asleep and take a nice rest until I touch your hand and call you by name."

As she subsided, eyes drifting closed again, Adam took the sketch pad from her slack hands and shifted his attention to Peterson, intending to compliment him on his work. The police artist looked bewildered and just a little distressed. McLeod had noticed it, too, and laid a sympathetic hand on his shoulder.

"What's the matter, son?" he asked.

Peterson ducked his head, just missing a shiver. "Sorry, sir," he said with some difficulty. "It's just that—if you don't mind my saying so, this is pretty spooky stuff. Would you mind if—if I went and got a cup of coffee?"

"Not at all," Adam said, before McLeod could reply. "I think that's a very good idea. But would you close your eyes for a moment first, please? I think you may have gone a little into trance there, and I want to make sure you're fully back to waking consciousness. It's perfectly normal," he added with a smile, at Peterson's delayed look of startled surprise. "Happens quite frequently."

"But I—"

"Close your eyes, Alec," Adam commanded, leaning forward without warning to lay his hand across the artist's brow. "Don't fight it; just relax and let that breath all the way out. That's right," he added, dropping his hand as Peterson subsided without resistance—indication that, indeed, he had been in trance and still was. "You're perfectly fine, and nothing happened at all out of the ordinary. There's nothing frightening about hypnotic regression; it's simply a tool like any other. Between your efforts and Claire's, we may well bring our man to justice. You've both done very well. You can take pride in your work. It was very well done, indeed."

He cast a cautionary glance at McLeod as he went on, sitting back in his chair.

"Take another deep breath now, and let it all the way out. And when I count backward from five to one, on *one*, you'll come back to normal waking consciousness, feeling fine, with what happened here just a little hazy—which is just the way you want it to be. And five . . . four . . . three . . . two . . . and *one*. Open your eyes now, Alec, and have a nice stretch. You might like to go on down to the hospital café and wait there for Inspector McLeod, have that cup of coffee.''

''Aye, I'll join you in a bit,'' McLeod added, on cue, as Peterson's eyes fluttered open and he heaved a heavy sigh. ''Dr. Sinclair and I have one or two points yet to clear up, but it shouldn't take long. Just leave the sketch pad here for now. I'll bring it when I come down. And congratulations; you did a nice piece of work.''

''Thank you, sir.''

Without demur, Peterson packed up his art satchel and took himself off, clearly relieved to be going. As the door closed behind him, Adam murmured with a wry smile, ''I do believe we gave Mr. Peterson a fright.''

McLeod allowed himself a dour chuckle. ''Well, he isn't a Peregrine Lovat, but he did all right, didn't he? And we can hardly blame him for getting the wind up. I dare say this kind of thing would raise my hackles, too, if I'd never seen anything like it before—and it did, as I recall.''

''It did,'' Adam agreed with a smile.

''In any case,'' McLeod went on, ''I'll take Alec's sketch and get Donald to fax copies to all and sundry. It won't necessarily guarantee that our hit-and-run driver will be picked up, but it'll certainly help reactivate the search.''

''It will that,'' Adam said. ''In the meantime, there's still the question of Carnage Corridor. This should make the difference, break the dream cycle, but before I bring Claire fully out of trance, I'd like to find out if seeing that driver's face has made any difference in her outlook—and if it hasn't, see what can be done about it.''

Claire Crawford was sitting as Adam had left her, eyes closed and head slightly bowed, her hands at rest in her lap. Lightly touching her left wrist, he said, ''Claire, it's Dr. Sinclair again. I have one last task for you, before we bring today's session to a close. Now that you've given us a description of the man who ran you down, I'd like you to study his likeness and tell me what you make of him. I'd like you to try and imagine what you would say to him if you were to find yourself face to face with him in this room. Open your eyes and look at the picture of him. Use that as your focus, and tell me what you see.''

He put the sketch pad in her hands as she opened her eyes. For long seconds she stared at the likeness in front of her with silent, penetrating intensity. Then all at once she uttered a small gasp and rocked back in her chair.

''Dear God, I think I—I *touched* him!'' she breathed agitatedly. ''It was just for an instant, but I—actually came into contact with him—the man who killed my husband! The man who crippled me!''

McLeod glanced at Adam, suppressing a startled exclamation, but Adam was already leaning forward, setting a hand on her wrist again.

''I understand,'' he said quietly, his voice betraying none of his own rising excitement. ''Please go on.''

Claire took a gulp of breath, her words tumbling over one another in her excitement, but still focused, still deep in trance.

''So very strange,'' she murmured. ''What his name might be, I still don't know. All the same, for a second or two it was as if I was—inside his head! I could see what he was like—knew exactly what he was feeling—''

''Describe your impressions,'' Adam prompted, as she broke off with a shudder.

The sound of his voice seemed to steady her. ''He's younger than he looks,'' she whispered. ''And smart—so smart, he used to think there wasn't anything he couldn't do. He was ambitious . . . wanted to get ahead in the world. . . .''

''Do you know what he was doing out on the road that night?'' Adam asked.

She nodded. ''He'd just lost his job. He was angry and humiliated. He wanted to get back at somebody—anybody. That's why he stole that car. And he'd been drinking to bolster his courage.

''He—knows now what a terrible mistake he made,'' she continued. ''He lives under a cloud of guilt and failure. He knows he's done wrong, but he's terrified to own up. All he can do is sit around wishing that he could live that night over again and make it somehow turn out differently.''

''Interesting,'' Adam said, well aware that all this could

be a fantasy—though it might be true, too. "Tell me," he added neutrally, "even though the law has yet to catch up with him, are you in any way consoled, knowing that he is far from happy in his freedom?"

"I thought I would be," Claire said, "but I'm—not."

There was a note of perplexity in her voice. Adam merely waited, giving her time to analyze her own reactions. After a long moment, she began speaking again.

"I feel I ought to hate him, but I can't," she murmured. "We're too much alike, he and I. Whatever his thoughts and intentions on the night of the accident, he surely never meant for anyone to die—any more than I meant any of those other people to die. How can I demand that he be punished for what he's done, when I'm guilty of much the same crime?"

For her own sake, Adam had been hoping that Claire would find it in her heart to forego her thirst for revenge. Instead, she seemed to be compounding her own guilt—which did no one any good.

"No," he said, "to describe your own actions as criminal is inaccurate. A crime is a premeditated act of wrongdoing." He tapped the drawing with one well-manicured forefinger. "This young man knew full well that it was wrong to steal a car and go for a drunken joy ride, and that his actions were likely to put other lives at risk. At very least, he is guilty of willful negligence.

"You, by contrast, were acting unconsciously. And now that you're aware of your own actions, you're making an effort to control them. Don't be confused into identifying with the opposition on the basis of a faulty comparison. If you're going to put yourself in the same place as the man who injured you, let it be in a spirit of forgiveness that will benefit you both."

More than this he was reluctant to say, for fear of placing Claire under any constraint while so highly suggestible. But before she could voice any response, McLeod's voice interposed with sudden, soft urgency.

"Adam," he murmured, "this is awkward, I know, but there's another presence wants a word."

Glancing at him sharply, Adam immediately touched his hand to Claire's wrist.

"Hear nothing until I touch your wrist again, Claire," he commanded. "Close your eyes and go deep asleep."

She closed her eyes and breathed out with a sigh, and Adam returned his attention to his Second. McLeod's particular gifts as a Huntsman were those of a medium. More than once in their long-running relationship, Adam had seen the bluff inspector play host to spiritual entities seeking to communicate on the material plane. Usually they were summoned for a particular purpose; occasionally they volunteered their presence. When they did the latter, it was usually because they had something to contribute.

"Have you a name?" Adam asked.

"Aye," McLeod said in a tight voice. He had put on his Huntsman's ring as Adam dealt with Claire. "The name is Malcolm Grant."

The most recent crash victim from Carnage Corridor!

"Interesting," Adam said. "They don't usually come through so soon after passing over. Do you want me to guide you down?"

"I'm on the brink already," McLeod muttered in the same taut under-voice. "He's really strong. Just stay with me, Adam. I'm not entirely sure he knows what he's doing, but I get the feeling it's fairly urgent."

"All right," Adam said quietly, slipping his hand into his lab coat pocket for his own ring. "Close your eyes and relax, but don't open to him yet. I'll have a word with him, before I let him take you. That's good. Now, on my signal, go deep."

Reaching out with his ring hand, he touched his fingertips lightly to McLeod's forehead, watching the tension melt away as the inspector slid quickly and profoundly into trance. Maintaining that point of contact, unconsciously searching the air around them—though he knew his eyes would see nothing—Adam likewise became aware of another presence very near.

"Malcolm Grant," he said softly, "if you are here of your own free will, in good conscience and of beneficial intent, this man, Noel Gordon McLeod, gives you leave to enter the temple of his body, to speak with his voice. He asks only that you come and go in peace, doing no one any harm. And

I stand ready to defend him, should you seek to go beyond what is offered.''

Lifting his hand from McLeod's forehead, he sketched in the air a symbol of power that would give binding force to his words. A flash of blue light from the sapphire in his ring marked the completion of the gesture. McLeod gasped, and his grizzled head snapped back. When he straightened up again, the intelligence cautiously looking out from behind the gold-rimmed aviator spectacles was other than his own.

''You were there when I passed over,'' the newcomer said to Adam. ''You tried to help me.''

Adam inclined his head. ''I regret I could not do more.''

''You can do more now,'' said the entity who had been Malcolm Grant. ''You must let me speak with Claire Crawford. I have something to say to her, which I believe might help her.''

Adam inclined his head again. ''I will relay your message,'' he told the spirit inhabiting McLeod's body, ''but she will have to decide whether or not to hear you out. Please wait.''

His hand sketched a different symbol above Claire's head, of protection rather than binding, then lightly touched her wrist.

''Claire, the spirit of one of the crash victims is here: a man by the name of Malcolm Grant. He wishes to communicate with you. Are you willing to listen?''

''Has he come to accuse me?''

''He has said he wishes to help.''

''I will speak to him.''

She turned her face toward McLeod's body, obviously seeing beyond the physical.

''Malcolm Grant,'' she said. ''I recognize your name. I know you have come because I am responsible for your death. I caused you to run your car off the road. I can offer no excuse for my action. Though I had no intention of injuring you, the consequences to you were the same. That being so, I accept any blame you wish to lay upon me, together with any penance you may ask of me.''

McLeod's blue eyes searched her face with lively interest.

''You misunderstand,'' said the voice of Malcolm Grant.

"I haven't come here to condemn you—but rather to urge you not to condemn yourself."

"Why should you not condemn me? I cut your life short."

"Our paths crossed entirely by accident. If the consequences were tragic, that is neither your fault nor mine. By definition, an accident is an unforeseen event, something none of the parties involved might have intended or anticipated. Since you had no more foreknowledge of what was going to happen than I had, you can hardly hold yourself morally responsible for what happened to me."

"But I *was* responsible, if only indirectly," Claire insisted. "Surely it is only just that I should render you compensation?"

"What are you prepared to offer me?" Grant asked. "Can you give me back the rest of my life? Or take away the grief of my family and friends?"

The questions seemed to take Claire slightly aback. "I would, if only I could. But what you are suggesting is impossible."

"Then I will offer you another proposition—some other thing that you could give me," Grant said.

Claire's head lifted. "What is that?"

McLeod's craggy face assumed the trace of a whimsical smile. "Your promise," Grant said. "Your promise that you will put aside this burden of guilt you seem so determined to lay upon yourself. No amount of further suffering on your part will serve any useful purpose. By the same token, don't be afraid of your memories. If you wish to redeem your present life, the key to that redemption is to be found in your past."

"I—I'm not sure I understand," Claire said, her voice faltering.

"Then ask your mentor. He will guide you in life, as he guided me in death."

Claire turned her entranced gaze toward Adam, like a blind woman turning her face toward the heat of a sun she could not see.

"Dr. Sinclair?" she whispered.

"I cannot give you peace, but you can find it," Adam said softly, recalling the words of the Master, and grateful to

Malcolm Grant for this opportunity to apply those words. "You have the knowledge within you to release yourself from the guilt that binds you. There is a part of you which understands completely everything that has happened to you. Welcome your past back into your present life—*all* of your past—and it will bring you all the strength and comfort that you need."

"But, how do I do that?" Claire asked, her eyes a-brim with tears. "Can you help me?"

"I can—but only if you truly wish and will it."

"Oh, I do!" Claire cried. "With all my heart, I do!"

Her consent, thus given, gave Adam all the mandate he required. In that instant he knew the images that would set her free, and his heart lifted as he realized that healing was now within her grasp.

"Very well," he said. "Close your eyes and go even deeper within your heart of hearts . . . deeper . . . and now deeper still. And now you find yourself standing at the bottom of a vast well. It represents the very depths to which your soul may sink in despair, but it also contains all the richness of your past, in all its times and facets and wisdom.

"High above, see the bright circle of light, which is your present life, and which holds revelation, if you will only rise to meet it. As you ascend, embracing your past, you will see your reflection mirrored above. When you get close enough to touch it, the past and the present will meet in you and become one, and reveal to you a truth that will give you strength to go on . . . but it is you who must choose to venture closer to the Light. . . . ''

"Yes . . . I choose!"

Claire's head fell back, her arms outflung and trailing to her sides. With her face turned upward toward the ceiling, she looked like a swimmer coming to the surface to breathe, her expression ever more joyous.

"Yes!" she murmured again, breathing out with a long sigh. "I see it. I see it all now. . . . ''

A small quiver rippled down the length of her relaxed body, and when it passed, she lowered her head slightly, her eyes opening dreamily to stare unfocused past Adam.

"How could I have forgotten?" she whispered. "Oh, I do

understand. There is no evil committed in this world that cannot be redeemed by a greater love. For a will to love will always find a worthy object. . . . ''

The voice was Claire's, but the words belonged to Annet Maxwell. Hearing this echo from Claire's historic past, Adam knew that the gap between these two aspects of her being had been bridged, and that healing now would come. It was only a matter of time. A smile stole unconsciously across his own lips as he briefly touched her hand again.

"You've been through a very great trial, Claire," he said gently. "In a moment I'll ask you to sleep—true sleep, deep and undisturbed, so that you may wake up later this afternoon, refreshed and clear-headed. You will remember nothing alarming in what was said and done today, but the essence of what has been accomplished will filter through to you in your dreams, replacing visions of destruction with visions of peace. Those visions will guide you, if you let them, helping you to find fulfillment in the future.

"Sleep now, deep and restful. A little later, I'll have the nurses put you to bed, but you will not rouse."

As he touched her hand again, Claire's blue eyes closed. She breathed out with a sigh, and her respiration shifted. Her expression in sleep was like that of a weary child. With his own sigh, Adam turned at last toward the witness still present in McLeod's body.

"Malcolm Grant, are you satisfied with what has been accomplished here today?" he asked.

"I am."

"Then go, as you came, in peace," Adam said quietly. "And may all the blessings of the Light attend you."

So saying, he raised his ring hand to touch McLeod lightly on the forehead with the sapphire. The inspector exhaled softly as the spirit of Grant withdrew, and sagged forward against the hand Adam shifted to steady him.

"Your guest has gone, Noel," he said quietly. "Draw a deep breath, take a moment to reorient yourself, and come back when you're ready. When you open your eyes, you will find yourself once more firmly grounded in the present, feeling relaxed and renewed."

Obedient to his superior's instructions, McLeod inhaled

deeply. A slight tremor registered in his extremities, and Adam sat back to wait. When McLeod roused a moment later, his gaze was fully awake and aware.

"Welcome back," Adam said. "How are you?"

"Not bad at all," McLeod said. "My visitor made a most courteous withdrawal. I guess he was more experienced than I first thought." He looked from Adam to Claire's sleeping form and back again. "What happened while I was out?"

Briefly Adam acquainted him with what had taken place. McLeod heard him out in thoughtful silence.

"Well," he exclaimed, when Adam had finished. "This has been a very busy day—and it's only half over. By the way, did I think to tell you earlier that the Scanlan post-mortem's at two?"

Adam rolled his eyes heavenward. "No, you did not."

"Sorry. Is it a problem?"

"No. It's—nearly eleven now, though," Adam said, consulting his pocket watch, "and I promised to look in on that other patient before lunch. If we hustle, though, we ought to just make it."

"Ready whenever you are," McLeod replied, getting to his feet. "At least it appears we've accomplished one worthwhile objective today."

As he glanced at Claire, Adam smiled and nodded.

"Quite true—and in a rather spectacular fashion. Unless I'm very much mistaken, when Claire next wakes, she'll be on her way to becoming a complete woman again."

"Aye, thank God for that!" McLeod murmured fervently. "And Carnage Corridor will be a safe stretch of road to travel again. Now all we have to do is hie ourselves off to Dumbarton. Your car or mine?"

CHAPTER SIXTEEN

T HAT same morning, in Glasgow, Peregrine Lovat was
completing his second orbit around a block near the city
center, looking for a place to park.

"I still don't understand why you were so keen to have
that roll of film developed," Julia remarked as he began a
third circuit. "What's so urgent about those Kintyre snaps,
that they won't wait till we get back to Strathmourne?"

Peregrine's eyes flicked ahead, still hopeful that someone
might leave. "If I said it was merely a fit of artistic caprice,
would that satisfy you?"

"I'm afraid you'll have to do better than that," she replied, with a lift of one fair eyebrow.

Peregrine summoned a sidelong grin and rolled his eyes
heavenward in an exaggerated show of resignation.

"All right, I'll come clean. I'm really a top secret agent
for MI5, and the photographer's shop is a front for our Glasgow operation."

Julia merely echoed his gesture of resignation and returned
his grin. They had arrived in Glasgow the previous night,
having booked into a period guesthouse not far from here.
This morning, after the usual hearty breakfast in which tour-
ists usually indulged, they had set out to begin touring the
city's museums, starting with the Burrell Collection, an
eclectic and sometimes eccentric assemblage of ceramics,
textiles, furniture, stained glass, and a particularly good selection of nineteenth-century French paintings.

But Peregrine had spotted the photography shop the night
before, as they pulled into their guesthouse; and it had been

an easy matter to slip out this morning, while Julia was in the shower, and drop off the roll of film in question for one-hour processing. He had also had the camera checked; it was working perfectly.

Now, with the necessity to collect the processed film, he was aware of a prickly feeling of anticipation that had nothing to do with his desire to shield Julia from whatever unpleasantness the photos might hold. Ever since leaving Kintyre two days before, he had found himself strangely preoccupied, haunted by the elusive ghost-image that he had sensed hovering over the body of the dead man—an image he had not been able to commit to paper. He wondered if there would be anything in his photos to show that the strange ghost-effect he'd observed was more than a mere trick of his imagination.

"Peregrine?" his wife broke in softly. "Is there something on that roll of film that you don't want me to see?"

The look that went with the question was as blue and unwavering as a kitten's, and Peregrine found himself incapable of dissembling.

"Actually, there is," he admitted with a sigh. "Back on Kintyre, while you were off fetching the police, I took some photos of the dead man. It occurred to me this morning that while we're here in Glasgow, we probably ought to turn the prints over to the Strathclyde Police, in case there's anything in them that might assist them in their investigation."

"Ah," said Julia. "Well, why didn't you say so in the first place?"

Peregrine grimaced. "I thought you could probably do without the reminder."

"Well, that's very gallant of you," she said affectionately, "but it isn't really necessary. How soon we forget! Whatever concerns you concerns me—for better or for worse!"

"Point taken," Peregrine agreed with a sheepish grin, "though I hardly think it need extend to ruining your honeymoon—*our* honeymoon."

"There you go again!" she declared, leaning over to kiss him on the cheek. "I told you it isn't possible to do that."

He was grinning as they completed their third circuit of the block, but he still had not found any legal place to park.

Switching on his left-turn indicator, he pulled the Alvis into a designated loading zone a short distance up the street from the shop and pulled on the hand brake.

"You'd better shift into the driver's seat, in case a traffic warden comes along," he told Julia. "I'll be back as quickly as I can."

Waiting for traffic before easing open the door, he alighted from the car and sprinted off up the sidewalk to the entrance to the photographer's shop. The premises seemed dim after the bright sunshine outside. The shop's proprietor was at the counter, offering advice to a middle-aged couple who spoke English with an accent that might have been Dutch. When at last they turned and started for the door, Peregrine darted forward and presented his claim slip.

"The name's Lovat," he murmured, watching as the man began rooting in a drawer beneath the counter. "I left in a roll of film earlier this morning for one-hour processing."

"Here it is," the man said, handing over a large yellow-and-orange film envelope. "That'll be six pounds eighty, please."

Peregrine gave the man a ten-pound note, received his change, and pocketed it as he stepped over to the window, pulling the prints out of their envelope to examine them. The photos on top were all views of Kintyre, most of them with him or Julia in the foreground, a few of them showing architectural details of some of the castles and country houses they had visited in the preceding days. These he hurriedly passed over in favor of the more sober forensic studies he was looking for.

The abrupt shift in motifs made him flinch. Though his first instinct was to avert his gaze, he forced himself to take a closer look—and was startled to discover that there was, indeed, more caught in the photos than he had been able to see clearly at the time.

The shimmer he had observed on the beach at Mull of Kintyre had resolved on film into a ghostly figure. Though the details still were a bit blurred, the robed form hovering over the dead man appeared to be that of a Hare Krishna, or perhaps a Buddhist monk, with shaven head and dressed in flowing orangey robes. The figure's hands were clasped as if in prayer, but there seemed to be an implement of some kind extending below the palm. Different aspects of the image appeared in the two closer shots, which had been shot from different angles.

Peregrine stared at the photos, hardly knowing what to make of them. Had the monk-image been confined to a single frame, he might have been able to convince himself that it was nothing more than a freakish trick of the light. As it was, that possibility was negated by the fact that parts of the mysterious secondary figure were present in all three of the shots he had taken. Conscious of a sinking feeling in the pit of his stomach, he began seeking other possible explanations.

Was it possible that his film had registered the presence of a ghost? If so, the likeness ought to have been that of the dead man himself, not some mysterious robed figure.

The resonance of some other past life of the dead man, then? Peregrine thought that equally improbable. While it was true that he had glimpsed ghostly reflections of other past identities in Adam and some of his fellow Huntsmen, those residual images had always been subordinate to the personality of the present day. Even in the days before Adam had begun teaching him to control his Sight, he had never known such resonances to linger after death—and the man in the water surely had been dead for several days, at least.

Besides that, the more he studied the photos, the more convinced he became that there was something sinister about the secondary figure in the pictures. Vainly he peered and squinted, even borrowing a magnifying lens from the shop owner, trying to discern what the strange monk might be holding in his hands—but he could not identify it.

Failure left him more convinced than ever that he had inadvertently stumbled across something that was going to demand further investigation. He considered asking to use the phone, but decided to wait and ring Adam from wherever he and Julia ended up having lunch.

"Listen, can you do enlargements in an hour, or do they need to be sent out?" he asked.

The man shrugged. "I usually send them out, but I *can* do them here. It'll cost you double, though."

"That's fine," Peregrine said. He slipped the innocuous

honeymoon photos back into the envelope and pulled out the negatives, which he laid on the counter beside the three photos in question. "How much for eight-by-tens?"

"For the three? Say, fifteen pounds," the man said, raising an eyebrow as he picked up the negatives and glanced at the photos.

"They're some trick shots I've put together for a photography class," Peregrine explained, suddenly aware how odd the photos might appear to a casual viewer. "I do need them back in an hour, though."

"They'll be ready," the proprietor assured him.

Outside, the Alvis was still where he had left it.

"No sign of any wardens," Julia announced cheerfully from the driver's seat, as he slid in beside her. "Where to now?"

Peregrine tossed the photos on the dash and took a moment to do up his seat belt.

"Lunch, I think," he said distractedly. "And I need to make a phone call. How about that pub we passed while we were orbiting, just up the street?"

"All right." She slipped the car into gear with a sidelong glance at him, released the brake, and eased out into traffic. "I do hope I'm going to get to see the photos that have gotten you all in a tizzy."

He glanced at her sharply, then returned his gaze to the pub coming up ahead of them.

"Not right now, I'm afraid," he murmured. "I left them in for enlargements."

"After lunch, then?"

"I don't know." He gestured toward the entrance to a car park just beyond the pub. "Put the car in there."

She parked the car in silence, refraining from further comment as they got out, though she did retrieve the envelope of photos from the dash.

"Sorry I barked at you," he murmured, already looking distractedly for the phone as they went in. "Listen, why don't you get us a table, and I'll join you in a few minutes. I promise I'll explain then. Meanwhile, you can order me a half of Smithwick's while you look at those."

The telephone was in a cubicle between the doors to the

men's and women's toilets. Closing the door behind him, Peregrine fished in his pocket for change and soon had dialled Adam's number.

"Strathmourne Manor," said a self-effacing voice from the other end of the line.

"Hello, Humphrey, this is Peregrine. I'm ringing from Glasgow. If Sir Adam is in, I'd very much like a word with him."

"I'm very sorry, Mr. Lovat, but Sir Adam has gone out for the day. I believe he planned to be at the hospital all morning, but he neglected to mention where he might be going after that."

Which suggested that Adam's plans for the afternoon had been in a state of flux. Peregrine suppressed a sigh of frustration.

"That's all right, Humphrey. I'll check with Inspector McLeod and see if he has any idea. If Sir Adam should happen to check in with you later, I'd be obliged if you'd let him know I'm trying to reach him."

"I'll certainly do that, sir."

"Thank you, and goodbye."

He had to look up McLeod's number at police headquarters. Here his call was received by McLeod's aide, Donald Cochrane, who seemed mildly surprised to learn who was phoning.

"Mr. Lovat? Congratulations on your wedding! No, the inspector's not here. He left about half an hour ago, along with Dr. Sinclair."

"Do you know where they went?"

"Aye, they're heading over to Dumbarton, to attend the post-mortem on that bloke you and your wife found washed up on the beach at Kintyre. It isn't due to begin before two o'clock, so I don't imagine they'll be back till late."

This was all news to Peregrine—and suggested that McLeod and Adam had, indeed, found cause to check further on the body Peregrine had found.

"I see," he murmured. "Do you know if Inspector McLeod took his cell phone with him?"

"He usually does. You could certainly try to reach him. Shall I give you the number?"

"No, thanks, I've got it."

"Well, then, you ought to be able to get through to him in the car, no bother."

Cochrane's prediction proved accurate. Scarcely had Peregrine dialled than he heard a responding click, and a familiar gruff voice saying, "McLeod here."

"Hullo, Noel. It's Peregrine."

"Peregrine? Good Lord! Where are you calling from?"

"From a pub in downtown Glasgow," Peregrine replied. "Listen, something else odd has come up, and I need to talk with Adam. Donald told me he might be with you."

"And so he is," McLeod replied. "Hang on and I'll hand you to him."

The next voice Peregrine heard was Adam's. "What's up, Peregrine?"

"Trouble, I think," Peregrine said, mindful of the need to be discreet. "I've just picked up a set of photos including some shots I took over in Kintyre. I thought you might be interested to know that the results were—rather extraordinary."

"Indeed?" Adam's voice took on a slight edge. "Can you tell me in what way?"

"They—ah—showed up what I was trying to draw. I think you ought to see them—perhaps before this afternoon's appointment. I'm having enlargements printed, and they'll be ready in an hour."

"I see," Adam said, after a brief silence. "You said you're calling from Glasgow?"

"That's right," Peregrine acknowledged. "Shall I try to meet you somewhere?"

"I think so," Adam said. "In fact, I wonder . . . Hold on a minute, would you?"

The sound went muffled for a moment, as if Adam had put his hand over the mouthpiece to consult with McLeod; then came on again, a note of apology in his voice.

"Listen, I hate do this to you, but do you think Julia would mind letting you out on loan for a few hours? I think it might be a good idea if you brought your sketchbox along to this afternoon's venture, if you can possibly manage it."

Despite Adam's bland tone and the ambiguity of his

words, Peregrine experienced a sinking feeling in the pit of his stomach, for urgency was there as well. And the thought of witnessing an autopsy—

"Oh, I'm sure she'll mind," he said gamely, "but I think she'll understand. I already have some explaining to do. We'd planned to do some browsing in Princes' Square, but I expect she won't object too strongly to being left to shop on her own. She did say something about wanting to surprise me with something she'd glimpsed in the window of an antique shop we passed on our way through the city center."

"Do whatever you have to do to buy yourself a temporary leave of absence," Adam said with a chuckle. "For my own part, by way of making amends, perhaps you'll allow me to take the pair of you to dinner tonight. What would you say to a meal at the Colonial?"

Peregrine grinned. The Colonial was a Glasgow fixture, with a reputation for serving fine Indian food.

"I expect that would be more than adequate compensation," he said, "provided she's still speaking to me. I just hope I'll be in a fit state to do justice to the menu. I've never attended a—ah—an examination like this before."

"I have every confidence in your fortitude," Adam said bracingly. "Now, about rendezvousing—Noel and I are still a good half hour out of Glasgow, and the noontime traffic will be heavy, once we get off the motorway. Why don't we aim to collect you outside the main entrance to the Central Railway Station round about half past one? We're in Noel's BMW."

"Right you are," Peregrine said. "See you then."

Having rung off, he stood for a moment with his hand on the receiver, collecting his thoughts, then made his way into the pub, where he soon spotted Julia ensconced at a table in a back corner. She was shifting through the photos and sipping at a half-pint. Another half-pint was set at the place across from her. She looked up as he slid into the seat.

"Did you reach him?" she asked.

"Aye." He took a long pull at his Smithwick's, then set it aside. "Listen, did you really mean it last night when you said you wouldn't mind giving me the slip for a little while today, in order to do some shopping for my birthday?"

"They want you, don't they?" she replied, question in her blue eyes. "Peregrine, what is going on? You promised you'd explain."

"So I did—and I shall," he said with a nod, mentally crossing his fingers against the things he could not explain. "The photos have some—details—that may be useful for the police investigation in progress. Adam's with Noel. They're on their way to the post-mortem on the man we found. It's at two this afternoon, up in Dumbarton. They'd like me to join them."

Briefly he outlined the rendezvous arrangements he had made with Adam, after which there was an awkward pause.

"Well, that sounds straightforward enough," Julia finally said. "I suppose you'd better go."

Peregrine eyed his wife uncertainly. "You really don't mind?"

Julia shrugged. "I'd prefer to have your company, of course, but I daresay I'll manage. Do you have time for a bite of lunch first? I've already ordered us steak and kidney pie."

Peregrine glanced down at his watch. It was ten minutes past noon. "It'll have to be fairly quick."

Even as he said it, a waitress appeared with their lunch, plunking down plates replete with generous servings of tender-crusted steak and kidney pie with roast potatoes, chips, and peas.

"Quick enough?" Julia said with a droll grin, when the waitress had departed. "I expected something like this might happen."

They began eating in silence, but after a few token mouthfuls Peregrine discovered he had no appetite for food. When he had pushed the peas around on his plate for several minutes, Julia reached over and laid a hand on his wrist.

"Will you please stop playing with your food?" she murmured, not unkindly. "If this isn't what you wanted, there's still time for you to get something else."

Peregrine shook his head, not meeting her eyes. "I guess I'm just not hungry," he murmured.

Julia studied his face for a moment, her own expression one of mingled sympathy and exasperation. "I can see you're not exactly thrilled about this autopsy thing," she observed. ''Why don't you bow out?''

Peregrine shook his head again. ''I can't.''

''Why not? It isn't as if your presence is vitally necessary. What would they have done if you hadn't called just when you did? You're an artist, not a forensics expert. What could you possibly be expected to contribute?''

''I won't know until I get there,'' he said quietly.

Julia subjected him to a long, searching look. ''In other words, you're going to wait and see.''

Peregrine looked up at her sharply. ''I'm not sure I follow you.''

''I'm not sure I know where I'm *going*,'' Julia admitted readily. ''Probably somewhere out of my depth. But I haven't been engaged to you for more than a year without noticing how often Noel McLeod calls on you and Adam to lend a hand in his police work—even though the police have their own forensic artists on staff, and Adam has more than enough to do in his psychiatric practice without taking on any extra commissions from outside.''

She gazed down at her plate, poking at a bit of crust. ''More and more often, I find myself wondering what it is that binds the three of you so inextricably together. Oh, I know you're friends,'' she went on, ''but even if you weren't, somehow I sense that this bond—whatever it is— would still exist.''

Peregrine felt his jaw drop.

''This same quality that you have in common with one other,'' Julia continued thoughtfully, ''seems to set you apart from everyone else in your professions. Maybe it's just the fact that each of you is exceptionally gifted at what he does. But it seems to have more to do with the way you use your individual gifts to help each other in your respective pursuits. Whenever you work together, you're like a well-rehearsed team—as if all your actions were dictated by some underlying goal or purpose. It's—'' She shook her head. ''I don't know how to ask this. Do—do the three of you perhaps belong to some sort of—of fraternal organization or secret society, maybe something like the Masons, but—help me, darling. I don't know exactly what I'm trying to ask, but I know there's something going on here.''

CHAPTER SEVENTEEN

PEREGRINE stared at his wife, hardly knowing what to say. Her speculations were disconcertingly close to the mark. An outright denial was out of the question; as his wife, Julia was entitled to his honesty. At the same time, he was uncertain how much of the truth Adam would countenance his telling her—or how much she would understand.

"I can't imagine what you mean," he said awkwardly. "We're certainly very good friends and professional colleagues. This bond you're alluding to may simply be the fact that we share many of the same . . . interests."

"Such as?"

Once again Peregrine found himself groping for an answer.

"Well—all manner of things," he said lamely, hoping he didn't sound as defensive as he felt. "History, antiques, objets d'art . . ."

As his voice trailed off, Julia gave him a dubious look.

"I suppose that's true enough," she said quietly. "Only I get the distinct feeling that for you, pursuing these *interests* is practically a vocation."

Peregrine gave a hollow laugh. "I suppose that being an artist does constitute a vocation—something you're *called* to do, as opposed to something you just do to make a living."

"No, it isn't just that," Julia said. "I know the difference between inspiration and—fascination, fixation. For instance, when we were going through the museum this morning, you stopped just outside one of those reconstructed gothic arches, and your eyes went all funny—sort of wide and vacant, but at the same time penetrating—as if you were looking at something far, far away.''

He shrugged. ''I guess I was distracted for a moment.''

''Distracted? I suppose you could call it that. But it isn't the first time I've seen that look in your eyes—and it isn't just an artist's way of looking at things. You get it almost every time we visit a museum or a monument. It always gives me the feeling that your perceptions aren't necessarily limited to the present time and place.''

''You know that I'm an incurable romantic,'' he said uneasily. ''Lots of artists get their inspiration from the past.''

''No, this is different,'' she insisted. ''I'll give you another example. That old tower house that Adam is restoring—the last time we rode out there with him, I accidentally overheard the two off you discussing how to decorate the laird's bedroom. He wanted to know if the original ceiling had been painted, and you said yes, it had, with garlands of flowers interspersed with verses taken from the Book of Proverbs. And you were able to tell him which ones, chapter and verse.''

She stopped short and looked at him expectantly, and Peregrine knew that only the truth would now suffice—or at least a portion of it. He poked at a chunk of steak with his fork, chasing it into a pool of congealing gravy.

''What you're really wanting to know,'' he said quietly, not looking at her, ''is, have I got some kind of special psychic ability. The answer is yes. Yes, I do.''

He could hear her little gasp, but he dared not look up at her as he went on.

''My particular gift is being able to 'See' things—visual echoes—*resonances*, if you like—from other periods in time. As an artist, I'm sometimes able to draw what I 'See' in this manner. When it first started happening, it scared the hell out of me. That was shortly before I met you.

''But then your sainted godmother introduced me to Adam. I don't think she had any inkling what was happening, but she knew something was wrong and thought he might be able to help me—and she was right. But I didn't go to him until after she'd died, and I was feeling almost suicidal.

You see, I'd foreseen her death, and a part of me was afraid that I'd somehow caused it.''

"But you couldn't have!" Julia breathed. "She had cancer, Peregrine."

"I know that now," he murmured, finally looking up at her, "but at the time, I was convinced there was some kind of causal connection. Anyway, Adam helped me pick up the pieces, and reassured me that what I had was a gift, not a curse. He taught me to control it, to use it in conjunction with my ability as an artist—and that ability now gives me the means to direct and control what I 'See.' ''

"So now you don't mind Seeing things anymore?"

"Not most of the time. Sometimes it's useful."

"For instance, in the investigation of a crime." It wasn't a question. Lacing her slim fingers together in front of her, Julia leaned forward on her elbows. "Is *that* what you're doing when you go out with Adam and Noel? Are they psychic, too?"

"Their talents differ from mine," Peregrine said reluctantly, "but yes, on both counts."

"And they use their abilities to solve mysteries that no one else can solve?"

"When the need arises."

"Psychic investigators." She quirked him an uneasy grin. "It sounds like something out of an old Hammer horror film." Levelling a penetrating look at her husband, she asked, "Why didn't you tell me this sooner?"

"Perhaps I should have done," Peregrine admitted. "But a lot of what we do has got to be kept confidential."

"Don't you trust me to keep a secret?"

"Of course I do—as far as *my* secrets are concerned," he replied. "But some of the secrets we're talking about aren't mine to disclose. Artists are allowed certain eccentricities— we're almost expected to be a little fey—but if either Noel or Adam became publicly connected with some of the things we're obliged to do, the methods we use—well, you can probably imagine the hue and cry that would be raised. Professionally speaking, they'd both be ruined."

She stared at him for a long moment, taking it all in, then ventured, "You aren't doing anything—illegal, are you?"

He snorted. "Of course not. If we stand for anything, it's the upholding of the law. But sometimes it's a higher Law than some folk are even aware exists—and believe me, we have to answer to a far higher Judge."

She shivered and put down her fork. "You make it sound almost—cosmic."

He searched her face with his eyes, shaking his head. "I know it's a lot to take in—and I wish I could tell you more, but I can't. I wouldn't blame you for having doubts about my sanity, but honestly, I didn't want to risk—"

He broke off, wondering if perhaps he had already said too much, and Julia pounced on the one word he probably should not have used.

"Risk?" she repeated. "Peregrine, does—what you do involve an element of danger?"

Squirming inwardly, he nodded. "Now and then."

"What about now?"

"I don't know," he admitted. "I don't think so. Not in the short term, at any rate. After all, what could happen while watching a post-mortem? Besides, Adam would never allow any of us to endanger ourselves without good cause," he added stoutly.

"I'll have to take your word for that," she said, "at least for the moment. And it appears that Adam's behind all of this. He's your leader, isn't he?"

At his reluctant nod, she cocked her head thoughtfully. "What would happen if you decided to give up this line of work?"

"Adam would have to find someone else to do what I do. But I don't believe I could give it up, even if I wanted to."

"Why not?"

"Because the work itself would almost certainly find me out, with or without any active solicitation on my part," he said, "in much the same way that this talent of mine was asserting itself long before I learned how to harness it."

"But you didn't ask for the gift. It just came to you."

"That's precisely the point," Peregrine said. He frowned, groping for words. "Possessing a talent like this is a bit like being factor or manager on a big estate. Once you've been entrusted with something—money, property, whatever—you are thereafter responsible for making right and profitable use of it. And the only authority that can legitimately relieve you of that responsibility is the one who imposed it on you in the first place.''

''Who, Adam? What right had he—''

''No, not Adam,'' Peregrine interjected. ''Julia, you know that I'm not a particularly religious person, at least outwardly, but I—think I'd honestly have to say that it was God, in this case, Who gave me the assignment. And I don't see any sign that He wants to withdraw it.'' He squeezed her hand in appeal. ''Is this making any sense at all, darling?''

Reluctantly she nodded, confusion but also acceptance lighting the blue eyes. ''In a roundabout way, I suppose it does. I'll probably have to go away and think about it—perhaps while you're off at this post-mortem. Would it be out of line to ask what you're supposed to be looking for on this occasion?''

Peregrine relaxed just a little, bringing her hand to his lips in a fond kiss. ''Adam just wants me to *look*,'' he said with a shrug. ''That's usually what I do. If I See anything, I'll draw it. After that, it will be up to him and Noel to decide where and how we proceed.''

''All right,'' Julia said, very matter-of-fact. ''In that case, I'll go shopping and leave you to your work. Are you going to tell Adam about this conversation of ours?''

''I'll have to,'' Peregrine said. ''It's important that he knows how much you know—for all our sakes. Besides, I wouldn't want to have any clouds hanging over us at dinner time; Adam's invited us for a meal tonight at the Colonial.''

Julia's eyes widened slightly. ''The Colonial? Very nice, indeed! Is this one of the perks of the job?''

Peregrine managed a droll smile. ''I suppose it's one of the perks of being Adam's friend,'' he said lightly. ''In this case, it will also be a salve to his conscience, for borrowing me when you and I should be on our honeymoon. Will you forgive him?''

She smiled. ''Of course. And I didn't mean to sound ungrateful. He's always been the soul of generosity.''

''Yes, he has,'' Peregrine replied, wondering whether the

day would ever come when he might reveal just how far that generosity extended beyond the physical—for despite the privileges that Adam's wealth provided, his life was one of constant sacrifice.

"I'd better go now," he murmured, with a glance at his watch. "I've got to collect those photos before I meet Adam and Noel."

She nodded. "Do you want the car?"

"No, you take it. It'll be easier for me to taxi over to the Central Railway Station. Do you know how to get back to the guesthouse from here?"

"I'll manage. Where and when do you want me to meet up with you?"

"How about seven o'clock, at the guesthouse?" Peregrine suggested. "If anything comes up that spells a change of plans, I'll phone in and leave a message there. In the meantime, promise me you'll try to enjoy yourself!"

"I'm going off to spend some of our wedding money," she said with a coy grin. "Of *course* I'll enjoy myself!"

He paid the bill and accompanied Julia back to the car to pick up his portable sketchbox, continuing on toward the photo shop when she had driven off in the opposite direction. When he collected his enlargements, he continued to the next cross street, where he managed to hail a passing taxi.

He gave the photos a cursory look in the back seat as the driver headed on cross-town to the railway station, but the enhanced detail suggested few further revelations. He closed the prints into his sketchbox as the taxi pulled into Central Station, for he had already spotted McLeod's black BMW standing at the curb, with McLeod and Adam waiting outside so he could spot them, conversing across the roof.

"You're very prompt," McLeod commented, as he opened the rear door for Peregrine and Adam got in on the front passenger side. "It's spot-on half past one."

"Just to show you that marriage hasn't addled my brain," Peregrine quipped. He gave the inspector a grin in the rear-view mirror as he settled into the seat. "I figured I'd better be on time, or I might find myself stranded."

"No danger of that," Adam replied, leaning an arm along

the back of the seat as McLeod and Peregrine buckled up. "Let's see those photos, so Noel can have a look before we head out."

Dutifully Peregrine produced the envelope containing the enlargements and passed them forward for his superiors' inspection. As Adam handed them one by one to McLeod, the expression on his aquiline face was thoughtful.

"Interesting, that these should come along concurrent with those shots from Carnage Corridor," he observed, with a sidelong glance at his Second.

"Carnage Corridor?" Peregrine echoed, as McLeod nodded his agreement.

"A case we've been working on in your absence," Adam said.

Briefly he summarized how their investigations had led them to become involved with Claire Crawford, directing Peregrine to pull the relevant photographs from his briefcase for comparison.

"It was her astral image appearing in the photographs that supplied us with the vital clue," he explained at the end of his short recap of the case. "Having seen these shots of yours, I'm inclined to think we may be dealing with a different manifestation of the same phenomenon. When we all get back to Edinburgh, it might be interesting to have you take a look at the accident site—though, with Claire just about sorted out now, I don't really expect you'll see very much. Still, one never knows."

"I'm not sure I'm with you," Peregrine remarked as he shuffled through the glossy five-by-eights with Claire's image circled in red. "You say these are pictures of this woman's *astral* self?"

"That's right." McLeod pushed the aviator spectacles farther onto the bridge of his nose and turned the key in the ignition. "Adam's got a theory about that, but I'd better drive while he explains. We're due in Dumbarton by two."

"Indeed," Adam concurred, as McLeod pulled smoothly into traffic. "As near as I can make out, Claire Crawford's astral presence registered on film because she was generating exceptionally intense emotional resonances at the time. It may be related to the way that ghosts sometimes show up on film.''

''Are you saying I saw a ghost?''

''Hmmm, perhaps something more akin to the historical resonances you See when you draw. Going on that assumption, it would seem to follow that this monkish character in your photographs was likewise generating personal resonances of a similarly powerful magnitude, perhaps at the time he killed Scanlan.''

''But—'' Peregrine glanced at the photos of Claire, then at the ones Adam had handed back. ''I don't understand. If you're right about all this, why is her image so distinct, and the image of this monk so misty? And for that matter, why couldn't I See him when I Looked?''

Adam arched an elegant eyebrow and partially turned back toward the traffic ahead as McLeod eased the car onto Waterloo Street, heading for the M8 motorway.

''I have no easy answer for you on that one,'' Adam said, ''but I can speculate. Claire Crawford was acting unconsciously, and for that reason was obviously making no attempt to conceal her presence—hence the projection and transmission of a clear visual image. Your monk, on the other hand, seems to have been operating from behind a screen of psychic defenses, warded in such a way that no Sighted observer—such as yourself, Peregrine—could have perceived who he was. Who could have predicted that his personal emanations might register on some impartially sensitive medium like photographic film?''

''Your theory explains the presence of a ghost-image in my pictures,'' Peregrine agreed. ''But it doesn't even *begin* to explain who and what this Oriental monk might be, or what he could possibly be doing hovering over the body of a dead Irishman in a survival suit.''

''You think *that's* odd?'' McLeod muttered. ''Try explaining what either of them could possibly have to do with a German U-boat, supposedly sunk off the Irish coast during the final stages of World War Two.''

''U-boat?'' Peregrine was thoroughly baffled now.

''I thought you'd appreciate that one,'' the inspector said with a dour grin. ''Wait till you hear the whole story.''

CHAPTER EIGHTEEN

B Y the time they had left the M8, heading north to cross
the Erskine Bridge, McLeod had filled Peregrine in on
the background regarding the *Kriegsmarine* flag found on
Mick Scanlan's body and the submarine it ostensibly had
come from. As they linked up with the A82 and began working their way westward toward Dumbarton, Peregrine was
shaking his head.

"And I told Julia this was probably going to be unevent-
ful," he murmured. "I'd better tell you about that, too," he
went on. "I had to tell her a little bit about us, Adam."

As they drove, Peregrine related the substance of his parting conversation with Julia. Only in the retelling did he fully
realize how effectively he had been outguessed and outma-
neuvered by his young wife.

"I tried to be discreet, Adam, but I guess those photos
had me more rattled than I realized," he concluded. "And
she'd deduced so much already, there didn't seem to be any
point to trying to sweep everything under the mat. She knows
me too well. If there was some better way to handle the
situation that escaped me, I'm heartily sorry."

"No, you did exactly right," Adam assured him. "Lies
are no proper foundation for a marriage. Quite frankly, I'm
surprised the two of you haven't had this conversation long
before now—though I've been grateful for the temporary
respite. Still, Julia's a very observant and perceptive young
woman—as is fitting, if she's to be your life partner. She
couldn't help but notice what she did."

"Yes—well, she reacted well enough this time, but what

about the next?'' Peregrine wanted to know. ''Clearly, she can't be privy to the details of our work, but there *will* be times when I'm in danger. I accept that danger—and I suppose I accepted it for her, unbeknownst to either of us, when I asked her to marry me—but it's hardly fair to keep her totally in the dark.''

''No, but it isn't fair to frighten her needlessly, either,'' Adam replied. ''There *are* dangers to our work, but I might even go so far as to say it's more 'difficult' than 'dangerous,' in the vast majority of cases—rather like more conventional police work, wouldn't you agree, Noel?''

McLeod gave a nod, catching Peregrine's glance in the rearview mirror. ''He's right, son. Certainly, a conventional police officer faces danger—there *are* occasional fatalities— but a lot more of the work is about solving problems, finding out answers, helping people. How did I hear someone put it? 'Stretches of routine punctuated by instants of sheer terror.' The work of the Hunting Lodge is little different in that respect, except that the work is rarely routine.''

''I'd have to agree with *that*,'' Peregrine said. ''Still— Noel, do you and Jane ever talk about your work as a member of the Hunting Lodge?''

''Not in so many words,'' McLeod said with a tiny smile. ''We worked that one out while you were still in short trousers.''

''But she *does* know all about your special abilities, and how you use them?''

''I wouldn't say she knows *all* about them,'' McLeod said. ''She knows the breadth of my—shall we say, 'hospitality'? And she knows that my writ as an officer of the law extends beyond the limits of the conventional legal system. If we decline to discuss the details, it's by common consent.''

Peregrine contemplated this disclosure in silence. After staring out the window for several minutes, he asked, ''How did it come about?—that she became aware of your gifts, I mean. Did you just decide one day to tell her?''

''Hardly as simple as that,'' McLeod said with a snort. ''No, as it happened, it came as a revelation to us both.''

Peregrine had never before ventured to ask how McLeod had originally become involved in the Hunting Lodge, so he listened avidly as the older man continued speaking of his own accord.

"It was a good twenty years ago. I'd just recently been promoted to detective sergeant, and was called out early one morning to investigate a burglary at a small country house museum, just this side of Dunbar. In fact, it was a lot like that place that had the Hepburn Sword stolen from it, just before you met Adam." Peregrine shifted to lean slightly forward between the two front seats as McLeod went on.

"Among the items reported stolen was a silver cross set with cairngorms, which had been handed over as part of the museum grant when old Sir Andrew Cockburn died, back in the early sixties. When I arrived at the crime scene, one of the curators told me the cross had been gifted to one of Sir Andrew's ancestors by Mary Queen of Scots herself—which made it a family heirloom beyond price.

"The job itself had been carried out by a team of professionals," McLeod continued. "No fingerprints, no wanton vandalism—just a clean sweep of everything worth taking. Burglaries like that don't leave the police with much to go on. When I drove back to Edinburgh that afternoon, I wasn't very sanguine about recovering any of the artifacts that had been stolen. Then, when I went to bed that night, I had a curious dream.

"I woke up—or thought I'd woken up—to the sound of somebody knocking at the front door. When I went downstairs to see who it was, I found an elderly white-haired gentleman standing outside on the step. He introduced himself as Sir Andrew Cockburn, and informed me that he could lead me to the crooks. He asked me very politely if he could come in, and without stopping to think, I said yes. The next thing I remember is waking up in the office of a priest who shall remain nameless, with my wife holding my hand."

At Peregrine's gasp, McLeod glanced back over his shoulder with a grin.

"Turns out, I'd been taken over by the spirit of old Cockburn himself," he continued reminiscently. "As keeper of the family cross, he'd developed an affinity with it over the years. With that affinity to guide him, he knew where the cross was to be found after the robbery, even if he didn't know who'd taken it. All he needed was the right person to use as a medium.''

''You,'' said Peregrine.

''Me,'' McLeod agreed. He gave a short laugh. ''Jane would be the first to tell you that it scared the hell out of her when she realized that the person sitting across from her at breakfast wasn't actually me. Oh, he promptly introduced himself, and assured her that I was in no danger, but he kept repeating that he had to give a message to someone in authority.''

He grinned. ''Fortunately, Jane was quick to realize that he didn't mean my police superiors—it would have been the end of my career. She also rightly surmised that this probably wasn't something that would make the minister of our kirk too happy.''

''I should say not,'' Peregrine murmured, spellbound.

''Anyway, she rang a lady friend who'd dabbled in seances and the like, and the lady friend referred her to a local Anglo-Catholic priest who was sympathetic to such occurrences and understood exactly what happened and why. He verified that the possession wasn't satanic or anything like that, then brought me safely out of my trance, after taking down the information that my 'tenant,' Sir Andrew, had to impart.

''And that information led to the successful retrieval of the cross and a number of other items from the robbery. I wasn't to learn until much later that the good father—who's dead now, God rest him, though he later became a bishop— was a member of the same Hunting Lodge as Philippa Sinclair.''

Adam's mother. As far as Peregrine was concerned, this single revelation supplied the answers to many hitherto tantalizing questions.

''I can see why you and Jane wouldn't have many secrets from one another,'' he said after a moment. ''But doesn't she worry about you?''

He shrugged. ''A cop's life can be dangerous; she knew that when she married me. I don't suppose that adding an extra dimension to my jurisdiction increases the danger all that much; after all, we do have astral tools for astral enforcement.''

"Am I really supposed to reassure Julia by telling her *that*?" Peregrine said.

"Of course not," Adam said, finally joining the discussion. "But don't sell Julia short. Beneath that fetchingly girlish exterior beats a heart of true steel—a quality for which you may have cause to be thankful one day.''

"So I shouldn't tell her any more?" Peregrine asked.

"I'd keep it on a need-to-know basis," Adam replied. "You'll know when more or less information is appropriate. In the meantime, I see the signs coming up for Dumbarton. Where's this hospital, Noel?''

"Actually, it's in Alexandria, a few miles past Dumbarton," the inspector replied, scanning the signs ahead. "The police mortuary is at Vale of Leven Hospital. Shout out when you see a sign. I know the central Glasgow area pretty well, but a lot of this is new out here.''

They whisked past the outskirts of Dumbarton, with its stone-built houses and crowstepped roofs, arriving at Vale of Leven Hospital with minutes to spare. The police mortuary was housed in a separate building from the main hospital, clearly signposted, and they parked adjacent to its entrance. They were met in the lobby by a young man in plain clothes who introduced himself as Detective Angus Murray, from L-Division of the Strathclyde Police. After giving McLeod's credentials a cursory inspection, Murray led them along a dimly lit corridor and through a glass-panelled door into a small room functionally furnished as a staff lounge.

Jack Somerville was there ahead of them, a husky, balding man half a head shorter than McLeod and muscled like a wrestler, heatedly discussing rugby standings with an athletic-looking younger man with an Irish accent. Listening indulgently was a diminutive grey-haired woman in horn-rimmed spectacles and green surgical scrubs who turned out to be Vale of Leven's resident pathologist, Dr. Margaret Gow. The Irishman was introduced as Detective Sergeant Ernan Ryan, sent over from the Garda Siochana in Dublin.

"We're only waiting on Dr. Macaulay," Somerville explained in his gravelly bass. "He's on staff at Southern General, coming across to be our independent consultant. He should be here any minute."

This announcement coincided with a stir back down the hall, followed by the sound of a door opening and closing.

"Och, just stay where you are, Detective," a tenor voice said good-naturedly. "I know my way well enough from here."

Muffled footsteps approached; then the door swung open to reveal a lanky, lantern-jawed man with bright, dark eyes peering out from under an untidy fringe of black hair. Though Dr. Macaulay would have towered head and shoulders above his female colleague if he stood straight, his posture was somewhat bowed from many hours spent bending over operating tables and peering through microscopes.

"Sorry I'm a bit late," he announced to the room at large. "Meg, if you'd be kind enough to introduce me to these gentlemen, we can suit up and get on with the afternoon's business."

A quarter hour later, with introductions tendered all around, both Macaulay and the police observers had exchanged their street attire for green surgical scrubs and seemingly incongruous rubber boots and shifted their venue to the theatre where the post-mortem would be performed. Peregrine had a sketch pad and pencil clutched to his breast. Scrubbed white tiles lined the walls and floors under a bank of high-intensity lights, and several stainless-steel buckets flanked a drain in the middle of the floor, directly underneath the stainless-steel table that occupied center stage. As a mortuary attendant wheeled in a green-sheeted form on a gurney, Peregrine found himself wondering whether the buckets were for the benefit of weak-stomached observers or were meant to contain more grisly offerings.

A faint whiff of decay tickled at his nostrils as Macaulay helped the attendant shift the body onto the stainless-steel table, and Peregrine retreated to the foot of the table with McLeod. The array of shiny surfaces reminded him queasily of a cross between a veterinary surgery and a prep-school biology lab, and the refrigerated air was cold enough to make the breath turn to frost between his teeth. Despite the sterile chill and the operative hum of the ventilating system, the air smelt strongly of clinical disinfectants—but not strongly enough. Detective Murray came to stand on McLeod's other side, already beginning to look unwell.

Meanwhile, Dr. Gow was slipping a series of X rays under the clips of a bank of light-boxes to one side, pulling on surgical gloves as she beckoned for Macaulay to have a look. Adam moved to the head of the table with Somerville and Ryan, also casting a professional eye over the X rays. As the two police surgeons came back to the table, taking positions on either side, McLeod casually interposed himself between Peregrine and Murray—which Peregrine realized would afford him a greater degree of privacy once he began sketching.

Pausing to switch on the overhead lights and video recorder at the head of the table, Dr. Gow stripped back the body's covering to the waist, announced the date and time, then began her description and external examination of the body.

"Subject is a well-nourished male Caucasian, approximately thirty years of age, previously identified by next of kin as Michael Alan Scanlan, an Irish national. Police surgeons attending: Dr. Margaret Gow, Vale of Leven Hospital, and Dr. Richard Macaulay, Southern General."

When she had also rattled off the names and functions of all the witnesses present—no mean feat, by Peregrine's reckoning—she and Macaulay examined the body's head injury, then got down to work.

Somewhat removed from too direct a view, Peregrine managed to remain reasonably detached through the initial phase of the procedure by working quick anatomical sketches; he had done similar exercises in art school. As the autopsy progressed, however, he found cause to be glad that he had not eaten much lunch. The cold room felt suddenly hot and stifling; he became aware of a roaring in his ears. The reek of decay and blood and other bodily fluids made the bile rise in the back of his throat, and he found himself swallowing convulsively to keep from gagging.

He glanced surreptitiously at his fellow observers to see how they were bearing up. Not unexpectedly, Adam's composure surpassed even the professional detachment evidenced by his medical colleagues, a compassion akin to reverence stirring his patrician features. Peregrine had the feeling that nothing, not even this clinical butchery, could make his superior lose sight of Scanlan as a once-living being, possessed of an immortal soul that would survive such violation of the earthly temple it had once occupied.

By contrast, the two surgeons seemed more casual, sometimes even flippant, though Peregrine soon realized that their apparent breeziness masked righteous dismay for the fate of this young man cut down so untimely. McLeod was stoically impassive, as was his heavyset counterpart from Strathclyde; Ryan looked a little queasy but determined to stick it out. When Macaulay fired up a miniature electric saw, and the stench of fragmented bone joined the other smells of the post-mortem theatre, Murray chose that moment to hurriedly excuse himself, decidedly green around the gills.

Looking away, Peregrine caught sight of his own face mirrored off various metallic surfaces round the room—pasty white, the eyes slightly hollowed behind their wire-rimmed spectacles, lips grimly set. To distract himself and regain some perspective, he turned to a fresh page in his sketch pad, shifting position as the two surgeons turned their subject onto his stomach to inspect the back wound. Taking a firmer grip on his pencil, Peregrine forced himself to resume sketching, not looking at the long probe that Dr. Gow inserted into the wound, testing the limits of the laceration, searching for anything left behind.

''Point of entry is between the eighth and ninth ribs, approximately eight centimeters to the left of midline; depth of the wound is approximately—eighteen centimeters. . . . ''

Peregrine's sketches from this angle began as anatomical studies like the first ones, though he was uncomfortably aware of the closer connection of death with the wound Dr. Gow was examining. By concentrating on details of contour and musculature he was able to regain some much-needed objectivity, but very shortly his perceptions began spontaneously to shift, mediating between levels of awareness. Almost before he was aware of what he was doing, he found himself drawing on the astral.

His physical eyesight grew blurred; the sounds all around receded. This blunting of his external faculties signalled the imminent release of his inner vision, insulating him from his earlier horror. Like a hawk upheld by the wind, he ascended out of himself to hover serenely within the stillness of the Inner Planes.

Increasingly detached, he watched as a few bold strokes defined the emergent image of the dead man suspended head-downward in midair, as if he were falling. Protruding from his back was the ornate hilt of a strange, clumsy-looking dagger.

Squinting at the body, Peregrine let his deep sight focus on the weapon, turning to another page. At once a more detailed sketch began to take shape beneath his pencil—first, a triangular cross section of the blade, with the slight indentations of fullers, or blood grooves; then a detail of the hilt attached to the blade embedded in the dead man's back—an intricately modelled collage of demonic faces, hideously contorted in a variety of snarls and leers.

He saw it clearly in his mind's eye; his hand obeyed him, sketching its details. But as he bent to the fine detailing, he became simultaneously aware of a growing strain on the silver cord holding body and soul together. With a final stroke to the sketch, he allowed the re-fusion, briefly closing his eyes against the now-familiar pang of disorientation and vertigo. Swaying slightly, he pulled himself up and realized that Somerville and Dr. Macaulay were directing curious glances his way.

Hastily he flipped over to another blank page to hide the dagger drawing and began another quick sketch. As he did so, he caught a look of unspoken inquiry from Adam, but his only response was a fleeting grin and a small shrug. He had Seen something, all right; but determining the significance of what he had Seen would have to wait until he and Adam and McLeod had a chance to review his drawings together in private.

Half an hour later it was all over. The official verdict handed down by the two pathologists was that Michael Scanlan had died from massive internal hemorrhage as a result of a stab wound to the back. Beyond this primary fact, however, many of the other aspects of the case remained open to speculation. As they gathered in the coffee room afterwards, shed of their surgical scrubs, Somerville and his medical colleagues were engaged in a debate on the possible identity of the murder weapon.

"We're definitely talking about something with a triangular cross-section," Dr. Gow observed, setting down her coffee mug. "In addition, the damage to the ribs at the point of entry suggests a degree of force more consistent with the penetrating power of a projectile weapon. The head injury was serious, but the wound was the proximate cause of death. There was virtually no fluid at all in the lungs. The man must have been dying even as he hit the water."

"Could the weapon have been some kind of spear—something like a harpoon, maybe?" Garda Sergeant Ryan asked. "We're working on the possibility that he and his partner ran afoul of illegal fishermen. It's the sort of weapon that might be used in a hot confrontation."

The two forensic surgeons exchanged glances. "That's not a bad guess, as guesses go," Macaulay said, "except that the wound itself is far too neat."

"A harpoon is barbed so that it won't come free without tearing the surrounding flesh," Dr. Gow pointed out. "Whatever implement made this wound came out as cleanly as it went in."

While the physicians and investigators continued to speculate, Peregrine quietly drew Adam and McLeod aside and showed them the drawings he had made of the dagger.

"*This* is what made the wound," he whispered, "though I obviously can't show it to them. I'm not sure what it is, though. Any ideas?"

McLeod gave a dissatisfied grunt and shook his head. "Beats me. I'd guess it's Oriental, though—or maybe South American."

"I'd vote for Oriental," Adam said, "but I don't pretend to be a expert on Oriental weaponry. Fortunately, there's someone in our immediate circle who is extremely well versed in Oriental artifacts—and I seem to recall something vaguely similar to this in one of her display cabinets. I think a call to Julian is in order."

"Aye, she'll know," McLeod concurred with a grim smile. "Or she can find out. Say, you don't suppose this is what Peregrine's ghost-monk was holding in his hand? Where are those photos, son?"

Opening his sketchbox, ostensibly to put away his sketch pad, Peregrine unearthed the best of the ghost-monk photos, with the blade-like extension between the monk's clasped hands.

"I think maybe that *is* what I was trying to see, when I took this shot," he said.

"I'd say you're probably right," Adam agreed. "And I'd say there's also an excellent chance that this is, indeed, the murder weapon. I'll certainly ring Julian before we leave here. And in the meantime, I wouldn't mind a look at that flag Somerville mentioned."

McLeod heaved himself to his feet with a nod. "I'll ask him about it," he said as Peregrine closed up his box. "Under the circumstances, I'm sure something can be arranged."

Somerville, when McLeod drew him to one side, proved as cooperative as predicted.

"Of course you can have a look," he murmured. "All Scanlan's personal effects are being stored in the local lock-up until the procurator fiscal agrees to release them to the family. I've got to go along there anyway, to make my report. Why don't you follow me there?"

At the station in nearby Alexandria, Somerville showed McLeod and his associates into a side office and then disappeared, returning a few minutes later with a large storage carton with Scanlan's name affixed to it.

"I hope you won't mind if I abandon you for a few minutes," he told them. "I've got some phone calls to make. You'd think no one at headquarters can do anything, judging by the number of messages I've got waiting. Take all the time you want to go through this stuff. If you finish before I can get back to you, and you need to leave, just give a shout for the desk sergeant and he'll return the box to the safe. I've signed it out, so I'm responsible."

Most of the box was filled with Scanlan's clothing—his bright orange life-vest, the black-and-orange survival suit he had been wearing, the knitted black boiler suit that went underneath like long johns, a few personal items from his inside pockets. Both suits had triangular tears in the back, though the sea had washed away all traces of his blood. Adam fingered the hole in the survival suit thoughtfully before laying it aside.

The flag was at the bottom of the carton, wrapped in a plastic bag. Pulling it out, McLeod shook out the folds of fine wool, stained by the salt water but otherwise as bright as the day it had been made. His expression was one of mingled fascination and distaste as he passed it to Adam for his inspection.

"I wonder if Scanlan *did* get this thing off a German U-boat," he murmured.

"I wonder, indeed," Adam agreed. "Peregrine, I don't suppose you can See anything that might be helpful?"

As Adam held out the flag, Peregrine found himself suppressing a shiver.

"Nothing immediate comes to mind," he whispered. "If you want, I suppose I could try handling it. . . . "

"Don't, if it makes you uncomfortable," Adam said.

"No, it's all right."

Drawing a deep breath to ground himself, Peregrine picked up the flag in his two hands. It was slightly stiff from its saltwater immersion; he could smell its mustiness, the salt tang of the sea, as he raised it closer to his face. Everything else around him softened and blurred as he centered his attention on the folds of scarlet and black and white.

The image of the flag itself grew harshly articulate, its color and design impinging on his inner sight with fierce intensity. But when he tried to penetrate beyond that image, the picture itself suddenly exploded.

CHAPTER NINETEEN

HE recoiled with a startled gasp, instantly muffled in the crook of one arm as he threw the flag from his hands. White light splintered behind his eyes like a splash of hot needles, but immediately dissipated. Only belatedly did he feel the bolstering pressure of a hand on his shoulder.

"Easy," came Adam's calm voice. "Did it give you a jolt?"

Coming out from behind his arm, Peregrine nodded and drew a shaky breath as he chanced a cautious look at the heap of crimson, black, and white. His two companions were staring at him in undisguised concern.

"Whew! I won't try *that* again soon," he mumbled. "The flag's protected somehow. I couldn't See past it. It's linked with something that doesn't want to be Seen."

"Perhaps the submarine it came from," Adam said slowly. "And *that* bears further thinking. It appears we aren't talking about a mere artifact of war here."

"Bloody hell!" McLeod muttered, exchanging a black look with his chief. "Do you suppose it connects with one of Hitler's Black Lodges?"

"The prospect looms increasingly likely," Adam said grimly. "I couldn't begin to be specific at this point, but *U-636* and its crew appear to have been bound up in *some* nefarious plan—which explains why it should have been brought to our attention."

"You mean, I was somehow *directed* to find Scanlan's body?" Peregrine asked.

Adam waggled one hand in a yes-and-no gesture. "I don't

know that I'd go that far—and I couldn't begin to tell you where your ghost-monk fits in. But there's no getting around the fact that Scanlan was murdered—probably by a man wielding what appears to be an Oriental dagger—and that he did procure a Nazi submarine's flag from *somewhere*. This all suggests that whoever originally sent out the sub—or their descendants—may well still be functioning—and still deadly.''

Peregrine swallowed loudly. ''But—Nazi Germany collapsed half a century ago,'' he said plaintively.

''True enough,'' Adam agreed. ''But the dark forces that fuelled much of its power still flare up occasionally. You surely haven't forgotten what we encountered in the Cairngorms.''

''Christ!'' McLeod muttered under his breath. ''You don't think it's *that* lot again, do you?''

''I hope not. But I *was* warned to expect the reappearance of an old enemy.'' Adam sighed. ''I think we'd better see about finding that sub.''

''More easily said than done,'' McLeod retorted. ''There's no way we can try that here, especially in light of the whammy Peregrine just got. And I certainly hope you aren't suggesting that we abscond with official evidence.''

''Not abscond, no; we'll ask,'' Adam replied. ''But the flag is the only direct link we've got to the sub. And if you can find out where Scanlan was patrolling, when he and his partner went missing, that should narrow down the location before we even start resorting to more drastic measures.''

''It's the drastic measures that are worrying me,'' McLeod grumbled, as Adam carefully gathered up the flag and began folding it. ''Even if I *could* borrow it, how do you propose to get past what zapped Peregrine?''

''I haven't figured that out yet,'' Adam conceded. ''Actually, I doubt it's the flag that's protected; more likely, we're talking about spillover from the sub itself, which *is* protected. But that can be got around, if I can trace the link back. What I *cannot* do is make the link without the flag.''

Before McLeod could respond, Somerville himself returned, waving a dismissive hand at someone in the outer office as he came in and closed the door behind him. He looked restive and harried, as if whatever business had called him away had not gone as well as he might have hoped.

"Bloody red tape," he muttered under his breath, jerking a chair out from the table and flouncing into it with a sigh. "I hope you gentlemen had better luck than I did."

McLeod glanced obliquely at Adam, who was tucking the flag back into its plastic bag.

"We've come up with a few ideas. But I'll warn you right now, they're nothing you could print in the newspapers without being branded a raving lunatic."

"Not another one of *those* cases?" Somerville muttered. "Never mind, I don't want to know. Just help me solve this case, and I won't ask any questions that might embarrass us all."

"I hope you mean that," McLeod said, "because in order to test our ideas, Dr. Sinclair and I need to borrow the flag for a day or two."

Somerville's grizzled eyebrows climbed. "That's asking rather a lot, considering it's my name on the sign-out. I can't alter the production book for you, Noel."

"I wouldn't ask it," McLeod said. "Forty-eight hours— and we'd be careful."

"I don't know . . ."

Adam was familiar with production-log procedure, and fully understood Somerville's concern.

"We'll be more than careful, Inspector," he assured him. "If it would make you feel any happier, Noel and I would be prepared to offer you a solemn pledge to that effect—for the sake of the widow's son."

His use of the Masonic phrase earned him a sharp look from Somerville, who glanced then at McLeod.

"Is he on the level?" he asked.

McLeod inclined his head. "And on the square. It's important, Jack."

"So I gather." The Strathclyde inspector pursed his lips. "If I *were* to let you have temporary custody of the flag, what exactly would you be planning to do with it?"

"Do you *really* want to know?" McLeod asked with a wry smile.

"On second thought," Somerville said, "maybe not." He

drew a deep breath. "Seeing as how it's you who's asking," he ventured, "I suppose I can let you have the flag on trust. You said forty-eight hours?"

"Hopefully, no longer," McLeod said, with another oblique glance at Adam.

"Quite hopefully," Adam agreed. "At the most, seventy-two."

"This keeps getting more complicated," Somerville grumbled, "but all right. Come on out to the front office while I take care of the necessary paperwork."

"Thanks," McLeod said, handing the flag to Peregrine to deposit in his sketchbox. "I'll make sure you don't regret this."

As the two police officers began heading for the door, Adam summoned Peregrine with a glance and then said, "I think we'll wait for you in the car. I'm going to use your cell phone to make a call."

Lady Julian Brodie's jewellery studio was situated on the upper floor of her handsome Edinburgh town house. Even on grey days, the big windows and louvered skylight kept the room flooded with natural light, sufficient for all but the most exacting work. The walls were lined with low counters supporting a wide array of tools and apparatus, including an enamelling kiln, rolling mills, and a centrifugal casting unit. The air was permanently redolent of hot metal, borax solution, and pickling acids, but years of exposure had rendered Julian cheerfully oblivious to the atmosphere associated with her chosen avocation.

Today, to the background accompaniment of an old D'Oyly Carte recording of *The Mikado*, she was finishing a commission for an old friend, a graduation present for his granddaughter, soon to receive her law degree. The piece was a golden miniature of a disk-shaped bronze mirror of the T'ang dynasty, the detailing inlaid in silver, the whole thing hardly larger than a 50p. piece. Creating the wax matrix for the design had been a fiercely demanding task, involving much close work under a magnifying glass; but though Julian Brodie was nearly seventy, the infirmity that now confined her to a wheelchair had done nothing to diminish the sharpness of her eye or the steadiness of her hands. She had just begun maneuvering a flawless blue-tinged moonstone into a bezel replacing the center boss of the original design when the telephone chirruped from across the room.

Humming a line from "Three Little Girls from School," Julian spun her wheelchair around and headed over to where she had left the portable telephone she habitually kept near her when left alone in the house, for Grace Fyvie, her live-in companion and housekeeper, had gone out to do the shopping. She turned down the stereo before picking up the phone.

"Bonnybank House."

"Julian, it's Adam," said a familiar male voice. "I hope I'm not interrupting anything critical, but have you got a moment or two to spare?"

"For you, my dear Adam, always," she said warmly. "What can I do for you?"

"I'm ringing on Noel's cell phone," came his tense reply. "I need to pick your brain."

"Of course."

His reminder of the need for circumspection, coupled with a friendship that went back to Adam's earliest childhood, warned her that what was to come was not a casual inquiry.

"I've stumbled onto a rather curious artifact that looks as if it must have come from someplace in the Far East," he told her. "Have you ever seen, or do you know anything about, a sort of Oriental dagger with a triple-edged blade and a hilt carved with some kind of grotesque heads?"

Julian's brow narrowed thoughtfully. "This begins to sound familiar. Can you tell me more?"

"I haven't got the exact proportions to offer you," Adam's voice continued, "but I would estimate this thing to be perhaps twelve to fourteen inches long, from pommel to blade-tip. The blade itself is heavy—almost more like a spear-head than a conventional dagger. The hilt reminds me a bit of a North American totem pole in miniature, with a succession of grotesque heads piled on top of one another. Each head seems to have more than one face. I wouldn't call the item at all attractive."

"I see," Julian said, at his pause. "I can't be sure without seeing it, of course, but it sounds not unlike a piece I picked up years ago at a bazaar in Katmandu. I'd like to have a look at mine before I commit myself to an opinion, though; I believe it's languishing on the back of a shelf downstairs. Can I ring you back? I'm afraid I'll lose you when the door closes on the lift."

"That's fine," Adam said. "You have Noel's mobile number, don't you?"

"Yes, I do," she replied. "Give me about ten minutes, and I'll get back to you."

While Adam waited for her return call, gazing distractedly at Peregrine's open sketch pad in his lap, Peregrine himself paced restlessly up and down outside the car. After about five minutes, still with no sign of McLeod, the phone gave a strident ring. Peregrine returned at once as Adam picked it up, leaning down to listen as Adam said, "Yes?"

"It's Julian, dear," came the expected silvery voice. "This dagger we're talking about—what would you say the blade was made of?"

Adam frowned. "I'm not sure; we're working from a sketch. Peregrine, what's the blade made of? Do you know?"

Peregrine shook his head. "Metal, I think. But I can't be more specific than that."

"He says metal," Adam repeated into the phone. "I don't suppose that's much help."

"No." Julian's voice sounded mildly frustrated. "Well, I can't be entirely sure, but judging from what's in my hand, I rather think that the object you're interested in is probably a *Phurba*."

"A *Phurba*?"

"It's a Tibetan ceremonial dagger," Julian explained. "As symbolic items—which most of them are—they're usually made of wood, but the ones created for serious ritual use are supposed to have blades of meteoric iron."

"That's very interesting," Adam said, scribbling a note of the name at the foot of Peregrine's drawing as Peregrine looked on. "When you say 'serious ritual,' what exactly are you talking about?"

"That depends on the practitioner," said Julian. "I've read of some Buddhist sects whose adherents regard *Phurbas* as votive objects. They accord them the same degree of veneration or even worship that Buddhists give to holy paintings and statues, and believe that such an object represents a physical locus for the saint or deity it depicts. On the other hand, there's a more primitive school of *Phurba* worshippers whose practices hark back to the shamanistic traditions that predate Buddhism. Students of this school view *Phurbas* as ceremonial objects to be used in the execution of certain magical rites." She added, "I don't suppose you've been offered one of these for sale?"

"Not exactly," Adam said.

"I see." Julian's tone conveyed an immediate appreciation for the restricted conditions under which he was laboring. "Well, I'm certainly not an authority in this area, but I can put you in touch with someone who is. If you want to know more in detail, you should talk to my old teacher, Lama Tseten *Rinpoche*."

"I sincerely hope you aren't suggesting that I catch the next flight out to Tibet," Adam said with a smile.

"Not at all," Julian assured him with a chuckle. "*Rinpoche* came to this country years ago. You can probably find him at the Samye Ling Tibetan Centre, down in Dumfriesshire."

Adam was familiar with the community's existence. "What's his name again?" he asked.

"Tseten," Julian repeated, and gave him the Anglicized spelling. "*Rinpoche* is the appropriate honorific. It's pronounced Rin-po-shay, and translates roughly as 'precious master.' The name Tseten means 'possessing long life'—a fitting appellation, I might add. He must be nearly a hundred."

"And you say he's down at Samye Ling?"

"He should be. He doesn't see many outside visitors these days, but I expect he could be persuaded to see you. Just mention my name. I'll warn you now, though, that you'll need an interpreter: Tseten speaks only Tibetan. If Tseten himself is unavailable, for whatever reason, I suggest you talk to Lama Jigme, who's a member of the same community. Jigme-la is only in his late thirties, maybe early forties, but he's Tseten's best student, and his English is excellent.''

Adam added the name Jigme to the notes in front of him.

"Thank you for the leads," he told her. "I'll let you know how we get on."

"I shall take that as a promise," she replied. "Take care, my dear."

Adam was finishing the last of several more calls by the time McLeod finally emerged from the police station, tucking a thick sheaf of forms into an inside coat pocket.

"I practically had to sign my life away, but at least we're semiofficial," he said brusquely at Peregrine's look of inquiry. "I also got the map coordinates on the stretch of coast where Scanlan and his mate went missing. What's going on?"

Before the artist could respond, Adam leaned out of the car and offered McLeod the cell phone.

"Why are you giving this to me?" McLeod muttered, adding fatalistically, "Don't tell me, let me guess: You want me to call Jane and tell her I'm not coming home tonight."

"Right the first time, I'm afraid," Adam said, "but I'll tell you what I've learned, before you make the call."

Inviting his two associates to join him in the car, he briefly recounted his conversation with Lady Julian.

"So I've spent the last little while trying to get in touch with at least one of the two men she spoke of," he informed them. "The route was not exactly direct, but I was finally able to get through to this Lama Jigme, who's agreed to see us.

"The bad news is that Jigme's not at home in Dumfriesshire, but out on Holy Island, off Arran, where he's been supervising some conservation work. The good news is that Julian's old master, Tseten, is there on the island as well, though he's on an informal retreat. Once Jigme has heard us out, he'll decide whether or not Tseten should be disturbed on our account. In any event, I've said we'll contrive to meet Jigme tomorrow morning, as early as possible."

"On Holy Island?" Peregrine asked.

''Correct. Which leaves us with the logistics problem of making the rendezvous. It's just past five now. I'm sure we could make the last Arran ferry—at this time of day, it's a couple of hours' drive down to Ardrossan—but aside from that being a bit unfair to Julia, whose honeymoon has already been interrupted, it would involve our trying find accommodation on Arran at very short notice. Under the circumstances, I think it will be better for us to spend the night somewhere on the mainland, with the intention of catching the first ferry out in the morning.''

''When is that?'' McLeod asked.

''Seven o'clock,'' Adam said with a raised eyebrow. ''Which means we ought to plan on being at the dock by no later than six forty-five—which, in turn, means a six-thirty rendezvous. That's why I'm suggesting we not go back to our respective homes for the night. Think you can manage that, Peregrine? Noel and I will find a B & B near the ferry terminal, so you're the one who'll have the really early start, if you're still in Glasgow tonight.''

With a groan, Peregrine settled back in his seat. ''So much for a leisurely breakfast with my wife, with bacon *and* sausage, and fruit scones with butter—''

McLeod choked back a snort and began punching in a number on his cell phone. ''With the breakfasts *and* dinners you've probably been putting away on your wedding trip, old son, I expect you can afford to skip one full breakfast. And at least you'll have the pleasure of your wife's company.''

''Speaking of which,'' Adam added, as McLeod waited for his wife to pick up, ''why don't we take a rain check on that dinner I promised? If I'm going to steal you away from your bride tomorrow, the least I can do is give you back some privacy tonight. Just don't miss the boat in the morning.''

Peregrine pulled a lopsided grin. ''I'll try.''

''Good. The main crossing takes just under an hour and I've been told there'll be a boatman to meet us at Lamlash just after eight o'clock. He'll run us out to Holy Island itself, where, hopefully, someone will be able to give us some of the answers we need.''

CHAPTER TWENTY

"I wonder what the weather's like in the Gulf of Corinth just now," Julia Lovat remarked with a sigh, as she turned west off the A78 the next morning, following the signs for Ardrossan and the Arran Ferry. The early morning sky was gloomy and overcast, with a light mist in the air, and she had the headlights and wipers on.

"Probably clear and balmy," her husband said around a yawn, hunched down in his seat beside her.

"Hmmm, yes." Julia down-shifted to overtake a milk float whose driver had stopped to make a delivery. "I find I have a sudden, unaccountable yearning to eat *baklava* and take a bus tour to Delphi."

The comment stirred Peregrine out of his early morning fog, and he removed his spectacles to rub at his bleary eyes. Despite an excellent meal the night before and a blissful evening spent in the arms of his loving wife, his sleep had been broken by fitful dreams, leaving him with a dull ache in his head and a flat metallic taste in his mouth. The disturbing quality of the dreams themselves was something he intended to take up later with Adam. In the meantime, blinking myopically out at the blustery Scottish dawn, he asked, "Are you regretting we didn't book a cruise of the Aegean?"

"Let's just say that I'm beginning to appreciate Jane McLeod's rationale for insisting that she and Noel take their holiday this year in Tenerife," Julia said. "As I recall, her words were something along the lines of, *The further away from home you go, the less likely you are to be recalled on business.*"

"You may be onto something," Peregrine agreed, yawning again. "The next time we plan a trip, maybe we should consider booking a sailing excursion to the Galapagos Islands, or a hiking expedition through the mountains of Sri Lanka."

"Well, it wouldn't hurt to file those ideas away for future reference," she said, "finances permitting."

"Consider them filed," Peregrine said with a grin that was slightly forced.

He huddled back down in his seat, retiring like a turtle into the bulky warmth of his high-necked Arran pullover.

"Are you sure you don't want to take a couple of paracetamol?" Julia asked, after negotiating a mini-roundabout. "I've got some in my bag."

"I doubt they'd help, but thanks anyway," Peregrine mumbled. "There's nothing wrong with me that won't improve once I've had a chance to wake up."

"I hope you're right about that," she replied, "because we're almost there."

Forcing himself upright, Peregrine put his spectacles back on and scanned ahead. In the gradually brightening gloom, the ferry and its landing loomed ahead against a windswept backdrop of whitecapped water and cloudy sky. The great bow doors of the ship gaped open, and about a dozen vehicles were already lined up on the access ramp in its shadow, including a familiar black BMW toward the end of the queue. Two figures in tan trenchcoats were just getting back into the car, both of them wearing flat tweed caps.

"There they are," he said, pointing, "and I forgot a hat. We'll just have to hope it doesn't bucket, or I'll drown. You can let me out right here."

Julia pulled the Alvis to the curb and stopped, and Peregrine reached over the seat for his waxed jacket and portable sketchbox. As he did so, the diesel-tainted air was riven by the loud hoot of a klaxon horn.

"You'd better hurry," Julia said. "They're starting to board."

Peregrine kissed her hastily on the mouth and scrambled out of the car, shrugging on his waxed jacket.

"Give us till lunch time, then try ringing me up on Noel's cell phone. The number's written down inside the cover of the road atlas. Hopefully by then, we'll know what our afternoon's schedule is going to be like, and I'll be able to suggest a time and place for us to rendezvous. Goodbye! I won't be any longer than I have to!''

'' 'Bye, darling.''

Aching head notwithstanding, Peregrine hurried off down the ramp, weaving his way in and out between the other waiting vehicles. He reached the BMW just as the car ahead was starting to move forward.

"Glad you could join us, Mr. Lovat," McLeod said over his shoulder as Peregrine flung open the back door and piled inside behind them. "You could have cut it a little closer, but not by much."

"Sorry," Peregrine murmured. "I thought I'd allowed plenty of time."

"You did," Adam replied, with a backward glance and a smile. "It's just now quarter to seven. I'm sure we won't leave early."

Peregrine merely nodded. The brief burst of activity had left him feeling slightly lightheaded. He took several deep breaths to steady himself, and was relieved when the pounding in his temples subsided to a dull ache. Mentally praying that this hangover sensation wasn't going to last all day, he gave Julia a wave over his shoulder as McLeod put the car into gear and began easing the BMW down into the shadowy confines of the parking hold.

Since motorists were not allowed on the car deck once the ferry was at sea, there was a general exodus of drivers and passengers toward the motorists' lounge as soon as the cars were secured. Leaving McLeod to join the queue for coffee at the beverage counter, Adam and Peregrine went off to secure a table. Peregrine chose one in a far back corner, dim and away from the rest of the passengers.

"You're looking a bit fragile this morning," Adam observed, taking a good look at his young associate as they settled down to await McLeod's return. "Perhaps you ought to think about getting something more substantial than a cup of coffee."

"I don't think so. The way I feel at the moment, breakfast would just about be the end of me. I spent most of last night having some pretty strange dreams about flying.''

''Something you ate?'' Adam asked lightly, though Peregrine's immediate gesture of denial dashed any hope of the dreams being inconsequential.

''Tell me about the dreams,'' Adam said quietly, his right thumb absently caressing the band of the sapphire ring on his right hand.

Peregrine sighed and leaned a little closer to Adam, resting his elbows on the table as he knit his long fingers together.

''I said *dreams* just now,'' he began, ''but actually it seemed to be just one dream that kept repeating itself all through the night. I kept dreaming I was imprisoned inside a round glass bubble, like a flying fishbowl. The fishbowl was hurtling through the air above a high range of mountains. I remember a loud humming sound, like a hornet's buzz, and the sensation of rushing wind. But nothing more than that seemed to come of it until early this morning, just before I woke up.''

''What was different then?'' Adam prompted.

''On the last recurrence, I caught sight of something new in the distance,'' Peregrine continued. ''It appeared to be some kind of monument on top of a cliff. As I got closer, I could see it was some sort of Oriental shrine with a statue in it. Then, as I got closer still, the statue seemed to come suddenly to life.''

He shivered and slid his hands up his arms as if against a sudden chill.

''It looked up and saw me. The glance it shot my way was like a laser beam. It hit the fishbowl—shattered it like broken crystal—and the next thing I knew, I was falling, plunging straight for the ground. I could see the ground rushing up to meet me, when someone suddenly grabbed me by the arm and called my name loud enough to wake me up.''

He broke off with a wan attempt at a grin. ''It was Julia. Apparently I gave a yelp in my sleep, and she was trying to get my attention to ask me what was wrong. I'm damned glad she did. I've had flying dreams before—and dreams about falling—but this was the first time I've ever really thought I was going to die.''

Another shiver accompanied this last disclosure, and Peregrine bowed his head over his close-clasped arms. If it had been anyone else, Adam might have encouraged him to make light of the whole experience. Where Peregrine was concerned, however, the occurrence of such a vivid dream had the makings of a worrisome development.

"This statue," Adam said thoughtfully, mentally reviewing everything the artist had just told him. "Can you describe what it looked like in any detail?"

"I can do better than that," Peregrine said. "As soon as I was wide enough awake to recover my wits, I sat down and made a sketch. Here, I'll show you."

Hefting his sketchbox up onto the table in front of him, he opened it up and pulled out one of his sketch pads, not opening it until he had set the sketchbox back between his feet. McLeod returned at that moment with three plastic cups of black coffee.

"Peregrine's done a sketch from a rather unpleasant dream he had last night," Adam murmured, taking one of the cups from McLeod as the inspector sat down across from him.

Peregrine flipped his pad open to the appropriate page and set it in front of Adam, then took a second cup of coffee off McLeod's hands.

"Anything familiar about him?" he asked.

Shaking his head, Adam cast his eyes over the figure of a princely male form seated cross-legged on a low throne. It reminded him at once of the votive images to be found amongst the shrines and holy places of India—except that the figure's face was blank. It wore the flowing robes of a *bodhisattva*, the head crowned with a peaked hat reminiscent of a bishop's mitre. But one hand cupped a drinking bowl made from a human skullcap; the other grasped an implement that Adam recognized as a stylized thunderbolt symbol, shaped something like a small, openwork dumbbell with pointed ends. The hands themselves were sheathed in gauntlet-like gloves which, like the robes and the mitre, had been given a watercolor wash of emerald green.

"Interesting," Adam murmured, angling the pad 180 degrees so McLeod could look at it. "Was this figure literally faceless?"

Peregrine frowned. "I don't think so—no. But I didn't

have time to make anything of the features, and I couldn't tell you now what I saw.''

''What made you color in the vestments?''

Peregrine's frown yielded to an expression of perplexity. ''I don't know. It just seemed—important.''

As McLeod wordlessly closed the sketchbook, casting a questioning glance at Adam as he pushed it back in front of Peregrine, Adam clasped his hands before him, the fingers of his left hand cupped over the sapphire on his right.

''Whatever else may be said of this 'dream' of yours,'' he said slowly, ''I think we may safely agree that it was no ordinary nightmare. We'll show the sketch to Lama Jigme, along with our evidence, but I expect he'll confirm that there is some connection. The clothing on the figure is similar to what you sketched before, except for the mitre and the gloves. The human skullcap makes me very uneasy. That's a thunderbolt symbol in the figure's other hand. In Sanskrit, it's called a *vajra*—I think the Tibetan term is *dorje*—and they're usually made of bronze. Both are suggestive of a cultural link, if nothing else, between whoever this individual may be and the kind of weapon used to kill Mick Scanlan.''

Peregrine gave a shudder and cupped his hands around his coffee. ''I was afraid you were going to say something like that,'' he murmured. ''I don't mind telling you, Adam, all this Oriental esoterica makes me more than a little queasy. I mean, I've just started to become reasonably comfortable with Western European magic, and now it looks like I've dragged us into something that *none* of us knows that much about.''

''That's why we're consulting experts,'' Adam replied with a wan smile. ''And I wouldn't say you 'dragged' anyone into anything. It's true that the involvement of the Hunting Lodge stems from your finding of that body at Mull of Kintyre. However, all of us serve as the catalyst for cosmic justice, on occasion; every assignment has to start somewhere. Having become Initiate, it was only a matter of time before you were judged sufficiently advanced to be dragooned directly by our mutual superiors on the Inner Planes.''

Peregrine looked at him a little incredulously.

''Is that meant to be reassuring?''

"Actually, it was," Adam replied, with a glance at McLeod. "Why don't you put your head down and have a bit of a nap until we get to Brodick? I assure you, you'll feel the better for it."

Without even attempting to argue, Peregrine took off his glasses and laid them on the table, slumping forward then to rest his forehead on his crossed forearms. He could feel all his tension and anxiety draining away as Adam's hand came to rest on the back of his neck, as if someone had pulled a plug; and the next thing he knew, that hand was gently kneading his neck and bringing him back to awareness. He could not remember any passage of time or any words spoken.

"Feeling better?" Adam murmured. "It's time to go back to the car. Don't stand up too quickly."

Peregrine found he did feel better as they made their way back down to the car deck, his anxiety largely replaced by eager anticipation. The ferry docked at Brodick a few minutes before eight o'clock. The weather had improved somewhat, but a fine mist still hung on the air, making rain gear desirable. They were off the boat within five minutes, heading south along the coast road, and another five minutes brought them to the harbor at Lamlash, a natural anchorage overlooking the Firth of Clyde, with the Holy Island looming out of the mist a mile beyond. Leaving the BMW in the car park, they made their way along the quay till they located a man in bright orange oilskins, helping hand equipment down to a second man in a large fiberglass dinghy equipped with an outboard motor.

"Morning," the boatman said, eyeing the three of them. "One of you called Sinclair?"

"I'm Sinclair," Adam replied. "I hope we haven't delayed you."

"Not so far," the man replied. "Got any equipment?"

"Just the sketchbox," Adam said, gesturing toward Peregrine.

"Come on aboard, then."

Already on board was a robust-looking bearded man with a Dodgers baseball cap crammed firmly down on his crown of curly black hair. Over the shoulder of his well-worn waxed jacket was a state-of-the-art Japanese camera. The pockets of the olive-drab gadget vest beneath the jacket bulged with auxiliary lenses and filters. A silvery equipment case lay on the deck at his Wellie-shod feet, along with a battered rucksack and a larger-than-average camera tote, out of which protruded the legs of a portable tripod. Next to the tote bag was a large flat box plastered over with notices that read FRAGILE, HANDLE WITH CARE, and THIS END UP. He nodded a tentative greeting to Adam and his companions as the boatman helped them climb down into the dinghy.

"Good morning," Adam responded, taking in the photo equipment. "I hope this mist burns off, or you won't get much in the way of photos."

The man gave a cheerful shrug and pulled off his baseball cap long enough to shake water off it.

"At least it makes for atmosphere," he said. His accent was vaguely Continental. "If you wait for the fine weather, you never get any work done."

"You must be a professional photographer," McLeod said as the boatman came aboard and made his way aft.

Their fellow passenger grinned and nodded, shifting some of his equipment so that everyone could sit. "That I am. The Ford Foundation sent me. The Holy Island Project is in the running for an important conservation award, and the organizers like to have a photo essay on each entry. I was doing some shooting over at Samye Ling yesterday. A fascinating place, very peaceful and serene. The Dalai Lama's speaking there next year. Do you know it?"

"We know *of* it," Adam said neutrally, as the boatman fired up the outboard and the photographer moved forward to cast off the bowline.

"Anyway," the man continued as he sat back down, "when word got around that I'd be coming to the island today, one of the staff asked if I'd mind delivering that." He gestured toward the flat box with a grin.

"What's in it?" Peregrine asked.

"Seedlings." Their informant looked inordinately pleased with himself. "I expect you know that the Buddhists are very ecology-minded. The Samye Ling people are doing a lot of tree-planting on the island—which is where my interest comes in. They hope to reestablish a fruit orchard on the same site where the old Christian monastic community had theirs, over a thousand years ago.''

The buzz of the outboard rendered further conversation difficult, so the four passengers subsided to gaze ahead as the boatman guided his small craft out to a larger vessel moored a hundred yards farther out. There they quickly transferred passengers and equipment to the larger boat, tying the dinghy to the stern before slipping the moorings to head on to the island beyond.

''We could make it in the dinghy,'' the boatman told them, ''but the island's just that far, and the weather's just chancy enough today, that I prefer taking the bigger boat.''

The wind was freshening as the larger boat cut a thin white wake across the steel-colored water, her passengers bracing themselves against railings and stanchions as she made for the rocky, mist-wreathed bulk of the island. Seen up close, Holy Island was even more rugged than it had appeared at a distance, though a shingle beach gentled the rock-bound shore where a jetty thrust a stony finger into the surf. Beyond the jetty, a weather-beaten farmhouse and a beached and battered fishing boat underlined the island's isolation, even though it was only a mile from the greater island of Arran, and less than fifteen from the Scottish coast. The mist lent the scene a surreal timelessness that the photographer, whose name was Thorsen, was already trying to capture on film.

A second short trip in the dinghy proved necessary to bridge the distance between the launch and the jetty. As they approached, Thorsen drew their attention to a splash of yellow-and-blue banner snapping in the wind atop a pole beside the jetty, vivid against the earth colors of the shoreline.

''I'm told that the flag symbolizes the meeting of earth and sky,'' he informed them. ''See the little wave-indentations in the dividing line between the yellow and the blue? And the little flags fluttering along either side of the path to the farmhouse are prayer flags. I gather they're meant to work rather like votive candles in a church.''

Further discussion was curtailed by the physical mechanics of transferring passengers and equipment from the dinghy to the jetty, aided by the brawn of a cheerful, shaven-headed young monk with a thick Glaswegian accent who introduced himself as Gregor. With blithe disregard for sartorial consistency, Gregor was wearing a navy anorak over his skirted robe of deep maroon, with a pair of mud-spattered green Wellie boots on his feet. When he caught sight of the box of seedlings, his wind-burned face lit up in a broad grin.

"Hah! I've been waitin' for these!" he exclaimed, happily hefting the box. "Many thanks for bringing 'em across for us, Mr. Thorsen. We'll try an' see that ye get some braw pictures while ye're here. Now, which one of you other gentlemen is Dr. Sinclair?"

"I am," said Adam. "And these are my associates, Mr. McLeod and Mr. Lovat."

"Ah, guid Scots names, all! It's a pleasure tae meet ye. If ye'll all come with me, I'll get Mr. Thorsen settled an' take the three of ye along tae meet Lama Jigme."

With no apparent effort, he swept the largest of the photographer's bags up onto one broad shoulder and tucked the box of seedlings protectively under the other arm before leading the way up a well-trodden gravel footpath that headed up to the farmhouse. The photographer fell in behind him, also laden with equipment, followed by the three Huntsmen, Peregrine carrying his sketchbox. As they passed between the rows of prayer flags flanking the path, Peregrine noted that some of the paper shapes were in the form of small horses imprinted with mandala-like designs in Tibetan script.

"They're called wind-horses," Adam said in an undertone, not wishing to deflate the photographer's earlier identification of the items, if he overheard. "It's believed that the fluttering of the breeze brings them to life, so they can carry the prayers inscribed upon them to their intended destinations."

"I wish I had time to sketch some of them," Peregrine murmured, continuing on at Adam's side, close behind McLeod. "This whole place has an incredible feel to it. If I could stop to concentrate for a moment, I'm sure I could resolve layers and layers of co-existent resonances, past and present. And oddly enough, they're all in harmony with what's happening now."

"Apparently the Oriental mysteries don't seen quite so daunting as they did back on the ship," Adam said with a droll smile.

"Maybe not." Peregrine cast a glance ahead at the shaven head of their guide. "Some of this is very different, but maybe what was bothering me has to do with why we're here—not the place itself. There's no question that this *is* a holy island."

"No, indeed," Adam replied softly.

Up ahead, perhaps as many as a dozen men and women in the more conventional work attire of jeans, Wellie boots, bright-colored parkas, and wooly hats were dispersing from the farmhouse. Several of them also sported the traditional maroon robes and shaven head favored by their guide. One of the shaved heads belonged to a woman. Most of them carried scythes, billhooks, and other cutting implements.

"They're goin' out tae cut rhododendron," Gregor remarked over his shoulder. "It turns into a weed if ye dinnae keep after it. It'll choke out everything else."

"I'm familiar with the problem," Adam replied with a smile. "My gardener fights the constant battle, along with the battle of the ivy. Are those all members of your community?"

"Hmmm, more like temporary lay members," Gregor allowed. "They're mostly conservation volunteers, here tae help with one of our reforestation projects. These are Scottish oak and whitebeam Mr. Thorsen's brought. They'll go in the old monastic orchard we're restorin'. There's a hellish amount of work to be done, but it's goin' to be worth it, to see the island come alive again." He grinned. "Come back again in five years, an' you'll scarce recognize the place."

As they approached the house, a faint sound of hammering grew gradually more distinct. Its source became immediately apparent as they came abreast of a sheltered side yard, where an energetic knot of workers were busy cobbling together a new weather stoop above an open side door.

When no one noticed their arrival, the Glaswegian monk stepped just inside the yard and gave a high, sweet whistle to attract their attention above the din of hammers. The hammering stopped and five pairs of eyes tracked to the sound. Four of them belonged to Westerners of assorted ages, several sporting shaggy beards, but the fifth carpenter, helping shoulder a heavy support beam into place, was a youngish-looking monk who resembled photos Adam had seen of the Dalai Lama as a young man.

"Ah, Gregor, I see our visitors have arrived," the monk said, gold-wire spectacles catching the light as he yielded his place to another and headed toward them, dusting off his hands. In common with the man who had just hailed him, he wore an open smile and a navy anorak over his maroon robe, though his Wellie boots were lemon-yellow.

"This is Mr. Thorsen, come to shoot those photos, Jigme-la," Gregor announced with a grin, sketching a bow that conveyed a mixture of affection and respect. "He's also brought the seedlings from Samye Ling."

"And we thank him for it," the monk replied, favoring Thorsen with a smile and a nod. His pleasantly modulated voice carried but a trace of an accent. "Welcome to Holy Island, Mr. Thorsen. I am Lama Jigme. We are very pleased to have you with us."

"I'm very pleased to be here, sir," Thorsen replied, raising his voice as the hammering resumed. "I'll try not to get in anyone's way."

"Not to worry." Jigme gave an apologetic shrug toward the intruding noise. "Please feel free to stay as long as you like. You've met the incomparable Gregor; he is one of my more promising students. He will show you to your quarters and see that you have anything else you may require that we can provide. I give you notice that he is one of our most knowledgeable conservation enthusiasts. May I suggest that, as an introduction to our work here, you allow him to give you a complete tour."

"Thank you, sir. I'd like that."

"Excellent. I shall look forward to seeing you again this afternoon."

As Gregor took Thorsen and his equipment into the house, Jigme turned a discerning gaze to his remaining guests, shrewd black eyes singling out Adam.

"You must be Dr. Sinclair," he declared, extending a hand in Western greeting. "I apologize for the distraction. Welcome to all of you."

Adam inclined his head and bowed slightly over the la-ma's slender hand.

"It's a pleasure to meet you in person, Jigme-la. These

are the associates I mentioned in speaking with you yesterday: Detective Chief Inspector Noel McLeod, of the Lothian
and Borders Police, and Mr. Peregrine Lovat, who frequently
assists us in his capacity as an artist.''

Peregrine found himself under close but friendly scrutiny
as Jigme turned from McLeod to shake his hand. Something
in the other man's aspect encouraged him to return that regard. A host of compound images blossomed before his eyes,
serenely unfolding before him like the petals of a lotus
flower, begging to be sketched. Then Jigme returned his gaze
to Adam, and all the manifold images coalesced into the
single image of a simple Buddhist monk, not nearly as young
as Peregrine had first supposed.

''I believe a cup of tea might be in order, to thaw out the
chill after your boat ride,'' Jigme said easily, gesturing toward the farmhouse. ''Please come inside, and we shall see
what can be organized.''

Leading them inside, he spoke briefly to a ginger-headed
man with a beard before continuing up a flight of wooden
stairs, beckoning them to follow. He shed his anorak as they
climbed, revealing a sleeveless gold jacket over his maroon
skirt. Upstairs, passing a closed door bearing a color poster
of the Dalai Lama, Adam saw Peregrine do a double take.

''This way, please,'' Jigme said, ushering them into an
alcove off a tidy landing, where a pair of stripped-pine
benches flanked another closed door.

Here Jigme paused to hang his anorak on one of several
wooden pegs above the benches, courteously inviting his
guests to shed hats, coats, and shoes as he sat to remove his
yellow Wellies. Before ushering them into the room beyond,
he wrapped himself around in a toga-like maroon mantle,
which he drew up over one shoulder.

''I hope you don't mind sitting on the floor,'' he said,
switching on an overhead light and bending to hand out flat
red cushions from a stack just inside the door.

Entering, Peregrine's first impression was one of orderly
simplicity. Pale straw matting covered most of the floor—
new, by the fresh smell of it. Everything was scrupulously
clean, the walls newly whitewashed where they were not
adorned with paintings of various Buddhas. One corner was

dominated by the presence of a graceful bronze Buddha seated in an attitude of serene contemplation on a low stand in the form of a blossoming lotus.

On the floor before the statue stood a bronze incense burner, a yellow votive light set on a rectangle of native slate, and a bronze bowl brimming with the purple and yellow of heather and gorse. The room itself carried a subtle fragrance of jasmine and wild honeysuckle. Though Peregrine found many of the images somewhat strange to his Western eyes, the peace prevailing in the room made him feel oddly at home.

Jigme had closed the door behind them, and now moved into the center of the room to plop his cushion down and sit cross-legged, inviting them to do the same. They did, Peregrine and McLeod sinking down to Adam's left and right. Though Peregrine again felt the urge to sketch their host, he merely laid his sketchbox at his left side, ready to produce their evidence to Jigme at the appropriate time. While they waited for their tea, Jigme offered a casual commentary about the room's function as a meditation chamber.

Very shortly, the ginger-haired man from downstairs brought in a wooden tray supporting four mismatched china mugs. The rich aroma of Darjeeling tea wafted upwards as, to an accompanying murmur of thanks, he deposited the tray at Jigme's left elbow and then departed, closing the door behind him.

"Please forgive the informality," Jigme said, as he distributed steaming mugs all around, "but our accommodations here are still a bit primitive. Jasmine tea is the traditional offering to guests, but I thought you might prefer something more substantial. I hope you don't mind it black."

"Not at all," Adam replied. "We're grateful for any consideration."

The gentle reminder of why they were there was acknowledged by a graceful inclination of Jigme's head. Raising his mug slightly in salute, he sipped from it cautiously, then set it on the matting at his feet to cool.

"Very well, Dr. Sinclair," he said quietly. "You indicated yesterday that you desired guidance on a matter of grave concern, and invoked the name of a well-loved student of my master, Tseten *Rinpoche*. Please acquaint me with this matter, so that I may advise him."

CHAPTER TWENTY-ONE

S OME eight hundred miles to the southwest, high in the
Swiss Alps, dawn had broken bright and clear, the
sharply angled rays of the rising sun striking fire off snow-
covered peaks that towered up like islands out of a sea of
milk. As the light broadened, the pulsing, mechanical drone
of a helicopter intruded on the early morning silence, carrying four passengers toward the remote Buddhist monastery
of Tolung Tserphug. Come from as far as Grenoble this
morning, after overnighting near there, the sleek executive
craft lifted up and over a summit pierced by a railway tunnel,
then veered eastward to follow a spur off one of the major
Euroroutes.

Mid-morning saw the red and white chopper climbing
once again, skirting the steel pylons of a modern funicular
railway. At the top of the mountain it served lay the clustered
roofs and frowning walls of the monastery. Here the chopper
circled once, its pilot gauging the updrafts by the flags flying
from the compound's many flagstaffs, then settled gently on
an expanse of alpine meadow outside the massively wrought
outer gateway.

As soon as the landing skids grounded, the door on the
passenger side of the cabin swung open. First to alight was
Francis Raeburn, his elegantly cut navy suit only slightly
creased after two days of travel, his fine, fair hair riffling in
the wash of the slowing rotor. Behind him, the men who had
become his keepers disembarked in a more leisurely fashion,
impassive as a pair of bronze statues.

Leaving Barclay to shut down the engine and secure the

chopper, Raeburn drew a deep lungful of the cold, pure air and looked around him, using this brief respite to get his bearings as he compared the citadel of the present day with his memories of thirty years before.

Designedly remote, the place had always been impressive, as much a fortress as a spiritual retreat. The concentric complex of buildings was perched on the brink of a precipice, alien to this part of the world yet somehow at one with the soaring vastness of such heights.

As a former inmate of the establishment's inner circle, Raeburn was in a position to appreciate how seamlessly the dual nature of the monastery had been integrated in outward appearance, with the casual visitor never the wiser. The outer bailey, with its communal residence halls, meditation cells, library, and reading and tutorial rooms, provided a scholarly environment in which innocent seekers from the outside world could acquaint themselves with the language and religious teachings of Tibet.

But beyond the shared opulence of the great temple, where anyone might sample Tolung Tserphug's public teachings, lay the guarded precincts of the inner court, adytums of sorcery where the darker, more seductive mysteries of black Tibetan magic were fostered on a far smaller number of carefully chosen initiates.

That much would not have changed since Raeburn's day, though technology had left its mark. Privileged to view the whole of the compound from the air as they came in, he had been interested to note an array of highly sophisticated telecommunications equipment on the roof of the abbot's residence, discreetly masked behind parapets and towers. The residence itself had been significantly enlarged since Raeburn's last visit, and embellished as well with a gilded roof to rival that of the temple.

Which did not surprise Francis Raeburn. Siegfried Hasselkuss had always cherished an inordinately high regard for his own importance.

A sonorous horn-call jarred Raeburn from his reflections, heralding a stirring of motion beneath the groined and shadowed arch of the monastery's entrance. Impelled by invisible hands, the heavy iron gate swung ponderously open on a small contingent of orange-clad monks, who emerged on the alpine meadow and began heading toward the helicopter with purpose. They arrived just as Barclay was lifting down the bags from the chopper's cockpit, one of them wordlessly taking the bags from him and two more setting their hands beneath his elbows to begin chivvying him toward the monastery entrance. The remaining two exchanged bows and a few murmured words in Tibetan with Raeburn's escorts.

"Stop a moment," Raeburn said sharply, catching the alarmed look Barclay cast back at him. "Where are you taking my pilot?"

"You need not be alarmed," said the eldest of the newly arrived monks, though a hand was on the *Phurba* thrust through the front of his belt. "Your servant will be taken along to the dining hall and offered refreshment after his labors. Thereafter he may sleep, if he desires. He will be returned to you in due course, once Dorje *Rinpoche* has spoken with you."

"I see." Raeburn did not bother to hide his irritation. "And when might that be?"

"*Rinpoche* will see you at once," said the second new monk, who also bore a *Phurba*, but on a cord across his breast, so that it hung beneath his left arm almost like a shoulder holster. "If you will please accompany us, we will take you to him."

Though the request was civil enough, it was not an invitation but a command. Seeing little choice but to comply, Raeburn allowed himself to be escorted inside the compound between Nagpo and Kurkar, old resentments fanned by the new presumption of the past twenty-four hours.

Beyond the gate lay an open courtyard paved with cobblestones, dominated by the temple with its golden pagoda roof. In keeping with Tibetan architectural design, the angles of all the buildings fronting the courtyard were trapezoidal rather than square, with stone walls sloping inward from a broad base. The effect was both exotic and benign, designed to foster the illusion that in entering Tolung Tserphug, the beholder was effectively turning his back on the fleeting present in favor of an ageless past.

But it was the immediate future that concerned Raeburn

now, as a touch at his elbow reminded him of his vulnerability as a most reluctant guest. Avoiding the broad, flag-decked approach to the temple steps, his escorts turned him instead up a narrow passage between two lesser edifices, passing then through a succession of two more open courtyards to emerge before the great gateway that gave access to inner sanctums, where the senior members of the community were accustomed to hold court.

He gazed up at the gateway with something like respect while one of his escort spoke in rapid Tibetan with the keeper of the gate. It was fashioned in the form of the Tibetan monument known as a *chorten*, this one a conscious imitation of the gatehouse guarding the entrance to the holy city of Lhasa. Like its Lhasan counterpart, this entrance embraced a square, block-like chamber, perforated by an archway and surmounted by a dome and spire. But where the Lhasan spire was crowned with a crescent moon surrounded by flames, betokening purity, the spire of this gateway was capped with a lightning bolt wreathed in clouds of thunder, a device which initiates of many different paths would recognize as a potent symbol of death and destruction.

Nor was the destructive potential vested in the gateway merely symbolic. Raeburn required no special effort of perception to sense the brooding energies emanating from the mouth of the arch, like exhalations from a dragon's lair. Sufficiently well schooled to recognize the nature of the forces at work, he was equally well acquainted with the measures necessary to counter them—though he had no intention of making a gratuitous display of his capabilities, thereby betraying his strength to his monkish guardians. On the contrary, the less Siegfried knew about what he had become, the better. Whatever else might transpire in the course of the next little while, Raeburn intended to retain the element of surprise in his own favor.

At a gesture of command from the gate's keeper, the power in the gateway smoothly shifted, like a veil being parted, and Raeburn's attendants hurried him through. Beyond a vaulted and lamplit corridor lay a windowless antechamber where he was instructed to remove his shoes and coat and don one of the toga-like orange mantles worn by all the other inhabitants of the place. The concession told him that he still had some standing here, despite his thirty-year absence. Once he had completed this change of attire, only Nagpo and Kurkar ushered him through another doorway onto a stone landing at the top of a descending spiral of broad stone steps.

He followed his escorts downward. Only once before, as a youth of sixteen, had he been privileged to come so far. After the initiation that followed, the last he had been allowed, his dreams had been haunted by images, simultaneously frightful and fascinating, of endless shadowy corridors full of lurking half-seen entities that knew no fixed form. Returning here now as an adult, veteran of many initiations in many dark traditions, he found those impressions both enhanced and clarified in the light of knowledge since acquired.

A doorway at the foot of the stair gave access to a maze of interconnecting passageways, the entrance guarded on either hand by a large triple-edged wooden dagger, taller than a man, supported point-downward in triangular mountings of meteoric iron. The faces carved around the hilts leered down at them in malevolent scrutiny, the eyes almost alive in the flickering light of butter lamps set in niches beside them.

Reverently, both Nagpo and Kurkar paused to salute each of the daggers in turn, raising both arms over their heads before pressing palms together and touching fingertips lightly to forehead, throat, and heart. As the two stepped through the doorway and beckoned him to follow, Raeburn performed the salute as protection rather than devotion, also drawing upon his own resources for reinforcement, for though not himself a dagger practitioner, he knew enough to recognize the force behind the dagger symbols as a focus of dangerous power. The initiation he had taken so long ago might preserve his life within the maze, but Dorje *Rinpoche* had never allowed him to receive the further empowerments that would have allowed him to function freely within the web of power he now entered.

He followed Nagpo and Kurkar into the maze. As he and his escort penetrated deeper, Raeburn became increasingly aware of the menacing presence of manifold dark energies, subliminally held in check beyond the bounds of conventional perception. Lengthening exposure and the mastery of parallel disciplines made him aware that the agency restraining those energies was the design of the labyrinth itself, the walls of which had been laid out in the form of a Tantric ideogram.

The forces thus channelled represented a formidable defense against any form of unauthorized intrusion, and set up a subtle interference that would make it difficult to initiate any action in opposition to its focus. Resigning himself to a passive role in the coming encounter, at least magically, Raeburn set his mind to keeping all the flexibility it could, as the bonds of the maze drew more closely around him.

A bewildering sequence of doublings and turnings brought them in due course to a different doorway than the one he had essayed in his only other visit to this place. Like the greater doorway, this one was likewise flanked by a pair of massive votive daggers. What most unsettled him, however, as he made his ritual salute and passed between them, was that the pommels crowning the two giant hilts were carved in the form of four *makara* serpents knotted together in the shape of a swastika.

There were more swastikas in the room beyond—a square stone chamber palely lit by an assemblage of butter lamps, fuming like burning chalices in niches ranged round about the walls. Between the niches, long, narrow banners of emerald-green silk hung in static cascades from ceiling to floor, each one charged with a white roundel overlaid by a black swastika in the form of two interlocking S's.

But the focus of the room was not the swastikas or the banners or even the green-draped dais that dominated the center; it was the figure seated amid a scattering of flat silk cushions, who clearly was master in this place. Raeburn would have known him anywhere, even after more than a quarter century.

And there was no mistaking that it was Abbot Dorje *Rinpoche*, not Siegfried Hasselkuss, who presided from the dais. In the years since Raeburn last had seen him, his old rival even seemed to have acquired an Oriental cast to his features, so striking as to suggest surgical enhancement beyond the illusion fostered by the shaven head and exotic attire—though the skin was still Nordic-pale, and he had not gone so far as to disguise the blue of his eyes. The illusion was strong enough to suggest that there was something to the old rumors, always discounted in the past: that not only had Siegfried Hasselkuss been *Lebensborn*, racially pure offspring of an SS officer embodying the Aryan ideal and a mother of similarly impeccable pedigree, but he had been deliberately conceived as a fitting vessel to receive the soul of the dying monk carrying the appellation Green Gloves.

The current bearer of this title, if not the dark force behind it, was presently arrayed in vestments befitting his station: a sleeveless jacket of cloth-of-gold over a black brocaded *chuba*, the whole accentuated by a mantle of brocaded green silk, a mitre-like hat, and a pair of gauntlet-cuffed green gloves. On a chased silver tray at his right hand reposed a teapot of translucent Fukien porcelain together with an attendant pair of eggshell-thin drinking bowls, each lidded with jade-inlaid gold. Scented steam, wafting up from the spout of the teapot, mingled lazily with the gauzy tendrils of perfumed smoke emanating from an incense-burner of enamelled bronze. The blended fragrance was subtly redolent of opium.

Advancing with Raeburn to the foot of the dais, the monks Nagpo and Kurkar paid their master the profound obeisance befitting a *tulku*—a lama of the highest rank—reminding Raeburn that, however improbable it might seem to Western minds, this scion of the Master Race commanded the unswerving loyalty of his followers here at Tolung Tserphug as Abbot Dorje *Rinpoche*, the recognized current incarnation of the legendary Man with Green Gloves. In acknowledgement of Dorje's temporal authority within these walls, Raeburn sank to both knees and inclined his head stiffly, but it was no gesture of homage of his own. He waited without speaking until the monks had received their master's gesture of dismissal and withdrawn. Only then did he counter the silent scrutiny of the man on the dais with a bland smile.

"Hello, Siegfried," he ventured, continuing in German, "It's been a while."

The use of his German name brought a flicker of displeasure to the abbot's ice-blue eyes.

"Absence has done little to mend your manners," he said

coldly, in the same language. "I shall thank you to remember to whom you are speaking."

Raeburn inclined his head again, carefully correct, but bordering on insolence. "Of course, *Rinpoche*. You must forgive me if I indulge in nostalgia. Not having been present to witness the crowning glory of your ascendancy, when you reached your majority, I still find it a trifle difficult at times to forget past associations."

The abbot's classically Nordic features hardened. "Do not think to trifle with me, Gyatso. My patience is short-lived when it comes to dealing with men who so consistently fail to reckon with their own limitations."

"Are you objecting to my lack of humility? I've always rather fancied that was one of my more useful qualities," Raeburn said.

"Perhaps you should consider discarding that illusion," the abbot said coldly. "Certainly your handling of that affair in the Cairngorms was nothing to boast about."

Raeburn levelled a reproachful look at his accuser. "Am I to be blamed for the mistakes of my betters, *Rinpoche*? You know yourself that the Head-Master had become the very soul of obstinacy, drunk with his own visions of power. If his authority exceeded his judgement, surely that is no fault of mine. On the contrary, perhaps if I had been accorded a greater degree of autonomy—"

"Enough!" The abbot cut him short with a curt, chopping motion of the hand. "I did not summon you here to bandy words. We are prepared to overlook the failure in question, provided that you perform for us a service for which you have been selected, and for which you should prove adequately qualified."

Raeburn's pale eyes showed a new glint of wariness.

"This is all rather sudden, after thirty years. What sort of service did you have in mind?"

CHAPTER TWENTY-TWO

BACK on Holy Island, Lama Jigme listened without comment, his tea long grown cold, while Adam unfolded the mysterious and troubling circumstances surrounding the death of Michael Scanlan. Having produced Peregrine's photographs and the Nazi flag, he then allowed McLeod to describe and to review the forensic findings from Scanlan's post-mortem and to review what Somerville had researched concerning *U-636*. Finally, Peregrine presented his various sketches, including the green-washed study based on his dream of the night before, and reiterated what he had described to Adam on the ferry earlier.

The three of them waited in silence while Jigme examined each of the items in turn, absently fingering an edge of the flag while he studied Peregrine's photos and drawings. A silence settled over the room, broken only by a faint clatter of domestic noises from other parts of the house. The monk's dark eyes were troubled as he set the flag aside and raised his gaze to his visitors.

"You were very right to come here, gentlemen," he announced gravely. "Apart from this flag—whose connection I must confess escapes me—all the other evidence you have shown me points to a debased and evil offshoot of that branch of Tibetan spiritual practice sometimes labelled 'dagger magic.' Some say it is pre-Buddhist in its origins—and in the wrong hands, even anti-Buddhist."

He indicated Peregrine's drawing of the falling Scanlan and the detail of the triple-edged blade piercing his back.

"Central to Tibetan dagger magic is the *Phurba* itself,"

the lama continued, "a blade endowed with mystical properties. The name can mean 'flyer' or 'rocket.' Amongst legitimate adherents to our doctrines, such daggers are relatively common as objects of devotion. Allow me to show you one."

Rising nimbly to his feet, he went to the Buddha figure in the corner and removed from behind it a bundle wrapped in soft folds of maroon silk brocade. This he unwrapped as he came back to sink down again before them, handling it through the silk as he displayed it for their scrutiny.

Like the dagger Peregrine had sketched, this one had a heavy, tapering blade of three edges. The hilt was likewise adorned with an assortment of grotesque demon-faces all around, whose ferocity sent a shiver up Peregrine's spine.

Their host did not offer the *Phurba* for hands-on inspection. Instead, still grasping the hilt through the silk, he gave the blade a light fillip with a fingernail. The response was a bright metallic chime. Jigme's expression as he laid the blade in his lap was slightly abstracted, as if he were listening for some distant echo.

"It is said that a blade possessing true power rings true to the music of the cosmos," he murmured softly, "and that the resonances that it makes are songs in praise of the Adibuddha."

"The Adibuddha?" Adam repeated softly in question.

"It is what we call the supreme source of all knowledge and truth, common to all Buddhist sects." Jigme smiled wistfully. "A Westerner might liken the blade's song to 'the music of the spheres.' "

"Ah," Adam breathed with a nod, though Peregrine found himself squirming uneasily.

"But the faces on the hilt are so—grotesque," the artist murmured.

"And aptly so," Jigme replied, "for they are meant to symbolize the wrathful destruction of delusion and evil. The blades themselves, of course, are morally neutral to start with, being creations of human beings. Their subsequent affinity for either good or evil comes about as the result of the interaction that takes place between the mind of the meditator and the intent toward which the practice is addressed."

"You speak of a tool, then," Adam said, "neutral in itself but usable in a variety of contexts."

"Yes, but it is more than that," Jigme replied. "To those who embrace the Dagger Cult, the *Phurba* is both an object and a meditational framework. We would call it a deity, but that term does not have quite the same meaning for us that it has in a Western perspective. In righteous hands, the *Phurba* can be a powerful force for good; turned to evil, a formidable weapon. Even His Holiness the Dalai Lama recognizes the *Phurba* practice. He is known to have a *Phurba* lama in his entourage," Jigme conceded.

"Then, these—dagger practitioners are within mainstream Buddhism?" McLeod asked.

"That is correct."

"Interesting," Adam murmured. "Then despite our evidence to the contrary, we must infer that in its optimal form, dagger practice is benign; if it weren't, the great lamas certainly would have nothing to do with it. Could you perhaps tell us more about its basic tenets?"

"Of course." Jigme's graceful hands gently turned the *Phurba* as he went on. "In the eyes of those who have received the teachings, *Phurbas* embody the active aspect of intrinsic awareness or enlightened mind. To more primitive believers, the *Phurba* constitutes a tool for the procurement of good fortune. This latter view is based upon the notion held by some that all forms of bad luck and unhappiness are caused by demons. By contrast, happiness and good luck are to be secured through the intercession of one who uses a *Phurba* in the enactment of special rituals designed to drive away or liberate the demons in question."

He paused to survey each of his visitors in turn. "You may notice that I avoid using the word 'kill.' This is because we believe that even demons belong to that broad category of sentient beings whom the Lord Buddha forbids us to harm, for all deserve our compassion."

"So, you don't—'kill' the demons?" Peregrine asked tentatively—though it occurred to him that Adam had not killed the demons guarding the Templar treasure.

A wry smile touched Jigme's lips. "I must admit that the distinction may be largely a semantic one. We use the term *sGrol,* 'to liberate,' rather than *sBad,* 'to kill.' The intention is to destroy only the bad qualities of the demon, thus liberating its intrinsic awareness into a higher realm.''

''Rather like the apostle Paul exhorting his followers to die to sin in order to be reborn into new life,'' Adam offered.

Jigme nodded approvingly. ''An apt analogy, in Western terms. To destroy only the entity's bad qualities is taken to be an act of Special Compassion. Liberating through compassion in this way is neither killing—an act of anger—nor suppression, the consequence of ignorance. I must confess, however, that my own experience with this fine distinction is mostly academic. I am more familiar with the aspects of *Phurba* having to do with protection.''

''Is that what the Dalai Lama's *Phurba* priest does?'' McLeod asked. ''Protection?''

The wry smile returned to Jigme's lips. ''I believe the priest in question sometimes performs workings for propitious weather. In Tibet, dagger men are also sometimes called hail-masters, because of their ability to avert hailstorms that could ruin crops. If this application seems a bit primitive,'' he went on with a trace of whimsy, ''it is also an indication of its antiquity. The first traces of the *Phurba* are said to occur at least a thousand years before the coming of the Lord Buddha—fifteen hundred years before the beginning of the Christian era—and not entirely in the Orient. Ritual daggers similar to this one have been found among the ruins of ancient Mesopotamia, in what is now called Iraq. It has been suggested that such implements were driven into the ground to mark out boundaries within which demons might not venture.''

''A form of warding?'' Adam asked.

''In a sense, perhaps,'' Jigme allowed. ''I have heard it said that these early ritual daggers are perhaps related to the pegs by which nomadic peoples anchor their tents to the ground.''

''The logic follows,'' Adam said. ''A three-edged metal tent-peg has obvious advantages over a wooden one, in that you can drive it into stony ground and keep it anchored against wind and weather.''

''Precisely,'' Jigme agreed, rewrapping the *Phurba* and

laying it aside. "And of course, iron and the working of it have long had their association with magic. Given the vast superiority of iron tools and weapons over bronze, small wonder that the first smiths who learned to extract the iron from its ore and forge it were viewed as magicians. In many parts of the world, blacksmiths still retain something of their ancient mystique. I should point out, however, that certain types of *Phurba* are still made out of wood, if they are meant to mark boundaries or serve as votary objects rather than as instruments for subduing demons."

"But it wasn't any wooden dagger that killed that fisheries officer we've been telling you about," McLeod pointed out.

"Indeed not." Jigme's tone matched the seriousness of his expression as he picked up one of Peregrine's photos. "And the fact that the attack was fatal proves beyond all shadow of a doubt that these dagger-wielders are operating outside the pale of our beliefs. No orthodox Buddhist would countenance the deliberate killing of another sentient being. The true perversion of those you seek is that they have exchanged the intended destruction of evil for the *promotion* of evil.

"The presence of this flag likewise troubles me deeply," he went on, not touching it as he laid the photo aside again. "While I myself was born too recently to have any personal memory of the Second World War, no one living and working in the West today could be wholly ignorant of the monstrous evils that were committed against mankind under the aegis of flags like this one. As for the possibility of a German submarine secreted in an Irish sea cave—"

He broke off with a deprecatory shake of his head. "I feel certain that Tseten *Rinpoche* will wish to see you," he announced, taking up the *Phurba*, then gathering up the flag along with Peregrine's sketches and photos. "You, in particular, Dr. Sinclair. In addition to these properties which make up the evidence of your case, may I presume upon you for the loan of some personal item that *Rinpoche* might handle? I believe I need not tell you why."

Without hesitation, Adam removed his Adept ring and handed it over, much to the shocked astonishment of McLeod and Peregrine.

"Thank you," Jigme said, bowing over the ring in his

closed hand. "I will return as soon as I may—certainly within an hour. In the meantime, please make yourselves comfortable. If you wish more tea, or there is anything else you require, just give a call and someone will assist you."

So saying, the young lama got to his feet and retired from the room. As the door closed behind him and his retreating footsteps died away, McLeod turned to Adam, his expression one of mingled shock and apprehension.

"Adam, your ring—" he said in a rare show of hesitation.

"It's all right," Adam assured him. "Believe me, I know exactly what I'm doing."

"But—I hope so," McLeod muttered, with a dubious shake of his head. "That ring of yours is probably the single most powerful psychic link to you that exists in physical form. If it were ever to fall into the wrong hands—"

"It won't. At least not through the offices of anyone here," Adam said firmly. "Don't be in any way misled by our host's youthful appearance, Noel. Even though Jigme may personally consider himself far short of his master's achievements, he's very advanced—a very old soul. And as for Tseten *Rinpoche*—"

He paused. "Gentlemen, we may well be about to be granted audience with a Buddhist saint."

Leaving the farmhouse behind him, clad again in boots and anorak, Lama Jigme set out briskly along a grassy footpath that soon changed to mud. Over his shoulder was slung a green canvas satchel containing the *Phurba* and all the items entrusted to him by Adam Sinclair. The mist was turning to rain, spattering his spectacles, and he squinted slightly against it.

The path meandered gently along the shoreline, gradually climbing, flanked with flowering gorse and patches of swaying sea grass. After following the path for nearly a mile, and surprising an Eriskay pony and her foal, he came upon a square outcropping in the rocks to his left, where a rough course of stone steps led upward to a slash-like horizontal opening in the face of the cliff.

Hitching up the skirts of his robe, Jigme clambered swiftly

up the steps toward the cave mouth. Below a sandstone cliff overhang, more stone steps descended into one end of a roughly crescent-shaped cave, perhaps ten feet wide and thirty feet long. Several feet beyond the bottom of the stair, on a straw mat rolled out on the floor of the cave, a bright-eyed and venerable figure in maroon robes and a red anorak looked up expectantly. Dark eyes sought and held Jigme's for a moment as the younger man gave a sign of respect, penetratingly keen amid a matrix of wrinkles. At once their owner wordlessly signalled the other man to approach.

Jigme paused to slip out of his muddy boots before hunkering down on the mat in front of his elder, bright red socks briefly flashing beneath him. Divesting himself of the green canvas satchel, he delved into it to produce Peregrine's photos and sketches, including his dream-sketch of the man in green vestments. To these items he added the Nazi flag.

The old man fingered each of the properties in turn, though he avoided the flag. His face darkened as he allowed his regard to linger for a moment or two over the drawing of the man in green. The flag he did not need to touch. When he had withdrawn briefly into silent meditation, he looked up expectantly at Jigme, who presented him with Adam's ring.

With a gentle exhalation, the old lama enfolded the ring in one graceful, fine-boned hand and bowed his head over it for a long moment. As he did so, his lined face underwent a change, one eyebrow lifting in thoughtful speculation. He gave his younger counterpart a wordless nod as he emerged from his short reverie.

Jigme acknowledged the unspoken message with a respectful bow, folded hands touched to his forehead, before rising to his feet and stepping back into his boots, departing the way he had come.

Jigme was absent for the better part of three-quarters of an hour. The waiting weighed heavily on Peregrine, but Adam appeared relaxed and composed, evidently confident of the outcome of Jigme's inquiries. After assuring his colleagues of Jigme's benign intent, Adam swivelled round to contemplate the graceful Buddha figure in the corner of the room, open palms cupped one atop the other between his splayed knees, and soon eased into a meditative trance. Though such composure eluded Peregrine, he tried to at least follow McLeod's example, either dozing or also meditating, head nodding over clasped hands; but as the minutes ticked ponderously away, the young artist found it increasingly difficult to hide his own impatience.

At length, unable to keep still, he got to his feet and wandered over to the room's one window, which looked out toward the north of the island. The sky was glowering, and a light rain blurred the vista of rocky heights and wind-sculpted trees and shrubs. To keep his hands from fidgeting, he thrust them into his trouser pockets—and encountered the cool metallic shape of his own Adept ring. As he surreptitiously slipped it on, he realized that McLeod had done the same. He could not decide whether he found that dismaying or encouraging.

Just when Peregrine was beginning to think he could bear the suspense no longer, his straining ears heard the front door open and close, followed by the sound of footsteps coming up the stairs. As all three men turned toward the doorway, it swung open to reveal Lama Jigme, now empty-handed, clad for the weather outside. He carried with him the outdoor scents of sea salt and wild heather, and his face held an odd mixture of satisfaction and concern.

"*Rinpoche* has agreed to see you," he announced. "He invites you to attend him at once at Saint Molaise's cave. I'm afraid it's almost a mile from here, but the trip will be worth your trouble. The accumulated power of many centuries of holy men has made it a secure retreat where you and he may speak freely, without fear of any intrusion from outside."

Adam was already on his feet, eager yet composed.

"We'll come at once," he told Jigme. "Thank you very much."

They donned their shoes and outerwear in silence, McLeod and Peregrine exchanging uneasy glances as they followed Jigme and Adam down the stairs. Outside, a stiff breeze had risen to accompany the rain, tugging at hats and coats as they set out southward along the grassy coastal footpath. After half a mile, a leftward bend to the path revealed a distant gleam of white thrusting upward from a far promontory.

''The old lighthouse,'' Jigme noted, gesturing in that direction as they negotiated a patch of mud. ''When funding permits, we plan to refurbish the keeper's house as part of the retreat facilities. The lighthouse itself has been disused for some time, but the sea jetty will provide a useful second landing place for bringing supplies to the island.''

They continued walking, kept from chill by their exertion, though a light rain continued to fall. The footpath became more mud than grass, not improved by the hooves of four shaggy, dun-colored Soay sheep with lambs at heel, who skittered off in alarm when McLeod's trenchcoat gave a particularly startling snap in the wind. A hundred yards beyond loomed a square rock outcropping that Jigme identified as the Judgement Stone, said to be the seat where the sixth-century St. Molaise had been wont to give his judgements to the pilgrims who came here to seek his guidance. Skirting the stone, Jigme led the party left up a succession of irregular steps paved with flat stones, to approach a wide, irregularly shaped cave-mouth opening in the cliff side.

The sea breeze died and the rain ceased as they climbed. The ensuing hush was deep and profound. Both McLeod and Peregrine pricked up their ears, listening intently to the silence. For all its outward calm, the air here was strangely vital, charged with expectancy.

Adam was likewise aware of the change in the air, so was not surprised when, following Jigme expectantly to the crest of the path, he found himself suddenly brought up short at the lip of the cave only barely visible from below. But it was not the cave but its occupant who immediately caught and held Adam's attention. Amid the dimness, seated cross-legged on a straw mat similar to the one back at the farmhouse, Lady Julian's old teacher was physically unimposing—only a diminutive, shaven-headed figure of ageless appearance—but one look at him, as their eyes met, told Adam that the vision of Tseten *Rinpoche* extended far beyond the need for any earthly source of illumination. Dressed much as Jigme, but with a red anorak instead of a navy one, his left hand was resting lightly closed on his knee, the right fingering the black beads of a *mala*, or rosary. The items Adam had sent with Jigme lay before him.

Going down the steps, Jigme gave him reverent salute over joined hands and began addressing the old lama in Tibetan. Hearing his name and those of his associates among the foreign syllables, Adam realized that the three of them were being introduced.

Tseten favored each of them in turn with a keen glance, and Adam set his palms together in the traditional gesture of respect and stepped forward, bowing slightly over his joined hands. As McLeod and Peregrine echoed the salute, the old lama's gaze warmed in response and he glanced at Jigme expectantly.

"*Rinpoche* invites you to be seated," Jigme said, indicating the straw matting. "I shall interpret."

CHAPTER TWENTY-THREE

A T this invitation, Adam bowed again and descended the steps, pausing to slip his shoes off and remove his cap before venturing onto the straw mat to sit cross-legged before the old lama. McLeod and Peregrine followed suit, sinking down to either side of him. Jigme positioned himself at Tseten's right. Smiling, the old man began to speak in Tibetan, opening his left hand to reveal Adam's Adept ring cradled in its palm.

"*Rinpoche* says that this ring bears the psychic signature of an old friend," Jigme translated. "You will know her as Julian Brodie. He asks that you convey his warmest greetings to her, the next time the two of you should meet."

Adam smiled in his turn and inclined his head, impressed by the old lama's demonstrable keenness of perception. Julian had not made the ring, but she had made extensive repairs to it on one relatively recent occasion when it had been damaged in the line of duty. It was no mean feat of discernment that Tseten could have sensed her particular resonance in the midst of all the other powerful reverberations that the ring itself carried. Even thus might a master musician differentiate the voice of a single instrument sounding in the midst of a fully orchestrated symphony.

"Please tell *Rinpoche* that I will be very happy to do as he asks," he said as Tseten laid the ring beside the other artifacts. "It was Julian herself who first suggested that we seek his counsel."

Before Jigme could begin translating, Tseten murmured a few words in Tibetan, evoking a smile and a nod from Jigme.

"*Rinpoche* assures me that his understanding of English is sufficient for our purposes, Dr. Sinclair; it is his spoken English that is not so fluent. To save time, he suggests that you speak directly to him, and I will give his answers—and, of course, clarify if he does not understand."

At Tseten's smile of inquiry, Adam gave a grateful nod.

"I thank you, *Rinpoche*. To the point, then, I should be extremely grateful for any guidance you may be able to offer. You have seen the evidence assembled thus far." He gestured toward the photos and sketches and flag. "Please tell us, if you can: What is the connection that binds together all these elements?"

The old lama was silent a moment, as if still mulling his answer to the question he had known would be asked. As he began to speak, Jigme supplied the English translation in quiet counterpoint to the older man's voice.

"The connection you are seeking is this individual here," Jigme said, gesturing toward Peregrine's sketch of the man in green as Tseten turned it toward Adam. "He is known to legend as the Man with Green Gloves. To explain his significance, I must acquaint you with some history I had thought and hoped was dead and past."

Tseten sat back, his fingers again seeking out the black beads of the *mala* as he continued.

"Are you aware, Dr. Sinclair, that before the last world war, a number of people from my homeland found reason to emigrate to Germany?"

Adam shook his head.

"Tibetan colonies were founded in Berlin and Munich in the mid-nineteen twenties," Jigme went on, translating over Tseten's voice. "It was rumored at the time that at least some of the individuals involved were black *ngagspas*—evil magicians—who had been recruited to work for the rising National Socialist Party. One such individual was a lama calling himself by the ancient title of Green Gloves. Legend holds that he who bears this title is possessor of the Keys to the Kingdom of Agarthi—or Asgard. These are not keys in any physical sense, but certain non-Buddhist teachings."

At Adam's nod of understanding, Jigme continued.

"As time passed, it became clear that, through these keys,

Hitler and his followers hoped to obtain direct access to an Aryan root magic that they so ardently desired and sought. They sought it by other means as well. Whether or not these hopes were well-founded, *Rinpoche* does not know, but it is certain that the man then calling himself Green Gloves quickly gained a reputation for being able to predict the number of Nazi deputies elected to the Reichstag. Hitler is said to have consulted him frequently. Apparently he found reason to trust in Green Gloves's auguries."

Adam nodded. "Hitler's interest in such matters is well known," he said, "though I had not heard of a connection with Eastern disciplines. Did this extend into the war itself?"

Tseten shrugged and spoke again.

"*Rinpoche* was then a young monk in Tibet," came Jigme's translation, "so he has no direct experience of those days in Germany to speak with authority. However, it is said that when the Russians entered Berlin in 1945, they found one thousand Tibetan bodies in German uniforms, suicides all, bearing no rank insignia or identification. When this rumor came to *Rinpoche*'s ears, he surmised that the individuals in question must have borne some connection with the Berlin Colony, which was suspected of practicing black magic—but he cannot affirm this for a fact."

The mention of Tibetan suicides stirred Adam's memory of his own clash, in the not-so-distant past, with a black magician also claiming Nazi connections, who called himself the Head-Master. On that occasion, a number of the Head-Master's initiates had yielded up their lives to their elemental patron in order to secure for their leader a measure of extra power with which to defend his citadel. Adam wondered if the thousand Tibetans found in Berlin might have been party to some similar working of black magic, designed as a last-ditch attempt to turn the tide of victory against the Allies.

Peregrine, meanwhile, was staring hard at his sketch of the figure from his dream, his hazel eyes owlishly round behind the gold-framed lenses of his spectacles.

"What about Green Gloves himself?" he whispered. "Did he survive the war?"

Tseten's response was a troubled frown as he shook his head and began to answer through Jigme.

"His fate is unknown," Jigme said, his eyes on his master's face. "*Rinpoche* presumes that the man then calling himself Green Gloves is dead by now, for of necessity, he would have been of mature years during the twenties and thirties, in order to have achieved what he did.

"As for the colonies we have noted—*Rinpoche* says it is probable that these were dispersed, their members left to fend for themselves as best they might. It was a time of great turmoil. It is possible that at least a few of these refugees found their way to Switzerland, black *ngagspas* among them. A number of Buddhist communities flourish there today—though he cannot imagine any of them having Nazi connections. Certainly, no Buddhist known to us would be involved with something like this," he finished emphatically, gesturing toward Peregrine's photographs and sketches. "Our beliefs demand that we respect all life. We do not kill anything."

McLeod heaved a gusty sigh. "Well, whatever else may be going on here, it doesn't sound like Green Gloves himself is likely to be a threat."

This utterance earned him a sharp look from Tseten, who immediately rattled off a vehement response in Tibetan. Jigme listened impassively, then turned back to McLeod.

"Are you aware how successors to such great lamas as the Dalai Lama and the Karmapa are chosen, Inspector?" he inquired.

Looking slightly nonplussed, McLeod shook his head.

"You do know about the Tibetan Buddhist practice of deliberate reincarnation?" Jigme said, continuing at McLeod's nod. "Very well. When a great lama dies, a search is instituted for a child with certain distinguishing physical characteristics who will recognize possessions of his predecessor and thus prove by this, and other means—perhaps visionary guidance and instructions left behind by that predecessor at his death—that he is the new incarnation of the spiritual Principle which uses the body of this official. A similar process is followed to establish lesser successions—even black magic successions, I fear."

Adam had sat forward during this recital, and spoke as soon as Jigme had finished.

"Are you saying that a reincarnated version of this Green Gloves could be at the bottom of all this?"

Both Tseten and Jigme responded with emphatic nods, and Tseten began speaking again in Tibetan.

"It is definitely possible," Jigme translated. "Such a successor, discovered just before the war and since trained up for that purpose, would now be in his prime—a formidable enemy of the *Dharma*, or Law, if he is not kept in check. Such a man, equipped with powers carried over from previous lifetimes, could as well have access to information about a submarine sent out at the end of the war specially designated to preserve and hide—"

The old lama abruptly stopped speaking. Left without the means to finish the sentence, Jigme glanced inquiringly at his master.

"To preserve and hide what?" Adam prompted.

There was an extended pause, during which Tseten appeared to weighing up his answer. Jigme stared at him intently. When Tseten slowly began speaking again, it was clear that Jigme's halting translation was exactly literal, that Tseten now was venturing even beyond Jigme's knowledge.

"It may already have occurred to you to wonder how and where I might have come by the information we have been discussing," Jigme said. "I sense that it is appropriate that you be told. By no means were all of the members of the Berlin and Munich colonies of which I spoke allied with Hitler. After the collapse of the Reich, some did seek refuge in Switzerland, but a few succeeded in winning their way back to their native homeland. One of these found his way to the monastery where I myself had become abbot. He it was who told me most of what I know about Green Gloves and his involvement with the rise of the Third Reich.

"Among the tales that he had to tell," Jigme continued, "is that Green Gloves was reputed to have brought with him from Tibet a chest containing a fabulous treasure. Opinions varied as to what that treasure was—my informant favored precious gems, which were gradually sold to finance certain activities of the Berlin colony—but mere physical wealth would have meant little to a man who possessed what they call the Keys to Agarthi. I do not suggest that the chest contained these so-called Keys—for we have already established that they have no physical dimension. What I do fear is that this chest may have contained the means by which to access the Keys.''

Tseten paused, apparently gathering his thoughts, and Jigme likewise paused, in rapt anticipation.

''Which is?'' Adam finally asked, in an attempt to restart the narrative.

The old man sighed and went on, Jigme softly echoing him in translation.

''We have in our tradition something known as *Termas*, or Treasure Texts, which are discovered from time to time to advance enlightenment and keep our religion evolving. In opposition to the *Termas*, there also exist false *Termas*—you might call them Black *Termas*—anti-Buddhist texts whose mastery could be said to produce reverse enlightenment. Endarkenment, if you will, or black magic. Not only does the use of such texts result in evil, but such involvement precipitates the practitioner into horrific realms in the next life.''

Tseten indicated the sketch of Green Gloves, where it lay beside Peregrine's photos and other sketches and the flag. ''I believe that Green Gloves may have possessed some of these false *Termas*—that these were what constituted his treasure. Given the outcome of the war, it is doubtful he was able to put these false *Termas* to their evil use—perhaps he died before he could do so. If so, and if he knew death was approaching, he would have made provisions to safeguard his most precious possession, to transport it to a place of safety—a place from which his successor is presently attempting to recover it.''

''Are you saying that *U-636* may have been carrying these false *Termas*?'' Adam asked.

Tseten nodded.

''I can think of no other possible connection between this man''—he indicated the sketch of Green Gloves—''and any German submarine. All the evidence before me points to an enterprise laid, if not by Green Gloves himself, then by his followers on his behalf, to recover the submarine's evil cargo. As their strength lies partly in secrecy, we can be sure they would not risk calling attention to themselves for the sake of any ordinary treasure of gold and jewels.''

His listeners traded glances, and Adam returned his gaze to the old lama, mulling what he had just heard.

"This is certainly consistent with what we know of attempts to smuggle other valuables out of Germany after the war," he said. "It's common knowledge that many art treasures and other objects of value ended up in South America, and many top Nazi officials also made their escape there. In many instances, the safest form of transport by far was by submarine.''

McLeod glanced at him uneasily.

"If I'm following you, it sounds like you think Mick Scanlan and his partner may have been killed because they stumbled on this submarine. The question is, Did their killers get what they were after?''

Tseten's gaze returned to Adam, and Jigme continued translating as he replied.

"I think not—at least not yet. But I cannot overemphasize the danger, if the false *Termas* are retrieved by those who seek them. If those who killed your young Irishmen were willing to profane the *Phurba* to achieve their ends, it is doubtful they will recognize any other ethical constraints. Should they succeed in obtaining and mastering the false *Termas*, they will have at their disposal a power equal to their ambitions. To gain some impression of the scope of those ambitions, you have only to recall Nazi Germany at its height.

"You must go to Ireland, Adam Sinclair—you and your associates. You must find the submarine that yielded up this flag, and rescue or destroy the Black Treasure Texts before these evil men can appropriate them for their own use.''

Adam inclined his head. "I will accept this charge, *Rinpoche*, and I am prepared to be guided by you. I believe the sub can be located, using the flag as a focus. Can you tell us what kind of resistance we might encounter?''

In a guarded sanctum at Tolung Tserphug, the author of the expected resistance unfolded his instructions to the man selected to execute them.

"I'm not certain I understand," Raeburn said, still kneeling at the foot of the dais where sat the Man with Green Gloves, Dorje *Rinpoche*. "You say you know where the sub is—it isn't even underwater—but you want *me* to go and retrieve the cargo, when any decent demolition man could be hired to blow the hatches and get you in. Why drag me into this, after so many years?"

"Those I would trust not to bungle the assignment are all Oriental," Dorje said with tart candor. "Their very presence in the area would be cause for comment, and would draw unwelcome attention to the undertaking. No, the salvage work must be handled by a Westerner like yourself."

"There are other Westerners."

"None so qualified as you; do not interrupt. The cargo she carries, long thought lost, is both valuable and precious. I wish to retrieve it. I have reason to believe that you are the person best suited to arrange it."

Wincing as he shifted from one aching knee to the other, Raeburn shook his head dubiously.

"There's more you haven't told me," he said. "May I sit? My knees aren't what they were last time we met."

Without waiting for permission, he eased his hip onto the dais and stretched one cramped knee, moving at a gesture from Dorje to sit on a cushion the other tossed in front of him. After stretching both legs, one after the other, Raeburn settled himself in the same cross-legged posture as his host.

"Thank you," Raeburn said, relishing even this small triumph. "Tell me more about this cargo."

Dorje inclined his head indulgently.

"It will consist of several smallish wooden crates, each easily carried by one man, and a somewhat larger one, requiring two—but getting the contents out of the country could present certain difficulties. That is another reason I desire your expertise. I should prefer that no explanations need be given to local authorities."

"Is it Nazi gold?" Raeburn asked bluntly.

"No, it is not."

"What, then? You've suggested that the cargo is—questionable. Since some risk clearly is involved, I'd like to know what I'm dealing with."

He cocked an inquiring eyebrow and waited. The abbot, for his part, turned his attention to pouring tea into the translucent china bowls, one of which he tendered to Raeburn with a faint smile.

"The cargo is diamonds, dear Francis," he said softly. "A veritable fortune in cut and uncut stones."

"Indeed?"

Raeburn's gaze narrowed slightly as the abbot settled back on his cushions and lifted his drinking bowl to his lips in green-gloved hands.

"Do you think I would go to so much trouble to bring you here if I were making this up?" Dorje asked over the rim. "I assure you, I shall make it worth your while. The diamonds came mainly from Amsterdam. They were a convenient form of portable wealth, far more handy than gold. During the latter stages of the war, when it became apparent that Germany was in danger of falling, many different caches of treasure were amassed, with the intention of dispersing them to places of safety in the event of disaster. Some were intended for Swiss bank accounts, where it was hoped they could eventually be retrieved and used to finance the ultimate rebirth of the Reich.

"But Germany was overrun before most of the treasures could be moved. Rather than allow them to fall into enemy hands, orders were given to dispatch much of this wealth to South America by submarine. Many reached their destination, but many did not. When *U-636* disappeared off Northern Ireland, it was reported that she had been sunk by British warships; indeed, two Royal Navy frigates claimed the kill. Now we know better—and can make good use of that knowledge."

The story made sense—of a sort—but Raeburn sensed that there was more to the tale than had been told.

"You said you would make it worth my while, if I agreed to help you," he said. "Assuming I'm prepared to do as you ask and direct this undertaking, what are the benefits in it for me?"

The abbot's eyes went cold, like chips of ice. "You should be grateful merely to escape reprisals for the destruction of our base in Scotland and the attendant loss of an irreplaceable artifact. However,'' he amended in a milder tone, ''I am willing to make some concessions for your trouble. If you succeed in salvaging the cargo, half the diamonds are yours to do with as you wish.''

''A generous concession.'' Raeburn's pale eyes flicked round the room. ''You're obviously doing well, but I'm surprised you can afford to part with that much wealth. Unless, of course, the diamonds are only a side issue. Unless,'' he concluded thoughtfully, ''there is something else aboard that submarine that you want to get your hands on—something of even greater value than diamonds. I wonder what that something might be.''

He raised his eyes to meet those of his former schoolmate and encountered a piercing glare. After a bristling silence, the abbot said coldly, ''The question of worth is purely subjective. Most men would consider the diamonds to be of paramount value and importance. The submarine was also carrying a number of Tibetan manuscripts. But those have value only to someone able to fathom their secrets.''

''Manuscripts.'' Raeburn's tone was thoughtful, but his long, lean body was taut with sudden expectancy. ''Would they be anything like the one that was in the possession of the Head-Master?''

The abbot's jaw tightened, then relaxed. ''The document to which you are referring was from a similar source,'' he acknowledged with a curl of his lip. ''The Head-Master removed it without authorization. It is no wonder that he failed in the work he set out to do, for his information was incomplete. Only the Man with Green Gloves, the Keeper of the Keys of Agarthi, has the knowledge and the power to make use of these manuscripts.''

Raeburn let this declaration pass unchallenged, only gazing at the abbot with an air of bemused satisfaction. After a moment, Dorje resumed his revelations, almost as if under some compulsion to do so.

''The full collection of these ancient texts was housed at Munich until the changing fortunes of the war dictated that they should be consigned to a safer haven,'' he said. ''My guardians were similarly persuaded that the single best hope for smuggling the texts out of Germany was by submarine.

Out of that shared conviction was conceived the idea of a joint venture intended to preserve two treasures for the Fatherland.''

''Your guardians let themselves in for quite a gamble,'' Raeburn said, toying with the dregs of his tea. ''If that sub was supposedly bound for Brazil, something must have gone seriously wrong in transit.''

The abbot paused to replenish his bowl from the teapot, avoiding Raeburn's eyes—why?

''Possibly,'' he conceded. ''Perhaps merely a change of plans. But that hardly matters now.''

''No, I suppose not.'' Watching the other man closely, Raeburn added, ''Forgive me for speaking bluntly, *Rinpoche*, but once you've given me the location of this sub of yours, what's to prevent me from taking the whole hoard, diamonds, scrolls, and all?''

''My assurance,'' said the abbot, ''that you would not survive the attempt.''

''Indeed.''

Dorje stared at him long and hard before continuing.

''Do not provoke me, Gyatso,'' he murmured. ''I think and hope that you are intelligent enough to realize your own limitations where you are dealing with me. Content yourself with what I am offering you in diamonds. I assure you, even a quarter of the trove will suffice to set you up in splendor for the rest of your life, with ample means to expand your personal operations far beyond your present scope. The manuscripts, on the other hand, would be of no use to you, for you lack the transmission of power to unlock their secrets. To tamper with them in ignorance would be to court a fate worse than that which befell your Head-Master.''

Seeing Raeburn silent, he relaxed a measure of his severity. ''I shall send Nagpo and Kurkar with you. As you have already observed, their talents are not inconsiderable. Beyond that, you are free to choose your own men, so long as they all are Westerners and not likely to call attention to themselves.''

Raeburn sat very still, fingertips drumming lightly on the rim of his empty cup.

''You say that this sea cave is in Ireland?'' he said. ''Your men have no doubt that the sub is there, and that it's intact?"

"This is not an exercise to vex you, Francis," the abbot said sharply. "You will be provided with detailed maps, and Nagpo and Kurkar will meet you there. I suggest that you approach by boat, and that you plan to make a direct transfer of the cargo from the sub."

"I thought you said it wasn't accessible by sea," Raeburn said.

"It will be. My two dagger-masters are quite capable of blasting open the cave so that the sub can pull out at high tide."

"Whoa! Wait just a minute! No one said anything about moving the sub!"

"I am saying it now," Dorje replied. "Kurkar reports the hull appeared sound. One of the fuel tanks has ruptured, but there will be enough remaining to run the diesels."

"This is ridiculous," Raeburn muttered. "Even if the sub were entirely seaworthy, I couldn't run it alone! Even to run on the surface, I'd need at least a skeleton crew."

"And you shall have one." The abbot's smile was very cold. "They have been at their posts for nearly fifty years."

For the first time, Raeburn felt real fear clutch at his entrails.

"What are you saying?" he whispered. When Dorje only stared at him, he ventured, "Surely you aren't seriously proposing to reanimate the dead?"

The abbot reproved him with a superior look. "Not I, but it can be done, as you are well aware. You need not act so incredulous. One of your own followers performed a similar operation, I believe, on a corpse far longer dead than these, who yielded up their lives a mere half-century ago."

Through his shock, Raeburn was more than a little surprised and not especially pleased to discover how well-informed his rival was about his doings. The operation in question had actually been performed by one of his more promising lieutenants—highly successful, for what it was, and of course Raeburn himself had trained Geddes—but the subject had been one man, not an entire submarine crew—even a "skeleton" one.

"That was different," he said defensively. "Only information was required. We didn't need him to do anything."

Dorje dismissed this objection with a wave of his green-gloved hand.

"Be at ease, Gyatso. You need not concern yourself with this aspect of the undertaking. Go now and begin working out your requirements for opening the submarine and conveying its cargo to safety. You will be provided with whatever you need by way of resources and communication. By tomorrow, you must be ready to put your preparations into operation."

"Tomorrow? What's the hurry?"

For the first time since the outset of their conversation, Raeburn thought he could detect a hint of uncertainty behind the other's maddeningly self-confident façade.

"The portents regarding this venture are auspicious at present," Dorje said, "but there are certain indications of instability if we wait too long to act. I have been warned of enemies afoot—servants of the Light, with the will and perhaps the knowledge to meddle to some constructive purpose, if we do not take advantage of the moment. I have waited nearly the whole of this present lifetime to reclaim this legacy!" he concluded with sudden sharpness. "I do not intend to allow anyone or anything to cheat me out of it."

He levelled a long look at Raeburn. "Have you ever before had dealings with anyone who might be described as a *Hunter*?"

Raeburn stiffened slightly, his right thumb nervously fingering his Lynx ring as a queasy chill went up his spine. "Why do you ask?"

"It was a symbol cast up to us in the midst of divining the outcome of this venture," the abbot replied, his eyes narrowing as he searched Raeburn's face. "In attempting to interpret the significance of the sign, my seer spoke of a *longtime adversary who must be killed if he cannot be eluded.*"

Raeburn's jaw clenched, and a venomous expression crossed his face.

"That's very interesting," he said softly. "The group that

defeated the Head-Master goes by the name of the Hunting Lodge. Their Master Huntsman is a man called Adam Sinclair.''

''You have encountered him yourself, then?''

''Only indirectly,'' said Raeburn, ''but that doesn't alter the fact that he's cost me a lot of trouble in the past. If he's in any way involved in this affair, I will welcome the chance to even the score.''

CHAPTER TWENTY-FOUR

"CAN you tell us what kind of resistance we might encounter?" Adam had asked Lama Tseten *Rinpoche*.

And when Tseten did not immediately answer, Peregrine stirred uneasily, no longer able to contain himself.

"Please, *Rinpoche*," he dared to whisper. "You can't just send us in blind. This is way beyond our experience—mine, at least. How do we protect ourselves against this black *Phurba* magic?"

The old lama ventured a faint smile before answering, settling back a little as Jigme began translating his reply.

"Patience, youngling. I was about to speak of that. It is certain that Green Gloves will send his dagger priests to secure the false *Termas*. They will be capable of wielding vast amounts of power, commanding demonic forces beyond your imagination.

"Countering such power is a matter of separating the wielder of the magic from his protectors, so that he is vulnerable to attack by his own demons. The Western magic resident in your chief is equal to the task, dagger to dagger. Dr. Sinclair knows—though he does not know that he knows."

This cryptic observation drew a questioning look from Adam, but instead of speaking, Tseten reached out and took him by the right hand. The old man's touch sent a faint electrical shock tingling up Adam's arm, accompanied by an almost irresistible compulsion to let fall all defenses where the venerable lama was concerned.

"If you will permit it, I can teach you to know what you

know," Jigme translated, as Tseten deftly picked up Adam's sapphire ring and slid it back onto his hand. Turning that hand upward, the old man slowly began to trace a decreasing spiral in the palm with the tip of his right index finger.

"You need not fear." Jigme's words were a soothing caress. "*Rinpoche* says you have the ability to resist his direction, but he prays that you will not, so that he may guide you to a higher level of consciousness."

The old lama's touch and the spiralling circle being traced on his palm were drawing Adam into trance. Almost without his volition, he could feel the tension draining out of his body, as if Tseten somehow had opened a tap. To either side of him, he sensed concern tensing McLeod and Peregrine, but he paid them no mind; he had nothing to fear from the master before whom he sat, and to whom he now yielded up his will.

"Grant me your teaching, Master," he whispered, lifting his gaze squarely to Tseten's. "I give you leave to guide me wherever I must go."

The spiralling on his palm ended with a brief caress. Taking both Adam's hands in his, Tseten gently folded them together, palm to palm, in an attitude of prayer, and held them in his own. As Adam closed his eyes, a sensation of calm expectancy stole over him, a centering and slipping into familiar patterns of quiescent readiness.

The old lama's hands left Adam's as he softly began to chant, Jigme's voice also joining in.

"*Om mani peme hum! Om mani peme hum! Om mani peme hum...*"

The familiar mantra lulled and reassured, enjoining surrender in the blissful contemplation of the lotus-jewel of compassion, a heady melding of self with the Supreme Allness that shaped the universe. Reinforced by a faint clicking that Adam dimly identified as Tseten's rosary beads, the quietly reiterating syllables filled the surrounding air with hypnotic resonances.

Breathing deeply, Adam let those resonances wash over him in waves, carrying him out of the phenomenal world and into the interior realm of a profound, free-floating trance. At first that realm was void, and without form. But then, across that interior void, the blended voices of the two holy men moved like an echo of the first syllable of creation.

A spark of pure, unbroken light appeared in the darkness behind Adam's closed eyelids, vital as a newborn sun. As his inner vision yearned toward it, the heart of that sun exploded, flooding the void with a particle-storm of polychrome radiance. Colors of the metaphysical spectrum spiralled round him in a corona of many-colored lights.

With his next indrawn breath, the corona flowed into his body, circulating throughout his entire being. The chain of braided lights penetrated every nerve with vital, tingling energy. In an instant of revelation, he perceived the colors in their true light, manifold expressions of the sixfold classes of sentient beings.

The black strand represented the creatures of the purgatorial realm. The red one stood for the *yidag* and *mi-ma-yin*, the lesser spirits; the green for the *tudo*, the animal world. The realm of men was represented by the yellow strand, that of the *hlamayin*, or greater spirits, by the blue. Encompassing and crowning them all, as origin and source, was the purity of white, the imperial aura of primordial awareness, subordinating all lesser colors to itself in timeless unity.

The corona flowed out of his body on his exhaled breath, but each successive cycle of respiration renewed the pattern, simultaneously experienced and perceived. As his concentration deepened, Adam became aware that the chain of lights was lengthening. With each successive cast, it seemed to draw him out of himself in ever-expanding reaches of consciousness till at last he became at one with the chain.

The instant of complete assimilation was accompanied by a sudden shift in the fabric of the cosmos. Though Jigme's voice continued to drone the syllables of the mantra, Adam heard Tseten's voice not through ears but through heart, through soul, speaking the transcendental language of the Inner Planes.

Unthinkable, unchangeable, the great perfection of Wisdom . . . unborn, unceasing, in essence like the sky . . . self-arisen, enlightened awareness knowing each and all . . . I bow before the Mother of all Buddhas!

The origin of the chain of being withdrew, contracting in

a spiral toward the star-point whence it had come. Obedient to the promptings of his guide, Adam divested himself of all imagistic ties with the material world. Anchored now only by the silver cord of his present lifetime, he joined the spiral recession toward the birthpoint of the universe. As the wheel of the cosmos drew him ever closer toward the heart of that original light, Tseten spoke to him again, mind to mind and soul to soul.

Open to me, O Seeker, and receive the Transmission.

In a timeless moment of eternity, Adam found himself recalling all his manifold past lives, many yet unexamined and even unguessed in ordinary consciousness. Here, each was like a separate strain of melody, blended together with its counterparts in patterns of complex harmony.

To that intrinsic symphonic unity now was added a new strain, plucked from Tseten's own being. Adam trembled, but not with fear, as the new music was introduced and brought into accord with the pre-existent motifs, pairing note with note and theme with theme until his very being resonated with augmented sound. The voice of his guide made itself heard against a background of diminishing crescendos.

The many forms of knowledge are merely kindred aspects of Wisdom, he was told, *different tunes played on the same set of strings. The art of the performer lies in the ability to transpose, adapting one form to another. Remember then, that Wisdom is a unity, and do not be afraid. For what you know, you know in the essence of the Truth. . . .*

Watching from either side of Adam, themselves lulled into stillness by Jigme's continued low chanting and the faint click of Tseten's rosary beads, McLeod and Peregrine could only guess at Adam's inner vision. Adam himself remained almost frighteningly motionless, hardly breathing, eyes closed and dark head slightly bowed, apparently oblivious to his surroundings. He did not react as Tseten leaned forward to loop the rosary beads over his head, still chanting.

The movement roused both McLeod and Peregrine to greater watchfulness, but did not seem threatening. But then, as Tseten reached behind his back, a flash of metal emerging in his hand, Peregrine could not suppress a gasp. A *Phurba* now lay in the old monk's hands.

Peregrine's first instinct was to interpose himself between the blade and the helpless Adam, or at least to cry out a warning. To his dismay, he found himself incapable of doing either. Beyond Adam, McLeod seemed similarly immobilized, blue eyes wide behind the aviator spectacles. Paralyzed, both men could only look on in growing apprehension as Tseten began to roll the hilt of the *Phurba* between his palms, point down, precisely the way the man had done who had killed Michael Scanlan.

As the words of Tseten's chant shifted, Jigme fell silent, head bowed. Light flashed from the turning *Phurba* blade, and Tseten's voice rose and fell in a rhythmic singsong that both caressed and commanded. Somehow the new chant did not alarm, though Peregrine thought he *should* be alarmed; Adam did not seem to be concerned, but nor did he seem aware of what was taking place.

Tseten's chanting continued for several minutes, then suddenly stopped. In the pregnant silence that followed, broken only by the distant screech of a sea gull, the old lama bowed low to the *Phurba* and touched its pommel lightly to his forehead, throat, and heart-chakra. Straightening then, he shifted the hilt of the weapon into his right hand and reached out to touch the triangular blade to the crown of Adam's head. Though Adam's eyes remained closed, the touch brought him upright, straight-backed, inhaling deeply, as if about to speak.

But before he could utter a sound, a deep, gong-like note seemed to fill the cavern, reverberating from the walls to echo and re-echo all round them, resonant with intimations of benediction and empowerment. Hearing it, Peregrine felt all his anxiety drain away, to be replaced by a sense of profound well-being. With bated breath he watched as the old lama gently laid the *Phurba* across Adam's hands, which opened of their own accord to receive it.

Left hand still resting lightly on the hilt, Tseten then raised his right hand to Adam's forehead. Firmly his first two fingers tapped out an odd, rhythmic tattoo between the younger man's eyebrows, directly over the location of the traditional Third Eye. As he tapped, he murmured again the words of the mantra he had spoken before. A palpable tension began to grow until, after a moment, Adam's chiselled nostrils quivered and his breath caught in a sudden, explosive sneeze.

Adam was sensible of an odd prickling in his sinuses an instant before the sneeze propelled him back to consciousness. Dizzy and slightly breathless, he weathered a passing wave of disorientation before the world righted itself around him and he found himself back in the remembered confines of St. Molaise's Cave. The realization that he was holding something in his hands came as something of a surprise, which deepened when he looked down to discover that the object resting across his outspread palms was a *Phurba*.

His waking memory could supply no explanation as to how it might have gotten there, though logic suggested that the *Phurba* had been instrumental in Tseten's efforts to forearm him against the devices of the enemy he was about to go seeking. It made sense, if he and his were going to have to face black *Phurba* practitioners. A quizzical look at McLeod received only a baffled shrug by way of response. He had no clear recollection of what had transpired during his period of trance, but he was nonetheless possessed of a vague but reassuring confidence that some form of universal knowledge had been imparted that would come to the fore in the event of need.

While he was still pondering this new reassurance, Tseten reached over and gently lifted the *Phurba* from his hands. Once his hands were free, Adam paused to knuckle the lingering haze from his eyes. His sleeves brushed the *mala* beads as he did so, and simultaneously he became aware of Jigme's attentive observation.

"Welcome back to us, Dr. Sinclair," the younger lama said with a smile. "You are a most attentive pupil. You may be sure that you are now appropriately fortified against whatever confrontations lay ahead."

Adam let one hand caress the *mala* beads on his breast, still a little disoriented.

"The *mala* is *Rinpoche*'s gift to you," Jigme said. "I suggest that you use it as a link and a tangible reminder of the transmission you have received."

Adam nodded mutely, conscious of a sudden, almost overwhelming desire to remain in the stillness. Glancing again at

Tseten, he saw that the venerable master had closed his eyes and was likewise nodding where he sat, his lined face showing slight traces of strain.

"It is best that you go now," Jigme said quietly. "I shall accompany you back to the farmhouse, where the boatman will take you back to Lamlash. *Rinpoche* is very tired, as you can see—and I expect that you, too, will feel the need for rest before the day is out."

"I confess I feel the need already," Adam said, covering a yawn. "I do beg your pardon, Jigme-la. It isn't the company, I assure you."

"Ah, but it *is*," Jigme said with a faint smile, "and a sign that much has been accomplished here. Perhaps you will rest on the drive back to your home."

"A suggestion I endorse wholeheartedly," Adam agreed, clasping a hand to McLeod's forearm. "Fortunately, my trusty Second is also my driver today."

"I'll make certain he is all right," McLeod murmured, motioning for Peregrine to help him get Adam to his feet.

While the three of them put their shoes back on, Jigme gathered up Peregrine's photos and sketches and put them and the flag back into his green canvas satchel. Though Tseten did not rise, his dark gaze met them as they turned to bid him farewell.

"Tseten *Rinpoche*, we are extremely grateful for your guidance," Adam said, raising joined hands to his forehead in a final gesture of respect. "You have my solemn assurance that we will do everything in our power to thwart the designs of our common enemy."

Solemnly Tseten returned the salute.

"The blessings of the Buddhas and Bodhisattvas attend you and your work, Sinclair-la," he said in heavily accented English. "And your *chelas* show promise," he added, with a nod and a smile at McLeod and Peregrine, who also bowed.

At Tseten's added comment in Tibetan, Jigme added, "*Rinpoche* also reminds you to please convey his greetings to your Lady Julian when you return home, Dr. Sinclair."

✦ ✦ ✦

Adam relayed Tseten's greeting by phone from Glasgow's Central Railway Station, where Peregrine was to rendezvous with Julia. At McLeod's insistence, he had settled into a back corner of the motorists' lounge and rested quietly for most of an hour during the ferry crossing back to the mainland, with his two lieutenants sitting wary watch and softly discussing the morning's work over sandwiches and coffee. He had withdrawn again once they returned to the car. By the time he roused a second time, as they approached the outskirts of Glasgow, a plan of action had started to take shape. The call to Julian was the first step toward setting it in motion.

"Well, that's arranged," he announced to the expectant McLeod and Peregrine, as he cradled the receiver. "She'll be expecting us around half past eight. Peregrine, I *am* sorry about the continuing disruptions," he added. "I wish I could absolve you from being there, but we may well need to call upon your talents."

Peregrine shrugged gamely. "That's all right. I'm starting to get used to having duty constantly hammering at my door."

"Yes, but it's wretched timing when it hammers at the door of the connubial bedchamber," Adam said with a smile. "Will Julia forgive you? Will she forgive *me*?"

A reluctant twinkle showed behind Peregrine's wire-framed spectacles. "Oh, she'll forgive *me*. She knows I'll make it up to her. And if you come through with a substitute for that curry dinner we had to scrub at the Colonial—say, dinner at Lancer's in Edinburgh—I expect she'll forgive you as well."

As Adam laughed aloud in acknowledgement, McLeod cast a wry grin at him.

"Looks like you can give your conscience a rest, Adam. I'd say the laddie has the situation well in hand."

"And how about you?" Adam asked. "Will this cause friction in the McLeod household?"

McLeod snorted and shook his head good-naturedly as they headed back out toward the taxi bays. "Since I didn't come home last night, I'm sure Jane will be almost expecting yet another demand on my time. Things like this have a way of happening when you and I are working together on a case.''

''Ah, there's Julia now,'' Peregrine said, gesturing toward the dark green Alvis just then pulling up at the curb opposite. ''Adam, shall I collect you about half-past seven? No point both of us driving back into town.''

''I'll ring you at the gate lodge, after Noel and I have had a chance to sort things out further. Realistically, though, I don't think there will be time to go home before we're due at Julian's. I may just beg a ride back with you, after we've finished.''

''Fair enough. If I don't hear otherwise, I'll see you there.''

Sketchbox tucked under his arm, Peregrine trotted off to join his new wife. Adam and McLeod both gave her cheery waves as she leaned across to open Peregrine's door, but as they made their way back to the BMW, McLeod allowed his jaunty air to lapse.

''I hope you know what you're doing in all this,'' he said as he unlocked the doors and they both got into the car. ''I'm bound to tell you that I'm none too comfortable about what went on back on the island. I find it less than reassuring that you haven't any clear recollection of what went on while you were in trance.''

''Ordinarily, I'd agree,'' Adam said as he buckled up his seat belt. ''I'm afraid you'll just have to trust me on this one. For what it's worth, I believe that Lama Tseten's intention was to introduce me to the universal templates underlying both our traditions. Certainly *he* believes that I now possess the basic intrinsic power with which to construct a defense against Green Gloves and his followers. And my own instincts are in favor of trusting his belief.''

''So you say,'' McLeod agreed dourly, turning the key in the ignition. ''What I don't like is that there's no way to field-test this before we come face-to-face with the enemy.''

''On the contrary, that's partly the reason I've set this meeting at Julian's tonight,'' Adam said. ''Whatever conceptual knowledge Tseten may have imparted to me, it was done at unconscious levels. There's still the job of bringing that information to consciousness, so it can be used. Fortunately, I have at least a vague idea what will be involved to accomplish that.''

With an unconvinced snort, McLeod guided the BMW out of the station car park and eased into the proper lane to take them onto the motorway, not speaking again until they had negotiated the interchange that put them back on the way to Edinburgh.

''Answer me this, and I'll say no more on the matter,'' he said, glancing sidelong at Adam. ''Do you still think Tseten qualifies as a Buddhist saint?''

''Now more than ever,'' was Adam's confident reply. ''And I expect our experience will demonstrate as much, before all this is over.''

They spent most of the hour-long drive back to Edinburgh beginning to develop the general form of their battle plan. En route, after checking in with his service—his presence would be required at the hospital before they went to Julian's—Adam rang Humphrey on the cell phone to have him begin investigating travel options—but one of the many details that must be worked out before they betook themselves willy-nilly to Ireland to seek out a derelict German submarine and its contents.

''There's one other thing I need you to do for me, Humphrey,'' he said, before ringing off. ''Before seven, I'd like you to deliver my medical bag to Mr. Lovat down at the gate lodge—the bag reserved for very special house calls. He isn't there now, but he should be home in a couple of hours.''

He waited until they got to McLeod's home before making several calls of a more sensitive nature on the inspector's secure line, all of them to Ulster numbers. McLeod managed to find a battered road map of Northern Ireland from a previous motoring holiday with Jane, and they spread it on his desk for reference while he and Adam alternated talking with their counterparts across the North Channel. Although the exact destination for the forthcoming mission had yet to be determined, probably until they were actually on Irish soil, at least the physical requisites for dealing with an antique submarine could be guessed at. The degree of psychic investment remained to be seen.

''Right, Magnus. I'll ring you as soon as I have our flight

details,'' Adam said, when he and McLeod had outlined their likely requirements. ''Do you need to talk to Noel again, or have you two got that part sussed out?''

''Oh, I know what needs to be done at this end,'' came the reply, in the lilting accents of the Ulster province, ''but I won't have anything more to tell him until I've talked to my local contacts. Some of what you've asked for will take some doing.''

''I appreciate that,'' Adam replied. ''You know I wouldn't ask if there were any other options. We'll talk to you later.''

After further consultation and a check of the time, Adam had McLeod drop him at the hospital for a brief check-in on his patients, for he had been absent since the previous noon, and hoped to be away in the morning as early as possible. Meanwhile, McLeod made a foray to the bookstores along Princes Street and George Street to procure the appropriate large-scale Ordnance Survey map of the Donegal coast. When he returned to Adam's office at half-past six to collect him, he found his chief on the phone again, looking none too happy.

''More problems?'' he asked, as Adam rang off and cradled the receiver.

''You might say that. I certainly hope the timing on this mission isn't critical, because I don't see a way in hell we're going to get to Belfast before mid-afternoon tomorrow. I have a nine o'clock lecture that I can't cancel and can't get anyone to take for me—I've already cancelled once this week with this class. Not that it makes much difference, because the first flight Humphrey can get us on goes at three-twenty in the afternoon. The earlier flights are booked out, even if I didn't have that lecture, and the odds against three standby seats becoming available don't bear thinking about.''

''What about the ferry, then?''

''The ferry connections are no better—we'd just be driving instead of waiting, and still get in late in the afternoon. Of course if I dump my lecture, we could drive through the night and catch the first boat—but I don't think we dare shortchange ourselves on sleep, going into something like this.''

''Sounds like we go at three-twenty then,'' McLeod said.

"I doubt Magnus can get his arrangements squared away much before then anyway."

"You're probably right—which is why I discarded the idea of hiring a plane," Adam agreed. "My resources aren't unlimited, and it's foolish to squander them just to gain a few hours that can't even be used." He sighed. "The clock is ticking, though. I don't think we can afford to waste very much time."

"Aye." McLeod glanced at his watch. "Speaking of which, if we waste much more time here, we'll have to skip supper—and the sandwiches and coffee I had on the boat gave up the ghost hours ago. You didn't even have that; you must be starving. Jane said she'd have something holding for us, whenever we can spare half an hour to wolf it down. The other option is a Big Mac."

"I'll opt for Jane's cooking any day," Adam replied, rising to collect his coat. "Let's get out of here before someone pages me; they know I'm in the building."

They made their escape without being apprehended. Jane McLeod had a simple supper waiting when the two of them returned just after seven o'clock. Over modest helpings of silver-side of beef with cabbage and boiled potatoes, McLeod told her of the beauty of Holy Island, and the environmental work going on there, but nary a word of who they had gone to see, or why. Nor did Jane ask. McLeod's announcement of a trip to Ireland on the morrow elicited a raised eyebrow, for even Jane knew that Ireland was totally outside her husband's police jurisdiction, but her only comment was to inquire what kind of bag she ought to pack for him.

At a quarter past eight, after rendering appreciation for the meal and apologies for having to eat and run, Adam bade her good night as he and McLeod betook themselves and their maps off to Lady Julian's, pulling up in front of her Edwardian townhouse just before half-past. Peregrine's Morris Minor was already there, parked directly underneath the street light that lit the sidewalk and steps up to Julian's front door. Two spaces farther on was the dark green Volvo Estate usually seen running errands in Father Christopher Houston's parish.

Of Christopher himself there was no sign, but the door

was just opening to admit Peregrine, his blond hair agleam from the brass carriage lights to either side of the door. Returned to the more formal and genteel milieu of Edinburgh, he was kitted out in classic navy blazer and grey flannel bags tonight, instead of the more casual attire of earlier in the day, but the battered sketchbox under one arm was the same that had gone to Holy Island. Adam's medical bag was in his other hand. Behind him, a lean figure in clerical attire pulled the door wider and partially emerged.

"Well, your timing is impeccable as usual, the lot of you!" said Christopher. "Come in, come in, don't stand on ceremony. Julian's given Mrs. Fyvie the night off, so I'm playing butler; she's out in the grotto with tea waiting. Peregrine, I distinctly remember marrying you to a smashing young woman, not a week ago. This is *not* what you're meant to be doing on your honeymoon!"

He took the medical bag from Peregrine and hustled them inside, shaking hands all around. Like the rest of them, a sapphire shone on his right hand. Still nattering of social small-talk, he closed the door behind them and led the way through the vestibule and green-damasked hall to the spacious and airy sun parlor at the back of the house, where Julian Brodie spent much of her time when not at work in her jewellery studio.

The drapes were drawn across the bowed French window that made the room so bright during daylight hours, and the room was lit tonight primarily by candles, though a high-intensity lamp was goose-necked over a rolling table in the center of the room, at present occupied by a straw-encased teapot and a tray of delicate *famille vert* porcelain cups. Lady Julian was pouring, herself like a porcelain doll, enveloped in a graceful sky-blue sari that softened the lines of her wheelchair. The clean aroma of jasmine wafted upward with the spice-smells of sandalwood and cinnamon, soothing and reassuring.

"Come in, my dears, and we'll start with a cup of tea," she said, beckoning them with a smile and a nod of her silver head. "Adam, you've had me absolutely on tenterhooks all day, wondering how you got on with Tseten."

She had already warded the room, though not against

them. After taking his bag from Christopher, Adam sketched a Sign with his ring hand before crossing the threshold, feeling the protection coil around him before it let him pass. After saluting Julian with a kiss on the cheek, he settled obediently beside her as she chivvied the rest of them into seats around the table like a mother hen, making certain everyone had tea.

He was struck, as always, by the sheer opulence of the room, a delicious hotchpotch of every kind of Orientalia, that delighted the eye but never quite overwhelmed. Against walls hung with figured yellow silk, fans and silk embroideries vied with scrolls done with brush and ink and exquisite Oriental watercolors. Tabletops and shelves displayed a variety of rare and curious objects from every Oriental culture from the Indian Ocean to the China Sea—jade and cloisonné, porcelain and lacquerwork, ivory and bronzes, most of it garnered during the course of her late husband's business sojourns in the Far East. Underfoot was the gleam of parquetry lavished with the jewel-tones of Oriental rugs.

Adam was recalled from his appreciation of Julian's bower by her voice bidding Christopher remove the teapot and tray to one side, leaving the table clear for their use. McLeod spread out the general map of Donegal and the rest of Northern Ireland. Peregrine had set his sketchbox on his knees and was laying out his photos and sketches, finally producing the Nazi flag, which he handed to McLeod before standing the sketchbox on the floor beside him. Briefly opening his medical bag, Adam retrieved his *skean dubh* and slipped it into a coat pocket before setting the bag on the floor, for Tseten had spoken of the coming confrontation being one of "dagger to dagger."

"So that's where we now stand," he said, when he had briefed Julian and Christopher on the background of the present situation, the events of Holy Island, and an assessment of the mission now facing the Hunting Lodge. What tea had not been drunk was long gone cold. "If the Black *Termas* are recovered by Green Gloves and his henchmen, and their teachings put into force, the resultant endarkenment will constitute a major encroachment against the Light. Tseten felt that prompt action was essential, though he stressed the folly of charging into the situation before we're properly prepared.''

''One can't argue with that logic,'' Christopher said, putting down the sketch of Green Gloves with a faint shiver. ''What did you have in mind to do here tonight?''

''That's a more difficult question to answer,'' Adam admitted, pulling Tseten's rosary out of his coat pocket. ''I have this from Lama Tseten, in token of his teachings and blessings. I think it's meant to be a key of some sort—whether mnemonic or visual or tactile, I couldn't begin to tell you. He also gave me to understand that my *skean dubh* will play a part in the proceedings—'dagger to dagger' was the way he put it.''

Julian had picked up Tseten's rosary to thoughtfully finger the black beads, and now laid it back on the table beside the *skean dubh.*

''Black *Termas*,'' she said with an eloquent shudder. ''What an appalling thought.''

''I'll say,'' Peregrine murmured. ''Just out of curiosity, what is a Black *Terma* supposed to look like?''

''Much like a true *Terma*,'' Julian replied, ''and I can show you one of those.''

Turning her chair around, Julian wheeled herself over to an intricately carved teakwood cupboard in one corner of the room, opening one door before maneuvering closer to peer inside. While she rummaged, Adam picked up Tseten's *mala* and wrapped it around his left wrist, as he had seen Tseten wear it. When Julian returned, she had across her lap a long, narrow wooden box, perhaps four inches wide by twenty long, and a slightly smaller object of less regular shape, wrapped in swathings of maroon silk. She held a steadying hand on both as her chair whirred back into place between Adam and Peregrine.

''This is just my *Phurba*,'' she said, as she set the maroon bundle on the table. ''We'll get back to that later. *This* is the treasure I want to share with you first.''

As she laid the wooden box open on the tea table before them and lifted the lid, an elusive whiff of Malaysian spices wafted upward. Leaning in, Peregrine saw that what lay inside was an oblong-shaped bundle, lovingly wrapped in an age-darkened envelope of antique yellow silk.

The perfume of spices grew stronger as Julian unfolded the wrappings to reveal what Peregrine took at first sight to be a large, folded Oriental fan, except that it was not tapered at one end. Closer inspection revealed that what would have been the end sticks were, in fact, the stiffened brocade cover boards of a long, very narrow book, perhaps two inches wide and eighteen inches long. Its parchment pages were not actually bound together, but merely sandwiched between the brocaded cover boards. The boards themselves were held in place with a silken cord tied in an intricate knot.

"This transcribed *Terma* is said to have been written personally by the ascetic Nyima," Julian said, carefully loosing the knot and turning back the uppermost cover, "written by his own hand. His name means 'radiant sun.' The text itself is a treatise on spiritual discernment—the capacity to perceive the true road to enlightenment in the midst of many illusory possibilities. It was given to me by a very old friend, long since passed on, with the injunction to keep it safe until such time as I could hand it into the keeping of one who would make himself known to me as its destined custodian."

She fingered the ancient parchment with gentle reverence. "That was almost forty years ago. I am still waiting for that custodian to appear. In the meantime, however, please feel free to acquaint yourselves with Nyima in the semblance of his handwriting. He was an artist as well as a sage."

She lifted the *Terma* and presented it to Peregrine. He received it gingerly, keenly aware of the text's antiquity. Though smaller, the characters on the uppermost page were as much a work of art as any of the hangings on the walls around them.

After lifting several more pages covered with the graceful script, Peregrine passed the *Terma* to Christopher, who handed it on to McLeod. The inspector paid it but a cursory examination before giving it into Adam's hands.

A faint tingling set up in Adam's left hand as he received the text, as if the rosary looped around his wrist were emanating a mild electrical charge. One winged eyebrow rose as he hefted the text in his hands.

The tingling intensified, spreading swiftly up his arm, reminding him of the sensation he had experienced back in St. Molaise's Cave, when Tseten first had taken hold of his hand. Even as the comparison sprang to mind, the *Terma* before him seemed suddenly to come alive, pages lifting and sighing as if with the passage of a breeze otherwise beyond perception. In that same instant, Adam felt an urgent tugging at his senses, like the pull of invisible fingers.

The room around him seemed to blur and fade, except for the *Terma*, objects and even the people in the room wavering on the brink of transparency. Even as Adam blinked his eyes, trying to clarify the vision, there reappeared before him, superimposed upon the image of the room, the shimmering Lotus Wheel of heavenly lights he had envisioned during his trance on Holy Island. Slowly the lotus began to unfold, revealing at its heart a light-shrouded human form.

CHAPTER TWENTY-FIVE

D IRECTLY across from Adam, Peregrine heard his chief
draw a sharp breath and saw him recoil slightly, dark
head flung back, his surprised gaze focused—or perhaps unfocused—somewhere beyond Peregrine, perhaps even beyond the confines of the room. No one else seemed to see
anything except Adam's reaction, but Peregrine, glancing
over his shoulder, caught just a glimpse of a ghostly shimmer
in the air, like gossamer in moonlight. When he himself tried
to capture it, however, the impression dissolved as if written
on water.

"Does—anyone else see him?" Adam murmured huskily.
"Dear God, the *goodness* that accompanies him . . . But too
bright . . ."

As one hand lifted to shade his bedazzled eyes, the other
brought the *Terma* to his breast in an awed embrace. The
mala wrapped around his left wrist dangled free, its black
beads clicking against the tabletop, and McLeod leaned in
tentatively, his blue gaze flitting between Adam's face and
the empty space beyond Peregrine, then shifting to Julian in
question.

"Shall I offer myself as a vessel?" he asked her. "I'm
willing, if the sage needs a voice."

Lady Julian shook her hand gently, her gaze not shifting
from Adam and the *Terma*.

"Thank you, Noel, but I think not. This is a test—and
Adam must prove for himself the measure of Tseten's teaching. What we *can* do is provide a bit of support. Christopher,

please bring me an incense-stick and that holder, from over by the jade Buddha.''

McLeod looked none too convinced, for he was well aware that Adam's psychic gifts ordinarily did not run to mediumship, but he made no objection as Christopher rose to comply, instead lending a hand with Peregrine to clear the empty cups from the table. When the priest returned, handing Julian a box of matches and then inserting the incense-stick in its holder, Julian bade him position it directly in front of Adam on the map-spread tabletop.

Their chief ceased shading his eyes as she bade McLeod switch off the gooseneck lamp, but his gaze remained unfocused, abstractedly intense, still squinting against a glare that only he could see. He did not seem to notice as she struck a match and touched fire to the incense-stick.

"Adam, look at this light," Julian said with calm authority.

He complied, his gaze tracking immediately to the flame, but even in the diminished light of her match and the candles around the room, his pupils were contracted to mere pinpoints. He blinked as she extinguished the match and then blew out the incense-stick, his gaze now fixing on the ruby-like glow that remained at the tip, flitting briefly to the tendril of spicy smoke that began to curl upward.

"Look at the light," Julian repeated softly. "Let nothing else intrude upon your field of vision. Let that single point of light represent to you the totality of all that is. It is the *om*, the beginning and the ending, the seed of all diversity and the sum of its reunification. It is the inexpressible Absolute, infinitely many and primordially One. In beholding it, you behold all things."

Her voice lulled and urged calm and detachment, a silvery net of sound inexorably drawing Adam out of himself and into profound trance. He could feel his body relaxing visibly, eyelids drooping, yet his soul was still tinglingly aware of that other Presence waiting beyond any physical dimension, entreating his attention. Only vaguely was he conscious of Julian's touch, gently drawing his hands down, bidding him lay the *Terma* on the table, letting his fingertips still rest lightly upon it.

His respiration slowed, growing more and more shallow until he seemed scarcely to be breathing at all, though still he stared at and through the point of light. After a moment, her own expression one of complete absorption, Lady Julian leaned over and touched him lightly on the heart, throat, and forehead, letting her fingertips linger just above the bridge of his nose, between his eyebrows. Each touch seemed to release a faint chime of distant temple bells deep at the core of his being, rousing distant memories almost to conscious levels.

"Answer me this now, Adam." Julian's voice was at once a caress and an anchor to the here and now. "Where is the physical seat of your consciousness?"

His chest rose on a slow intake of breath, and his answer only barely whispered past his lips.

"In the head, behind the eyes?"

"Then you must move it to a new locus of perception," she said. "Be aware of your left arm—the arm that bears the *mala*. Imagine how it would be to see through the tips of those fingers, to hear with the palm of that hand. Let what you see draw your mind to another location."

Adam's physical gaze was still focused on the jewel of fire tipping the incense-stick. Sunk deep in trance, he had bade his own volition recede into drifting quiescence, malleable to Julian's direction. He drew a deep breath, imagining that he and the fire were being drawn together in a single unified point localized just between his eyebrows. The fusion was sensible as a tingling feeling in his forehead, anchored by the feather-touch of Julian's fingertips. With it came the fleeting recollection that Tseten also had touched him thus.

As Julian took her hand away, the tingling sensation began to spread toward the back of Adam's head, creeping down his neck and out along the length of his left arm toward the center of his left hand. It seemed to intensify as it passed through the coils of black beads wound around his wrist. A companion image rose up from the *Terma* beneath his hands, spiralling up like a whirlwind and resolving into the clearly discernible shape of an elderly Tibetan ascetic with a refined face and graceful, expressive hands, who might have been Jigme in old age.

The figure beckoned with grave urgency. Joyfully Adam's spirit rose up to meet him. His arm with the *mala* lifted in entreaty, the hand snapping shut as if attempting to grasp something not easy to hold.

"A pen," Adam murmured breathlessly. "I need a pen and paper. . . ."

Peregrine was already delving into his sketchbox, turning one of his sketch pads to a blank page, pushing it across the table to Adam and then rummaging for a pencil. Before he could find one, Christopher produced a ballpoint from an inner pocket and set it in Adam's left hand. Adam blinked once, deeply, then set the pen to the blank page in front of him and began to write, his gaze never wavering from the glowing point of light atip the incense-stick, his pupils now gone wide and dilated.

Allowing for the difference of writing implement, the characters that appeared beneath Adam's pen might have been inscribed by the same hand that had penned the *Terma* beneath his other hand, centuries before. Gradually the Tibetan characters filled most of a page. Adam's hand was shaking by the time he finished, and the pen slid from his relaxing fingers as he subsided back into the stillness of deep trance.

"Adam, rest now," Julian murmured, "but remain in trance, and hear and remember everything that's said. There may be further work for you."

Quietly she took the sketch pad from under his hands, bidding McLeod switch the lamp back on as she tilted the page for the others' inspection.

"Can you read that?" McLeod asked Julian, a grizzled brow raising in question.

Julian shook her head. "Not really. Perhaps a word here and there. Like Nyima's *Terma*, this is written in a variant of Lantsa, which I've also seen in old stone carvings. But this dialect is antique—as different from modern Tibetan as Old English is from modern English."

Clearing his throat, Christopher reached across to take the sketch pad.

"It's just possible I may be able to shed some light on this," he said quietly, countering Peregrine's look of faint surprise with an almost embarrassed little smile. "No, I don't ordinarily read obscure Tibetan dialects. But Saint Paul observes that among those instructed by the Holy Spirit, some have the gift of tongues and others the gift of interpreting the same. I happen to be one of the latter—sometimes, at least."

Ignoring Peregrine's look of astonishment, Christopher cast a practiced eye over the page of script, shaking his head slightly, then tore a fresh page from the pad underneath it and set both on the table before him, also scooting his chair closer.

"Well, let's see what we can do with this," he said, pulling closer the pen Adam had discarded and then crossing himself. "Care to give me a jump-start, Julian? It saves time if someone else takes me down—and I have a feeling that time is one thing we may not have much of."

"Always happy to oblige," Julian replied, and wheeled around behind Peregrine to pull between him and Christopher. "Do you want the light back out?"

"No need. This either works or it doesn't."

"Suit yourself. When you're settled, take a good, deep breath and let it out."

The priest complied, laying both hands flat on the table before him and closing his eyes.

"Breathe in again, very deeply, and let it all the way out," Julian said. "And when I give your signal, you will let yourself sink profoundly into meditation, ready to open yourself to the gift of the Holy Spirit. One . . ."

She traced the sign of the cross on the back of his right hand.

"Two . . ." She signed his left hand in the same way.

"And three."

As she touched his forehead on the count of three, he gave a faint shiver and appeared to relax more deeply into himself, though he made no other movement for several seconds, only breathing shallowly in and out. At length, however, his lips parted.

"Let the words of my mouth and the meditation of my heart be acceptable in Thy sight, O Lord, my strength and my redeemer," he said softly, quoting from the Psalms.

When he opened his eyes, it was as if a candle had been kindled within him, lighting up his whole aspect with inner luminance as he turned his gaze to the page of text Adam had transcribed.

As Christopher scanned down the page, his lips silently sounding out the syllables, Peregrine at first feared that the text was beyond the priest, despite his reputed gift. But then Christopher took up the pen and began to write on the fresh sheet of paper, never faltering, covering most of the page with his neat, disciplined handwriting until, with a flourish, he inscribed a circled cross at the bottom and laid down the pen.

"*Consummatum est. Deo gratias,*" he murmured, letting his eyes drift closed again.

At once, Lady Julian leaned in to lay her hand on one of his.

"Thank you, Christopher. You've done very well. I'm going to count backwards now from three, and that will be your signal to return to normal consciousness, remembering in detail all of what you have just read and written. Three . . . Two . . . One." She gave his hand a squeeze. "Come back now."

Christopher drew a deep breath and opened his eyes, blinked once, then absently crossed himself again as he exhaled and reached for the page he had written. He suddenly sat forward as his eyes skimmed down the page.

"Good God, when I remarked about not having much time, little did I realize how true that was," he said, his glance flitting briefly around the table. "And it was, indeed, Nyima who spoke to Adam through the link of the *Terma*— though he sounds a good deal like our own Contact. Listen to this."

"Adam, pay close attention," Julian interjected, before Christopher could begin reading. "Remain in trance, but listen very carefully. Go on, Christopher."

With a nod, Christopher began reading.

"*Those who will oppose you are known of old, the evil ministers of many incarnations who seek dominance over devils and demons in the name of that one who is master of the masters of evil. The teachings of the false* Termas *they now seek spell gathering darkness in all its forms: the ignorance that comes from the rejection of wisdom; the blindness that comes with the refusal to see; the evil that comes from the abjuration of truth.*

"By this time tomorrow, their agents will be poised to recover their long-hidden prize. If this cannot be prevented, then great will be their victory—perhaps even a victory of Shadow over Light. But in Sinclair-la lies the knowledge and the power to resist the evil ministers, to separate them from their demonic protectors and keep the false Termas *from their hands."*

As Christopher lowered the piece of paper, McLeod was rubbing at his eyes behind his glasses.

"By this time tomorrow," he muttered bleakly. "And he's essentially reiterated what we already knew: that Adam has the power and the knowledge to pull this off—except that we still don't know how to access it. That's why Adam had us come here tonight: to help him bring Tseten's teaching from the unconscious to the conscious."

Julian had leaned across to take Adam's transcription from Christopher, and now began to compare it to the *Terma*.

"I'm a little surprised that the sage wasn't more forthcoming, then," she murmured. "Obviously, it's intended that we've been given enough information to make it all work. Equally obviously, we're still overlooking some key."

"I wonder whether it was form rather than substance Tseten was talking about," Peregrine said after a short pause. "I know something's meant to have happened on the island—that Tseten indicated he'd done *something*—but what do you suppose he meant when he said he proposed to *teach Adam what he knows*?"

Julian looked up, one grey eyebrow lifting in inquiry.

"Is that what he said? He proposed to teach Adam what he already knows?"

McLeod nodded, his gaze suddenly intense as he stared at her. "I can quote him verbatim. He said, 'The Western magic resident in your chief is equal to the task, dagger to dagger. Dr. Sinclair knows—though he does not know that he knows.' And then he said to Adam, 'I can teach you to know what you know.' "

Julian nodded, a faint smile touching her withered lips as she laid transcript and translation aside.

"Now I understand," she said. "It's precisely what I might have expected of *Rinpoche*. All of the world's great spiritual traditions have certain concepts and principles in common—what Jung called archetypes, the conceptual foundation stones of all mythologies, regardless of cultural origin. The power and purpose of ritual is to discover and unlock a psychological doorway that will admit the individual to the primordial realm. Many such doorways have been discovered over the history of man's long and hungry quest for the Divine. The point to remember here is that all of them work by way of analogy and metaphor."

Peregrine shook his head. "I'm glad you understand, because I don't."

"Look at it from another angle," Christopher offered. "The trick is to identify the effective principle at the heart of a ritual, and make a translation based on that recognition."

"You mean, like rubbing two sticks together, as opposed to striking a match?" Peregrine suggested.

"Precisely," Julian said. "In both instances, the necessary element common to both operations is to generate sufficient heat friction to start a combustion reaction. Once you know that much, you can set up an analogous procedure that will do the same thing yet again."

"Then, what you're saying," Peregrine said, "is that Adam will be able to take what he knows and convert it into a form that will be effective against these black *Phurba* magicians?"

"More or less," Julian said with a smile. "It's basically a matter of transference—finding a new method to produce a desired result, possibly by taking a familiar tool and using it in a new way. Yes," she mused, her face suddenly thoughtful. "A familiar tool. And you did say 'dagger to dagger,' didn't you, Noel? Now I know why I got out my *Phurba* when I brought the *Terma* over."

So saying, she leaned forward to retrieve the *Phurba* in its maroon swathings, deftly unwrapping the folds of figured silk until its bulky form was revealed. It was not so fine a specimen as the one on Holy Island, but it radiated something of the same kind of authoritative aura.

"Yes, indeed," Julian breathed, as she took the *Phurba* in her hands. "The use of ritual blades for the direction of energy is common to many magical traditions. The link between a *Phurba* and a *skean dubh* like Adam's is so obvious, I'm amazed I didn't think of it right away. Both are intended for ritual use, and both have blades forged from meteoric iron. I believe Tseten may have intended that we should exploit the analogy, to channel the teaching he had to impart."

She reached across to lightly touch Adam's near hand with hers.

"Adam, dear, open your eyes. I hope you've brought your *skean dubh*, because I should like to introduce it to my *Phurba.*"

Slowly Adam nodded, still deep in trance as he opened his eyes, though he made no move to bring out the *skean dubh*, for she had not asked him that.

"Nyima is still with you, isn't he?" she asked.

He nodded again, too deep to initiate more response than was required, and not at all concerned about that fact.

"That confirms my suspicions. Adam, take out your *skean dubh*," she said.

Without speaking, he reached into his coat pocket and produced the little Highland blade, half its length sheathed in a close-fitting scabbard mounted with silver interlace at throat and tip, the whole no longer than the span of outspread thumb and little finger. A clear blue stone almost the size of a pigeon's egg graced the end of the pommel, gleaming with a blue fire to match the sapphire in his ring.

"Unsheathe it now," Julian prompted.

As Adam complied, McLeod took the silver-mounted sheath from him and laid it aside, motioning Peregrine to sit well back. Christopher had already scooted his chair back a good six inches so that McLeod could also retreat.

"Now, pay close attention," Julian said, taking her *Phurba* in her right hand and turning her chair to face Adam squarely, knee to knee, as he did the same. "I ask you now to let your blade greet mine. Let Nyima be your guide, that the traditions vested in each of the blades may come together and comingle in the crucible of shared need and common purpose.''

His movements measured and deliberate, Adam closed the hilt of the *skean dubh* in his right hand and presented it, point upward, as a fencer might salute an opponent. With a softly worded invocation to the Light, Julian raised her *Phurba* in like manner, then turned the blade sideways and laid it across that of the *skean dubh* to form a cross.

The moment of contact was accompanied by an invisible crackle of energy, like a discharge of static electricity. As Julian held the two blades together in contact, focusing her mind through the matrix of their joining, the energy began to build, intensifying until the air in the room was humming with the reciprocal buildup of unseen forces.

The feedback culminated in a soundless detonation that impacted on the eardrums like the shock waves from an underground explosion. Abruptly Julian broke contact, bringing the *Phurba* back to her breast in another salute, Adam only a touch behind her.

Reverting thereafter to slow motion, Julian then embarked on a series of feints and passes resembling *t'ai chi* katas, each movement studiously formal and exact. Raising his *skean dubh* like an extension of his hand and arm, Adam copied her every movement, the two blades moving like partners in a complicated dance.

The speed of the drill increased. Julian's hand was steady as a rock as she took Adam through an accelerated round of move and countermove—strike, parry, and riposte—though the blades never touched metal or flesh after that first crossed, meteoric kiss. The exchanges became gradually more complex, an elegant dialogue of demand and response, each engagement more intricate than the last, the blades' deadly interplay all but invisible to the following eye of the beholder.

The exercise climaxed in a sudden musical tone as the two blades finally came together again, with a ringing reverberation like the striking of a temple cymbal. The after-peals resonated within the physical confines of the room like a hail of crystal bullets.

As the echoes subsided, Julian slowly lowered her arm and bowed her head over the *Phurba* in an attitude of humble thanksgiving. Adam, too, had subsided, head bowed in his hands, the flat of his *skean dubh's* blade pressed to his forehead. Julian was breathing hard, her thin, ivorine face showing every line and shadow of its age as she pulled herself together and straightened her spine; but when Peregrine would have leaned toward her in concern, Christopher laid a hand on his shoulder in warning.

"It is accomplished," she declared, in a voice ragged with exhaustion. Her arm was shaking as she extended it to lay the blade of the *Phurba* on Adam's left shoulder. "Let all the holy powers commanded by these blades henceforth recognize Adam Sinclair as their master. And let all who seek to oppose the Light beware the weapon in his hand, for it is consecrated to the Light, now and forever."

As she spoke these words, Christopher Houston rose silently to come around behind her, making a sign of benediction in the air above her and Adam, lowering his hand then to lay it gently on Julian's bowed shoulder, eyes closing, his lips moving silently in prayer. Her arm was trembling as she withdrew it to cradle the *Phurba* in her lap, but she visibly drew strength from Christopher's touch, her breathing easing and the color beginning to return to her cheeks. After an interval, she smiled up at him and gave his hand a pat.

"Thank you," she murmured. "I believe I'm all right now."

Her voice had regained its briskness. Nevertheless, Christopher gave her a searching look.

"Are you sure?"

"Quite sure. Don't flutter, Christopher." Turning to Peregrine and McLeod, she pulled a rueful *moue*. "It's times like this that I remember I'm not as young as I used to be. Still, I think we've done some good work tonight. Now, to see what our Adam has to say for himself."

Setting the *Phurba* back in its nest of silk, she turned to Adam and laid both hands on his shoulders.

"The Work is accomplished, Master of the Hunt," she stated formally, as Christopher returned to his place. "*The night is far spent, the day is at hand: Let us therefore cast off the works of darkness, and let us put on the armor of light.''*

So saying, she gave both his shoulders a squeeze and then withdrew. Adam lifted his head and drew a swelling breath, then let it out again in a gusty sigh, his dark eyes finally focusing once again on the material world.

"I sense that we've been very busy," he said somewhat huskily, absently fingering the *skean dubh* still in his hand.

"Some of us more than others," Christopher replied, with a sidelong glance at Lady Julian.

Tight-lipped, McLeod handed Adam the sheath for the *skean dubh*, which was slid into place with a nod of thanks before Adam pocketed the weapon.

"I gather you don't remember much," the inspector said dourly. "You'd better read this."

He handed Adam the transcript and Christopher's translation, both of which Adam looked over in silence while he fingered the beads of the *mala* still wrapped around his wrist.

"It appears our timetable may *just* be adequate," he said grimly, when he at last looked up. "I expect we won't have much time even to breathe, once we meet up with our opposite numbers in Belfast, but at least we know that things won't get critical until tomorrow night."

"Opposite numbers?" Peregrine said. "You mean—more of us? More Huntsmen?"

Adam smiled wearily as he unwound the *mala* from his wrist and dropped it into a coat pocket.

"Did you think only Scotland had a Hunting Lodge? I've been in touch with several of our Irish counterparts. They've agreed to give us their full cooperation and assistance. God willing, we should be able to find our missing submarine and recover its contents before our adversaries even know we're onto them."

"*Are* we onto them?" Peregrine asked. "I mean, Tseten told us *what* they'll try to do, but we still don't know exactly where. Are we going to dowse for the sub's location tonight? I can try it, if you're too tired."

"I am, and I do appreciate your offer, but you have a very short memory," Adam replied. "What happened before, when you tried to link up with the flag?"

Peregrine gave a sheepish grimace. "Then, how are you planning to find it?"

"Fortunately, Tseten seems to have given me an alternate dowsing technique that should get around that little problem—and remember that we do know the general area of the Donegal coast where Mick Scanlan was patrolling." He gestured toward the map still spread on the table. "Given the day I've had, I'm content to let the exact location slide until we've crossed to Ireland tomorrow. I expect there will be less interference, once we're on the same island."

"Is there anything else we *can* do tonight, then?" Christopher asked. "And would you like me to come along tomorrow?"

"No on both counts, but the offer is duly noted and appreciated," Adam replied. "After the last couple of hours, I'm reasonably confident I'll have what it takes to see this one through, with just Noel and Peregrine to back me up with the Irish crew; but if I'm wrong, mere numbers won't mean anything.

"What you *could* do, however, is look in on a patient of mine while I'm gone." Briefly he outlined the circumstances of Claire Crawford's case. "We seem to be past the immediate crisis, in that I don't think she'll be causing any more accidents along Carnage Corridor, but I want to make sure she's dealt with the guilt. Once that's accomplished, we can see about the possibility of putting her psychic talents to better use."

"I'll be happy to do that," Christopher agreed.

"Thank you. That will put my mind at ease on that score, at least." He cast his gaze around the rest of the company and sighed wearily. "And on that note, I think it best if the three of us bid you both good night and head for our respective beds for some sleep. Peregrine, I'll give you a full briefing on our travel plans on the way back."

CHAPTER TWENTY-SIX

DAWN found Francis Raeburn alone in the chill, sparsely furnished quarters allotted him by the master of Tolung Tserphug. He had not slept. Seated cross-legged on the straw mat meant to serve him as a bed, elbows resting on his knees, he steepled his fingers and contemplated the sum of his work over the last twenty hours—an array of notes, maps, and diagrams laid out on the bare flagstone floor before him. His most valuable reference had been an original manual of technical specifications and operation for a Type VII C Atlantic U-boat, in mint condition. The compact cellular telephone beside the manual had given him his link with subordinates in several countries, though he harbored no illusions that his many calls had gone unmonitored.

He was not so sanguine as to suppose that he dared risk open defiance of his host. The service being required of him had not come with the option of refusal. Had he been allowed full access to Tolung Tserphug's training thirty years ago, he might now dare to challenge his boyhood rival with some chance of survival or even victory; but a direct confrontation with the mature and fully empowered Green Gloves was another matter entirely.

Then there was the threat of possible intervention by an old adversary—which almost had to be Adam Sinclair, the only man who had ever presented a serious challenge to Raeburn's occult endeavors. It seemed unlikely that a Scottish Master of the Hunt could have become aware of an operation taking shape in Ireland, but Sinclair had been known to work far afield of Scotland in the past; the writ of an astral enforcer of Sinclair's apparent stature ran beyond mere national borders.

So the possibility could not be dismissed lightly. Raeburn had heard it said that once a Master Huntsman took the scent of a quarry, breaking that scent was almost impossible until the final confrontation. If Sinclair had established that sort of link, doubtful though it might seem, Raeburn would need to ensure that the "Master" met his match, when Lynxes teamed with Eastern quarry to turn on the Hunt in unfamiliar territory, with unfamiliar weapons. In such an event, Ireland could well become the killing-ground that would end Adam Sinclair and his Hunting Lodge, once and for all.

Against that possibility, and to ensure that his grudging service to Green Gloves at least netted some degree of personal gain beyond what the master of Tolung Tserphug had in mind, Raeburn had laid his plans with meticulous care. He both feared and respected the power of the dagger priests that Dorje had said would accompany him, but hopefully their efforts could be channelled to suit Raeburn's purposes. Coded instructions had been given to trusted henchmen, and preparations now would move forward with each passing hour. He tried not to think about the methods Dorje had suggested might be employed by the dagger-men. Suffice it to get the cargo off the submarine, into the boat, and onto the seaplane being arranged for—never mind Dorje's boast that the submarine itself must move from its resting place for one final voyage.

Shivering slightly as he indulged in a yawn, Raeburn pulled his orange mantle more closely around him, still greatly annoyed with the situation, despite its promise of gain. He did not like Oriental austerity, despite his boyhood aspiration to partake of Oriental esoterica. As an extremely successful practitioner of Western occult disciplines, if canted decidedly toward what his opponents would refer to as the Left-hand Path, he had developed a taste for pleasure, even personal indulgence.

His present situation was neither pleasant nor indulgent. Though the compound was wired for electricity and many other modern conveniences—including a sophisticated computer linkup in the next room, to which he had been given free and unlimited access for making his travel arrangements—this room had no heat or even a light bulb in the overhead socket. He supposed it was Dorje's way of reminding him who was in charge. Faint warmth and illumination came from the fitful flames of an array of butter lamps set out along the four walls, with more useful light provided by a chimneyed oil lamp at his left elbow.

The flames cast his own shadow oddly against the walls, whose sole adornment in the north, before him, was a rather gruesome portrait of the dread god Shinjed, who was perhaps another aspect of Taranis, the Thunderer, whose votary Raeburn had become while under the aegis of the now-departed Head-Master lamented by Dorje. But he could not believe that Taranis meant him to pay more than token lip service to the arrogant Man with Green Gloves.

As he shifted to relieve a cramp in one knee, his shadow rebounded around the walls and his hyperacute hearing caught the light patter of sandal-shod feet approaching from the door behind. Without the preamble of a knock, the door to the room swung open, silent on its hinges but accompanied by a whisper of air and the faint rustle of robes. Unhurriedly, Raeburn turned his head, his sardonic gaze lighting on the two younger dagger priests who had met the chopper when he arrived. He had expected Nagpo and Kurkar.

"You will please come with us, Gyatso-la," the nearer of the two said, favoring him with a nod. "Dorje *Rinpoche* wishes a final word with you before you depart."

Noting the "please" and the honorific, Raeburn gathered himself to his feet with less resentment than he might have felt, wondering whether the courtesy betokened Dorje's approval of the plans undoubtedly monitored during the night. He could read nothing from the priests' faces as he gathered up his notes and the technical manual. After wrapping his orange mantle around himself with a flourish, he padded stocking-footed to the doorway and paused to slip into his waiting Guccis before following his escorts along the passageway that led toward his new employer's private quarters.

It was a different chamber to which they led him this time. After passing through double doors flanked by painted dragons and two more subordinate priests, his escorts bade him leave his shoes in the ensuing anteroom before leading on to a second set of doors, these covered with figured silk of an emerald-green hue.

Raeburn passed through these alone. The chamber beyond was dim, of modest size, wreathed in a dense haze of aromatic smoke. Dorje was sitting enthroned on a carpeted dais amid a wealth of silk cushions, dressed informally in a *chuba* of emerald-green silk, with a profusion of lacquerwork tiles spread before him and a heavy bronze incense burner at his left elbow. A pair of green gloves lay beside it, in pointed reminder of who he claimed to be. His blue eyes were heavy-lidded, the extreme dilation of his pupils suggesting the recent use of a potent narcotic, but his gaze had lost none of its sharpness as he subjected Raeburn to his searching scrutiny.

"You have not slept," he noted, gesturing for Raeburn to approach.

Raeburn inclined his head and mounted the dais. "I can sleep in the chopper, and then on the flight to Ireland. I trust my pilot has slept?"

"Rest assured that he did," Dorje said, with a tiny smile, as Raeburn folded to his knees and then back on his hunkers before him. "I trust that all your preparations are complete?"

"They are," Raeburn replied. "Of course, one cannot predict all permutations of such an operation, but I am confident that any trifling details will be resolved as the plan unfolds."

Dorje's expression hardened. "They had better be trifling."

"What do your auguries tell you?" Raeburn countered, indicating the tiles. "Surely you know better than I, the odds for or against the success of this mission."

"I have never cared for your impertinence," Dorje said icily.

Raeburn quirked his rival a faint smile. "I haven't cared for this mission, from the very beginning," he said lightly, "but you needn't concern yourself that I'll sabotage it, just to defy you. Remember that I, too, have a stake in this venture. I am hardly likely to endanger my own profits."

A sardonic smile curled the other's lip. "Ever the materialist, Gyatso. I begin to see why you have yet to transcend your limitations.''

"I may yet surprise you."

"I doubt it. Acquaint me with the arrangements you have made.''

With a shrug, Raeburn began to relate the timetable and form of his preparations. He had scarcely begun, however, when Dorje cut him off with a gesture.

"Why have you not arranged to fly into Belfast?" he demanded. "Dublin is twice the distance from your destination.''

"True enough," Raeburn conceded. "Unfortunately, I have reason to believe that quite a credible likeness of me has been circulating in British police circles over the last year or so. By contrast, the Irish Republic has no record of my existence. I thought you might prefer me not to risk calling attention to myself.''

With Dorje's grudging nod of agreement, Raeburn continued.

"One of my associates will be waiting to meet me with a car when I arrive in Dublin," he went on. "The coastal village I've chosen for our staging area is only a few hours' drive from there, and the sub a few more hours beyond, by boat. A suitable vessel and crew are being hired.

"Meanwhile, my pilot Barclay will meet another associate in Brussels, and they'll fly via London to Belfast, where separate arrangements are being made for them to charter a seaplane. Once the sub's cargo has been salvaged, Barclay will fly in to collect it and me. Do you wish me to detail the means of getting the goods out of the country?''

At Dorje's gesture of agreement, Raeburn proceeded to outline the succession of boats and other vehicles that would be used to convey the sub's cargo back into Europe, and subsequently to Tolung Tserphug. Dorje was nodding as Raeburn finished, but he did not speak, only staring distractedly into the coals of the incense burner at his elbow.

As the seconds ticked by into a full minute, Raeburn began to wonder whether his old rival had slipped into some narcotic stupor—the fumes were still heavy in the room, and beginning to affect his senses as well—but then Dorje looked up, the pale eyes still wide and dilated, all pupil.

"I have already sent Nagpo and Kurkar ahead to make their own preparations at the site," he said at last. "The auguries suggest that your preparations will suffice, so long as you exercise vigilance regarding the interference of which I have already warned you. When you arrive in Zurich, my agent will meet you and deliver sufficient cash to cover all financial outlays necessary for the execution of this operation. Have you any questions?"

Raeburn shook his head. "It wouldn't do any good to ask that I be released from this assignment, so no."

"I am glad we understand one another." Dorje allowed himself a small smile. "You may go, then. Your escorts are waiting to conduct you to one of the Western guest rooms, where you may shower and change clothes and eat, if you wish. Your pilot has already been instructed to prepare for the flight to Zurich. I send no one with you from here, but I suggest that you put firmly from your mind any attempt to cross me. I hold little patience with those who betray me."

The veiled threat was quite real, and Raeburn's bow, forehead to floor, conveyed real respect for the power wielded by the Man with Green Gloves, if not the individual who held that title. Dismissed with a curt wave, Raeburn got to his feet without further comment and departed, not looking back at the two dagger priests who followed after.

CHAPTER TWENTY-SEVEN

WHILE Raeburn and his pilot were winging their way over the Alps toward Zurich, Adam Sinclair was caught up in traffic on the approach to the Forth Road Bridge, coming into Edinburgh for his nine o'clock lecture. Crisis intervention was the morning's topic—an important aspect of psychiatric practice, but it also described much of his work with the Hunting Lodge, and certainly applied to the task awaiting him in Ireland. Humphrey had packed him a bag and was driving, which freed Adam to review his lecture notes, but slowing traffic soon had him glancing at his watch and then peering ahead in some concern, as Humphrey eased the Range Rover to a halt behind a long line of other cars making for the bridgehead.

"Looks like an accident up ahead, sir," Humphrey noted.

The distant flash of blue lights reminded Adam of his own accident approaching this bridge, little more than a year ago—no accident at all, as he later had learned, but an attempt by the Lodge of the Lynx to kill him. They had done him an unwitting favor, though they did not know it, for without the accident, he might never have met Ximena.

The Range Rover began to creep toward the lights, and Adam sat back with a faint smile curving at his lips, lecture notes temporarily forgotten. He thought about ringing Ximena when he got to the hospital—if he ever got to the hospital, in this traffic—but the timing was all off. It was just after midnight in San Francisco; and if she was not working the Emergency Room, she would be snatching some much-needed sleep, in between bouts of looking after her dying father. He wondered how much longer their relationship would stand the strain of separation.

The Range Rover finally rolled onto the bridge itself, and the cause of the delay at last became apparent. A holiday caravan had parted company with its tow-vehicle and ploughed laterally into the guardrail flanking the left-hand lane, blocking that lane and partially obstructing the other. No one appeared to be hurt—or if they had been, an ambulance must have already taken the victims away in the opposite direction—so at least Adam would not be obliged to stop and render medical assistance; but traffic officers in fluorescent orange windbreakers were diverting all in-bound traffic into the right-hand lane while workmen struggled to clear away the obstruction.

The sight of the officers from Traffic Division reminded Adam of Claire Crawford. He had looked in on her briefly the night before, when he checked in at the hospital, but there had been no time to follow up on their work with the forensic artist; nor would there be time today or even tomorrow. Nonetheless, her spirits had seemed much improved, even when he told her he must be away for a few days.

He tried not to dwell on the reason he must absent himself. The plans for *that* exercise were as well laid as could be done until he and his fellow Huntsmen actually arrived in Ireland. Meanwhile, he must not shortchange his patients or his students by letting himself be distracted from the morning's duties.

To that end, he returned to the review of his notes. Traffic opened up, once they eased past the knackered caravan, and Humphrey managed to make up the lost time and deposit his employer at the main hospital entrance with a full five minutes to spare.

"Thank you, Humphrey," Adam said as he tucked his notes into an inside coat pocket. "If you could take my bag up to my office and leave it there, I should just about make this lecture. I'll be in touch as I can. It may be Sunday before we get back."

"Very good, sir. And may I add, good hunting."

Experience and determination enabled Adam to make a

reasonably good presentation, despite his growing distraction, and the question-and-answer period that followed was lively and thought-provoking. When he emerged from the hall some two hours later, still engaged in animated discussion with two of his students, a young aide in a candy-striped uniform was waiting to hand him a pink telephone message slip.

"Mrs. Fisken said it was urgent, Dr. Sinclair," she said, "and that you're to ring back right away."

His first sinking thought, as he unfolded the slip, was that some complication must have arisen over the arrangements he had made to cover his absence. He was hardly relieved when he read McLeod's name and number.

"Sorry, Doctors, I'll need to attend to this," he said, tucking the note into a pocket. "We'll continue our discussion on Monday."

When he had reached the refuge of his office, he tapped in McLeod's number at police headquarters with some apprehension.

"It's Adam," he said, at the sound of McLeod's voice. "Is there a problem?"

"For a change, no," came McLeod's reply, a touch of excitement in his tone. "It may take more than this to make your day, but I wanted to let you know before you left the hospital. Donald just brought me a report that Carlisle Police faxed in early this morning. Guess what? Last night, about an hour after pub-closing, a bloke by the name of Avery Melville turned himself in at a local police station. He's claiming to be the man responsible for a drunken hit-and-run accident that took place up here in Edinburgh about a year ago, on the A70 road to Lanark."

It took but half a heartbeat for Adam to realize the import of what McLeod seemed to be telling him.

"This *is* is the Claire Crawford case we're talking about?"

"The very same."

The sense of relief that flooded through him was mixed with equal parts of wonder and astonishment.

"Well done, Donald! I expect he's as pleased as the rest of us. But before I go running off to tell Claire about this development, have we done any double-checking? How close *are* the facts? Could this really be the hit-and-run driver who killed her husband?''

"It looks a dead certainty to me," McLeod said, on a note of grim triumph. "McSwain down in Carlisle says this Melville's looks match up with the sketch we put out. And the account he gave of himself coincides at every salient point with the story as Claire told it. No, I don't think there's much doubt that Melville's the perpetrator, all right. Hit-and-run drunk-driving isn't a sufficiently glamorous crime to inspire a false confession."

"I see your point," Adam allowed. "All the same, I wonder . . .''

"You wonder what?"

"I wonder about the timing. Assuming this Melville *is* the guilty party, what do you suppose impelled him to make a clean breast of things *now*, after remaining at large for so long?"

"I was wondering the same thing," came McLeod's reply, "and so was Donald. He rang Carlisle and asked if they'd fax him a transcript of Melville's confession. Want me to read it to you? The pertinent bit isn't very long."

"Please do."

"*Ever since it happened,*" McLeod read aloud, "*I've been hating myself. Probably the only reason I'm still here is that I haven't got the courage to take my own life. I've often thought about turning myself in, but I was afraid of having to face up to* her—*the woman I hit. Then a couple of days ago, something . . . I don't know, something changed. I don't know what; all I know is that I suddenly realized I wasn't scared anymore. All I want now is to be out from under this weight of guilt.*''

"I see," Adam said, when McLeod finished reading. "Well. Off the record, I would have to say that it appears our last session with Claire may have produced something more than a sketch."

"The thought *had* occurred to me," McLeod agreed. "Are you going to tell her that?"

"I am, indeed. She deserves to know that the wheels of justice do, indeed, grind exceedingly fine—and she's been a worthy instrument, if what she did helped Melville find the courage to face the consequences of his actions. There may be hope for both of them now.''

Claire's reaction to the news did credit to her newfound freedom of spirit. After weeping briefly in Adam's arms out of sheer relief, she pulled herself together and, wiping away her tears, bravely raised her face to his.

''Dr. Sinclair, I feel as if you've lifted an enormous weight from my shoulders,'' she said, squaring those shoulders and dabbing at her eyes with a tissue.

He smiled and pulled a chair closer, to sit knee to knee before her wheelchair.

''I think it's you who've done the lifting,'' he said gently. ''How do you feel about what's happened?''

''Only relieved—and thankful,'' she replied. ''I thought I'd feel elated, but it isn't that. I feel—sorry for him—even after all the pain he's caused me.''

She glanced down at her hands, clasped in her lap and toying with her tissue.

''It was so easy to hate this man when I hadn't seen his face,'' she went on more slowly. ''But once I saw him clearly, it was obvious that he wasn't the monster I'd envisioned—just someone who'd let his own weaknesses betray him once too often. Maybe that's always the thing about hatred—that it's blind. And being blind, it feeds on illusions. Give me the truth any day, and let me see things for what they are.''

''That's an important insight,'' Adam said. ''Tell me this, then: On Wednesday, I asked you to consider what you might want to say to this man, if the law should ever find him out. Now that he's turned himself in of his own accord, I'd like to ask you that question again.''

A sad, wistful smile touched Claire's lips. ''To be truthful, I don't really know. Somehow it doesn't seem as important anymore. What I maybe *ought* to say is something along the lines of, 'I realize you didn't mean to hurt my husband and me. I can't ever forget the husband and the child that I lost, but if I didn't at least try to forgive you, I would lose myself as well.' ''

Her words echoed those spoken to him by Annet Maxwell

in the churchyard of Hawick: *Surely we were better advised, for the good of our own souls, tae forgive rather than tae demand retribution.* It was conclusive proof, if he needed it, that Claire Crawford had successfully reintegrated her past lives with her present. Smiling, he reached over and patted her hand.

"I hope you realize how far you've come," he said quietly. "We'll talk more about this when I get back. Meanwhile, I've arranged for a professional colleague of mine to look in on you while I'm gone—a clergyman, actually." He took out a business card and jotted Christopher's name and telephone number on the back. "He's an Episcopal priest; has a parish out in Kinross, but he does a bit of counselling as well. I think you'll like him. And when I get back, we'll talk about when you think you might be ready to go home."

Claire looked slightly startled. "You mean, *I* can decide?"

"We'll give it a few days, but yes, I think so. My major caution would be to deal gently with yourself in these next few days, after the euphoria wears off, and don't try to do too much too soon."

A shy but pleased smile lit Claire's face, giving Adam a glimpse of the pretty woman she had been before her accident.

"Can I call Ishbel and tell her the news?" she asked.

"Of course you can. I'm sure she'll be as pleased as you are."

Still smiling, she hugged her arms to her shoulders in wonderment. "Dr. Sinclair, I don't know how to thank you. I wish—I wish you didn't have to go away right now. But since you do, I hope everything goes well for you."

So do I, Adam thought as he bade his patient farewell and rose to depart, for resolution of the Irish affair was apt to be of a totally different level of magnitude than what he had managed to accomplish with Claire.

✦ ✦ ✦

"This thing you bought in Glasgow," said Peregrine to his wife as they headed toward Edinburgh Airport a few hours later. "Is it bigger than a breadbox?"

Julia Lovat clucked her tongue in mild derision. "Of

course it's bigger than a breadbox. If it were *smaller* than a breadbox, I wouldn't have had to make arrangements for having it delivered.''

''Just checking,'' said her husband. ''Is it bigger than a fridge-freezer?''

Julia considered. ''Equal volume, different proportions. And please look out for that farm machine.''

The machine in question was a heavy-duty tractor towing a seed-drill behind it, just coming out of the Gogar Roundabout ahead of them. It was rumbling along at a snail's pace, its bulky wheels overlapping the broken yellow line at the center of the westbound carriageway.

''He's got a perfectly good lane of his own,'' Peregrine complained loftily. ''I don't see why he should want half of mine as well. And what's a combo like that doing out on the city bypass, anyway?''

''Bypassing the city, I would imagine,'' Julia said drily. ''Even farmers occasionally have to get from A to B.'' Pausing to whip a glance over her shoulder, she added, ''Here's your chance to overtake, if you want to.''

''Just watch me,'' said Peregrine. ''This is what Morris Minors were made for.''

The Morris Minor in question was the Lovats' workhorse vehicle, a miniature estate wagon with wood-panelled sides and enough space in the rear to lay paintings flat and accommodate Peregrine's artist's paraphernalia. Today it held only an olive-green canvas carryall, his sketchbox, and a green waxed jacket. When Peregrine applied pressure to the accelerator, the little car leapt forward, bypassing the tractor with a clear yard to spare. A sign pointing the way to the Turnhouse Airport Exit loomed ahead.

''And about time!'' Peregrine declared.

He decelerated into the exit lane just as a British Midlands jet roared in low overhead on its way to land. Julia glanced at her watch.

''It's only half past two,'' she announced. ''You've still got a bit of time to spare, if you want to keep guessing.''

Peregrine had been relying on the game to provide a distraction from darker, more unsettling thoughts about his impending trip. Concerning its object, he had told Julia as much of the truth as he dared—that it had to do with the body they had found, now known to be that of an Irish Fisheries officer named Michael Scanlan. It was police business, and Peregrine had been asked to assist McLeod and Adam. He had mentioned the *Kriegsmarine* flag found on Scanlan's body, and that they hoped to find the German U-boat from which it came, but of the Black *Terma* he had said nothing. There seemed to him no point in acquainting his wife with the more ominous aspects of their quest, when there was nothing she could hope to do to offset the danger.

"Well?" Julia asked, on a patient note of challenge. "Don't you have any more questions to ask me about our mystery acquisition?"

Peregrine sighed. "Wouldn't you rather just put me out of my misery and tell me what it is?"

"Where's the fun in that?" Julia demanded. "No, if you're determined to be lazy, you'll just have to wait until you get back. You *are* planning to come back, aren't you?"

The sudden shift in his wife's tone of voice caught Peregrine off guard. "What kind of a question is that?"

"A serious one," Julia replied. "Is there anyone out there who might object to your going in search of a Nazi ghost-sub?"

The question left Peregrine feeling more than a little disconcerted.

"Nobody I could put a name to," he said guardedly. "But you needn't worry; Adam will see to it that I stay out of trouble. If you don't believe me, just look at Noel. He's been Adam's Second for years, and *he's* never come to any serious harm."

"There's always a first time," Julia said. "Do me a favor, darling, and don't let this occasion be the one that breaks the record."

Peregrine reached over and lightly stroked her cheek. "I won't," he promised. "Especially now that I've got you to come home to."

After leaving the Morris in one of the outlying car parks, husband and wife made their way arm-in-arm to the terminal building, Peregrine wearing his jacket and with the carryall slung over his shoulder, Julia carrying his sketchbox. They found McLeod pacing up and down in the vicinity of the Aer Lingus service desk. A navy-blue duffel was pushed up close against the counter, with a twin to Peregrine's waxed jacket laid atop it.

" 'Lo, Noel. Where's Adam?" Peregrine asked.

McLeod shrugged and gave Julia a peck on the cheek. "On his way here, I presume. I've gone ahead and picked up all our tickets, just in case he's running late—"

"Isn't that him now, just getting out of that taxi?" Julia asked, pointing out through the plate-glass wall of the concourse.

An old-fashioned black taxi was just disgorging a fare at the curb, and the tall figure in a grey three-piece suit was unmistakable.

"It's about time," McLeod muttered, in undisguised relief.

Any further comment was drowned out by the public address system, coming on to deliver a boarding announcement.

"Is that our flight?"

"Aye."

While McLeod fidgeted, Peregrine took the opportunity to draw his wife aside for a proper goodbye kiss, then wistfully watched her departing figure until McLeod came over to tell him of the latest development in the Claire Crawford case. A moment later, Adam joined them, a lightweight leather carry-on case in one hand and a medical bag in the other. The three men traded greetings on the way to the airport security checkpoint. When McLeod produced his police identification, he and his companions, together with their bags, were whisked through the gate and onto the waiting plane.

Conversation in flight was sparse, of necessity. Peregrine had the window seat, and spent his time peering out at the grey cloud-cover, thinking about Claire Crawford and trying *not* to think about Michael Scanlan, all too aware that the flag for which Scanlan had paid with his life was still tucked into his sketchbox, right under his seat. Beside Peregrine, McLeod had lain back in his seat as soon as they were airborne, eyes closed and arms folded across his chest with the air of a seasoned campaigner taking what rest he could before an expected engagement.

On the aisle, Adam gave every outward appearance of calm, but Peregrine noticed that one forefinger kept tracing spirals on the arm of his seat in a gesture that was almost ritual in its formal repetition. He wondered if the pattern might represent some kind of mnemonic device, reinforcing the teaching Adam had been given at the hands of Tseten and Julian. Adam was wearing his ring, as was McLeod, and Peregrine surreptitiously dug his from his pocket and slipped it on, just before they landed.

The plane touched down at Belfast City Airport just on an hour after takeoff. Deplaning with the rest of the passengers, Adam and his companions made their way through to the arrivals hall. Here they were hailed by a stoutly built man in a tweed jacket, with a flat cloth cap perched jauntily atop a thatch of snow-white hair. With him was a pert, grey-eyed woman in designer jeans and a rust-colored pullover under her navy duffel coat, whose abundant auburn hair was dramatically threaded with silver. Smiling, Adam strode forward to meet the pair, shifting his medical bag under one arm to free a hand.

"Hello, Aoife," he said, saluting the woman on both cheeks. "It's good to see you again, but we've got to stop meeting like this! And Magnus," he went on, turning to trade handshakes with the man. "How is life treating you, now that you're supposedly retired?"

The white-haired man grinned. "If you can believe it, I'm busier now than ever I was while I was still with the Force." His rich baritone carried the distinctive lilt of Ulster.

"He isn't joking," Aoife said in the same accent. "He's thinking of running for Parliament. I keep telling him he must be mad!"

"*Someone's* got to take a stand," Magnus returned.

"Aye, they do," Adam agreed, turning to make introductions. "You both remember Noel, of course, from the last time we had business in common, but you won't have met the latest addition to our ranks. This is Peregrine Lovat, a professional portrait artist with a rather interesting sideline in historical studies. Peregrine, I'd like you to meet Aoife Kinneally, my opposite number here in Northern Ireland, and Magnus Buchanan, her Second. Aoife's a stringer for *Sky News*. Until recently, Magnus was with the Royal Ulster Constabulary."

To Peregrine's discerning gaze, both members of the Irish Hunting Lodge displayed a characteristic aura of subtle, overlapping images—proof of their far-reaching personal pasts. Resisting his instinctive urge to pursue and capture those images, Peregrine concentrated instead on upholding his part in the exchange of civilities as they headed out of the terminal building. A travel-worn red Hi-Ace passenger van stood at the curb, casually watched over by a young RUC officer wearing body armor and a pistol, and carrying a compact submachine gun. At a nod from Magnus, he faded on along the road.

"My son's set of wheels," Aoife explained as she unlocked the back door so they could stow their luggage. "It was either this or the Carerra, on such short notice, and I wasn't sure how much gear you might bring."

"I'm grateful for transport in any form, Aoife," Adam said as he stashed his bags. "Before this night is over, I'm probably going to owe you half a score of favors."

Aoife laughed, a deep chuckle. "I'll remember that, the next time my editor hits me up with a demand for a personal interest story. In the meantime, we'd better be on our way. You did indicate that the time clock in this affair is running."

They closed up the back and piled into the van. Upon leaving the airport, Aoife headed west, skirting Belfast itself and picking up the M2 motorway north and westward toward Antrim. From the seat beside her, Adam spent the next half hour updating their Irish allies and outlining his battle plan.

"Our timetable *is* tight, then," the Irish chief said, at the end of Adam's briefing. "Fortunately, all our physical arrangements are in place; we just need to nail down the exact location. We'll stop at my house—it's on the way—and you can change clothes as well. I hope you brought warm things, because it's apt to be cold, out there in the West."

Very shortly, they were turning off the motorway to Templepatrick, a pleasant village not far from the town of Antrim.

Aoife's home was at one end of a narrow lane—a substantial stone-built cottage with a detached garage flanking one garden wall. Leaving the van parked in the drive, she shepherded her guests and their bags through a wicket gate into a lushly tangled garden, where pink and white roses climbed untrammelled through thickets of flowering brambles. A mossy path meandered to a side door to the house. Entering, Adam and his companions found themselves in a tiled service porch, between a washer and dryer on one side and an array of coat-hooks and Wellie boots on the other.

"Just leave your coats anywhere you see a space," Aoife said over her shoulder, shrugging out of her own. "Adam, you and Noel can go on through to the living room to change clothes while I put the kettle on. The toilet's beyond and to the right, if you need one."

Peregrine was already dressed for the coming foray, in a turtleneck and navy guernsey over denim jeans and sturdy hiking boots, so he merely went on into the big country kitchen and subsided onto a chair with his sketchbox as Adam and McLeod disappeared in the indicated direction. Aoife had made tea and was pouring it into two large thermos flasks when the pair returned, Adam wearing a dark tweed jacket over a polo-necked sweater and cords. McLeod was less formally attired in a navy fatigue sweater and baggy green army surplus trousers bedecked with multiple pockets.

The inspector ducked out to hang Adam's waxed jacket on a peg beside his own and Peregrine's, while Adam came and laid an Ordnance Survey map on the big kitchen table and sat down beside Magnus. A red Aga cooker set into the hearth of a former fireplace provided both a focal point and welcome warmth in the large room.

"Do you need more space, or can this be done right here?" Aoife asked as Adam began unfolding his map.

"This should be fine," Adam said. "As I indicated on the phone last night, we know where Scanlan and his partner were patrolling, so the sub has to be somewhere along here." He indicated a section of Donegal coast centered on Sheep Haven. "This is where their land backup last made contact, and their boat was later found up by Malin." His hand swept up the coast.

"So she's somewhere along here. And here's what we're looking for." He tossed a photo of a Type VII C German submarine in the center of the map that Peregrine had found and photocopied earlier that morning.

"Now, we do have a flag that we believe came from the sub, that we'd hoped to use as a link. The complicating factor is that someone didn't want the sub to be found, and put a rather impressive whammy on it to make sure of that. I've been given a method for getting past that, but I'll need a bit of help."

While he explained what he proposed, Peregrine opened his sketchbox on his lap and produced the flag, wrapped in its plastic bag. He laid it on the map and set the sketchbox at his feet as Adam delved into a pocket of his tweed jacket and produced Tseten's rosary, which he laid atop the map.

"Now, we're all only too well aware of the evil this flag came to betoken," Adam said, dumping the flag out of its bag without touching it, and laying the empty bag beside his chair. "However, I'm given to understand that Tseten's *mala* can be used as a buffer, to keep the negative energies associated with the flag from interfering with my tracking function. So Aoife, I'll ask you to put some protection on me and then lay the flag around my shoulders."

Aoife nodded, coming around behind him as he took up Tseten's rosary and wound it around his left wrist, then turned his palms upward in his lap. His eyes closed as Aoife briefly set her hands on his shoulders and then extended both hands palm-downward a few inches above his head, the fingertips overlapped. Peregrine caught the wink of a dark emerald at the heart of the gold Claddagh ring on her right hand, and suddenly realized that the green stone in Magnus's signet was also a cloudy emerald, engraved with his coat of arms.

"Ye holy ministers of grace, rulers of the four cardinal elements, riders upon the winds of Heaven, confer upon this your servant the benefits of your guidance and hold him inviolate against the principles of darkness," Aoife murmured, eyes closed and face uplifted in an attitude of supplication. "Though he walk for a time in the valley of the shadow of death, let not that shadow fall upon his footsteps, but let the Light be his companion, to his soul's comfort and salvation. Amen, so be it."

She bowed her head, as did Adam, and Peregrine stifled

a gasp to see a spark of scintillating fire spring into being beneath the crossing of her hands. As she slowly drew her hands apart, the spark blossomed into a dancing wreath of colored flame that flickered blue and red, gold and green, descending to encircle Adam's brow in a prismatic coronal. An instant it hovered there, before contracting and descending as a single tongue of flame to glow over his heart. Then it dispersed toward his extremities, thinning out as it travelled, until there was nothing more to be seen of it but a rainbow shimmer clinging about his fingertips.

Aoife lowered her hands until they came to rest lightly on the crown of Adam's head. Then, with a final whispered benediction, she took them away. Adam knew that instant, despite his closed eyes. The moment of release was accompanied by a sense of lightness, and he drew a deep, lingering breath to savor gratefully a newfound sense of being strongly protected. That sense of protection was damped but little as Aoife took up the Nazi flag and shook it out, laying it like a stole around his shoulders.

It was like shouldering some noisome living creature, slick, venomous, and cold. His skin crawled at its touch, but the chill had no power to penetrate. Drawing strength from the unseen sources of protection he could feel surrounding him, eyes still closed, he drew off his Adept ring and laid it on the table, setting the tips of both forefingers lightly upon it. He could feel the *mala* tingling about his left wrist as he projected his consciousness down through his arms and into his fingertips, to wrap around the focus of the ring.

"That which you bear comes from that which you seek," Aoife murmured, lightly touching her hands to his shoulders. "Beneath your hands lies a map encompassing the location of that which you seek. Picture the submarine now, in as complete detail as you can. Let its image form in your mind's eye, and let the link that will lead you back to it focus through the ring beneath your fingertips, drawing it to the place where the submarine now lies—as above, so below."

Adam paused a moment to draw a deep breath, calling up Peregrine's photo of the U-boat, visualizing as much detail as he could. The tingling in the *mala* increased almost to the point of discomfort, but he refused to back off. Projecting his vision into the image, he narrowed his interior focus until he could read the serial number painted on the conning tower: *636*.

Recognition of this detail was accompanied by a slight tug at the ring beneath his fingertips. Obedient to that directive, Adam let his fingers exert the lightest of pressure to push the ring across the map.

"Keep the image of the submarine in your mind's eye," Aoife's voice urged. "Let the link of the flag draw you toward its home, toward the vessel where that flag once flew. . . ."

The ring moved more, somewhat jerkily, then did not seem to want to move any more.

"Tory Sound," came Magnus's voice from off to one side, as hands lifted Adam's hands, though he did not open his eyes. "Horn Head."

"It's plausible," McLeod said. "There's Sheep Haven, where Scanlan's backup lost him."

"Aye, and there was quite a lot of submarine activity in those waters during the war," Magnus replied. "The bottom's littered with wrecks."

"Let's try it again," Aoife said. "Peregrine, turn the map, so it's oriented differently, and let's see if he hits that same location again."

Adam had to stretch across the map the second time, before the ring seemed content to stop. No one commented as his hands again were raised and the rustle of paper told of the map being turned again. Adam could not tell from their reaction whether he had confirmed his first hit or not.

"Let's give it one more try," Aoife murmured, letting his hands rest on the map again.

The third time, when the ring came to rest, Adam opened his eyes and immediately leaned forward to look underneath his hands. His ring encircled Horn Head.

"Three hits," McLeod murmured, looking pleased with his chief's performance. "It looks like that's where we're going."

A little distractedly, Adam slid his ring back onto his finger and pulled the Nazi flag from his shoulders, handing it off to Peregrine to fold and return to its plastic bag.

"How far is that from where we are?" he asked, glancing up at Magnus and Aoife as he unwound Tseten's *mala* and dropped it back into his pocket.

"About two hours to where we can pick up the boat we've arranged," the Irish Second replied. "Aoife's nephew keeps a thirty-foot cabin cruiser at Portstewart. We had him run it over to Malin Head last night. From Malin, it's only about twenty-five nautical miles to Horn Head—say, another couple of hours."

"And it's nearly six now," Adam said. "That puts us on target around ten. What about dealing with the sub, once we locate it? At very least, I expect we'll need to blow some hatches to get in; and probably it would be best to just destroy it, once we've secured the cargo. I don't think it would serve either government's interests if its existence were to become known."

"We've provided for that," Aoife said. "Magnus had to call in some heavy-duty favors, but one of our contacts with the security forces has lined up some appropriate ordnance— nothing fancy, but it ought to do the job on both counts. Magnus can supply the know-how, of course."

"I did a stint with bomb disposal," Magnus offered, at Peregrine's startled glance. "That was back in my young and foolish days. Now and then, though, the experience does come in handy."

He turned to Adam. "There wasn't time for our man to deliver the goodies here, but he's going to meet us en route— which means we ought to get moving."

Rising, Adam acknowledged this information with a sober nod and began folding up his map.

"I can't thank you enough for all your help," he said, as McLeod signalled Peregrine to join him, already heading for the service porch, and their jackets. "This operation would have been doomed at the outset without your assistance."

"Think nothing of it," Aoife said with a tight smile. "Forewarned is forearmed. If you hadn't been in a position to give us advance notice of the danger on our doorstep, Magnus and I and the rest of our people might have found ourselves with real trouble on our hands."

"I only wish I could have posted the warning sooner," said Adam. "As it is, we've still got a close race to run."

CHAPTER TWENTY-EIGHT

THE sun was going down beyond the horizon, sparkling the calm surface of the harbor with flakes of copper fire. In the fishing village of Derrybeg, the copper glow was picked up and reflected back from the windows of the houses facing the water. Most of the working boats were still out at sea, leaving the harbor empty except for a handful of small pleasure craft anchored in the shallows. The only large vessel standing in at the dock was a forty-foot converted fishing boat with the name *Rose of Tralee* picked out in peeling paint across her stern.

Her skipper, one Dennis Plunkett, was lounging in the stern, leaning against the taffrail while he smoked a cigarette—a beefy, big-bellied man in his middle fifties, with a rusty spattering of freckles across his face and the backs of his hands. As he scanned the sky from east to west, pushing his captain's cap back off his forehead, he figured that maybe twenty minutes of daylight remained. Already the sky to the east was dotted with stars, with the full moon shortly to be on the rise.

He glanced down at his watch, then took a final drag on his cigarette and flipped it into the water past the diving platform fixed to the stern, just missing the inflatable dinghy tied there. A light footstep approached from behind, emerging from the cabin, and a tenor voice spoke to his back.

"It's getting late, Skipper. So where's this client of ours got to?"

With a shrug, Plunkett turned to address Liam O'Rourke, the younger of his two crewmen.

"He said he'll be here. After all, this is his party. And it's already half paid for, whether he shows or not."

O'Rourke heaved a sigh and ran a sun-browned hand through his bristle-cut thatch of light brown hair. A former girlfriend once had told him he looked like James Dean, and he had made every conscious effort since to live up to that image. After a moment he sat down on one of the stern lockers.

"I don't know," he said doubtfully. "This whole job begins to smell a little. I'd give a lot to know where Kavanagh's boss came by his information about this wreck we're supposed to be checking out tonight. I mean, you've been running salvage operations in these waters for nearly twenty years, but you tell me this is the first you've ever heard of it."

"It is. That still doesn't mean a rat's arse. What the hell, Liam, you know as well as I do, how cutthroat this business can be. If you get a good lead, you'd bloody well better keep it to yourself, because if you don't, some other shark will try to move in and jump your claim. Why else do you think Kavanagh's boss is planning to show us the way to this wreck of his in person, rather than just giving us the map coordinates? It's because he doesn't want to risk letting us in on the secret any sooner than he has to."

"Must be some secret," said O'Rourke. He chewed his lip thoughtfully. "What kind of wreck is it, anyway? Do you know?"

Plunkett nodded. "Kavanagh had to tell me that much, just so we'd know what kind of gear to bring with us. It's a German U-boat, Second World War."

O'Rourke looked disappointed. "Is that all? Hell, with all the destroyer action that went on around here, dead subs are practically a ha'penny a dozen. But nobody's ever yet found one with any sunken treasure in it."

"No," Plunkett agreed. "Still, there's always a first time."

Before he could say anything more, Seamus Dillon, his first mate, came up from the hold.

"That's everything stowed away, Skipper," he reported. "All the air tanks are recharged, and the cutting gear is packed and ready. Wish we'd had time to get some explosives, though.''

At the mention of explosives, Plunkett pulled a face.

''I don't know what you want me to do about that. This job came up at short notice. We'll just have to make do with what we've got.''

Dillon gave a rub to his jaw, shadowed with evening stubble.

''Well, I just want you to know it makes me nervous, going down on a dive like this without 'em. I don't suppose you could talk our mysterious client into postponing this operation for a few days?'' he said without much hope.

Plunkett shook his head. ''Not from the way Kavanagh was talking. He says tonight.''

''After all these years, what's the bloody hurry?'' Dillon wondered sourly.

''Kavanagh says his boss might be expecting trouble from a rival party,'' Plunkett replied, ''but my guess is that they want to be in and out of this wreck before the authorities get wind of it and start throwing in legal obstacles.''

''Bloody bureaucracy,'' O'Rourke muttered. ''*We* do all the work, take all the risks. Seems to me it ought to be 'finders-keepers.' ''

''Well, it is, if we get there first, and the authorities don't know,'' Plunkett said with a sly smile. ''Assuming, of course, that there's anything worth finding and keeping.''

''Assuming, of course,'' Dillon said drily, ''that this whole thing isn't just a front for some gun-running scam.''

''That thought *had* crossed my mind,'' Plunkett said, ''but I don't see how that's any concern of ours, as long as we get paid.'' He spat over the railing in a gesture of patent indifference.

''As long as they don't blow our brains out, once we've served their purpose,'' Dillon pointed out.

Plunkett merely grunted.

''I think it's too late to back out now,'' O'Rourke said, standing up to gaze toward the landward end of the dock. ''Would that be your Mr. Kavanagh?''

He pointed toward a grey Mercedes saloon just pulling up, with a driver and two passengers. The first passenger to

alight was manifestly Kavanagh himself, the dying light
picking out a darkly handsome set of features above a pair
of shoulders that would have done credit to a Rugby center
forward. As he fetched a large duffel bag from the boot,
shouldering it with ease, the second passenger emerged:
taller and slighter, a willowy figure with a briefcase who
might have been anything from a university professor to a
certified accountant. He bent to speak briefly to the driver,
then turned to follow Kavanagh toward the dock as the car
pulled away.

"I think you can stop worrying," Plunkett said to Dillon.
"Unless the driver's coming along, there's only the two of
them, and the 'boss' looks to be the executive type."

Kavanagh led the way down the dock. Dillon and
O'Rourke faded back against the taffrail as Plunkett came to
the side to meet their new clients. Kavanagh boarded with a
bound, depositing his duffel bag on the deck with a metallic
clunk.

"My diving gear," he announced as he turned back to the
taller man following at his back. "And this is Mr. Raeburn.
From this point onward, you'll be taking your orders from
him."

Handing his briefcase to Kavanagh, Raeburn stepped
lightly down into the boat, then paused to give a fastidious
twitch to the cuffs of close-fitting grey leather gloves as his
pale eyes scanned his new employees. He was kitted out in
grey, from his polo-necked sweater and leather bomber
jacket to his grey cords and grey deck shoes—not half so
impressive as his employee, in Plunkett's unspoken opinion.
Kavanagh had the build of a prizefighter, and his clothes
spoke loudly of financial success, from the flash designer-cut
of his jacket and trousers to the heavy gold and carnelian
signet ring he wore like a knuckle-duster on the third finger
of his right hand. Plunkett noticed with mild interest that the
device seemed to be the snarling head of some kind of big
cat.

"Good evening, Captain," Raeburn said. The tone left no
doubt in Plunkett's mind that Raeburn really was in charge.
"If everything is ready, as Mr. Kavanagh requested, I suggest that we get under way."

Within five minutes, the *Rose* was moving slowly away from her berth, nosing out of the little harbor and heading northward along the Donegal coast. Their course took them due north and then east around the point of land known as Bloody Foreland, so-named for the way the setting sun sometimes lit its heights, though the sun had already set tonight. By the time they were passing close by the cliffs of Inishbofin, the full moon had risen like a copper penny from behind the dark line of the shore, gradually silvering the water as Inishbofin dropped away off to port.

Leaving Kavanagh to keep an eye on the movements of the crew, Raeburn repaired to the tight confines of the cabin, setting his briefcase on the scarred wooden table adjoining the tiny galley and then extinguishing the cabin lights. During the course of the next half hour, he watched from the cabin's starboard window as the coastline became increasingly rugged, massy headlands rising up from moon-drenched water.

At length Raeburn roused from his contemplation of the coast and returned to the table, plucking off his gloves and then opening his briefcase. By moonlight he removed a Walther PPK pistol from one of the cutouts in the foam lining of the case and tucked it into a special holster sewn into the lining of the leather bomber jacket, then pocketed several spare ammunition clips and a miniature two-way radio. He then removed a cylindrical black box as long as his hand and a handspan around, giving the cap a quick twist and up-ending the cylinder thus opened to shake out a small, tightly rolled scroll of parchment. After returning the cylinder to its place, he plucked out the scroll of parchment and closed the case, laying the scroll on the closed top as he pulled a chair closer to the table and sat.

The ring he slipped from the third finger of his right hand was a more elegantly crafted version of the one Kavanagh was wearing. The blood-red carnelian surmounting the heavy gold band bore the same device: the snarling head of a lynx. Setting it on the case before him, he pulled a small pocket torch from an inside pocket and took up the scroll, unrolling it to read four lines of Tibetan script.

He mouthed the words once to fix them in his memory,

then began slowly whispering the words as a mantra, replacing his torch in his jacket pocket and letting the scroll roll back on itself, twisting it narrower. Turning his focus to the *muladhara* chakra at the base of his spine, he began summoning up the serpent power. He could feel it gathering, an almost sexual tension building upward, as he took up his ring between the thumb and forefinger of his left hand and thrust the scroll through the circle of the band.

The parchment vanished in a consuming flash of flame, and as he inhaled the smoke of it, pressing the ring to his forehead and closing his eyes, he could feel the kundalini serpent uncoiling within him, pushing open the successive chakras at sacrum and solar plexus, breastbone and throat, finally fountaining up his spine to roil behind his eyelids, opening the sixth or *ajna* chakra, the aptly called Third Eye. As a prickling sensation broke out between his eyebrows, just above the bridge of his nose, he shifted the circle of his ring to the same spot and opened his eyes again, turning his gaze toward the moon-drenched shadows of the shore.

The minutes ticked by as the *Rose* continued to press north and eastward, running parallel to the rugged cliffs of Horn Head. They had rounded the point when all at once Raeburn's augmented vision espied an unearthly shimmer of green light emanating from amongst the rocks, just to the right of a narrow crescent of beach.

He stared at it for a moment, to fix its position firmly in his mind. Then, slipping his ring back onto his finger, he drew a deep breath to bank the energies, got to his feet, and went topside. He found Dillon operating the sonar, shaking his head as he studied the readings. Plunkett was at the helm, Kavanagh standing between him and Dillon. O'Rourke was up on the bow, keeping a lookout for the rocks that occasionally jutted out of the water farther inshore.

"Take her in to half our present distance from shore and drop anchor," Raeburn said.

"We've only got about thirty feet of water right now," Plunkett said, though he spun the wheel to take the *Rose* in closer. "You sure about this location?"

"Beyond all mortal doubt," Raeburn replied. "Have your men bring up the dinghy as soon as we've dropped anchor."

"But—"

"The wreckage is in a sea cave, accessible from the shore," Raeburn said, in a tone that did not brook further discussion. "We'll need your equipment ashore."

Plunkett said nothing until O'Rourke had set the anchor and the engines had been shut down, watching as Kavanagh brought two large canvas satchels from out of his duffel bag and laid them beside the stern lockers.

"We're only going to get three in the dinghy, with so much gear," Plunkett said, as Dillon pulled the dinghy closer to the diving platform suspended off the stern. "If you want all that to go ashore as well as the cutting equipment, I suggest that you go across in the first trip with Dillon and me, and then we'll send him back to fetch Mr. Kavanagh."

"That's entirely reasonable," Raeburn replied, much to Plunkett's surprise.

Plunkett boarded the dinghy first, settling in the stern beside the little outboard motor. Dillon followed with a canvas bag containing flares and a brace of electric lanterns. Next O'Rourke handed down a large duffel with acetylene tanks and cutting equipment, after which Raeburn climbed down, perching in the bow. He took the two canvas satchels Kavanagh handed him and set them at his feet, silent as Plunkett fired up the little outboard and O'Rourke cast off their bowline.

The moonlight cast hard shadows as the little craft buzzed toward the slender crescent of beach, the *Rose*'s running lights gradually fading against the bright glare of moonlight. Within a few minutes, the little inflatable was running up onto the sandy crescent, which was already narrower than it had been, with the tide coming in.

"I expect we're going to run out of beach before we run out of tide," Plunkett remarked as Raeburn sprang lightly to the sand and he followed. "Where's this sea cave of yours, Mr. Raeburn?"

Raeburn shouldered one of his satchels and gestured off toward the cliffs to their right, leaving Dillon to retrieve the other and draw the boat farther onto the sand.

"Up there. If you don't waste time talking, we'll be well above the high-water line before it becomes a problem. Just pull the dinghy up as far as you can and moor it. And bring the equipment.''

They followed these somewhat autocratic instructions without comment, Plunkett breaking out the electric lanterns and handing one each to Raeburn and Dillon before hefting the cutting equipment onto his shoulder and scooping up the bag with the flares. As they began trudging up the beach, heading for the cliffs with Raeburn in the lead, the tiny radio in his pocket beeped.

Plunkett stopped dead in his tracks, and Dillon said, ''What's that?'' as Raeburn pulled out the radio and lifted it to his mouth.

''Go,'' he acknowledged, also drawing the Walther as he turned.

''*Rose* secured,'' came the terse reply, even as the moonlight glinted off the gun-metal in Raeburn's hand.

''Stay where you are, gentlemen,'' Raeburn murmured, before lifting the radio to his mouth to acknowledge. ''Roger.''

''What the devil's going on?'' Plunkett demanded, as Dillon glanced back at him in alarm.

Raeburn moved aside and gestured with the gun for the two to come on past him.

''Please take the lead, Mr. Dillon,'' he said quietly. ''There's still a great deal of work to be done this evening.''

As Dillon sidled on past, keeping a wary eye on the gun, Plunkett followed, tight-jawed—and balked in his tracks as two outlandish human forms stepped suddenly between him and his first mate, out from behind an outcropping of rock. The pair had shaved heads, and were wearing what looked like bright orange sarongs. Though these men were old, Plunkett vaguely remembered seeing kids dressed like this in Galway one summer, amiably dispensing meditation tracts to passers-by.

But there was nothing amiable or meditative about the way these two moved briskly forward, each bearing a strange triple-edged dagger. As Plunkett uttered a croaked cry of dismay, one of the monks raised his blade in warning, pointed straight at Plunkett, while the other tapped Dillon's forehead with the point.

CHAPTER TWENTY-NINE

DILLON went rigid, quivering convulsively as if struck by an electric charge, his lantern glowing momentarily brighter before tumbling from his hands. Plunkett backpedalled frantically, slamming into the side of the cliff behind him and dropping his duffel bag. When Dillon's spasms abated, he crumpled to his knees in the sand, staring blindly ahead. The man who had touched him caught him easily under one elbow to keep him from falling over.

"Jayzus, Mary, and Joseph!" Plunkett muttered, and hastily crossed himself.

The gesture did not escape Raeburn.

"I doubt that will avail you very much, Mr. Plunkett, unless you are a man of far greater depth than I take you for. And I wouldn't even think about trying to run. I doubt my associates would take it kindly. Mr. Dillon, please leave your satchel, and go back and get into the dinghy. I shouldn't want you to drown when the tide comes in."

Plunkett blenched visibly as Dillon shouldered out of the strap on the satchel and got to his feet, oblivious to anything around him as he walked back to the beached inflatable and got in, sitting statue-like amidships. Running a dry tongue across his lips, Plunkett managed to whisper, "Who the devil are you people?"

Raeburn disdained to answer the question, only tucking his pistol into his waistband as he turned back to the two *Phurba* priests.

"I see you got here in good time," he said in German. "So, which way is this cave?"

The two Tibetans traded glances. Then Kurkar silently turned and pointed with his *Phurba* toward a shadowy section of the cliff fronting the cove. Frowning, Raeburn directed the beam of his lantern upward, where its glare lit up a jagged hole in the cliff-face, with the edges showing raw like a newly opened wound.

Smiling faintly, Raeburn turned back to Plunkett and gestured toward the satchel Dillon had left. Nagpo had retrieved the fallen lantern.

"All right, pick that up and come with me."

Plunkett's gaze flicked to the pistol in Raeburn's waistband, but at his captor's pointed glance back at the nearest *Phurba* priest, he bent to obey, awkwardly slinging the satchel alongside his bag of flares, then reshouldering the duffel bag. He staggered a little under the combined weight as Raeburn directed him toward a tumbled rockfall at the cliff's base.

"I can't climb that," he protested, faltering to a standstill. "Not carrying these."

"My associates believe that you can," Raeburn informed him. "And you *will*—unless, of course, you prefer to find out precisely what happened to your man. Personally, I would advise against it. I'm told that he will suffer no permanent harm—but I am never entirely certain, when dealing with another language and culture, whether the vocabulary is exactly equivalent. Start climbing, Mr. Plunkett—and do be careful. You're carrying explosives."

"What the—"

"You did indicate to Mr. Kavanagh that obtaining explosives on such short notice would be impossible—something about government red tape intended to foil would-be terrorists. Fortunately, Mr. Kavanagh is extremely resourceful. Climb, Mr. Plunkett."

As he gestured upward with his lantern, Plunkett made a noise between a groan and a sob, now convinced that Raeburn himself was one of those terrorists, but he was already readjusting the weight of the satchel and the flares, to counterbalance the duffel bag, and began immediately, if laboriously, to climb.

The rockfall had made a rude stairway leading up to a

diagonal ledge. Soon puffing and panting under his burden, Plunkett scuffed his way sideways along the ledge, now and then casting nervous glances over his shoulder at the moonlit beach below. Raeburn followed hard on his captive's heels, shining the electric torch onto the path ahead, his own thoughts carefully screened behind a mask of professional inscrutability. With Nagpo and Kurkar keeping close behind him, shadowing his every move, he knew he was as much a prisoner of the present situation as Plunkett. But with any luck, he might succeed in altering the circumstances in his own favor.

The threshold to the opening was choked with fresh rubble. Squeezing past Plunkett, Raeburn shone the lantern inside and then entered, bidding Plunkett to follow. With the two *Phurba* priests following after, the skipper of the *Rose* needed no further encouragement, though he stifled a curse as he stumbled on rough footing and nearly fell.

The opening became a passage that wormed its way into the fabric of the cliff. After a couple of tight, zigzag turns, the party arrived at the mouth of a second opening, where light from Raeburn's lantern dispersed into open space beyond. Peering ahead and past his captor, Plunkett gasped and nearly dropped his burden.

"Sweet Mother of Mercy!"

Even Raeburn had to admit that the submarine made an impressive sight. Framed by the vault of the surrounding cavern, it slumbered half-in, half-out of the shadows like some giant, armor-plated prehistoric creature. Leaning out from the entryway, Raeburn let the lantern-light play over the long, streamlined hull as Nagpo did the same. Bracketed between the deadly bristle of fore and aft gun-turrets, the conning tower reared up above the straddling swell of the fuel tanks like the dorsal fin of a hunting shark.

The incoming tide was being channelled into the cavern through an underwater rift. Already the sub was partially awash amid a gentle roil of greenish-black swells. The air stank of spilt oil and rotting kelp. The vibration of the surf, pounding at the cliffs from outside, sent echoes bouncing round the walls like the mutter of phantom voices.

There in the cavern mouth, with Nagpo and Kurkar looking on, Raeburn bade Plunkett put down his burdens and break out the flares. After planting one to either side of where they stood, he had Plunkett toss half a dozen more among the rocks opposite the conning tower to provide general illumination. The harsh, actinic glare sent monstrous, magnified shadows leaping toward the cavern roof as Plunkett reclaimed his somewhat lightened load and reluctantly followed Raeburn down toward the bow-end of the sub. Smoke from the flares hung wraith-like on the stale air as the four men sprang across onto the foredeck and made their way carefully aft, pausing beside the forward hatch.

"Have a look at this one first," Raeburn said, shining his lantern on the rusted hatch and wheel. "You can put the gear down here while we decide what to do. The hatch in the conning tower is probably going to be easiest, but our friends may simply not have had the physical strength to shift this one."

Plunkett gratefully obeyed, donning a pair of work gloves that he pulled from a rear pocket and then bending his back to the wheel that dogged down the hatch. It refused to budge.

"Try the one aft," Raeburn said, handing Plunkett his torch.

He and the monks accompanied Plunkett as far as the salt-corroded ladder that led up into the conning tower, but the second deck hatch proved no more cooperative than the first. As Plunkett reluctantly returned, Raeburn took back his lantern and shone it up the ladder.

"Up you go, Mr. Plunkett."

Plunkett climbed carefully, testing each rung. Raeburn followed right on his heels. The skipper of the *Rose* was already straining at the wheel atop the hatch as Raeburn came onto the bridge.

"Nope, can't budge this one, either," Plunkett said nervously, bidding Raeburn bring the lantern closer as he continued to inspect the hatch. "It—ah—*is* cleaner than the others, though—probably because it hasn't been submerged twice a day for fifty years."

"So, what do you propose?" Raeburn asked.

Plunkett sat back on his heels, fearful of meeting Raeburn's gaze beyond the glare of the lantern.

"Well, we might chisel our way in, but that would take a while. I'd rather try the cutting gear before we resort to explosives. I don't even know what you brought."

"Standard SBG and Cortex fuse—exactly what you're accustomed to working with," Raeburn replied.

Plunkett raised an eyebrow. "Well, that'll get you inside in next to no time, all right, but the concussion could bring the cave down on us."

"I think not," Raeburn said, with a glance down at the *Phurba* priests, who shook their heads impassively.

"Right." Plunkett drew a nervous breath, then exhaled gustily as he considered the matter.

"All right, this may not be as bad as I'd expected," he allowed. "Not being underwater makes life *much* easier. Since you seem to be in a hurry, I think we can manage just by binding a length of Cortex round the hatchway and setting it off."

"I'll bring you what you need," Raeburn said with a faint smile.

He left the two *Phurba* priests to keep an eye on Plunkett while he went back to the pile of equipment by the forward hatch and fetched the smaller of the two canvas satchels. Kavanagh had briefed him on what would be needed, depending on circumstances. He watched Plunkett carefully as he deposited the satchel beside the hatch.

Unpacked, the Cortex looked like nothing so much as a coil of white plastic washing line, but Plunkett's heavy face was beaded with sweat as he measured off the requisite length of fuse and cut it loose with the Swiss Army knife from his pocket. After pressing the fuse down around the hatch, he connected it up to a detonator that Raeburn handed him. The detonator, in turn, he wired to a 9-volt battery.

"We'd all better get well back from the conning tower," Plunkett advised as they came down off the ladder. "This stuff packs a wallop when it blows."

At Raeburn's gesture, both the *Phurba* priests retreated with them as far as the forward hatch, Plunkett stringing out wire as they went.

"Brace yourselves," Plunkett muttered, and made the final connection.

The Cortex exploded with an earsplitting crack. The deck underfoot gave a violent answering shudder. After a brief, smoldering rain of rust particles, everything fell silent.

"Now, let's see just how good you are," Raeburn muttered, urging Plunkett back toward the conning tower with a push.

He made Plunkett go first back up the ladder. The hatchway showed a blackened fringe of torn metal where the Cortex had ripped away the surrounding matrix of rust and corrosion. Slipping his work gloves back on, Plunkett gingerly seized hold of the hatch-wheel and gave it an experimental tug. There was an answering grating noise as the hatch shifted.

"It's free," he announced.

"Excellent," Raeburn said. "Let's have it open, then."

Gritting his teeth, Plunkett heaved the hatch-cover up the rest of the way. The exertion left him gasping as he dropped forward onto his knees to peer inside—and came face to face with a mummified corpse lodged on the inside access ladder.

The corpse was bearded, and wearing the grey uniform of a German naval lieutenant. It had one withered arm wound tightly around the uppermost rung. The other had dropped away from the underside wheel of the hatch-cover with a loose rattle of finger-bones against the ladder below and the flap of an empty grey sleeve. Plunkett recoiled with a yip, then froze as he felt the sudden, icy pressure of a gun barrel against the back of his head.

"Thank you, Mr. Plunkett," Raeburn said softly. "You've been very helpful. Unfortunately, your services are no longer required."

The Walther's blast sent echoes reverberating in the cavern and in the depths of the boat as the big Irishman collapsed forward, blood and brain matter seeping from the hole in the back of his skull and the larger exit wound in the center of his forehead. After pausing to holster his weapon, Raeburn hauled the body up by its jacket and sent it tumbling over the conning tower railing. It bounced heavily off the deck and slid into the water with a sucking splash as the two impassive *Phurba* priests started up the ladder to join him.

Eager now to be on with it, Raeburn turned his attention

to clearing the hatchway. A couple of kicks knocked the German corpse loose from the ladder, sending it tumbling back into the dark womb of the ship. He stood back as the first of the two *Phurba* priests entered the hatch and started down, the second lighting his way and then handing down a lantern. Raeburn followed more slowly, fumbling with his own lantern until he could gain floor-level.

The hatch gave access to the control room. As he stepped off the ladder, Raeburn's wary gaze met an eerie tableau. The two *Phurba* priests were standing motionless near the periscope column in the center of the control room. But beyond them, the probing glare of the two electric lanterns picked out nearly a dozen mummified corpses in grey German naval uniforms, all loosely slumped at their duty stations as if death had taken them unawares.

A thin current of fresh air, filtering down the hatchway, stirred up the dust of nearly five decades and reawakened the reek of old decay. Raeburn studied the scene for a long moment, momentarily at a loss to read the riddle.

"They were gassed," said Nagpo, speaking from the shadows.

Raeburn shifted his gaze. "Why?"

"It was necessary that there should remain a command crew on board," the monk replied.

"Why?" Raeburn persisted.

This time he got no response. Impervious to the stench and the shadows, the two *Phurba* priests moved off toward the aft section of the control room. Raeburn followed them with the second light. Skirting the base of the periscope, he fetched up short at the sight of a third monkish figure, attired like his companions in robes of orange silk, one bony shoulder bare, seated cross-legged on the floor in an attitude of meditation.

Like all the members of the bridge crew, this monk was long dead, reduced to a mummified corpse. The hairless skull was bowed over the sunken chest as if in prayer, and the claw-like hands were curled about the dusty hilt of a *Phurba* much like those carried by Nagpo and Kurkar. With all the decay, Raeburn could not tell whether the blade Nagpo reverently lifted from the desiccated fingers had been the means of death or only seemed to broach the abdomen. He started slightly as Nagpo gravely saluted his living companion with the blade, then presented it to him with bowed head.

"Now is your past sacrifice made good in this present day," he declared in Tibetan. "Receive what is yours, that you may resume your destined task."

Kurkar accepted this cryptic tribute with an inclination of his shaven head, taking the *Phurba* that Nagpo held out to him and running a stroking hand down the blade.

"That which was surrendered now is reclaimed," he replied.

Closing his eyes, he concentrated for a moment, the blade of the *Phurba* pressed flat against his cheek; then the hand with the *Phurba* lashed out to strike the mummified skull of its previous owner. A bright flash left Raeburn blinded for a few seconds, only able to see in afterimage the outline of the bowed body engulfed in a white-hot flame that consumed all. When he could see properly again, only a fine powdering of white ash remained where the body had rested, and Kurkar was tucking the *Phurba* into the belt of his robe beside the other one.

"Now for the rest," the *Phurba* priest declared, as he turned back to the forward section of the control room.

There were four of the wooden crates shoved against the grey-painted bulkhead, each about a cubic foot in size, all with German eagles and SS markings boldly stencilled across them in red and black. With the boxes was a somewhat larger chest of brass-bound teakwood, its lid and sides intricately decorated with grotesque and fanciful carvings.

Smiling slightly, Kurkar approached the chest and lifted the lid. Though kept from Nagpo from approaching too close, Raeburn could see that the chest was full of Tibetan texts, each one swaddled in a band of green brocade. As Nagpo shone his light upon them, Kurkar lifted out the top-most one and deftly removed the wrapping. He let his fingers linger briefly over the pattern carved on the wooden cover, then turned to the first page inside.

The script was not unfamiliar. Raeburn had seen other examples of its type amongst the collection of manuscripts jealously guarded by a former superior, self-styled the

Head-Master. Kurkar read out a phrase that Raeburn took to be a title. The dialect was one he had heard the Head-Master use in the pronouncement of certain arcane magical formulae.

Even this brief utterance had the effect of generating unsettling resonances throughout the long-dead air of the control room. The two Tibetans traded inscrutable smiles. Still smiling, Kurkar lowered the cover and replaced the wrapping before turning back to Raeburn.

"This chest and its contents do not concern you," he said in German. "Your present duty is to examine this vessel and ascertain to what extent it is operational."

The arrogance in the order was no less offensive for being delivered in a tone of cool indifference, but Raeburn made himself bite back his anger.

"It isn't operational at all," he said stiffly. "I told Dorje—"

"Just do as you are told," Nagpo interrupted. "Or do you wish to dispute the matter?"

With a snort and a gesture of resigned disbelief, Raeburn gave up the argument and set about performing a survey of the boat's mechanicals. With the sub's vast running batteries as dead as her crew, none of the automatic gauges were registering, so he had to activate them manually to get a status reading. It was a time-consuming operation, but eventually he was able to determine, in theory, that the compressors and the diesels were still in working order.

"She has fuel enough left in the saddle tanks to get her moving, if she weren't sitting on the bottom," he reported to his Tibetan supervisors. "That aside, I must remind you that I can't initiate a first-start arrangement by myself—I told Dorje that. There are too many systems involved."

"How many crewmen will you require?" Kurkar asked, as if determining catering arrangements.

"Pretty much all of your 'skeleton crew,' " Raeburn said with some acerbity, still unconvinced that Dorje's boast had been legitimate. "The captain and exec, the chief engineer and his second, a couple of junior mechanics—I told Dorje what was needed. I still think it would be just as easy to take the crates to the dinghy and—"

Nagpo calmly held up a hand. "*Rinpoche* informed you correctly," he said. "This necessity has been anticipated. You will now leave us and wait outside. Remain well clear of the hatch. Our work will require no little concentration."

Much as he might resent such a cavalier dismissal, Raeburn knew there was nothing to be gained by questioning it. Biting back an acid remark that would be wasted, he turned on his heel and made for the ladder.

Back out on the conning tower, he wondered what it was that the *Phurba* priests were going to do. It was just possible that they might, indeed, be able to reanimate the crew—though doing it on such a scale was beyond Raeburn's ability. But reanimating a submarine was a different matter entirely. Dagger magic dealt with primitive animistic forces that were sometimes difficult to direct or contain. This being the case, Raeburn could not imagine how forces of this kind could be induced to interact harmoniously with such a complex product of technology as a submarine. By his reckoning, the very incongruity could be potentially very dangerous.

He was half-minded to use his enforced withdrawal as an excuse to withdraw entirely, and make good his escape. What prevented him was the promise of a share in the sub's cargo. He had seen the crates, and knew what Dorje had said they contained. If even half the volume of each really was diamonds, such a prize was not lightly to be dismissed. And then there was the matter of the manuscripts. . . .

After a moment's further deliberation, he set his lantern on the slimy floor of the conning tower and stationed himself at the forward railing, well back from the hatch, and settled in to wait and see what would develop.

At first all was silence. The eerie light of the flares began to get on his nerves. As the minutes ticked away, however, the hush became pregnant with eerie expectancy, like the prelude to a storm. Very occasionally, Raeburn became aware of a whisper of chanting coming from within.

Then all at once he became aware of a deep-toned rumbling that seemed to be travelling up from the sea-floor. As it grew louder, the light of the electric lantern began to flicker, as if something were interfering with the power in the batteries.

The atmospheric pressure inside the cavern was changing. Raeburn could almost feel the barometer dropping. His eardrums began to throb, filling his head with a dull tattoo like distant artillery fire. He pressed his palms to his temples, then gave an involuntary start as something whisked past him.

He wheeled instinctively toward the open hatch. There was nothing to be seen. Another passing flit raised the hackles on the back of his neck. Then suddenly the surrounding air was full of invisible movement.

Like water disappearing down a drain, the phantoms were sucked down through the hatchway into the belly of the ship, and Raeburn was assailed by a sudden, fleeting impression of voices shrieking in protest somewhere above and beyond the registers of normal sound.

The screams drained away like leaves caught in a whirlpool. Then the whirlpool turned itself suddenly upside down, its concentric forces rising up out of the depths of the sub in a cone of elemental power.

Like the tail of an inverted cyclone, the storm of power lashed out at the cavern's roof. There was a sonorous boom, like the report of a mortar. Looking up sharply, Raeburn saw a sudden rift appear in the cavern's roof. Out of that rift descended the first crackling rain of unearthly energies.

CHAPTER THIRTY

THE full moon was well up in the sky by the time the
Lady Gregory cleared the northernmost tip of Horn
Head. Adam stood alone in the bow of the big cabin cruiser,
dark eyes narrowed to mere slits as he scanned the serrated
line of the shore. He had exchanged his tweed jacket for a
waxed one, and he pulled the corduroy collar closer against
the sea-spray as the *Lady Gregory* forged on, skirting the
unbroken chain of sea-cliffs that stood frowning in the moonlight like the ramparts of some huge, forbidding fortress. So
far, they had spotted no sign of their quarry.

But they were getting close. In the last half hour, all of
them had begun to detect the first telltale signs that dark
forces were building in this vicinity. Those emanations were
growing with each passing minute—all the proof any of them
needed that time was running short, and not in their favor.

The sound of soft footfalls and the rustle of a waxed jacket
heralded McLeod coming up from the stern to join Adam.
The inspector was carrying a pair of infrared binoculars, one
of two supplied by Magnus's undercover contact. Another of
Magnus's contacts had ensured that they were not detained at
any of the border checkpoints coming out of Londonderry—
which was just as well, because the cache by then secured
in the back of the Hi-Ace van had included numerous tightly
controlled items, the most innocuous of which were the half-
dozen spare ammo clips for the Browning Hi-Power auto-
matics that both McLeod and Magnus now were carrying.
His nerves raw-alert, Adam reflected grimly that it was going
to take something more than conventional firepower to stop

whatever dark work their adversaries had in progress—but they must be prepared for conventional resistance as well.

McLeod trained the binoculars on the shore, scanned long and intently, then muttered, "Nothing!" in manifest frustration. "Damn it, we can all but *smell* them! If we don't find them soon, there's going to be hell to pay."

While his two superiors were keeping a lookout from the deck, Peregrine was up in the pilot-house with Aoife's nephew, Eamonn, owner and operator of the *Lady Gregory*. While Eamonn skillfully piloted the *Lady G* around and through the maze of offshore rocks and shoals, keeping an eye on his depth-sounder, Peregrine was using the second pair of night-binoculars in an attempt to get a high-angle view of the passing landscape. So far he had seen nothing worth mentioning.

"What exactly are you looking for?" Eamonn asked.

"I wish I knew," Peregrine sighed. "I'm just hoping I'll recognize it, if and when I find it."

Though he did not say as much to Eamonn, he was beginning to feel like a fifth wheel. His artistic abilities seemed of little use or relevance in their present circumstances, especially when compared with what some of his more senior companions were doing. Magnus, he had learned on their drive to Malin Head, had clairvoyant talents—the ability to visualize distant occurrences. At the moment, the retired RUC officer was below deck with Aoife, hoping to gain an extrasensory impression of who their adversaries might be and, even more importantly, what exactly they might be doing.

Which couldn't be anything good, Peregrine thought moodily. Even without Magnus's longer-range brand of perceptual acuity, he was himself queasily aware of shadowy forces on the rise. Even brushing the edges of that thickening miasma of evil was like being forced to wade at the edges of a polluted lake. What Adam must be experiencing, he could only guess.

Jagged rocks loomed ahead, too close for Eamonn's taste, and the young skipper expertly put the wheel over to navigate the *Lady G* safely past them. As they nosed around the next headland, Peregrine found himself starting to wonder if perhaps they ought to go ashore and proceed on land. That consideration evaporated an instant later, as his questing gaze was drawn toward a triangle of lights suspended between the moonlit water and the surrounding crescent of shadowy cliffs.

The source of the lights was a large fishing boat bristling with booms, slightly larger than the *Lady Gregory*. She was anchored several hundred yards out from a narrow strip of beach, her hull rising and falling on the shallow swell of the incoming tide. Down on the foredeck, McLeod gave a wolfish growl of discovery and subjected the newfound vessel to a close sweep with his binoculars.

"*Rose of Tralee*," he read out. "Do you suppose she's really just fishing?"

"Not for fish," came Adam's terse reply.

He and McLeod retreated aft, keeping an eye on their quarry, as the *Lady G* nosed toward the other vessel, gradually slowing. Two sets of feet came thudding up the steps from the lower deck. Magnus arrived first, with Aoife right on his heels.

"What've you got?" the Irish Second asked.

"You tell me," McLeod muttered, handing him the binoculars. "Name's the *Rose of Tralee*. Do you think she's doing some moonlight fishing, or is this our bird?"

Magnus swept the glasses along the length of the other vessel, riding at anchor between them and the shore. As Aoife joined him by the railing, Peregrine came scrambling down from the pilot-house.

"I think there's somebody on board," he whispered. "I saw movement against the cabin lights."

The cabin lights suddenly winked off, even as he said it, and Magnus lowered his binoculars.

"This is your call, Magnus," Adam said quietly. "How do you want to play this?"

"By the book, I think, until we know what we're up against." He handed the binoculars to Aoife and glanced pointedly at McLeod. "Unless anybody else has a better suggestion?"

The Scottish detective shook his head. "Go for it."

Nodding, Magnus made a trumpet of his two hands.

"Ahoy!" he called in a loud voice. "*Rose of Tralee*, this is the *Lady Gregory*. Is anyone aboard?"

His hail boomed out across the intervening water. Before he could shout a second time, the cabin door opened and a broad-shouldered figure emerged into the moonlight.

"This is the skipper of the *Rose*," a rough voice called back. "What do you want?"

The Irish accent went with the locale, but the tone was suspiciously hostile, and the silhouette proclaimed "city," not the rugged attire one would expect on a fishing boat.

"We were just passing by when we saw your lights," Magnus shouted. "Are you in any difficulty?"

"Nothing we can't handle for ourselves," came the curt reply.

"Do you believe that?" Magnus whispered to Adam.

"No."

"Neither do I. Peregrine, go tell Eamonn to take us in closer. We'll see what happens if we refuse to take the hint."

As the young artist darted off toward the pilot-house, Magnus cupped his hands again.

"If it's engine trouble you're having, we've a mechanic on board," he shouted. "Why don't you let us come over and see if we can give you a hand?"

The *Lady Gregory*'s engines changed pitch, and she began to nose closer.

"Why don't you go to hell?" snarled the self-proclaimed skipper of the *Rose*. And punctuated the retort with a sudden burst of gunfire.

Everyone aboard the *Lady Gregory* hit the deck as a stream of bullets swept across her bow, pinging off her steel hull and scattering shattered perspex from a forward cabin window.

"Jayzus, what's he got? A bloody Uzi?" Magnus gasped, from a prone position on the deck.

"Something bigger than that," McLeod replied, already drawing the Browning Hi-Power from his belt and snapping back the slide to chamber a round.

Aoife wormed across the deck on her elbows as far as the foot of the ladder that led up to the pilot-house.

"Eamonn, are you two all right up there?"

"Aye, thank God for steel bulkheads," came a voice from above. "Though heaven only knows what my insurance adjuster's going to say, when we get back to port!"

Magnus had taken cover behind the shelter of the superstructure, his own pistol now in hand, and was working his way toward one side, keeping his head well down.

"I don't think we need to ask any more questions," he muttered, getting his feet under him. "I don't care whether they're Nazis or the bloody IRA, they aren't meant to have firearms. Let's see what they've got."

Rearing up from cover, he squeezed off three quick shots over the forward bulkhead and ducked back down from a fierce blaze of return-fire. Bullets ricocheted and fiberglass flew in splinters.

"I guess that answers your question," McLeod muttered, keeping his head down. "Why do the bad guys always wind up with the biggest guns?"

He started to rise, then flinched back with a sharp imprecation as a bullet burned past his left cheekbone. The spiteful chatter of automatic weapons-fire continued, coming in fits and bursts.

"Are you all right?" came Adam's sharp inquiry.

"Aye, just a scratch."

"Somebody needs to teach that feckless bastard the difference between quantity and quality," Magnus said, as the strafing abruptly petered out.

"Maybe he's out of ammo," Adam said hopefully.

"Don't count on it," McLeod muttered.

Cautiously he lifted his head. The response was a short, resurgent salvo that sent him diving for the deck. As he did so, Magnus reared up again and squeezed off a double round of two in the direction of the muzzle-flashes, immediately ducking down again. When the echoes subsided, there was only silence.

The two policemen traded glances.

"Either he's playing possum, or you've hit him," said McLeod.

"Only one way to find out," Magnus replied—and heaved himself to his feet, weapon poised.

Too late to prevent it, his fellow Huntsmen tensed in dread

anticipation, McLeod ready to lay down cover-fire. When the silence held, a collective sigh of relief whispered among them and Magnus ducked back down.

"That's appears to be round one to our side," Adam said, "unless, of course, this isn't our quarry at all. Eamonn," he called up to the pilot-house, "take her in slowly. We'd better board and see what the damage is."

As Eamonn cautiously brought the *Lady Gregory* alongside the *Rose*, the two policemen took the opportunity to reload.

"How the devil did you get to retirement age taking chances like that?" McLeod demanded.

Magnus pulled a wry grin. "Just lucky, I guess."

"Better keep some luck in reserve," McLeod recommended. "It isn't bullets I'm most worried about."

He and Magnus went aboard the *Rose* first, weapons at the ready, Adam following cautiously with an electric torch. They found the gunman sprawled on the deck amidships, an assault rifle trailing loose from his lax fingers. The right side of his face was bloodied from a crease-wound above his right ear.

"Well, this could well be one of our common, garden-variety, home-grown terrorists, after all," Magnus muttered, kicking the rifle away from the man's hand. "That's Libyan shit—a Kalashnikov AK-47—all too easy for them to get. I'll check below to make certain he hasn't got any buddies."

While McLeod kept the gunman covered, and Magnus went below, Adam knelt down to check the wound.

"He seems to be concussed, but there isn't much bleeding," he reported. "He'll keep until we can get the rest of this sorted out."

With an unsympathetic grunt, McLeod leaned down to confiscate the rifle, recoiling in the next instant as if he had been stung.

"Bloody hell!" he muttered, kicking the weapon farther out of the way. "Adam, look at this."

As he lifted the gunman's hand by the cuff of his jacket, light from Adam's torch touched off a glassy glint of red from the gold ring worn on the third finger of the right hand. The intaglio device incised on the underside of the stone was one all too well known to them in recent years: the snarling, tufted head of a big cat.

"So much for home-grown terrorists," Adam murmured. "And that explains the warning about an old enemy."

"Aye, we should've guessed as much," McLeod agreed.

"Not necessarily. Lynx involvement is not *in*consistent, given their previous Nazi connections, but Tseten was convinced that other forces are at work here—and I'm inclined to believe him. I'd guess this man is hired muscle—which is not to say he mightn't have been dangerous on other levels. Whoever the real boss may be remains to be seen."

"Adam?" came Magnus's voice from below. "Could you come down here?"

As Adam glanced in that direction, McLeod held up a hand in warning and got to his feet, raising his pistol at the ready beside his head as he moved toward the opening. Magnus' white head emerged from the doorway before McLeod could do more, and the Irish Second held up both hands, his weapon in one of them, and gave them a sheepish grin.

"Sorry, I just realized how that must've sounded. We've got another man below, but he's unconscious—drugged, I think. He may be one of the crew. There's something else you ought to see, though—and maybe have Peregrine take a look, if his talents run the way you've described."

Leaving McLeod to guard their unconscious prisoner, Adam summoned Peregrine to come aboard, then headed down into the cabin. Peregrine had been standing by anxiously at the rail with Aoife, who was scanning the shore with binoculars, but at Adam's summons he moved to the gap in the rail and leaped across to the *Rose*, stepping cautiously around McLeod's prisoner, to follow. He found Adam kneeling beside a man sprawled in one of the cramped berths below. Magnus was backed into the tiny galley, eyes closed.

"He isn't dead; just sedated," Adam said softly, glancing back at Peregrine. "See what you can pick up in here. I can almost *taste* the residuals."

Closing the cabin door behind him, Peregrine leaned against it and let his gaze sweep around the cramped room, immediately zeroing in on the scarred table adjoining the ship's galley. A faint, telltale shimmer in the air in this part of the room hinted at the presence of powerful resonances.

He drew a long breath to center and let his deeper sight take over. The shimmer grew more distinct, resolving into the ghostly image of a tall man with fair hair. With it came a palpable aura of restless ambition and consuming malice.

Hardly daring to breathe for fear of losing the impression, Peregrine groped hastily for his pocket sketchbook and began to sketch. As oftentimes before, the very act of drawing served to fix and clarify the image. Temporarily oblivious to everything else in the room, he worked with rapid concentration, only venturing to look down at the page when he judged he was finished.

The face that gazed back at him was that of a lean, fair-haired man with chiselled lips and sharp cheekbones flanking a patrician blade of a nose. It was a likeness Peregrine had seen before in photographs, but never in the flesh. Even so, he was in no doubt as to its owner's identity.

"Francis Raeburn!" he said aloud.

Instantly Adam came to join him.

"What did you say?"

Instead of repeating himself, Peregrine mutely held out the sketch he had just made. Adam stared at it intently, then handed the sketch pad across to Magnus, who had roused at their words.

"This begins to make more sense," Adam said, gesturing for Peregrine to open the cabin door. "Now I think I understand the Nazi connection, given that Raeburn is the son of David Tudor-Jones. What I do *not* understand is how Raeburn hooks in with Eastern esoterica—though I expect we're going to find out."

They emerged from the cabin to find Aoife aboard the *Rose* and pointing out something on the shore to McLeod.

"Right there, in the lee of that outcropping," she said, as McLeod took the glasses and began to scan. "I think I'm seeing the stern of the *Rose*'s dinghy. I couldn't spot anyone moving around, but that probably means they've already gone into the cave—wherever *that* is."

As Adam joined them, McLeod handed him the glasses.

"Straight ahead at eleven o'clock," he muttered. "You

can see just a glint of moonlight on the outboard at the stern.''

Adam found it easily, then scanned farther along the beach and upward, searching for an opening.

"That beach looks like it disappears at high tide," he said, "which is not long from now, if I'm not mistaken. Magnus, can we get ashore? I don't see a cave, but it almost has to be in those cliffs off to the right.''

"Aye, just let me get chummie below and cuff him to something," Magnus grunted, as Adam headed back to the *Lady G.*

"First let me have that ring he's wearing," McLeod muttered, tucking his pistol into his waistband.

"What, spoils of the Hunt?" Magnus asked.

"Hell, no." McLeod gave his Irish counterpart a decidedly feral grin as he pulled the ring off and hefted it. "How deep is it here?"

"Oh, probably thirty feet or so."

"Deep enough, then," McLeod said—and tossed the ring overboard. Magnus chuckled, then lifted their unconscious prisoner under the arms and dragged him below. By the time he re-emerged, Aoife and Peregrine had reeled in the *Lady G*'s dinghy and drawn it alongside, and Adam was watching McLeod climb aboard, handing down a pair of the infrared binoculars.

"I've cuffed both of them, for good measure," Magnus said to Adam, with a jut of his chin back to the *Rose*'s cabin. "They'll not be going anywhere. Shall I come with you and Noel, or do you want to keep your team together?''

"Ordinarily I would," Adam said, "but in this case, I think Peregrine ought to stay with Aoife and you come with me. You aren't armed, Peregrine," he added, at the artist's crestfallen look. "The backup you and Aoife can give us doesn't depend on brawn or firepower.''

"Take one of these, then," Aoife said, handing Adam a pocket-sized walkie-talkie. "I'll put Peregrine in charge of the link aboard the *Lady G.* And be careful, all of you."

Nodding his thanks, Adam tucked the walkie-talkie into an outer pocket of his waxed jacket, then climbed lightly down into the dinghy beside McLeod. His *skean dubh* was safely zipped into an inner pocket. Magnus handed down a pair of electric torches, then came aboard and settled in the stern. The little outboard came to life with a healthy whirr, and as Aoife and Peregrine cast off the bow and stern lines, Magnus goosed the throttle and swung the bow around to begin heading toward the shore. McLeod put the binoculars to his eyes and scanned the cliffs ahead, then glanced aside at Adam.

"You don't suppose that Lynx chap back on the boat will come to, and try to cause trouble, do you?"

"I doubt it," Adam replied. "He may come to, but he's going to have one hell of a headache—hardly conducive to any serious concentration. Why do you ask?"

"Oh, I just took a bit of a precaution, that's all," McLeod said, returning to his scanning. "I tossed his Lynx ring into the drink; figured a little salt water would go a long way toward cleaning the nasties off it."

"He did; I saw him," Magnus confirmed, satisfaction in his tone.

Adam allowed himself an amused chuckle. "It's fortunate for you that our Lynx was unconscious," he said. "You both do realize, of course, that it was a valuable ring, and he's apt to scream 'Theft!' when he sees it's gone."

"Ring? What ring?" Magnus retorted. "When I arrested what I took to be a terrorist gun-runner, he wasn't wearing any ring."

McLeod did not turn, but his grim chuckle floated just above the sound of the little outboard.

They fell silent after that, though, for the air had begun to tingle with uncanny fluctuations of energy. As the dinghy neared the shore, heading for the now-visible second dinghy, Adam could feel that energy crawling over his skin like an assault of marching ants. He scanned the cliffs ahead and to the right, where an area of darkness just below the cliff-top drew his gaze like a magnet.

"Look there, Noel," he recommended, pointing. "Is that an opening?"

McLeod turned the glasses in that direction and gave a grunt.

"It's an opening, all right," he agreed, handing the binoculars back. ''And I'd bet my next paycheck Raeburn's already inside.''

''You won't get any takers here,'' Adam said, confirming with the glasses. ''Magnus, let's get this thing ashore.''

A rev of the outboard and an incoming wave swept them through the last of the shore-break. A moment later, they grounded on the sand mere yards from the other inflatable. At close range, they now could see a motionless form sitting hunched inside it.

''Bloody hell,'' McLeod muttered, drawing his pistol. ''Is he dead?''

Leaving Magnus to secure their own boat, McLeod scrambled ashore with weapon at the ready, Adam following with a torch. The man in the boat was alive but unconscious, even comatose.

''Another of the legitimate crew of the *Rose of Tralee*, I would guess,'' Adam said, checking the man's pulse and peering under eyelids.

''There doesn't seem to be a mark on him,'' McLeod said. ''Why is he not responding?''

''It appears to be some form of magical entrancement I've never encountered before,'' Adam replied as Magnus came to join them. ''He's practically reeking of it—but I won't know how to counter it until I meet up with the person who cast the spell in the first place.''

Magnus glanced nervously over his shoulder at the cliffs beyond.

''Well, he ought to be safe enough here, until we get things sorted out. Shall we?''

Back on board the *Lady Gregory*, standing shoulder to shoulder with Aoife at the side rail, Peregrine could see nothing of the shore party, though he could just make out the two dinghies. He lifted the spare binoculars to his eyes, but the moonlight itself confounded him, leaping fluorescently from rock to rock in some places, elsewhere leaving deep clefts of impenetrable shadow. As he fiddled with the sights, trying to get a clearer view, he became aware of the distant mechanical drone of a propeller-driven aircraft.

It seemed curiously out of place—a fugitive from some distant world of daylight and sanity. He looked up as he realized that the sound was coming closer—and glimpsed its swollen belly as it passed across the face of the moon. The shape did not register until it banked into the wind and he saw the pontoons fitted to its high wings.

"Aoife?" he breathed. "What the devil is a seaplane doing out here at this hour? You don't suppose it's going to land?"

CHAPTER THIRTY-ONE

IN the cavern above which the seaplane circled, nascent lightnings crept along the hull of *U-636* in a flurry of fluorescent green. Huddled far forward in the conning tower, Francis Raeburn ducked low as a javelin of light crackled down the periscope above his head. His lean face tight with tension, he darted a hand into the front of his jacket and took out a slender rod of stripped ashwood.

The rod was tipped with an iron-bound lump of rock crystal. With a muttered incantation, Raeburn used it to trace a sign of personal warding around himself, between him and the open hatch. Another lightning bolt sheered off before it could hit the railing and struck the radio antenna instead. It hung there writhing like a serpent for the space of a heartbeat, then dissipated downward through the fabric of the deck.

The power of the storm grew. Though apparently insulated from its brunt, Raeburn could feel the static electricity stirring the fine hairs on the backs of his hands, crawling on his scalp. Thrusting tongues of wildfire invaded every valve and outlet of the vessel beneath him, burning away five decades' worth of filth and corrosion until the air grew choked with the reek of charred barnacles and scorched metal. Freed from their bondage of rust, the deck-guns swung crazily on their pivots as if chasing ghost targets. From deep down in the bowels of the ship came the liberated groans of other systems coming back on line after half a century of paralysis.

The water beneath the keel began to boil, tossing up angry gouts of foam. Feeling the sub shudder beneath him, Raeburn clutched at the nearest railing for support. As he did so, he heard dimly through the hiss of the electrical storm another unmistakable sound: the hard rattle of gunfire.

Raeburn's jaw tightened at this latest complication. The noise was coming from outside. It could only mean that Kavanagh had encountered opposition. Commanding his zone of protection to move with him, he grabbed up his lantern and scrambled down out of the conning tower, making a dash toward the bow, for the need to find out who the new arrivals might be outweighed all other considerations of safety. He dared not look back as he sprang across the gap between the deck and the rocks and sprinted for the base of the ledge.

Sparks rained down on him from the rift in the cavern roof as he began his ascent. He scaled the gradient in leaps and bounds, dodging fiery hailstones as he went. Fending off a last, blazing shower with a sweep of his wand, he won through to the passageway at the top and made his way out into the sanctuary of the open air, keeping low and to one side.

The *Rose of Tralee* was standing offshore where he had left her, but a second boat was now drawn alongside, showing lights fore and aft. That meant that Kavanagh probably was neutralized. Drawing a deep breath, Raeburn pocketed his wand and pressed the stone of his Lynx ring to his forehead, forcing himself to concentrate, to re-engage patterns established earlier. As his perceptions sharpened, he scanned the scene below, seeking some clue as to the identity of the newcomers.

One of the figures aboard the second cruiser was a woman, but not anyone he recognized. Her male companion was some years younger than she, slender and fair-haired, but he could not see the face because the man was looking through a pair of binoculars trained in the direction of the cliff below. A third man was in the pilot-house, also gazing intently at the shore and pointing. At that moment, Raeburn's own attention was diverted by a flicker of movement near the water's edge, not far from where he had left the *Rose*'s dinghy.

Keeping close to the wall, lest he show a silhouette, he bent his gaze downward, bringing deeper levels of awareness into play as he attempted to pierce the obscuring distance and moonlight. He located the dinghy easily enough, and the crewman he had left behind unconscious, but a second dinghy now was drawn ashore beside it, and three other figures were skirting the base of the cliffs, heading his way. Their faces were obscured in the shadows, but not the aura of authority that centered on the tall, dark man who led them.

The signature of power was one that Raeburn had encountered before. Sucking in breath, his teeth drew back from his lips in a silent snarl of recognition as he acknowledged that presence by name.

Adam Sinclair: Master of the Hunt.

Mentally cursing his luck—and Dorje had warned him of this possibility!—Raeburn ducked back into the sheltering darkness of the cave mouth. As he did so, he became aware of the distant drone of aircraft engines. He spotted its source as the distinctive silhouette of a Grumman Widgeon passed across the moon. In the same instant, the comlink in his breast pocket gave a subdued beep.

Raeburn snatched it out and upped the volume. Barclay's drawl came through on a wave of static.

"Sea Wolf, this is Sky Hawk. Do you copy?"

Raeburn darted a venomous glance at the enemy ship below and eased slightly closer to the entrance to enhance reception, keeping to the cave wall.

"This is Sea Wolf," he muttered, as he thumbed the button to transmit. "What the hell is going on?"

Another rattle of interference intruded before Barclay's voice made itself heard again.

"Good to hear from you, Sea Wolf. I've been getting nothing but static for the past quarter of an hour. What's your status?"

"We've located the parcel," Raeburn said. "Our partners still say it will be delivered as scheduled. I have my doubts, but that's what they say. Unfortunately, we've got company."

"I see 'em, Sea Wolf. Want me to keep 'em busy while you get things under way?"

"Negative." Raeburn was vehement. "Give me about ten minutes, then bring the plane down as close as you safely can and stand by for further orders."

"Understood, Sea Wolf," came the response. If there was anything else to follow, it was lost in a blanket of electronic noise.

The seaplane banked, circling gently away from the boats. Raeburn wasted no more breath or energy cursing the damnable perspicuity of his Hunters. Leaving Kavanagh to whatever fate might await him, Raeburn turned on his heel and made his way back toward the cavern. Though he had no intention of serving Green Gloves any further than he had to, self-interest demanded that he warn his unwanted Tibetan associates that the success of their joint enterprise was now under threat, unless they could move quickly to conclude it.

The electrical storm was subsiding as he regained the cavern. Steeling his courage, Raeburn sprang back aboard the sub amid the fading glare and trotted back to the conning tower, quickly negotiating the ladder up to the command bridge. He almost faltered as he saw the well of sickly green-white light gaping to receive him.

"I'm coming back down," he called. "We have a complication."

He started down, overstepping the last few rungs to land with a clatter in the middle of a scene from a nightmare. The control room now was feverishly lit from all sides, control panels softly aglow, gauges pulsing. Through the soles of his shoes, Raeburn could feel the fabric of the deck vibrating with restored power.

But what sent a chill down his spine was the sluggish movement of half a dozen gaunt, grey-clad figures now standing erect over the consoles, wasted hands tending an array of switches and levers and valves. Nagpo was standing in their midst, surveying his work with apparent satisfaction.

Both awed and aghast, ignoring the Tibetan's amused glance in his direction, Raeburn slowly made himself approach the back of the nearest figure, which wore a peaked, once-white cap. As he cautiously set a hand to its shoulder, the figure turned, and he found himself staring at the bearded face of the dead U-boat commander. The sunken eyes burned with an unearthly greenish light, and as the dead lips parted, a hollow groan escaped from between the yellowed teeth. As Raeburn snatched his hand away, memory from his days at

Tolung Tserphug supplied the Tibetan term for such creatures, and he spoke it aloud in disgust.

"Rolag!"

Nagpo's dissonant laugh mocked his response.

"You demanded a crew, Gyatso. They are here as *Rinpoche* promised—right where they have been since the end of the war."

Swallowing his distaste, Raeburn let his gaze flick to the others moving sluggishly in the background. Until this very instant, he had not been willing to believe that Dorje was serious.

"You are—very resourceful," he acknowledged, tearing his gaze from the *rolag* captain only with an effort. "I just hope you can maintain your control long enough to get us out of here in very short order, because I'm here to tell you that there's a Hunting Party assembling outside, preparing to come in and challenge this operation. Its leader is a man I've encountered before, and I must warn you that if we allow him time to prepare himself, to realize what he's up against, he might conceivably be able to marshal the resources to stop us."

"I very much doubt that," Nagpo said condescendingly. "Our resources extend far beyond your limited comprehension."

He gestured. Following the line of the other man's pointing finger, Raeburn discovered Kurkar sitting cross-legged at the far end of the control area, deep in trance, his eyes turned upward in their sockets so that he looked almost like a *rolag* himself. He was rolling his *Phurba* between his palms, his lips framing an ongoing chant in an effort of total concentration.

"Kurkar-la prepared these men half a century ago," Nagpo explained, "when he occupied the spent body you saw before. He is one of the reincarnating ministers, reborn nearly half a century ago for this hour and this moment. I am accomplished, but I stand in awe before such mastery."

Raeburn could almost feel the force of Kurkar's will outpouring to keep the *rolag* crew on their feet and under his control. The magnitude of the achievement elicited a grudging admiration.

"If you look around you, you will see that this vessel is now fully operational," Nagpo went on. "We must prepare to move out. I trust you to give appropriate orders to the captain. When you have done so, you will please to join me on the bridge."

Nagpo turned without further comment and began to retreat up the ladder into the conning tower. With a nervous glance at the entranced Kurkar, who might or might not be fully aware what went on in the control room, Raeburn cast his glance across the controls. The readouts on the accompanying gauges told him that the sub's diesel and electrical systems were, indeed, flashed up, with power levels restored to maximum. Resigned to the part he must play in Dorje's mad charade, at least for now, he turned to address himself to the *rolag* captain. He could find it in his heart to pity the man—all these men: soldiers once faithful unto death, now recalled to agony in bodies animated only by the darkest of sorceries.

"Listen carefully," he said in German. "I am aware that you are suffering. If you disobey, those who have commanded you here have the power to imprison you in these bodies until they rot into nothing. However, if you do as you are told, you will be released as soon as this vessel's cargo has been transferred to the flying boat that is coming in to land outside this cavern. Do you understand?"

The *rolag* captain executed a jerky nod, the eyes luminescent with dread comprehension.

"Good. Then blow all ballast and prepare to move out on my command. And as soon as we're underway," he added, with a darting glance at the oblivious Kurkar, "load both stern torpedo tubes and come to the bridge. I shall give you a target on which to vent your vengeance."

He edged toward the ladder to follow Nagpo, but he paused to watch with morbid fascination as the captain moved, whispering among his *rolag* crew. Accompanied by a sepulchral chorus of hissing and groaning, the resultant movement was jerky and slow as levers were shifted, switches thrown, valves opened, but with ponderous deliberation the interlocking systems began to engage. A rush of compressed air hissed through the pipes, followed by the start-up hum of the DC generator.

The hum built to a powerful drone as the ballast compressors began blowing air into the ballast tanks. The captain
was swaying on his feet, sometimes staggering, his agony
apparent, but at a sign from him, the helmsman engaged the
rudder, testing, and the planesmen followed suit with the
hydroplanes. Satisfied that his orders were being carried out,
Raeburn mounted the ladder.

Nagpo was waiting at the aft railing of the conning tower,
Phurba already in hand, and bade Raeburn come and stand
beside him as he turned purposefully toward the stern.
Throwing his head back slightly, he closed his eyes and began to chant, rolling the hilt of the dagger between his palms
as he did so. After a moment, still chanting, he slowly raised
the *Phurba* so that the point of it was directed toward the
seamed rockfall blocking the sub's egress to the sea. Raeburn
found himself almost holding his breath.

Nagpo's chant gained force, waking whispering echoes off
the surrounding rocks, the *Phurba* a blur of motion between
his swiftly moving hands. His voice rose sharply to a pitch
of command, and in that instant, his hands sprang apart and
the *Phurba* launched from his grasp like a tiny missile.

With only a whisper of displaced air, it raced toward the
summit of the seam and struck. Raeburn cringed from the
resultant explosion, but none of the falling rubble touched
the sub as the rock-face split and separated. With a secondary
explosion, he suddenly found himself looking out across
open water through a rift like the mouth of a tunnel.

Almost too fast for mortal vision, Nagpo's *Phurba* returned to his hand. Clasping it to his breast, the Tibetan
turned to Raeburn.

"The way is open," he announced. "Instruct the captain
to proceed."

Swallowing down his apprehension, Raeburn crouched
down to the hatch.

"Both engines, back one-third," he said in German.

There was a brief delay while the message was relayed to
the control room. Then with a rumble of propeller blades and
a churning of white water under the rudder, *U-636* began
edging backward through the jagged opening, making for the
moonlit sea beyond.

CHAPTER THIRTY-TWO

OUTSIDE the cave, the roar of the explosion rocked the cove from end to end. With a heavy rumble of shifting rock, an entire seaward section of the southwest cliff blew itself apart, raining down rubble like an artillery barrage.

Eamonn had drawn the *Lady Gregory* apart from the *Rose of Tralee*, standing in closer toward where the shore party were just preparing to ascend the cliff-face. Aoife and Peregrine were with him in the pilot-house. As an eight-foot shock wave smacked into the cruiser's starboard quarter, the big boat slued sixty degrees around, heeling over dangerously and then righting herself as she plunged into the trough at the wave's back.

Eamonn braced himself against the wheel, and Aoife managed to snag the nearest railing, but Peregrine lost his footing and tumbled through the pilot-house doorway, trying simultaneously to grab onto something and protect his head and glasses as he bounced down the ladder-stairs. Something slammed him hard in the ribs on the way down, and the world momentarily went red.

He came around gasping, his breath knocked out of him, with someone pulling at his clothes to hoist him upright. The boat was still rocking crazily, and his glasses were askew. Momentarily panicked, he grabbed his benefactor's sleeve and hung on.

"Easy, it's Aoife," said a familiar voice as he forced his eyes open to look at her. "I was afraid you might have broken your neck. Did you hit your head?"

Still gasping, he shook his head and righted his glasses.

His left side was aching as if he'd been bounced off the front of a bus. He took a deep breath, winced at the pain of it, and made an effort to drag himself upright.

"No, my ribs," he managed to whisper, grimacing as he slid a hand inside his waxed jacket to brace himself. "I think I maybe cracked a few. I'll be all right, though. What the hell happened? Are Adam and the others all right?"

"I don't know yet," Aoife said, pulling out her walkie-talkie. "I haven't tried to raise—"

She broke off short, suddenly alert and listening, rearing up on her knees to peer over the railing toward the shore. Somewhere above the ringing in his ears, Peregrine became aware of a deep, throbbing rumble, like the growl of a waking sea monster. He heaved himself up beside her as the moonlight picked up a leviathan surge of movement, black and silver, from out of the jagged archway left gaping in the cliff-face.

"Aoife, look!" came Eamonn's urgent cry, from up in the pilot-house.

But the two of them were already staring in disbelief as a lean and deadly shape began easing stern-first into the moonlight, contoured like a torpedo, until every feature was fully visible, from the white churn of foam about her tail-rudders to the dark hulk of the conning tower to the bristling bastions of her gun-turrets.

"Dear God, it's coming out," Aoife whispered, as Peregrine gave an incoherent exclamation of mingled awe and dismay. "Adam, where are you?" she demanded into the grid of the little radio. "Adam, are you seeing this? It's the bloody sub! Raeburn and his cronies must have gotten to it—and somehow they've got it moving!"

Adam was lying on his back, where the concussion from the explosion had thrown him. Aoife's voice reached him through a haze of static and numb shock. Cautiously, in case of broken bones, he eased himself up on his elbows, looking for the others as Aoife's voice came again, sharp with anxiety.

"Adam? Magnus? Can any of you hear me? What's happening over there?"

Sitting up at last, Adam spotted McLeod a few yards away, making a determined effort to pull himself together. Magnus was on his hands and knees, but looking none too stable.

"Everybody all right?" Adam asked, painfully delving into his outside pockets for the radio he knew must be there somewhere.

"Just shaken up," came McLeod's reply.

"Aye," Magnus agreed, somewhat shakily. "Just give me a second to catch my breath. What was that, a bomb?"

"I don't know yet." Adam finally found the little radio and pulled it out of his pocket, clumsily thumbing the transmitter button.

"Aoife, this is Adam. We're more or less intact. What's that you say about the sub?"

Her voice came patchily back to him. "It's backing out of the cave under its own power. Don't ask me how, but this Raeburn of yours seems to have found a way to reactivate it. If you've got any suggestions on how you planned to stop him, now would be a good time to clue me in."

Adam's gaze darted seaward and his jaw dropped in disbelief. A solid black shape like a humpbacked whale was backing slowly away from the base of the cliffs, accompanied by the low growl of laboring diesels.

"There's nothing I can do from here," he told Aoife, getting to his feet. "You'll have to pick us up. Have Eamonn bring the *Lady G* in as close as he can. We'll put the dinghy back in the water and come to meet you."

McLeod was already on his feet, and lumbered over to offer Magnus a hand up.

"What about our mystery man?" he asked, jutting his chin in the direction of the *Rose*'s dinghy. "We can't very well leave him here, in the state he's in."

"I'll bring him along in his own boat," Magnus said, already heading for the second vessel. "Let's move!"

✦ ✦ ✦

On board the *Lady Gregory*, Peregrine was dividing his anxious attention between the submarine, which seemed to be coasting to a stop several hundred yards out, and the seeming snail's-pace of the approaching dinghies. As Eamonn tried to ease in closer for the pickup and Aoife tossed a line to Adam in the first boat, the seaplane they had spotted earlier buzzed them and continued on out to sea, descending toward a stretch of open water half a mile beyond the sub.

As it touched down in a spume of spray and running lights and coasted to a standstill, and the sub's bow began to swing away from them, the intent became immediately obvious. Quite clearly, such a rendezvous had been the plan all along—and *that* they must prevent.

"She's turning, Adam!" Aoife shouted, as he and McLeod clambered aboard the *Lady G* and Magnus brought the second dinghy alongside. "She's going to rendezvous with that plane that just landed!"

"At least the business-end is turning away from us," Peregrine gasped, snubbing the second dinghy's line amidships as McLeod helped Magnus drag his unconscious passenger up into the *Lady G*.

"What makes you think she doesn't have aft torpedo tubes?" Magnus muttered, climbing aboard. "And if she can move, she can maybe fire them! Noel, let's get this guy below. Eamonn, hit it!—before her stern crosses us."

On the bridge of the *U-636*, Francis Raeburn was waiting for precisely that to happen.

"Flood both stern torpedo tubes," he called down the hatch. "Prepare for surface firing and lock on target as she comes into range."

The periscope was extended beside him, turned in the direction of the *Lady G*, and he could hear the sepulchral hiss of commands being given below, bearings and ranges being set. Slowly the stern of the sub continued swinging toward the approaching cruiser, turning the sub on her bow. But as the *Lady G* continued to close, still clear of the angle of the sub's stern tubes, Nagpo turned with almost contemptuous deliberation and pointed his *Phurba* at their pursuer, rolling the hilt between his palms.

The *Lady Gregory*'s engines spluttered and died, coughing diesel fumes. There came the whirr and grind of turbines laboring as her skipper made a vain attempt to rev her up again, but she lost headway and stuttered to a halt, beginning to drift with the tide.

"Now finish them, if you wish, Gyatso," Nagpo said coldly. "But let that not delay you in your primary task."

Coupled with the effortless demonstration of power just displayed, this arrogance left Raeburn speechless. But before he could even contemplate a rejoinder, the sub's stern at last swung into line with the *Lady G*, and he felt the boat shudder under his feet.

He turned just in time to see the first torpedo streak away toward the cruiser lying dead in the water, its wake silvery in the moonlight. And as the deck shuddered a second time, the *rolag* captain came up from below, to pull himself painfully to the rail to watch the torpedoes' course.

On the *Lady Gregory*, as Magnus and Eamonn labored below-decks to restart the engines and Aoife manned the pilot-house, Adam and his own Huntsmen watched in mingled horror and dismay as the bright wakes of twin torpedoes streaked toward them in the moonlight. The first one went wide, buzzing past the *Lady G* in a wide arc to detonate against rocks father inshore; the second was off by only inches, and grazed their bow to skitter along the metal hull and off the stern, its detonator failed after fifty years. Seconds later, they saw it run up on the beach and plough into a sandbank.

Nearly limp with relief, Peregrine brought his binoculars to bear again on the submarine, now moving unmistakably toward the distant seaplane, trailing her heavy wake behind her like a train of tattered lace. Muttering, McLeod went aft to see whether either of the outboards in the dinghies would run. Aoife reported from the pilot-house that everything electrical seemed to be dead. Peregrine gasped as he finally got a good look at the three strangely assorted figures grouped together up on the conning tower, clearly visible in the moonlight. Fortunately, they no longer seemed to be concerned with the *Lady G*.

"Adam!" Peregrine muttered huskily. "Look at this!"

He thrust the binoculars at his mentor, but Adam already had another pair trained on the three, increasingly aware of the evil that accompanied them.

"The one is Raeburn," he acknowledged, as the moon's gleam caught the sheen of pale, fine hair and a supercilious profile, familiar both from Peregrine's sketch and from photographs in McLeod's personal case files.

And Raeburn was travelling in odd company, indeed. To his right stood a short, shaven-headed Oriental in fluttering orange robes—perhaps the man of Peregrine's sketches. An unearthly shimmer in the air about the man's clasped hands drew Adam's attention to the *Phurba* he was holding before him, pointed toward the submarine's bow. It was not unexpected.

But it was the third man who caused Adam's blood to run cold, standing at Raeburn's back. The once-white submariner's cap marked him as the captain—which was not possible. But as Adam noted details of the uniform—fifty years out-of-date—and the pale fire glowing in the hollow eyes, he realized it was possible, indeed. He found himself bristling as the significance registered, and he slowly lowered his glasses.

"What is it?" Peregrine whispered. "What have you seen?"

"I very much fear," said Adam, "that *U-636* is being crewed by dead men. And that tells me what kind of power we're going to have to deal with before this night is over— if we can even get to them for a confrontation. Technology fails in the face of sorcery. Noel!" His voice suddenly had more of an edge to it than Peregrine could ever remember hearing before.

"Aye?" came a response from one of the dinghies.

"Noel, we've *got* to get something moving here! They mustn't be allowed to escape!"

✦ ✦ ✦

Up on the bridge of *U-636*, Raeburn watched with satisfaction as the waiting seaplane grew gradually larger in the moonlight ahead, now less than one hundred yards away. He had never really expected the torpedoes to rid him of Sinclair—he was surprised that even one had detonated—but he regretted that the *rolag* captain had not had at least the small comfort of a final kill. As something like compassion stirred within him for his unlikely ally—well-leavened with self-interest—a change of plan began to take shape in his mind.

He hazarded a sidelong glance at Nagpo, gazing impassively ahead as the submarine crept closer. He wondered whether it was Nagpo or Kurkar or the pair of them keeping the sub afloat, the crew animated; but it wouldn't really matter, once the treasure was safely transferred aboard. By the Widgeon's cabin lights, Raeburn could see the reassuring face of Barclay at the controls, staring in his direction, a microphone held to his mouth; and with him a tested lieutenant, much welcome on this present venture. Klaus Richter would well understand what was at stake here.

Hiding a secret smile, Raeburn retrieved his radio and lifted it to his mouth. Far astern, the cruiser was still drifting helplessly.

"Have Richter break out the inflatable," Raeburn instructed. "Stand ready to fetch the cargo across as soon as we heave to, and be prepared to repel boarders, if necessary."

Barclay acknowledged the order with a cheery, "Roger that," and signed off. Raeburn held back a moment longer, watching the distance dwindle to perhaps fifty yards, then turned back to the open hatch.

"Both engines, stop."

With only little delay, the engines subsided to a faint idle and the sub coasted to a standstill. Peering out across the moonlight, Raeburn spotted the snub-nosed outline of a rubber dinghy plumping into shape just outside the aircraft's cargo door. As the neat, compact form of Richter swung down into the boat and took to the oars, Nagpo stirred, his wizened ivory face evincing satisfaction.

"I am glad to see that your people know how to take their orders," he observed in his precisely accented voice. "Take the captain below, and have the crew begin bringing up the cargo.''

Aboard the *Lady Gregory*, Peregrine had his binoculars trained on the now-stationary submarine. Magnus had come up out of the engine compartment in disgust, and he and McLeod were considering whether oars might be sufficient to get one of the dinghies to the sub in time to do any good.

''They're bringing wooden boxes up on deck!'' Peregrine said indignantly. ''They're stencilled with something. God, I've never felt so helpless!''

Adam interrupted his agitated pacing to commandeer Peregrine's binoculars and have a look for himself. A rubber dinghy from the seaplane had drawn alongside the sub on the side opposite from them, and two undead crewmen were in the process of handing its occupant a cubical wooden crate, which he stowed in the stern. There was no way of telling what might be inside.

''I see what could be German eagles and swastikas on the crate,'' Adam said, as McLeod came to listen, ''but I couldn't tell you what's in it. We can only hope that it isn't the scrolls, that they're still to come.''

''The mere fact that Raeburn wants something is reason enough why he shouldn't be allowed to have it,'' McLeod growled. ''Damn it, Adam, isn't there *anything* we can do to get this tub moving again?''

In the control room of *U-636*, the third of the crates of diamonds had gone aloft and crewmen were lifting the chest of manuscripts into the hatchway that led into the conning tower. Raeburn was standing forward of the periscope with the submarine's commander. After a casual glance at Kurkar, still sitting entranced at the rear of the control room, he drew the captain closer to one of the duty stations.

''Listen to me,'' he murmured in German. ''I can only imagine the kind of agony you and your men are enduring. I must warn you that there is no guarantee that my associates will release you from that agony when your task here is done.

On the contrary, the only way for you to liberate yourself and your men is with this.''

With his body blocking his movement, Raeburn drew the Walther from inside his jacket. Thumbing off the safety catch, he pressed its grip into the captain's cold hand.

''The man who summoned you back from the peace of death—and who betrayed you unto death half a century ago—is aft, working his unholy sorcery to keep you bound here,'' he told the *rolag*. ''His power over you will cease, once and for all, when he himself is likewise dead. Do you understand?''

The captain's head executed a stiff nod of comprehension, and his gun hand fell to his side, shielded behind his thigh as he turned away and started back toward the ladder where his men were preparing to hoist the last crate of diamonds aloft.

Beyond them, Kurkar sat cross-legged on the floor where his predecessor had sat, blind to his surroundings, still rolling his *Phurba* between his palms, in the throes of deep trance. He stirred as the captain's arm lifted, pointing directly at his forehead at point-blank range, eyes opening wide in mingled fury and alarm, but in that same instant, the captain squeezed the trigger.

The Walther went off with a bang that reverberated throughout the ship. Kurkar gave a convulsive jerk, now possessed of a bloody third eye, then crumpled forward, the *Phurba* tumbling from his hands and skittering across the metal floor. As it parted company with its master, the reanimated crew of *U-636* collapsed in their places and Raeburn's pistol fell from the hand of a German naval officer half a century dead.

The sub's idling engines fell silent, but the lights merely dimmed and then stabilized, powered by the battery reserves. Pale eyes glinting, Raeburn made a dive to recover the *Phurba*, thought better of it, then scooped up the Walther instead. As he did so, he heard the swift slap of sandalled feet descending the ladder from the top of the conning tower.

CHAPTER THIRTY-THREE

RAEBURN faded into the shadows beside the main instrument panel, the Walther pointed in the direction of the ladder while his free hand began tripping switches. In that same instant, Nagpo dropped down off the ladder to the floor of the control room, *Phurba* in his hand.

Even as Raeburn's finger tightened on the trigger, the *Phurba* was lifting to point directly at him, tracing a darting symbol in the air. The fusillade that Raeburn loosed went wide, as if deflected by an invisible wall, the ricochets clattering about the confines of the control room and sending Raeburn himself cringing for cover. As the echoes died away, Nagpo turned his dark gaze around the room, the *Phurba* still held between himself and his adversary, and noted the body of Kurkar lying face-down in a congealing pool of blood. The barely checked anger contorting his face as he turned back to Raeburn made him look almost like the German corpses sprawled about the room.

"This was ill done, Gyatso," he rasped. "Whatever satisfaction it may have given you, I do not think you will find it worth the price."

As he took a step forward, Raeburn again lifted the Walther and pulled the trigger at point-blank range, only to have it click on an empty magazine.

"You fool!" Nagpo said witheringly. "What did you think to accomplish by betraying us?"

"You would have betrayed me!" Raeburn blurted, retreating as far as he could against a bulkhead. "Do you think I ever believed Dorje would let me walk away from this?"

Nagpo's gaze glinted. "It seems that *Rinpoche* may have underestimated you after all," he said. "It is true that he always intended to dispense with you, once you had served your purpose. But you are wrong to regard it as a betrayal. On the contrary, justice will be served. Whatever your excuses, your failure in Scotland could not be allowed to go unpunished. Now, kindly drop your weapon."

Instead, Raeburn hurled the empty gun at Nagpo's face. The Walther bounced aside harmlessly, deflected by the magic of the dagger, but its flight bought Raeburn the split-second of distraction he was hoping for. Thrusting his hand into the front of his coat, he pulled out the wand of ashwood and snarled a word of cold command as he levelled it at Nagpo.

The monk flinched, but only slightly, the *Phurba* already moving to counter the attack. As a burning shock numbed Raeburn's right hand, the wand itself ignited in a burst of green flame.

With an involuntary cry, he cast it from him. The wand vaporized in midair, its ashes sifting to the floor in a scattering of grey powder. Now within reach, Nagpo touched the tip of the *Phurba* to Raeburn's breast. Pain radiated outward from the point of contact in a wave of cold that strangled his breath in his throat and paralyzed all voluntary movement. The next thing Raeburn knew, he was flat on his back on the floor, helpless to move or speak, as Nagpo came to stand over him, now gazing down impassively.

"Did you really suppose you could succeed in your betrayal?" he said coldly. "*Rinpoche* had intended that your death should be quick and painless, for the sake of the boyhood you shared. Now I think he will prefer it slow and lingering, and that he will wish the pleasure of feasting on your agonies."

Aboard the *Lady Gregory*, the distant crack of what sounded like a single gunshot penetrated through the low thrum of the submarine's idling diesels. As the echoes of the report faded out across the water, the diesels abruptly stuttered and died, leaving behind an almost uncanny silence.

"Good Lord, what was that?" Peregrine murmured, as McLeod muttered, "Gunshot," and Adam swung his binoculars back to the conning tower. The one undead-crewman on deck had collapsed over the box he had just brought down from the conning tower, and an orange-clad figure was disappearing down the hatch.

"A possible mutiny below decks, I do believe," Adam murmured, as more shots reverberated from within the bowels of the submarine. "Listen."

"I make that thirteen shots," McLeod whispered, as the firing ceased. "Somebody's played their trump card."

Aoife was also raking the superstructure of the sub with her binoculars. "I don't see any other signs of movement," she reported. "Maybe our friends have—"

Before she could complete her speculation, the *Lady Gregory*'s engines roared to life.

"That's it!" came Magnus' joyful yell from the open engine compartment, as Eamonn burst forth and scrambled back toward the pilot-house. "Let's get this tub moving!"

As Magnus, too, emerged, his tight smile matched those on the faces of his fellow Huntsmen, boding no quarter for their adversaries as the *Lady Gregory* began to move out. Delving into a stern locker, Magnus produced a pair of Ingram submachine guns and tossed one to McLeod. Adam handed his binoculars to Peregrine and withdrew Tseten's *mala* from his pocket, quietly wrapping it many times around his left wrist. At last they were to be allowed to engage the enemy.

The distance between the two vessels began to close. Magnus quietly joined Eamonn in the pilot-house, to give himself a higher vantage point. Off beyond the submarine, the seaplane still rode the swells like a delicate sea bird, its rubber raft drawn up under the wing. Peregrine's view of it was partially blocked by the hulk of the conning tower, but it appeared that a man inside was helping the man in the boat lift one of the crates up into the plane's cargo hatch.

"They've got that first crate aboard the plane," he announced.

Instead of answering, Adam turned to Aoife. "Do you know if Eamonn has such a thing as a loud-hailer on board?"

"I'll get it," she said.

When she put it in his hands, a few seconds later, Adam raised it to his mouth. They had closed their range to fifty yards, and Eamonn held the *Lady G* at that distance.

"Ahoy there, *U-636*!" he called, his deep voice reverberating across the water. "Anyone who can hear me, come out and show yourselves. You stand accountable for breaches of the peace on this and other levels. As acting head of this enforcement team, I require you to divest yourselves of any and all weapons, and to surrender yourselves into our custody. Otherwise, we will board you and take you by force."

Silence answered, broken only by the idle of the *Lady G*'s engines and the lapping of the waves. Then all at once, the shaven head and orange-clad shoulders of a man with Oriental features emerged above the edge of the conning tower, silken robes fluttering about him like tongues of fire in the moonlight.

Adam was already drawing his *skean dubh* from an inside pocket, handing off the loud-hailer to Aoife so he could unsheathe the little blade, quietly pocketing the sheath as a new voice made itself heard across the gap between the two vessels, accented and precise.

"Whoever you may be, do not think to intimidate *me* with threats of force," the man said, though strain showed in both face and tone. "I have power at my command that the likes of you can scarcely comprehend."

No simple pointing of the *Phurba* would suffice to still the *Lady Gregory* this time. The light of the moon caught the dull sheen of the metal blade as its owner began to roll the hilt between his hands, the gutteral words of a deep-toned chant rolling from his lips like the rattle of dead men's bones. The sound woke dissonant echoes off the surrounding waters, joining the chant like a supporting cacophony of demon voices, till the air itself grated on the eardrums like scrabbling fingernails dragged across a slate.

"Get back!" Adam warned, lifting his *skean dubh* to the sky in appeal to the Light as McLeod, Peregrine, and Aoife faded back from him, hands clapped to their ears—for sound was building like a rising wave, voice and echoes racing up and down the scale in screeching counterpoint. The *Lady Gregory*'s engines sputtered and failed again.

Undaunted, Adam repeated his entreaty. The blue stone set in the *skean dubh*'s pommel seemed to draw the moonlight like a magnet, wreathing his hand in a shimmering aureole of moonbeams as he executed a sign before him in the air with his blade. As he completed the gesture, Peregrine heard—or thought he heard—an elusive chime, like the faraway peal of temple bells. But that delicate, ethereal sound was swallowed almost instantly in an earsplitting crack of thunder.

A shrieking gust of wind swept the deck of the *Lady Gregory*. Circling back, it clothed itself in a sudden manifestation of shadowy form. Even as McLeod uttered a hoarse warning cry, the wind swooped down on Adam with a scream like a banshee's shriek, sweeping him into a savage embrace.

Pain slashed and stabbed at him. Instinctively Adam struck back with his *skean dubh*, but his stroke sliced only air. The shadow-thing enveloped him, absorbing his efforts to throw it off, heaving its bulk against him to hurl him to the deck. Its weight settled on his chest, cutting off his breath.

Half-suffocated, he continued to flail. The weight on his chest pressed harder, driving him closer to the brink of unconsciousness. Though he redoubled his struggles, he began to sink into a well of darkness.

He could feel the power focused through the other members of the Hunting Party trying to win through to him, was dimly aware of McLeod and Peregrine and Aoife huddling together with linked hands, Magnus pouring energy toward him from the pilot-house, but all their efforts were in vain. Spawned from dimensions outside their experience, his attacker seemed impervious to their assault.

His left arm was crushed against his chest, trying unavailingly to ward off the weight as his right arm sought a point of attack. The pressure of the prayer beads pressing into his wrist, against his sternum, recalled the beads' former owner. As physical consciousness dimmed, Adam momentarily cast himself free of his body in a desperate appeal to the Light. That appeal, resonating through the astral planes, was answered by another voice that seemed to call him back to Holy Island. Homing there in spirit, he became aware that the summoning presence was Tseten's.

Remember, you must separate the servant of evil from his

demonic protectors, came Tseten's instruction.

Simultaneously came the words of exorcism that would make that separation, ancient words in an ancient language that spilled from Adam's lips as he was catapulted precipitously back into his body.

The pronouncement lent him a sudden surge of fresh strength. His attacker gave back, hissing in fury and alarm. Yanking his blade-hand free, Adam repeated his exhortation, slashing not at what pressed his body to the very brink of oblivion but at the submarine, and the man who directed the attack.

With a rending screech, what lay upon his chest withdrew in a writhing medusa-knot of serpents, coiling and recoiling, then rocketing skyward in a dissipating whirl. A third time Adam repeated his exhortation, now rising onto his elbows to stab his *skean dubh* toward the distant Tibetan monk in a gesture to answer that of the *Phurba* in his attacker's hand.

In that moment, a torn veil of cloud passed over the moon. The light dimmed on the surrounding water. As all eyes aboard the *Lady G* cast anxiously skyward, more clouds came boiling up over the horizon.

They converged on the two vessels from all sides, gathering density as they came. Colliding, they formed a churning vortex directly overhead. From the top of the submarine's conning tower, a bolt of blue lightning leapt skyward. Speared from below, the clouds split open, emptying a thunderous shower of hail down on the vessels below.

Ice-pellets the size of golf balls battered their way across the *Lady Gregory*'s foredeck with a sound like machine-gun fire. The onslaught drove the Hunting Party back under cover as the projectiles hammered down from all sides. The hailstones grew larger, cracking off the roof like a rain of horseshoes. The waves rose in answer, leaping about in a welter of flying spume.

More lightning flashed, scything through the hail like serpents' tongues. One searing strike carried away the *Lady G*'s radio antennae, sending blue fire crackling along the metal railings like corposants, the St. Elmo's fire of legend. Another stroke sheered off the after-rail, leaving a smoking hole in the metal bulkhead. Crowded next to Adam under the overhang of the cabin roof, Aoife shrieked at him through the din, wordlessly entreating him for respite.

Nothing in Adam's living experience had prepared him for this. But as his thoughts turned once again to Tseten, there came to him another unspoken directive. In that instant of communion, he saw himself once again suspended in inner space, encircled by the dance of the universe. With a Word, he plucked a star from the midst of that swirling pavane and set it aloft on the point of his *skean dubh*.

Stepping out into the storm, he lifted the blade over his head. A lotus blossom of supernal light opened outward from its point, unfolding above him like an umbrella. Hail bounced harmlessly aside, rolling off the deck into the sea. Still unfolding, the umbrella continued to expand, bringing the rest of the ship under its protection.

The storm of ice became a storm of fire. Hailstones ignited as they fell, smacking into the waves with bellows of rising steam. The sea began to seethe. From out of the depths came a serpentine stream of twisting flames, resolving as they surfaced into a phalanx of demonic forms. Hard-pressed, Adam began to waver.

"Huntsmen, to me!" he called to his companions. And braced himself to withstand the onrushing attack.

Eyes burning, mouths slavering, the demons bore down on the ship in a flying wedge. Cutting, thrusting, and parrying, Adam fended them off with sweeps of his blade as McLeod and Peregrine, Aoife and Magnus, came to stand with their backs to his, also drawing Eamonn into their protection.

But though they might lend defense, it must be Adam who essayed the attack. Bolstered by their fresh energy, by the full force of their combined wills, he took a renewed grip on his *skean dubh* and channelled into it all the power that was now at his command. Wielding that power like a scourge, he left his body behind and hurled himself in spirit across the intervening gulf of astral space, to strike where he sensed his adversary to be.

The Hailmaster saw him coming and rose to meet him. There was a ringing explosion like shattering bells as blade met blade on the astral. The Hailmaster parried Adam's first thrust with contemptuous ease. He struck back, and Adam uttered a cry as his adversary's blade point passed breathlessly close to his heart.

Even the near-miss seemed to burn. Teeth clenched, wholly focused, Adam renewed his attack, seeking for an opening that would enable him to disarm his opponent.

Instead, he found himself drawn into a bind. He tried and failed to pull out of the deadlock. As the Dark rose up triumphantly, Adam caught a glimpse of eyes of molten ruby, and a wrathful, multilimbed presence intent on breaking him, devouring him. Though all his being quaked with the effort, Adam summoned the full of his remaining strength and gave his blade a final, desperate wrench, knowing he would get no second chance.

But miraculously, his opponent's weapon gave way, the physical blade spinning from his hand in a glittering arc to splash into the sea even as its astral counterpart exploded in a shower of burning shards. In that instant, the bonds retaining Nagpo's demonic protectors were severed, and the entities fled away in a sudden implosion of black light.

The backlash slammed Adam backwards across the void with a dizzying sense of free-fall, followed by a jarring shock as his spirit-self re-entered his body. Arm benumbed to the elbow, he folded to his knees as the deck of the *Lady Gregory* swam back into focus around him. He raised his head to find himself surrounded by the faces of his friends. Before anyone could speak, there was a sudden rush of wind across the bow and an ear-piercing shriek from across the water.

Adam struggled to his feet and lunged for the forward railing, arriving in time to see a dark moil of darker shapes converge on the conning tower of the submarine. With no weapon left to defend himself, and stripped of his demonic protectors, the Tibetan dagger priest was screaming as, with bare hands, he attempted to beat away the other demons he himself had called.

But to no avail. His scream edged briefly into a gurgle as he went down behind a screen of jostling wings and flailing tails. Within seconds, no trace of the *Phurba* priest remained.

Then, out of the deadly silence, the cloud of demons roiled and lifted, hovering aloft expectantly above the conning tower of *U-636*, a predatory congeries of eyes and teeth and thrashing limbs that did not bear too close a scrutiny.

"Now what?" McLeod muttered.

"We can't just let them disperse," Aoife whispered. "If they get away from us, they'll start hunting."

"I know," Adam said. "I need a few seconds to think . . ."

He cudgelled his tired brain for inspiration, and once again the teaching he had received on Holy Island came to his aid. He remembered the words of Lama Jigme, even before he had met Tseten: *We use the term* sGrol, *to liberate, rather than* sBad, *to kill.*

That remembrance served as the key to unlock his deeper knowledge of what finally must be done. Shifting his grip on the hilt of his *skean dubh*, he turned to Aoife and gave her a fleeting smile.

"I remember now," he told her. "Stand back, everyone, and pray this works."

As they moved back, several of them dropping to their knees in an attitude of formal prayer, Adam gathered his *skean dubh* to his breast and paused an instant to compose himself, head humbly bowed as he silently invoked the protection of the Light. Then, with nary a hesitation, he raised his blade to sketch the outline of a circular door in the air above him, willing it to open.

Drawn by his movement and the scent of his power, the cloud of demons lifted higher above the submarine and moved quickly toward him. Undaunted, he lifted both outstretched arms in a gesture of invitation. He fancied he could feel the heat of demon-breath curdling at the edges of his soul as the cloud began to descend, but he held steady the image of the open door as he raised his voice.

"Denizens of darkness, I offer you liberation, passage to the realm of Supreme Bliss. Cast off your burdens of delusion, hatred, and blood-lust, which cause you only suffering, and enter freely through the door."

The hovering shadows hesitated, jostling and vacillating, a murmur of discordant voices and anguished souls. Then all at once, in a sudden flurry of dark wings against the luminous backdrop of another sky, they began pouring through the doorway Adam had opened.

When the last one had passed through, the door simply dwindled like a closing iris, a final star-point flaring against the night sky before all was silent once more, with only a thin mist of grey smoke dissipating in the moonlight.

CHAPTER THIRTY-FOUR

FRANCIS Raeburn came to his senses with a feeling of having been drugged. He was still aboard the submarine, but he had no idea how long he had been unconscious. The sub seemed to be listing slightly to starboard, and the lights in the control room were starting to flicker, an indication that the sub's power was fast fading. Of Nagpo, there was no sign.

He gathered himself to his feet, wondering what had become of his captor, and nearly fell over the fourth and final crate of diamonds. The discovery jogged his sluggish memory back to full acuity. Groping into the front of his jacket, he was relieved to find that he still carried the comlink. Thumbing the call button, he called softly, "Barclay? Are you there?"

There was an immediate return crackle as the pilot came back to him. "Right here, Mr. Raeburn. You okay?"

"Yes," Raeburn snapped. "What's going on?"

"There's been a helluva storm up here, sir. That Tibetan shaman and a party of Huntsmen have been mixing it up in a big way. You better get up here fast. I can't see any sign of the dagger priest, but the Hunting Party's got their boat running again. I expect they're getting ready to board you."

"I'm on my way topside," Raeburn said, bending to test the weight of the last crate. "Send Richter over to pick me up, and make sure he's armed."

He retrieved the Walther before he started back up, and jammed a fresh clip into the butt.

✦ ✦ ✦

Aboard the *Lady Gregory*, Adam was still laboring to catch his breath when suddenly Magnus started up and pointed back across the water toward the submarine.

"Who the devil is that?" he exclaimed.

The rest of the party followed the line of his finger as a tall, lean figure emerged stiffly through the conning tower hatch, glanced their way, then hefted up another of the cubical crates and pushed it toward the ladder on the opposite side of the conning tower. Beside Adam, McLeod snatched up one of the pairs of binoculars for a closer look, then uttered a growl of outraged discovery.

"I'll be damned! It's Raeburn! Eamonn, take us in closer."

As the *Lady G*'s engines revved in response, and Magnus shifted his Ingram to cover the sub, McLeod retrieved the loud-hailer from the deck. Adam drew Peregrine closer into cover, and Aoife withdrew to make her stealthy way up to the pilot-house with Eamonn.

"Francis Raeburn! This is Detective Chief Inspector Noel McLeod. Stop right where you are. You can consider yourself under arrest!"

The blond head turned toward them, and a maliciously well-modulated voice floated back across the water.

"Inspector McLeod, is it? So you're here as well as your chief. Nonetheless, I must thank all of you for disposing of our mutual adversary. I had no more use for him than you did. But you must forgive me if my gratitude stops short of compelling me to hand myself over to you. As it happens, I have more pressing business to attend to."

Starting down the ladder, Raeburn pulled the remaining crate toward him and disappeared behind the conning tower. Bristling, McLeod turned to Adam.

"Now what?"

Adam sighed grimly. "It appears we're going to have to do this the hard way."

Aoife glanced down from her vantage point in the pilot-house.

"Raeburn's not alone," she informed them. "You can't

see it, because he's hidden behind the conning tower, but that man from the seaplane is on his way back to the sub, and he's got some kind of submachine gun. If we don't hurry, this could get really nasty."

At a sign from Adam, Eamonn nudged the *Lady G* throttles and began slowly easing closer toward the submarine's starboard side, deliberately keeping the conning tower between them and the gunman in the approaching raft. The distance between the two craft dwindled until they were separated by a gap of no more than twenty yards. Taking the loud-hailer from McLeod, Adam called out across the water, "We're coming aboard, Mr. Raeburn. For your own good, I would advise you to abandon whatever resistance you may be contemplating and surrender yourself without any further violence."

Raeburn had gained the deck level behind the conning tower, and poked his head out from the left to fire three rounds in their direction before ducking back into cover. Magnus and McLeod returned fire, and all aboard the *Lady G* took cover, well-protected by her metal hull and bulkheads.

"I'm not falling for that claptrap," Raeburn shouted. "I see no personal advantage in my making things easy for you."

Peering cautiously from behind a locker, Adam saw Raeburn stack another crate atop one of the two waiting beside a larger chest with metal fittings, just forward of the conning tower. It was the chest that abruptly drew his gaze like a magnet, and he was left with no doubt in his mind that it contained the Black *Termas* that Tseten had so greatly feared and abominated. Here, at last, was the reason for their presence here tonight; and whatever else might transpire, Raeburn must not be allowed to escape with the chest in his possession—or with any of the other crates, if they could help it.

Beyond the submarine, the inflatable raft from the seaplane was slowly drawing closer, Raeburn casting an anxious glance in its direction as he crouched in the shelter of the stacked crates and the conning tower, pistol still in his hand.

Beside Adam, McLeod was growing restive. Dispensing with the loud-hailer, he made a trumpet of his two hands.

"Raeburn, this is your last warning," he shouted. "Don't be stupid and add to the charges you'll be facing when we pick you up."

The response from Raeburn was a derisive laugh. "And what charges are those? Defending myself? And I think that conventional authorities would be hard-pressed to prove even that."

"I think a jury might decide otherwise, given the fact that you've been involved in quite a lot of gun-play tonight," Adam pointed out. "I don't know who shot whom, down below, but the fact that you're still alive suggests that you have at least a few questions to answer."

Raeburn drew himself up, his fine fair hair feathered by the wind as he surveyed his accuser with scorn.

"Dr. Sinclair, I believe. We've not met formally, but of course I know who you are. You've given me a great deal of trouble over the past few years, as I trust I've given you.

"Right now, however, that's neither here nor there. I don't intend to stick around while you satisfy your curiosity at my expense. Should you care to board my vessel after I've left, please feel free to investigate the shooting to which you've just referred. I believe you'll find that it was carried out by a dead man—a *very* dead man—not something *I* should care to attempt explaining to the press, especially in view of the fact that Inspector McLeod is presently out of his jurisdiction, bearing a firearm in another country."

Aoife edged closer to Adam.

"He's grasping at straws, playing for time," she murmured.

"That's all right," Adam replied. "So are we."

With a glance, he measured the remaining distance between their own vessel and the deck of the submarine, which seemed to be riding lower in the water than it had been.

"If we can keep him distracted, we'll soon be close enough to board," he murmured. "Noel, try to keep him talking."

"With pleasure," McLeod grunted. Raising his voice, he

called, "Go ahead and try and leave the sub, if you think you can get away with it. But you're not taking those boxes with you."

Raeburn cast a glance over his shoulder at the approaching raft, then back at his challengers.

"Nonsense," he retorted. "These boxes are my property, by right of salvage. Interfere with them, and I'll have you up on charges of piracy."

McLeod raised his pistol, calmly taking a bead on Raeburn, who ducked behind the conning tower.

"We can split legal hairs later," he told Raeburn. "In the meantime, you'd best keep back from those boxes."

The raft was still several meters distant, still mostly shielded behind the conning tower. The man leaning into the paddle was blond like Raeburn, and hard-eyed, with an Uzi slung around the neck of his leather flying jacket. After darting a glance at him, Raeburn cast an appraising look at the cruiser easing ever nearer the sub, then ducked down to pick up one of the crates of diamonds, brandishing it before him.

"Do you know what's in here?" he cried. "Diamonds." Without further preamble, he pitched the crate into the water on their side, where it immediately sank from sight. "But if I can't have them, then neither can you."

As Peregrine started up with an exclamation of surprise and indignation, Raeburn picked up a second crate.

"The only way to stop me from doing this is to shoot me," he stated, "and you won't do that, because your kind can't kill in cold blood."

The second crate splashed down and sank with a gurgle.

"How inconvenient for you, that you believe in justice and fair trials," Raeburn observed, and bent down for the third crate.

As he did so, McLeod levelled the Browning and squeezed the trigger.

The crate seemed to leap in Raeburn's hands, partially exploding in a fountain of wood splinters. His balance momentarily disrupted, the crate slipped from his hands and smashed against the deck before sliding into the water, Raeburn flailing after it. Diving instinctively, as both McLeod and Magnus began firing, he surfaced some distance out from the sub, where the man in the inflatable raft was returning cover-fire. A second dive brought him up gasping behind the raft, where he clambered aboard and took over firing as his associate began paddling furiously back toward the seaplane.

It was just enough to keep their pursuers pinned down. The two policemen kept firing after the raft when they dared, but the pitch of the cruiser's deck played havoc with their aim.

Adam's attention, meanwhile, was reserved for the brass-bound chest still riding on the submarine's deck, which was settling ever lower in the water. Peeling off his waxed jacket, he directed Eamonn to bring the *Lady Gregory* as close as he could, for the sub clearly was sinking. Peregrine shucked out of his jacket as well, jamming his spectacles into a pocket before tossing it to Aoife, he and Adam swinging over the cruiser's port-side rail and dropping to the sub's deck as the *Lady G* came alongside the conning tower.

They landed ankle-deep in water, for the entire deck was now awash, waves breaking over the bow and rolling aft with every swell. The chest shifted ominously, and a spatter of Uzi fire from the direction of the raft warned them that Raeburn was still a danger.

"Keep as low as you can!" Adam shouted, as a chance burst churned the water between the two of them, and Peregrine recoiled.

Following his own counsel, Adam made a dash for the chest, and got a hand on it as a passing wave smacked it broadside. Even then, he feared for a moment that he was going to lose it.

Then Peregrine came to his aid, seizing hold of the other handle. Still ducking Raeburn's bullets—though his aim was becoming more erratic, the farther he got from the sub—they managed between them to manhandle the chest toward the dwindling island that was the conning tower. By the time they reached it, the water was past their knees.

Eamonn was fighting to hold the *Lady Gregory* in position, still hiding behind the conning tower as a shield and using it to keep the *Lady G* from grounding on the sub's sinking deck. Leaving Magnus to keep up the fire-fight from far forward, McLeod joined Aoife at the railing. Adam and

368 ✦ *Katherine Kurtz and Deborah Turner Harris*

Peregrine hoisted the chest aloft as their companions leaned out, ready to receive it. Even as the weight of it left their arms, the submarine's deck sank out from under them and left them swimming. The water was icy cold.

"Hang on a sec and we'll throw you a line," Aoife shouted down to them, as she and McLeod hefted the chest off the rail and onto the deck.

As they trod water, hampered by heavy shoes and clothing, Peregrine hazarded a look over his shoulder, where the conning tower was slipping deeper, a wash of phosphorescent green bubbles streaming upward from her rapidly vanishing hull.

"This thing isn't going to suck us under, is it?" he gasped, with a wild glance at Adam.

"I hope not."

"What about sharks? Are there sharks in these waters?"

Before Adam could answer, the depths below them were suddenly suffused with a blooming burst of opal-green radiance. A split instant later, the shock of the explosion hit the surface. The booming roar tossed them skyward on a geyser of sheeting foam. Neither Adam nor Peregrine remembered coming down again.

The blast hurled a wall of water toward the shore, catching the *Lady Gregory* and spinning her around, dangerously canted over. Looking down from the pilot-house, Eamonn could see nothing of the deck but a shelf of racing foam as the water crashed over her port rail and swept across her decks.

Magnus alone managed to hang on to the forward railing. Farther amidships, the chest containing the Black *Termas* skidded the length of the deck and lodged itself against the stern rail. Aoife and McLeod were swept off their feet and carried after it, and only just managed to keep from being washed overboard. For a foundering moment they seemed certain to capsize; but then, with a shudder, the *Lady Gregory* righted herself, shedding water in sheets as she settled back on her keel.

McLeod had lost track of the number of times tonight that his ears had been set to ringing, and almost missed the distant drone of aircraft engines picking up speed as he got to his feet. Turning numbly toward the sound, powerless to stop it, he swore audibly to see the seaplane lumbering away from them, gathering speed and lifting off, making for the open sky. But a shout of alarm from Aoife forestalled his dwelling on Raeburn's escape.

"There's Adam!" she shouted. "Where's Peregrine? Does anybody see him?"

Looking down in the water where she was agitatedly pointing, McLeod spotted a second puppet-like shape floating face-down in the waves a short distance away. Neither was moving.

"Eamonn, get a spotlight on them!" he called up sharply to the pilot-house, already struggling out of his jacket and kicking off his shoes.

CHAPTER THIRTY-FIVE

ADAM came groggily to his senses to find himself lying
face down on the deck of the *Lady Gregory*. His chest
felt bruised and his mouth tasted of bile. His ears were ringing. He heard someone coughing beside him and lifted his
head to see Peregrine, half on his hands and knees, retching
as a water-logged Magnus grabbed him around the middle,
helping him clear his lungs. The artist's face was a pasty
shade of green, similar to the olive-drab blanket Aoife laid
around his shoulders, and he hugged it around him, shivering, as Magnus helped him collapse to a sitting position.

Rolling gingerly onto his side, Adam tried to speak, but
nothing came out but a soggy-sounding cough.

"I'd stick to breathing just now, if I were you," said
McLeod's gruff voice.

Strong hands helped him sit, as another blanket was drawn
around his shoulders. A coughing fit brought up what seemed
like gallons of sea water and left him wheezing, lightheaded.
When he could focus again, he saw that McLeod, like
Magnus, was drenched to the skin, and guessed that the two
must have been responsible for pulling him and Peregrine
out of the water after the explosion. Part of him wanted simply to lie down and sleep off the shock and the chill of near-
drowning. But there were too many things he wanted—and
needed—to know.

He cleared his throat and tried again. "Where's
Raeburn?"

"Flown the coop," McLeod said sourly. "There wasn't
much we could do to stop him, by the time we were sure

the two of you hadn't drowned. Magnus called the mainland on the cell phone and put out an APB on the plane—our radio's kaput—but I doubt it'll do much good. This part of the coast is honeycombed with places where he could have hidden another boat to take him well away from here.''

''And the chest?'' Adam's voice was starting to come back to him.

McLeod allowed himself a brief, wolfish grin. ''We've still got that. Raeburn didn't have it all his own way.''

Moving cautiously, Adam edged himself back to lean against the side of a locker. From where he sat, he could see the open sea through the *Lady G*'s railings. There was no sign of the submarine. McLeod glanced in the direction of his gaze, then looked back at him and answered the question Adam had not yet summoned strength to ask.

''I don't know whether Raeburn actually rigged that explosion, or whether all that jostling was enough to set off one or more of those fifty-year-old torpedoes,'' he said. ''Or maybe it was some after-reaction from all that magic being released. Whatever the case, the sub is history again.''

''Which is all for the best,'' Aoife said, leaning down to press a mug of hot coffee into Adam's icy hands. ''Can you imagine the flap it would have caused if she'd been found adrift and intact?''

Adam managed a shaky swallow of coffee, suppressing another cough, then nodded.

''Requiring a nimble display of press-obfuscation, at very best,'' he agreed.

''I do love your understatements,'' Aoife said with a chuckle. ''Fortunately, Tory Sound is littered with old wrecks. If any of the wreckage from *U-636* should eventually turn up, it will be assumed that it came from the sea-bottom—just one more wreck among so many others.''

''What about the cave?'' Peregrine asked hoarsely, over his own steaming mug.

''I'm about to deal with that,'' Magnus replied, getting to his feet. ''First, though, I want to check again on our guest below.''

In the heat of battle, Adam had forgotten the crewman from the *Rose of Tralee*.

''Is he awake?'' he asked.

"Aye," said Magnus, "and pretty shaken up to find himself under lock and key. I'd cuffed him to a berth, just for good measure, since we didn't know who he was. I've given him to understand that the outfit he and his mates were messing with was a band of terrorists out to recover a cache of arms. When the cache goes up—in, say, about two minutes from now—I think he'll be relieved enough at the thought of staying out of jail not to pry too deeply into the matter. He hasn't said anything about seeing any monks with funny knives, so maybe he doesn't remember.

"The chaps on the *Rose* present different problems, but I'll think of something before the authorities get here. The one's no problem; the terrorist story will stick, so far as he's concerned. And the Lynx chap can't very well tell the truth without digging himself in deeper. We might make a hijacking charge stick, if the crew from the *Rose* are cooperative, but I expect we'll eventually have to let him skate. At least we'll have given him a scare, and we'll know to keep an eye out for him in the future."

He disappeared down into the hold. While he was gone, Adam prevailed upon McLeod to help him move around to the other side of the ship. To his surprise, the *Lady Gregory* was standing several hundred yards off the dark entrance to the sea cave opened by the departing submarine. Peregrine retrieved his glasses from his coat pocket and came limping to join him at the rail, gazing silently at the cave and the *Rose of Tralee* still lying at anchor off the little crescent beach. When Magnus returned a few minutes later, he was carrying a shoulder-fired rocket-launcher and a small but heavy canvas satchel.

"A parting gift from my friendly armorer," he explained as he set it up and aimed a charge at the shore. "We've only got two shots to get this right, so keep your fingers crossed. And it would be nice to have the second shot to dispose of that torpedo that ran up on the beach. Hold your ears, everyone."

He succeeded with his first shot. A rumbling blast inshore collapsed the remains of the cave where *U-636* had slept hidden for so long with its dangerous cargo. The second shot accounted for the inconvenient torpedo. As the Hunting Party watched the dust clear away in the moonlight, Peregrine alone appeared dissatisfied.

"What's the matter?" Adam asked, as Eamonn advanced the throttles and began easing the *Lady G* in the direction of the *Rose*.

The young artist sighed and adjusted the set of his blanket, turning to ease back down on the deck with his back against the rail.

"This is all very well and good for cutting short all the official loose ends," he complained, "but I can't help wondering what Raeburn will be getting up to next. We know he got at least one crate of diamonds aboard that plane— enough of a fortune to keep him in business for a good long time to come."

"True enough," Aoife agreed. "On the other hand, he didn't get all the diamonds and he didn't get the *Termas*."

Peregrine's gaze shifted uneasily toward the sodden trunk in the stern.

"I suppose you're right," he acknowledged. "Only now we've got the *Termas*, what are we going to do with them? I mean, Lama Tseten certainly seemed to think they're very, very dangerous. Maybe we should have just let them sink to the bottom, along with the sub."

"We couldn't have been sure they'd be destroyed," Adam said, crouching down beside him as Aoife and the two policemen headed for the bow, to deal with the occupants of the *Rose*. "It simply would have postponed the day when someone else would have to reckon with the danger they represent. Things like this have a way of resurfacing—no pun intended. If true *Termas* can be expected to turn up when they're needed, who's to say that these false *Termas* may not do the same?

"No, the proper custody of these texts belongs to Tseten *Rinpoche*. If they *can* be destroyed, he'll know how to do it; and if they can't, I can think of no one I'd trust more, to negate their dark powers and see that they don't fall into the wrong hands again. As for the diamonds," he continued, "count them lost along with so many other treasures. Except for this."

Digging into a soggy trouser pocket, he dragged out a sparkling blue-white gemstone. Rainbow fire winked behind its facets as he handed it into Peregrine's shrinking palm. The artist's eyes went wide as he lifted it closer to his astonished gaze.

"Adam, this thing must be five or six carats!" he exclaimed. "Where did you get it?"

Adam smiled wearily. "I felt it roll under my foot as we were heading off up the deck to retrieve the chest full of texts. It must have come from the crate that Noel shot. It seemed wasteful to leave it, so I scooped it up as I went past. Give it to Julia as a wedding present from the Hunting Lodge—though I shouldn't call it that, if I were you. Maybe it will be some compensation for her having so many interruptions on her honeymoon."

Peregrine looked at the diamond again. "It's glorious," he said, "but I don't really think I ought to accept it. Even if it wasn't such a valuable stone, I don't think I'd feel right giving Julia a Nazi diamond to wear."

Adam smiled inwardly. It was a worthy sentiment.

"In that case, let me suggest that you sell it and use the proceeds as a down payment on your first home. As I recall, there's a lovely little chapel just a few miles from Strathmourne that's just been made redundant. I'm not eager to kick you out of the gate lodge, by any means," he added, at Peregrine's almost hurt glance. "You're welcome to stay as long as you like, but you and Julia will want some privacy to start out your marriage; and I'm thinking the chapel would convert to a splendid residence for an up-and-coming portrait artist who'll be wanting to start a family. I doubt the church commissioners would want much for it—and the work involved in restoring and converting it would provide a lot of local employment."

"I don't know," Peregrine said doubtfully. "I'm not sure it would be right."

"Let's consider the other options, then," Adam said, easing his back and trying to find a more comfortable position. "If we toss that diamond overboard with the rest, nobody benefits. Or it might be appropriate if at least part of the proceeds went to Tseten, to further the work on Holy Island."

"It seems like if anyone's entitled, he is," Peregrine allowed.

"In a sense, perhaps," Adam agreed. "However, Tseten will receive guardianship of the false *Termas*—which is worth far more than any financial consideration, for however good a cause. And while he gave me the teaching that enabled us to effect the capture of the *Termas*, *we* were the ones to put our lives on the line."

"That's true enough, I suppose."

"There's no 'I suppose' about it," Adam declared. "It isn't often that we benefit financially from one of our operations; and when we do, I prefer that we take care of our own. You're just newly married. You could have been killed here today. I know you took the risk willingly, and I can only be thankful for your courage and commitment, but I'd like to know that Julia has been provided for, if you're someday called upon to make the ultimate sacrifice—and we've all pledged our willingness to do so, if it should ever come to that. You might ask Lady Julian about it, if you'd like another perspective."

Peregrine found himself rolling the diamond against the engraved band of his Adept ring—the ring that had belonged to Julian's husband, fallen in the service of the Hunting Lodge many years before—and he closed the diamond in his hand, bringing his fist to his lips.

"I understand what you're saying," he whispered. "It's just that—"

"I know," Adam said quietly. "It's something you've never had to think about before. It's something *I'll* have to consider, if ever Ximena consents to be my wife. Why don't you give yourself a day or two to get used to the idea? It isn't charity, and it isn't plunder. The stone can finance a lot of worthy objectives for a lot of people, but there's no reason why you and Julia shouldn't be among those who benefit. You can still make a handsome donation to the Holy Island Project, if you like.

"But when we get back home and you've had a chance to catch your breath, take Julia out to see the chapel. See if it appeals to you. If the pair of you decide it's what you'd like, I'll be happy to speak with the bishop on your behalf. . . . "

AFTERWORD

The Holy Island of this novel is, of course, fictional, as are Lama Tseten *Rinpoche* and Jigme-la (though one might wish they were real), but readers interested in the ongoing work of the Samye Ling Tibetan Centre in Scotland, including its conservation work on the real-world Holy Island (you can sponsor a tree!), may write to:

Mr. Thom McCarthy
Kagyu Samye Ling Tibetan Centre
Eskdalemuir
nr. Langholm
Dumfriesshire DG13 0QL
SCOTLAND

SARVA MANGALAM!
"May all beings be happy"